Don't miss Rage: Book One

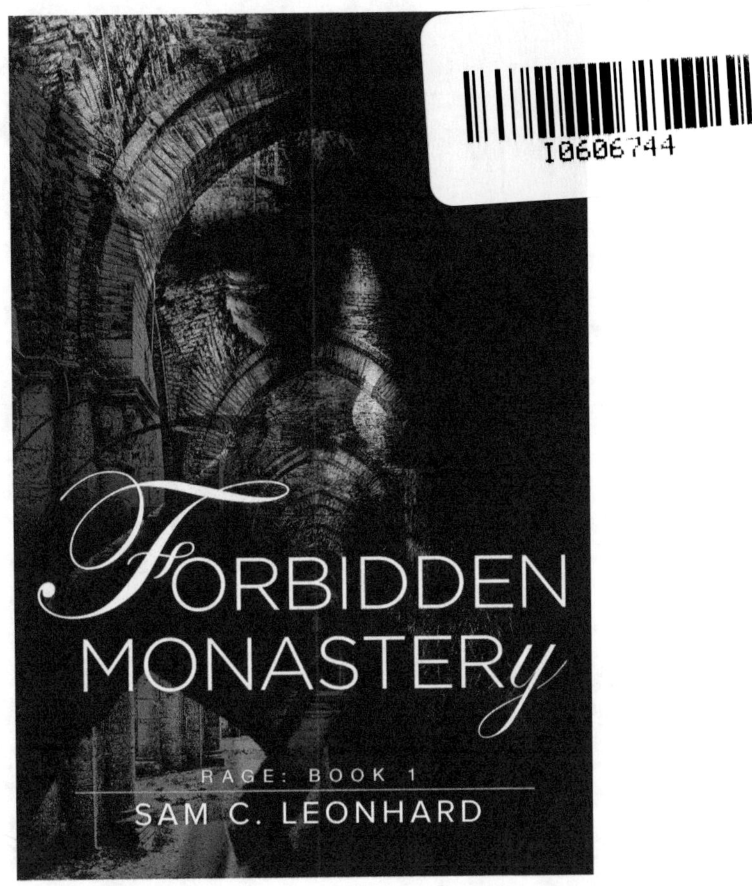

"*Forbidden Monastery* is a well-written, fast moving chase wrapped in magic and mayhem. The main characters are gratifyingly rendered and incredibly engaging. The book has a sequel pending, which I will anxiously be waiting to read. In the meant time, I think this one is definitely worth checking out!"

—Joyfully Jay

EMPRESS AND CHILD

SAM C. LEONHARD

DSP PUBLICATIONS

Published by
DSP PUBLICATIONS

5032 Capital Circle SW, Suite 2, PMB# 279, Tallahassee, FL 32305-7886 USA
http://www.dsppublications.com/

Empress and Child
© 2015 Sam C. Leonhard.

Cover Art
© 2015 Aaron Anderson.
aaronbydesign55@gmail.com
Cover content is for illustrative purposes only and any person depicted on the cover is a model.

ISBN: 978-1-63476-112-3
Digital ISBN: 978-1-63476-113-0
Library of Congress Control Number: 2015930655
First Edition September 2015

Printed in the United States of America
∞
This paper meets the requirements of
ANSI/NISO Z39.48-1992 (Permanence of Paper).

Special thanks to my wonderful betas Mary M. Ardagna, DreamyDragon, and Tom. You all did a terrific job in a ridiculously short amount of time, and I cannot say how grateful I am to all of you. Also, thank you to everyone who read the story in advance and gave the much needed feedback. However, without the team at DSPP—Rose, Yv, and Joanne—I couldn't have hoped to shape it into the form it is now. Thank you, all of you!

ROLOGUE

I T WAS late at night when Luca woke up. *Stomach cramps again,* she thought wearily. *Don't I just love them.*

Nausea washed through her body, and she retched, pressing one hand to her mouth and fumbling with the other for the bowl that stood next to her bed just for those occasions. It wasn't the first time she was sick, although usually it happened closer to morning.

In the end, she didn't have to throw up, but slightly shaky anyway, she put the bowl on her bedside table. She was sweaty, her nightshirt was sticking to her clammy body, and she pondered if she should get up and get changed. Most likely she would be sick again; most likely she wouldn't stop sweating, either. And her warm bed was much more comfortable than the idea of freezing night air sending a chill down her spine whilst hunting down a clean garment.

Sighing, Luca fell back onto her pillows. Once awake, she hardly ever managed to find her way back into dreamland, and staring at the ceiling was what she usually did in such a case. One out of three nights, she didn't sleep through. Tonight, apparently, was one of them.

Besides, being awake wasn't that bad at all. When awake, she couldn't dream, and if she didn't dream, no nightmares could bother her. "Damn them," she muttered, not for the first time cursing her overactive brain, which insisted on plaguing her with dark images of blood and loss. Even worse were the dreams of Keiran. Keiran's voice, pleading for help. Keiran's hand, reaching out for her. In those dreams, she always tried to reach him before he was lost in the abyss.

Of course, she always failed to save him, just as she had failed to save him three months ago.

Luca thought of Rage as well. During the day, he hardly ever crossed her mind. He'd abandoned her, hadn't he? He'd sunk to his knees at the spot where Keiran had fallen, not responding to her plea to come home with her. When she'd turned her back on the cursed monastery, she had believed he would follow her. At first, she'd been sure he'd get up at any moment, getting across the bridge and away from this horrible place.

But he hadn't. She'd left him behind, unable to persuade him to follow her. For all she knew, he might still be kneeling at the edge of the abyss.

He might have even jumped.

He surely is dead, Luca thought, sleep tiptoeing closer. *He either jumped to join Keiran, or he stayed in the monastery and went mad. No one can survive up there.*

Only she was quite sure he was alive.

Stupid thoughts. She had a manor to run, and there was simply no time for useless daydreams.

So why do I think I should go and find him?

The branches of the tree outside her window rattled against the glass, causing the small hairs on her neck to stand up. It sounded like bone fingers begging to be let in.

Luca shuddered and pulled the blanket a bit higher. *This is my room*, she told herself. *I grew up here. It is safe. No one is outside. No one wants to get in. Keiran is definitely dead. Rage is probably dead. Get used to it.*

Not that it was an easy task to accomplish.

Right, sleep wasn't as close as she had hoped. Even trying to keep her eyes closed was a lost fight. So instead of continuing to try, she lit a candle and found the book she'd been reading earlier. If she read for an hour or two, she might be able to take a nap shortly before sunrise, and if not, she would at least be so tired by lunchtime that she could doze off at the table.

But instead of opening the book, she pulled her knees up under the cover. Wrapping her arms around her shins, she thought of how she had managed to get away from the Forbidden Monastery. She had found the horses; she had packed Sammy into one of the saddlebags and had headed home, not leaving one horse for Rage. He was used to walking, and the horse wouldn't have stayed behind alone anyway.

Not once had she looked back. She'd been terrified of seeing Keiran's ghost accusing her of abandoning him. Had she looked back, she might have climbed down into the abyss to at least get his corpse back.

An impossible task. She'd stood on that bridge for less than half an hour, and it had driven her nearly mad. Getting closer to the river—never. Keiran would have to stay down there, alone.

She didn't know how she'd made it back to the plains, and she had next to no recollection of her journey home. One day, she had just ridden through the gates of Babylon Manor, haggard, pale, and dirty. A servant had seen her, and he had nearly chased her off, thinking she was a beggar. The servant lowered his ax only when he recognized Gus, a horse who had been born on the manor. When he had recognized her as well, he'd dropped his tool just in time to catch her.

She'd spent two weeks in bed.

Four weeks later, the nausea had begun.

"Damn you, Rage. I wish you were here so I could shout at you," Luca said to the flickering shadows dancing across the ceiling. "I'm so tired of doing this on my own. Running the manor isn't as easy as I had thought, but that's not the point. You left me alone! You are out there somewhere—if you aren't dead, that is—and I bet you don't waste a single thought on me. I bet you even forgot we are legally married. I could do with your help, you know? I could—"

No. She wouldn't walk down that path. Only grief waited there, and truly, she'd had her share of grief recently.

Maybe she should get up. There were some of last year's apples down in the kitchen, old and wrinkly and meant to go into an apple pie tomorrow, but suddenly those apples made her mouth water. She wanted them. Now.

Her dressing gown was on the floor where she had dropped it, but when she couldn't find her slippers, she put on some thick, warm socks instead and sneaked out of her room.

As expected, the corridor was cold. Only a few candles were burning. They barely cast enough light to see where to put her feet.

The carpets were always somewhat ruffled up and more than once, she nearly stumbled over one of the folds. Saving money, though, was her most important goal. She'd use as few candles as possible until she had found a way to secure her status as Lady of Babylon and her right to rule her manor the way she thought fit.

When she reached the kitchen, she heard someone move and groaned inwardly. She didn't want company, but when she entered the kitchen, ready to throw out anyone who dared to be in there at that time of night, she saw it was only Sammy. Busy chasing a slender, ginger-colored cat, he didn't even stop to acknowledge her. He swooshed past her and followed his playmate out into the corridor.

All that was left was silence and some pots gently dangling from where the cats had brushed past them.

Fine. She went to bed alone, she woke up alone, and there was no reason why she couldn't eat an apple alone too.

Her feet were cold despite the socks, so she went to get her apple, sat on one of the chairs, and took a bite. It tasted just as good as she had imagined, sweet and juicy despite its looks. But now that she was fully awake, the problems came back as well. Usually she managed not to think about them during the night, but then, usually she stayed in bed, pretending to be asleep after her stupid stomach had woken her up. "I hope this stops soon," she sternly told her body but knew all too well it wouldn't.

Placing the hand that didn't hold the apple on her flat belly, she continued, "I am sick of being sick, do you hear me? It is bad enough I am facing a trial concerning my somewhat dubious status as a married woman without a husband. I am still only sixteen, you know. In theory, I need a legal guardian until I am eighteen. But I *am* married, which changes things. Or would change things if I could present an actual husband." She crunched the last bite of the apple, looked at the core, and ate it too. The dark seeds were bitter, the stem hard, but what the hell.

Now a glass of milk laced with powdered chocolate seemed a good idea.

"Imagine that only a few months ago, my biggest concern was to prevent Lucius from hitting my best horse. And now he is dead, my best friend is dead, Rage is the Lady knows where—or dead—and I am pregnant." Sternly she looked at her belly as if staring could change the facts. "And I don't know who your father is. My dead friend or a most likely dead assassin. If the court finds out you might have been conceived outside of marriage, they will put me in with the sisters until you are born, and then they will take you away from me. You will grow up in an orphanage. Babylon Manor will be sold. Luckily, Lucius didn't have any relatives. It would kill me, knowing I have to pray all day for forgiveness of my sins whilst someone related to that bastard lives here and takes what is legally mine."

It would kill me to give up my baby, she thought.

Luca flattened her nightgown over her belly. Apart from her, no one knew she was pregnant. She would be able to conceal it for another two, maybe three months at the most, but afterward, she'd need—

Help me!

Luca jumped up from her chair; it fell and clattered loudly to the floor. Bewildered, she looked around, searching for the voice's source. Someone had called: someone in pain, someone scared. From outside, a cold breeze sneaked into the dark, silent kitchen. The cats must have pushed the window open, and she hadn't noticed until now.

Please help me!

"Where are you?" Luca barked out, cold shivers running down her back. She wasn't used to bodiless voices in her own kitchen. She had left all those voices behind in the abyss belonging to the Forbidden Monastery.

Then the truth dawned. There was no one in or near the manor pleading for help. She'd fallen asleep, and she was dreaming of Keiran calling for her.

Wearily she wiped a tear off her cheek. "Stop it, Keiran," she murmured, knowing he couldn't hear her and hoping she would wake up soon. Once her eyes were open, the voice would vanish. "You are dead. You cannot call me, and anyway, even if you could, I cannot help you. Stay in your grave, however wet it might be, will you? I've got enough problems without you disturbing my sleep."

By the Lady, her feet were cold. Even the socks couldn't warm them up, so Luca pulled her legs up and began rubbing her numb toes. The rest of her body was warm enough, the tiny spark of life growing inside her miraculously serving as a very special oven, but her feet were a different matter. Hopefully spring wasn't that far away anymore.

Rubbing her feet heated up her hands, but her toes stayed immune to their treatment. She even banged her elbow to the table in front of her. It hurt worse than she'd expected, and she cursed.

Then she froze in midmotion, left foot tucked in the hollow of her hands, her hair half escaped from the braid she'd woven it into.

Help me! the voice whispered into her mind.

She wasn't dreaming. In a dream, one couldn't feel pain that clearly. In a dream, one couldn't reason one was only dreaming.

She was awake.

But then—where did the voice come from?

"Keiran?" she whispered, horrified as well as wildly ecstatic at the implications of that voice, which wasn't a dream voice anymore. "Are you... don't tell me you are still alive!"

CHAPTER
One

DESPITE HER initial plan, Luca didn't sneak away that night. Although she wanted to run to the stables, get a horse, and take off immediately, she realized it was impossible before she'd as much as crossed half the yard. Because if she left the manor behind without a good explanation, there would be no chance she could keep her property. A sudden and unexplained disappearance would cause too many questions, and she couldn't afford any more of them. Her status as Lady of Babylon was shaky at best; Lord Barnard, her neighbor, was already rubbing his greedy hands in expectation of taking over her property. He lived three days' journey away and had more land than he could actually control, but that didn't stop him from wanting a little more.

Waiting until morning was hard. She'd gone back to her room and paced restlessly from wall to wall until dawn. In between, she threw clothes onto her bed and talked to herself to anchor her somewhat crude plan in her mind so she wouldn't give the wrong orders once her servants were awake. "I'll pretend to go to the High Court to present my case in person," she told the walls of her bedroom. "That means a week's journey to the capital, another week to get an appointment, a day to present my case, and one week for the journey back here. Three weeks and a bit."

In three weeks, she *could* try to find Rage, tell him about Keiran's calls, and persuade him to come back to the monastery with her.

She also could go to the monastery directly. Only she didn't know how to find the path leading up to it. And she was scared to go up there alone. Finding Rage made more sense. "He might be dead," she murmured, trying to find a pair of shoes that would go with the red dress. At the High Court, everyone needed to wear the best clothes they owned, and that included shoes as well as jewelry. And as everyone would believe she'd go there, she needed to pack accordingly.

Not that she had a lot of jewelry. Her mother had left her a few necklaces, a pearl bracelet, some rings. They'd have to do. And the black shoes—they'd also fit with the green dress.

"Ridiculous." Luca snorted in disgust at the heap of clothes on her bed. So many things being packed for nothing. She'd take the carriage until she was out of sight, then swap it for a horse and plain, warm clothes. "And there's the problem of taking a maid," she muttered under her breath. "Can't leave here without a maid. I think… I think I'll take Jean. She's as daft as a girl can be without being called dimwitted. She'll believe whatever I tell her. Yes, Jean is a good choice."

Rummaging through the clothes covering the bottom of her wardrobe, she found her rucksack, the one she had made the moment she'd come back from the mountains. When she'd ordered it from the bag maker, she hadn't been able to give him a reason as to why she wanted it. It wasn't a thing a lady owned; it was a traveler's bag, large and light and with many pockets to store all sorts of things. It resembled Rage's rucksack, only his had been as black as his eyes and clothes whilst hers was of a dark brown. Stuffing a pair of trousers, a shirt and a jumper, knife and money, matches and matchbox into it took her less than five minutes. At last, she added the apples she'd taken from the kitchen, half a loaf of bread and some cheese, a leather bottle filled with water, and a jacket.

Damn, how long would sunrise take today? She wanted to leave!

In the back of her head, faintly, ghostlike, she could hear Keiran calling for help. It made her shudder. It made her pray she'd gone mad.

When the first rays of sun chased the night away, she opened her door and called for her servants. They were fast to obey her calls—she was known to have a temper and could reduce the weaker of them to tears in a matter of minutes. "Send for Eli," she told one of her maids, and as ordered, her caretaker was with her in a matter of minutes. She'd picked him herself, as a replacement for Jeeve who had been killed by the same man who'd been responsible for Keiran's fall into the abyss.

Eli was younger than Jeeve had been, and he'd come with a family. A wife, two kids, and a thief's branding on his left shoulder, he'd been about to go to prison when she'd claimed him for herself. It was her right to do so—whatever happened in any of the villages belonging to Babylon Manor was under her jurisdiction—and although there had been grumbles and growls from the people, she'd taken Eli home with her, having seen at first sight he was just the man she needed. Broad shouldered and ugly, he clearly was willing to do anything to save his family from starving. When Luca had offered him a job, he'd accepted without a moment's hesitation.

So far, he hadn't disappointed her.

"What can I do for you, my lady?" he now asked, nervously shifting from one foot to the other. Usually she didn't give him direct orders, having explained to him on his first day at the manor what she expected of him. That he'd been called to her in person worried him visibly. "I hope I didn't do anything wrong? I know I could have gotten a better price for those sheep, but I know you don't want me to sell the young ones to the butcher, so I thought—"

"I'm going to the empress's city," Luca interrupted him. Out of the corner of her eye, she saw the rucksack's handles sticking out from behind another bag. Quickly, she pushed it down a bit deeper. "I'll be gone for a bit longer than three weeks, if everything runs smoothly. The High Court needs to be informed about my case and that Lord Barnard is trying to steal my property. Can you run Babylon Manor during the time of my absence? Do you think you are capable of keeping the others in check, collecting the fees, dealing with the village people, and telling Lord Barnard to f—to wait until I am back should he appear on my doorstep?"

The maids—she hadn't even noticed them coming in—giggled. Everyone knew that Luca occasionally swore like a banshee. It was a habit she'd cultivated whilst traveling with Rage, but nowadays, she sometimes managed to rein in her tongue just in time.

She knew that especially the maids hoped Lucius was gone and wouldn't come back. A lot of blood had been found in his bedroom. Some believed him dead; some hoped he'd been taken by the Lady herself and dragged directly into hell. But there was no corpse, and Luca hadn't told anyone that she knew what had happened to it, afraid she would be accused of having killed him or at least of having been involved with his killer.

Lord Barnard would argue she wasn't to inherit Babylon Manor because there was no proof that the rightful lord was dead.

Or he might argue that Lucius was dead, and she was his murderess, despite the fact that apart from the blood and a bit of ash on the carpet, no body had been found. Barnard was a skilled man when it came to adding to his riches, and she had little experience with arguments that required legal knowledge.

Shit. She didn't have time to go on a journey, and one likely to end up in disappointment on top of it!

But she could not ignore the echo of Keiran's screams in her head either.

"Can you do it?" she repeated, interpreting Eli's silence as shock at her offer. "If I lose Babylon Manor, if Lord Barnard takes over, you will hang the same day he sets foot on my land. You know that. Your wife and the kids will lose their home. She'll end up as a whore in Windbrook, and your kids will be sold to the city. I assume you don't want that. Will you keep Babylon Manor safe until I am back?"

Eli raised his chin. A hard glance had crept into his eyes at her words. "Yes, my lady," he said. "I can and I will. Lord Barnard won't set foot onto your property, and I won't betray you, either. I swear by the life of my children."

Luca, remembering just in time she'd need proper boots if she were to ride after Rage and wondering how she could take them without anyone noticing, smiled at Eli. "I know you won't betray me. Now go and get my carriage ready. I want to leave as soon as possible. I'll take Jean with me. The capital will broaden her horizons, and she won't get bored waiting for me whilst I'm at court."

For a moment, Eli looked at her skeptically. "Jean?" he mused, clearly surprised by her choice. "You sure you want to take her and no one else? Billy would be a good choice for protection, or Sayar."

"Just Jean," Luca repeated. "After all, I'm going to the capital, not some place where I have to expect an ambush. Billy and Sayar are needed here."

I'm going to find an assassin. I'm going after someone who's died three months ago, she thought. *What do I need protection for?*

"As you wish, Lady Lucinda," Eli said. He knew her well; he knew it was impossible to talk her out of something if she had made her mind up. "Your carriage will be ready in half an hour."

Just enough time to grab some breakfast.

"Perfect," Luca said, then shushed her maids and Eli out of her rooms and began searching for a decent pair of boots.

TWO HOURS after sunrise, she was on the road, the big wooden case tied to the roof and her leather rucksack along with a pair of boots shoved under her seat. Jean was driving. She had been delighted at the prospect of going to the big city, was already planning a schedule to see all her relatives living there, and hadn't been surprised at all to be the only one to come along. "Sure I'll drive," she'd cheered and jumped up onto the coach box. Now she was leading the carriage toward the main road at high speed—if she continued like that, they'd reach the capital in less than five days.

Not that Luca planned to stay in the coach for another hour. The movement made her sick, and she feared they'd land in the next ditch at any moment.

Ignoring her upset stomach, Luca changed into trousers, shirt, and jumper. Lacing her boots was a challenge in the swaying carriage—she hadn't eaten much, but concentrating on the task made her wish she'd stuck with water before she'd left. But eventually she was ready, her rucksack only waited to be grabbed, and with the jacket on, it became too warm inside anyway. Time to leave; time to tell Jean she wouldn't be going to the capital, not yet, anyway.

She banged her boot against the back of the driver's seat. "Stop!" she yelled. "Jean, stop the coach!"

Luca expected Jean to bring the carriage to an immediate halt, so she braced herself so she wouldn't hit one of the walls. But Jean was a sensible girl, at least when it came to horses. Tugging gently at the reins, she slowed them down until they stood and began grazing. "What is it, mistress?" Jean called, then hopped off the coach box. "Something wrong? Did I drive too fast? Did you forget something?"

After pushing the door open, Luca jumped out, her rucksack swung onto her back. She'd rebraided her hair to a simple plait. She looked ordinary, like the next milk girl on the way to the market apart from not carrying a bucket of milk.

Jean's mouth fell open in surprise. "Mistress!" she stammered. "Whatever happened to your clothes?"

Careful now. If she acted wrongly, said the wrong things, Jean would have a fit. And an agitated Jean would never be able to do what Luca needed her to do. "My clothes are inside," she said, forcing a friendly smile to her face. "I had to change so no one would recognize me. Thank you for stopping the carriage, Jean. You did an excellent job. I knew you were just the right person to bring along."

Jean beamed. "Thank you, mistress."

Reaching back inside the carriage, Luca found the old hat she'd nicked from one of the gardeners and jammed it onto her head. The large rim overshadowed her face, and she could push her hair underneath it, too. "Look, Jean, I am sorry I have to put you through this, but you need to go to the capital on your own."

"But, mistress—"

"I know it is a lot to ask. Think about it, Jean. If I travel in that carriage, Lord Barnard will do everything in his power to stop me. He doesn't want me to go to the High Court and present my case. He wants Babylon Manor, he wants me in prison or wherever else, and so I must take a secret route. Hence the clothes, the hat, and the dirt in my face." Kneeling, Luca scooped up earth and smeared it onto her too clean cheeks, then wiped her hands off on the bottom of her trousers. "I'll get myself a horse and meet you at the Green Eel on Meadow Street. That's about half a mile from the city center. Everyone will be able to show you the way in case you cannot find it by yourself. You'll get the best room, and you will wait for me. Can you do that?"

"Yes, mistress, but—"

"Jean, I don't have time for further explanations. Lord Barnard surely saw us leave this morning. He'll be on our tracks, and the longer we stay here, the sooner he will find us. Do you want him to find me? Do you want me to lose Babylon Manor?" Urgently, Luca took Jean's hand, looking at her as openly and honestly as she could manage. "I need your help with this, Jean. Please don't let me down!"

Jean gulped, then nodded. "I will help you, mistress, and do what you say. But no one will believe me. I'm just a servant girl, I'm not that bright, and what if they say I stole the carriage?"

Luca smiled. "I thought of that. I've written a letter to the landlord of the Green Eel. Last year, I stayed with him for a few days, and I paid him generously. I'm sure he will remember me. And you will have enough money to pay for the room, any food you might wish to order, and a little extra to spend on yourself. You don't need to worry, Jean. Your name is in the letter and that you are acting on my behalf. Now get back to the coach box. Drive fast but safely, just as if I were still traveling with you. If Lord Barnard stops you, tell him you don't know where I am and that you left Babylon Manor alone. He will believe you and won't do you any harm. Understood?" Reining in her impatience, she led Jean toward the carriage and was more than a little relieved to see her climb up on the coach box.

"I'm not afraid of Lord Barnard," Jean said, raising her chin. "I can deal with him. But… the letter. Where is it, mistress?" Picking up the reins, Jean looked at her expectantly.

"Here." Luca took the letter out of her rucksack along with a pouch of coins and handed both to Jean. "I'll be with you as soon as I can."

Already about to leave, Jean, having stowed the letter in her own small traveling purse, had one last question. "What if you don't turn up, mistress? Do I just stay and wait, or do I go back home?"

Damn this girl, Luca thought desperately. *She's either brighter than I thought or much more naïve.* "If I am not in the Green Eel by the end of the month, go back home and let Eli know I have disappeared. He'll find a way to get all of you to safety before Lord Barnard takes over." *If I am not in the Eel, it will be because I'm dead,* was what she thought but didn't tell Jean. *I'll have been eaten by a bunch of ghosts.*

Luca watched the carriage swinging down the road and around the next bend. Then she took off in the opposite direction, away from Babylon Manor as well as away from the capital. Coldwell was east of her; if she were lucky enough to find a horse she could steal, she would reach the Shadows by nightfall the next day.

STEALING A horse was still surprisingly easy, and actually, it wasn't really stealing as in theory, everything on her grounds belonged to her. So when she saw the mare grazing peacefully, it didn't bother her much to sneak closer, cut it loose, and lead it away, although it was broad daylight, and the farmer who owned the horse might see her taking it. True, she looked like a thief, and even as Lady of Babylon Manor she didn't have the right to take whatever she pleased without at least giving an explanation, but those were details she could fix later. After all, she had no intention of keeping the horse. Once she found Rage, and once she found Keiran, she'd give it back together with a generous amount of coins outbalancing the worries the farmer might have suffered.

"Wish I could have taken Flash," Luca murmured, swinging herself onto the mare's back. She didn't have a saddle, but at least she'd brought the saddle blanket she always used and which Keiran had made for her many years ago. "I wish I could have come up with a plausible explanation for taking him to the capital. Groomed and saddled and with some decent supplies. I would kill for freshly baked bread with butter right now, horsy. Imagine the irony: for weeks and weeks I am sick, and as soon as I have nothing but stale bread, wrinkly apples, a piece of old cheese and plain water, I can't think of anything else but a feast."

The horse's back was hard, and briefly, Luca thought of the life growing inside her. At the moment it was barely more than a spark, too tiny to round her belly and far too small to survive outside her body. The journey ahead of her might be too much for it. She might lose the baby.

The thought was surprisingly devastating. When she'd realized she was pregnant some weeks back, it had taken her nearly a week to accept it. She'd argued with herself about how improbable it was to become pregnant after having sex only once—well, fine, twice—but both times under such unusual circumstances. The first time magic had been involved, and surely, conception was next to impossible when impersonating a man. The second time had been followed by horrible events, and surely, conception couldn't happen when so much else was going on.

But her period hadn't come. Instead, morning sickness had begun to plague her.

She'd even thought of getting rid of the baby by using magic, forbidden magic, of course, but still relatively simple to perform. It would have cost her half a day's work, a bit of lamb's blood and a dead frog. She would have been rid of the parasite growing inside her long before anyone noticed her pregnancy. She would have a lot less trouble explaining who had fathered the child; she would be able to eat without throwing up ten minutes later…. And still, she hadn't done it. The child might be Keiran's, and she'd loved him. Impossible to kill the only thing left of him. Or it might be Rage's, who was her husband, and who she could still hear crying over his lover's death in the small hours of the morning, when she lay awake and worried about her future and the future of Babylon Manor. She couldn't kill his child, either, because in a weird way, she loved him too.

"Hold on, little one," she said. "I'll go slow, and I will rest tonight instead of pressing on. That all right for you? I'm trying to find your father, sort of. Don't know which one actually is responsible for your existence, but for some reason, I want them both back."

The day passed quickly, and around evening, Luca became hungry. Luckily, riding hadn't upset her stomach further. The gentle trot she'd chosen, the fresh air, and the prospect of finally being on her way had cheered her up, and when the sun set, she chose a clearing in the woods she was crossing, lit a fire, and had dinner. She might have even dropped off to sleep—she was tired enough, she had only a few more hours to Coldwell to go in the morning, and it was unlikely outlaws would stumble over her during the night.

If only Keiran's voice had stopped calling for her.

Help me!

"I'm doing my best, Keiran," Luca said wearily. The smaller moon, Galadriel, had come up hours ago, and still she hadn't been able to get any sleep. "You know, if this goes on for too long, your calls will drive me mad." Sighing, she got up, stretched, and yawned. No use staying here. Keiran's pleas would keep her awake anyway, so she might as well get back on the road.

Whilst persuading the mare to part with the grass she'd been munching, Luca vaguely wondered whether she was losing her mind. "That's why I hear his voice: because I'm mad. Great. Maybe Lindsay can put me out of my misery if I manage to explain well enough why I am looking for Rage."

"RAGE? NO, love, he's not here. Not anymore, that is. Come inside, though. It's freezing outside, and you look as if you could do with my famous Health soup. Come inside, missy! No one here apart from Maria, my neighbor's newborn, and she's fast asleep. Come on, yes, that's fine. One step, and another step—by the Lady, girl, you look as if you haven't slept in days."

Luca, dizzy with fatigue, allowed Lindsay to lead her inside the small kitchen. It was early morning, the light outside not bright enough yet to see more than a few steps, and the two moons still hanging low just above the horizon. Galadriel cast her silver beams onto the streets, and Arwen added a green shimmer—Luca was barely aware of either as she had a hard enough time keeping her eyes open. Heavily, she sat on the bench in Lindsay's kitchen, suddenly glad beyond words that the landlady had opened to her knocks, that she was still the owner of this tavern, and that she had recognized her in her disguise. She hadn't even been overly surprised to see her.

"Here, honey, drink this," Lindsay said, placing a steaming mug in front of Luca. "It will warm you up quickly. Why on earth did you travel through the night instead of getting yourself a nice warm bed in a roadhouse along the way?"

"Couldn't do that," Luca mumbled. Her hands were wrapped around the mug, heat seeping into her body and making her shiver in anticipation of the hot liquid running down her throat and warming her from inside as well. She took a sip, and another one, then coughed—the soup wasn't only hot, it was spicy as well, and seemed to burn holes into her tongue.

Lindsay smiled. "The first time he drank it, Rage called my soup liquid fire, although it made him stay on his feet long enough to get some healing magic from Teddy. Glad you seem to like it better than he did."

Warmth spread through Luca, and she sighed with relief to be out of the wind and the night. Ever since she'd left home, she heard

Keiran calling for her, louder with every passing minute, and at times, she'd nearly screamed with frustration because she was unable to help him and equally unable to stop his pleas for help.

"I should apologize for calling at such an early hour," Luca said, gradually relaxing as the fire emerging from Lindsay's hearth warmed her even further. "Actually, I should apologize for a lot of things."

"Like running away in the middle of the night last time you were here and although you'd promised to stay at least a week?"

"For example."

"Or for stealing my bread."

"As well. Would it be all right if I paid for it now?" Her fingers were still numb from the night's cold when Luca searched for her purse, but eventually she was able to place a few coins onto the table. "That should cover about everything I took plus what you spent to heal Keiran."

A big smile spread over Lindsay's friendly face, and quickly, she scooped up the coins. "Rage already paid me," she pointed out with a grin. "But I'm glad to see you are a decent person after all and not one of those spoilt little brats who think everything is for free. And now tell me why you are looking for him."

Only a few short months ago, Luca wouldn't have even talked to a woman who owned a tavern. Back then, her only trouble had been her daily arguments with the man she'd thought was her father. But since then, a lot had happened, and most of it had been really, really bad. And Lindsay was a good woman despite her loud and sometimes rude manner. There was no reason not to trust her, and from out of nowhere, Luca felt an urge to tell the landlady everything.

Only upon opening her mouth, she realized she didn't even know where to start.

Lindsay misinterpreted her silence. "Look, girl, I don't know what this is all about, but Rage is well liked in the Shadows. Getting Teddy's corpse out of the burning house and saving his daughter on top of it was awesome. I won't betray his trust in me without a damn good reason." Impatiently, she slammed her hands onto the table.

"Remember, I was the one who kept the fire in check," Luca snapped. "It was me who saved your precious Shadows from burning to ashes, and anyway, I am married to the damn assassin!" She slammed her own hand onto the table. On her finger was a thin, unimpressive ring. It wasn't shiny, as it wasn't made out of metal, and it didn't hold a gem as it was woven from human hair. "I married him the old way up in your attic room, Lindsay. I have a right to know where he is."

Lindsay opened her mouth, then closed it again without having said a word. She got up, put some plates on the table, and added glasses and a jug of water as well as bread, cheese, honey, and half a ham.

"I'm not hungry," Luca said wearily. "Been up since…. Well. Cannot remember, really. I took it easy on the way here, walked on occasions, but I didn't sleep much. Either I lay awake half the night, or I woke up from nightmares the moment I dozed off. Please, just tell me when he's been here and if you know where he might be now."

Taking a knife, Lindsay began buttering a piece of bread. She added honey, breathed in deeply, and handed it to Luca, who took it out of reflex. "Eat," the landlady said gently. "You are with child, aren't you? A bit of food will do both of you the world of good."

CHAPTER
Two

"HOW THE... how do you know I am pregnant?" The bread forgotten in her hand, honey dripping on the table, Luca stared at Lindsay. "No one knows, and it doesn't show yet, either. You didn't weave magic. So how can you know this?"

Lindsay smiled. "Doing a bit of midwifing here and there. The kid in the cradle? Maria, her name is. Born last new moon, and with my help. Her mum had a hard time delivering her, so she's with me until Mummy is better. Don't need magic to know if a girl is pregnant. Can see it in your face and your eyes and how you react to smells. Ten weeks, maybe twelve?"

Sighing, Luca took a bite from the bread. The honey was sweet, the butter fresh—to her surprise, she realized she was ravenous. "About twelve," she replied, devouring the bread with a few bites and gratefully accepting the second slice Lindsay had prepared for her. "It is Rage's child, conceived on our wedding night. I would say that is reason enough for me to find him."

Strange, how easy it has become to lie, Luca thought. Not that she was unfamiliar with lies. Lying to Lucius had been a daily pleasure, lying to the servants, lying to the priest who took her confessions. She wasn't the most honest person, she had to admit. But those had been small lies in comparison to what she was telling Lindsay, and what she had been hiding from everyone else so far. No one apart from her and Rage knew, for example, that Keiran was dead—or should be dead, at least. She hadn't told his father and his stepmother. They believed he'd run away; they hoped he was well and didn't think of him much as far as Luca knew. Until a moment ago, no one apart from herself had known she was pregnant. Even she didn't know who the father was. And she hadn't told anyone what had happened at the Forbidden Monastery, either.

Anyway, she couldn't take back what she'd said, and she wouldn't tell Lindsay she'd slept with Keiran. In a way, she was embarrassed about it, but that was not the main reason. The memory of the morning when she'd been in bed with both Keiran and Rage was most precious to her, and she wasn't willing to spoil it by sharing it and facing a possible scolding.

Thoughtfully, Lindsay held her gaze before nodding slowly. "Guess it is. Why did you split up in the first place? Come on, girl, you know that there are too many open questions. Fill in the details, will you?"

Snorting, Luca pushed her empty plate away and took the mug instead. It was still half-full with the soup. Her stomach, still growling with hunger, demanded that she drink it, so she did. When she'd emptied it, she said, "The details? Are you joking? Telling you the whole story would take hours. I don't have hours. Did you know I am only sixteen years old, Lindsay? By law, I need a legal guardian until I am eighteen. My lovely neighbor Lord Barnard offered himself for the position. I declined, told him I am a married woman and that I don't need his help. But he insists on either meeting my husband or taking over my property until I'm eighteen. He says Lucius promised him my hand in marriage, and knowing Lucius, I fear it's possible. If he does marry me, I am sure I will have an unpleasant accident shortly after my wedding night. I can't even imagine what he would do if he found out I'm with child. I need Rage at my side, Lindsay. And I have no idea where he is. Last time I saw him… well, that's a different story. Until you told me he was here, I didn't even know for sure he was still alive!" Suddenly disgusted at the dregs showing at the bottom of her mug, she put it back on the table hard, nearly breaking it. Her eyes burned with unshed tears—not because of Barnard or the secrets she had to keep quiet, not because of her insecure status back home, but because of the voice in her head, begging her for help. It was such a scared voice, flat and hoarse, devoid of all hope. It would have broken her heart even if she hadn't known its owner. "Please, Lindsay, tell me when he was here. Tell me where I can find him."

The baby in the crib began to cry, the thin, wailing sound of a hungry newborn. Lindsay got up and brought the baby back to the table, rocking it, soothing it. "Shush, little one, no need to cry. Here, nibble on that for a bit." Gently, she slipped her little finger into the baby's mouth; immediately, it began to suck, its tiny hands balled to fists, the eyes squeezed tightly shut. "Won't last long, and she'll want her mum's breast," Lindsay said. "Maria here is a good girl, but when she is hungry, she can cry loud enough to make the stars tumble from the sky." With narrowed eyes, she looked at Luca. "So you and Rage are married, eh? I bet things didn't go entirely right, given he was heavily in love with the boy. Anyway, Rage is not here. Came by around midwinter feast. Looked as if he'd been through hell and back. He stayed in the attic room for less than a day, then wandered off in the middle of the night. Haven't seen him since, dear. Mike and Ben tried to track him down. Thought they might manage to persuade him to get back here given his sorry condition, but well, they couldn't find him. Here, take little Maria for a minute. Got to check on her mummy. Back as soon as I can, and try not to drop her."

Before Luca could as much as shake her head at Lindsay's request, the landlady had put the baby into her arm, patted her back, and left the kitchen through the back door. A rush of cold made Luca shiver. The baby began to cry again, louder this time and clearly angry at the still absent food. Helplessly, Luca began to rock her, and after an awkward moment of hesitation, began to hum the only nursery song she remembered.

Maria opened her eyes. They were stunningly blue. Under the cap she was wearing, Luca could see ginger locks, flattened to her head but as soft as down. Luca touched a strand, then brushed her fingertips over the child's face. "Soft as a peach," she whispered, wondering if her own child would be that beautiful, and if it would be born at all. So many things could happen in nine months, normal things like an accident or a simple miscarriage, nasty things like an attack, horrible things like climbing into an abyss where there were ghosts waiting at the bottom. Her child had about as much chance of getting born as this little girl had of becoming the empress's daughter-in-law.

Tears began to drop onto the baby's dingy blanket.

"There, there, honey, no need to cry!"

Great. Lindsay had come back and now saw her breaking down. "I'm fine," Luca tried to say, but it came out as a sob.

"You're obviously not, dear, or there wouldn't be tears running down your cheeks. Come, it is not that bad, having a child. You're young, I give you that, but not too young. I'm sure you will find Rage, and once he knows he will be a father, he'll forget about the boy."

Now that made Luca bark out a laugh. "Hardly, Lindsay," she said, wiping the tears from her face. "He loves Keiran. He doesn't love me. And that's not the reason for my tears, anyway. Too many problems, and a few hard weeks ahead of me. Here, take the baby to her mum. Would it be possible to go upstairs to the attic room? Maybe Rage has left something, anything, I can use to perform a Tracking spell." Holding the baby out to Lindsay, Luca wasn't overly surprised to find that parting with the tiny child was harder than she'd expected.

Maria in her left arm, Lindsay brushed a strand of hair out of Luca's face. When she'd taken off the hat, the string that held it back had loosened, and now the blonde locks were cascading down her back and obscuring her expression. "You can use the attic room all right, girl," the landlady said. "Ben will take you upstairs. Sleep well, Luca."

"I'm not tir—" Luca began, but for some reason, her tongue refused to finish the sentence.

"Of course you are tired." Lindsay's voice sounded odd, muffled as if she were speaking through a thick cloud of cotton. "You know, my Health soup has a different effect on each person who drinks it. For Rage, it dimmed down the pain and made him strong enough to walk to Teddy's hut. When my son Mike managed to hack off half his foot with the axe, it reduced the blood loss until I had him patched up. Keiran's wounds healed faster, and for you, it works like a sleeping draught."

"But—"

"No buts anymore. The bed is waiting."

No! Luca wanted to say, *I've got to go, I've got to find Rage and Keiran.* But no one listened. Maybe she hadn't said the words, and maybe she had and they just ignored her. In any case, she was picked up as if she were a child herself. Strong arms around her, and the faint smell of fish on the clothes of the man who carried her. One of Lindsay's sons, obviously, but where had he come from?

Upstairs, was it? To the attic room where she'd witnessed Rage and Keiran making love, where she'd seduced the assassin, where she'd married him the old way? Not a bad thing, sleeping in their bed. Maybe she would dream of him; maybe she would figure out whilst asleep how to find him.

LUCA WOKE up screaming around lunchtime. Sweat was pouring down her face, and she was shaking badly. Her throat was dry, her tongue rough and swollen. Greedily, she took the glass of water Lindsay had left on the bedside table and drank it in one long go.

Only then did she become aware of Ben sitting on the spare bed, the one she'd slept in the last time she'd been in this room. "Nasty nightmare that was," he said in his low, slow voice. "Care to tell me what it was about? Helps, sometimes, to tell. That's what Mum says, and she's often right when it comes to such things."

"I dreamed about Rage," Luca said after a moment of consideration. She didn't believe sharing her dream would make it less cruel. Instead, she hoped talking about it would keep it in her mind. In her experience, even the worst nightmares had a tendency to melt away in the daylight.

"What about him?" Like a statue, Ben sat on the bed. He was a large man with broad shoulders and a considerable beer belly. In his hand, he had a knife; he was cleaning his nails with it.

Swinging her legs out of bed, Luca stared out of the window, saw rainclouds gathering, and decided she hated early spring even more than she hated winter. "Rage was holding my father's head in his hands. He—my father—died a few months back, and not in a pleasant way." She didn't tell Ben that Lucius hadn't been her father, nor that Rage had really held his head in his hands. "The head was accusing Rage of having killed me. There were maggots coming out of its rotten mouth, and one of his eyeballs had slipped onto his cheek, and the next moment, I saw myself in a grave, and Rage was shoveling earth onto me although I begged him not to."

"Nasty dream," Ben confirmed. "Seems you weren't fond of the man. So why are you looking for him? Really, I mean. Overheard your talk with my mum. That you're married. Don't believe it."

Surprised, Luca stopped braiding her hair. Right now and with the prospect of being on the road for the next few weeks, she truly considered cutting it short might be a good idea. "Ben," she said, "you've got an eye for people. Do you know where he is?"

Ben shrugged. "He came here at the end of last year, sat on the same bed you sit on now. Didn't talk or sleep or eat. Didn't do anything. Sat with him just as I'm sitting with you now. Mum sent me, y'know? She likes to know what's happening under her roof. Didn't like the empty look in Rage's eyes. Told me to cheer him up a bit."

"Didn't work, I suppose." Luca sighed. She'd found her rucksack someone had put next to the bed and the hat as well. Jamming it on and pushing her hair underneath it, she then fished for her jacket. She was ready to go, although she had no idea where.

Ben held the door open for her. "Didn't work," he confirmed. "He was not really here even when you saw him standing in front of you. Figure Keiran died?"

Already halfway downstairs, Luca stopped, not looking at Ben. "That's why I have to find Rage," she said. "I believe Keiran is still alive. He's calling me. He's calling for help. I don't know the way to the abyss, not exactly, but I swear, if I don't find Rage soon, I will try to get into the mountains on my own."

Ben put his hand on her shoulder. "If I knew where he is, I'd tell you. But he didn't speak, not a single word. Just sat on the bed, and then he was gone in the morning. Don't know how he did it with me being there, but gone he was. Can't even tell you the direction he took."

Luca nodded. "The mountains are to the north. Finding him here was my only hope. I'll take the main road. And Ben? Thanks for watching over me whilst I was asleep."

"My pleasure," Ben replied, and then he put her blanket on her stolen horse, helped her up, got provisions for her from his mother's kitchen, and waved until she was gone.

As if the rain had heard her complain, it ceased half an hour after she'd left Coldwell. Instead, big, wet snowflakes drifted earthward out of low-hanging gray clouds. The weather was so very much like it had been the day she and Rage had gone into the mountains for the first time, it struck Luca like an omen.

There hadn't been a single thing belonging to him in Lindsay's attic room. Nothing to use for a Tracking spell. No way to find him.

She would have to find the hidden path to the Forbidden Monastery without his help. "Can't be that hard, can it?" Luca muttered, pulling the collar of her jacket as high as possible against the wind and the snow. "From the inn where Ethan kidnapped Keiran, we went northwards, into the mountains. Easy, really. No need to worry."

At least her horse didn't seem bothered by the snow. It wasn't a full-blood mare but long legged and with a beautiful head. This one still had its thick winter coat, a large bottom, and a lot of stamina. A horse made to pull carts loaded with barrels. A reliable horse that could go on for days without much to eat. Occasionally, it shook its big head as if chasing off flies. Other than that, it went on steadily and stuck to the road although the road was nearly invisible under the snow now. "I think I won't give you back to your owner," Luca told the horse. "I will keep you, and you won't have to do more than graze on my meadows. If I survive this storm, that is."

Luca rode on for hours, occasionally dozing off and only waking up when her body threatened to slip to the ground. Her feet and fingers were numb, her face felt as if the skin was frozen. Soon she'd become too cold to remember where she was going and why she was outside; soon, she'd lose a toe and the tip of her nose to the frost.

If she hadn't heard Keiran calling for her, stronger with every step her horse took, she would have given up hours ago.

She didn't even know whether or not she was still heading north. Or what time it was since the snow and the clouds made it impossible to judge the hour. There was only Keiran's call, tugging at her heart and her soul. "On my way," Luca mumbled. "Nearly there."

Which way did the horse go? Where was she?

The voice in her head was loud enough now to convince her she'd made it into the mountains already. She must be near the Forbidden Monastery, near the abyss where Keiran awaited her, or she wouldn't hear him so clearly. The mare just trod on. Probably, they had become lost hours ago, and the horse only hoped she'd know where they could find shelter.

No, there were no mountains anywhere in sight. The path ahead of her was as flat as her palm, and to the left, she could see the outline of a forest. Impossible to tell where was north and where south, impossible to choose a direction. She needed to get inside, or the storm would blow her away. Even her mare, patient as she was, neighed unwillingly when Luca forced her onward, across a ditch. She wanted to get into the woods, hoping she'd find an abandoned hut where they could stay until the storm had ceased. "Get along," Luca urged, but the horse remained stubborn. It wanted to go the other way although there was nothing there, not even a single bush to break the wind.

The reins slipped out of her fingers when the horse shook its head, and immediately, the mare walked away from the woods. Frantically, Luca fumbled for the reins. When she finally found them, she'd lost sight of the trees behind her.

No use turning around, no use because in this weather, she would have trouble finding her own nose, not to mention a forest that was already lost in the storm.

The horse neighed again and changed to a slow gallop. Luca nearly fell; she hadn't expected such a sudden change in pace. Obviously, the horse had better instincts than her, because through the snow, Luca saw something dark and large appear before her, something that hadn't been there a moment ago, something square and artificial.

A house. Or better yet, a wall surrounding a house.

"Horse, I will buy you a sack full of spring carrots if this is what I think it is," Luca mumbled, her lips cracking from the cold, her words barely audible in the whirling wind. "Make it two sacks. This is a nunnery, isn't it? Yes, of course it is. Great. Wonderful. Let's hope the nuns are at home and willing to open their gate to a stranger."

Barely feeling her legs, Luca slipped off the horse's back and led the mare to the gate. It was closed, of course, and when she banged against it, her impression was that she didn't make more noise than a fly banging against a window. They couldn't hear her. She'd freeze out here, only a few feet away from warmth and shelter and food.

Luca thought of her unborn child, she thought of Keiran, and she used her foot to make more noise. "Open this door, you stupid women," she yelled, outraged at the weather, the voice in her head driving her mad, and at Rage who refused to be found. "Open up, or I will break it down!"

Her outburst didn't last long. She was too hungry and too cold for that. Exhausted, she sunk against the door's solid wood and wondered if she had enough strength left to set the door on fire with a bit of magic when it finally opened, just a crack, and not nearly wide enough to let her in.

A pair of steel blue eyes looked at her. The rest of the face was hidden behind a veil, as it was custom for the sisters who served the Lady. "No need to become aggressive," the sister said curtly. "And no need for swearwords, either. If you seek our help, all you need to do is ask. Although, I do admit that the weather can drive even the most sensible person crazy."

"And I'm not sensible at all." Luca felt a smile tugging at her cracked lips. "Please, will you let me in? I've been outside for hours. I need shelter and food, if possible. And—hay for my horse?"

"Neither is any problem at all," the sister said and finally opened the door wide enough for Luca to get inside. "My name is Nicole. Would you care to tell me your name?"

Inside the yard, the wind was still blowing but with less strength, as the wall broke its power. Pushing her hat back and out of her face, Luca saw one low stone building with large windows and a smaller one, made of wood. The stone house would be the home of the sisters, she guessed, the wooden one the stables. "My horse has led me here. Without her, I wouldn't have survived. May I put her into your stables? And I'm Luca, sorry. My manners have frozen several hours ago."

Sister Nicole shot her a glance, amusement dancing in her eyes. "Clever horse. She'll get an extra big ration of hay. You, I think, could do with dinner, I suppose?"

"Tea would be great for a start," Luca mumbled.

Once the mare was safely put in a big box in the sisters' stables, Nicole led Luca into the kitchen attached to the infirmary. It was a small place, but then, the nunnery was small too. Near the capital, the sisters owned houses nearly as big as the empress's palace, enough land to rent it out, and enough cattle to feed an army. This place here was in the middle of nowhere, it seemed, and neither rich nor blessed with rich protectors.

Warmth embraced her. "I'm glad I found your nunnery," Luca sighed, dropping onto one of the benches that stood along the kitchen walls. She'd shed her heavy coat; it lay dripping wet on the floor until the sister picked it up and hung it on a peg near the fireplace.

There were five tables. Luca guessed the nunnery could feed up to twenty people, if necessary. Today, though, she was the only guest. Only one other sister was in the kitchen, stirring a pot hanging above the fireplace. The smell was delicious.

"Would you like some lamb stew, Luca?" Nicole asked, and placed a steaming bowl onto the table before Luca could even nod. Along with the stew came bread and a big mug of milk.

"I'm too cold to eat," Luca said helplessly, eying the stew and wondering if she would be able to keep it down if indeed she dared to eat it. Better delay that task for a while. "Can I change first, please?" With numb fingers, she fumbled the strings of her rucksack open only to find the spare clothes inside damp.

The nuns looked at her, and then at each other. "I'll go and get you some dry clothes," Nicole said, rushing out of the kitchen.

It took Luca a while to open the laces of her boots, but once they were off, she found her socks were soaked, too. "Great," she murmured. "Had I taken a bath, I couldn't be wetter. Damn snow."

"This is the last outburst of winter," the other sister said, sitting down opposite her. "Tomorrow the weather will be better. Nicole will be back any moment, you can get changed and then eat your dinner." She held out her hand. "I'm Laure, abbess of this place. I hope you like lamb stew. I cooked it myself."

Wiping her wet hair out of her face, Luca cast her a tired smile. "I used to love lamb stew, but for the last few weeks my stomach hasn't approved of food anymore. Ever since, I mostly live on apples and bread and water. Your stew smells delicious, though. I am looking forward to trying it."

Laure smiled, putting her head to one side. "You look familiar. Have you been here before? Oh, thank you, Nicole. Luca, take these clothes. They were left by one of our patients. She doesn't need them anymore, and they look as if they might fit you. It's quiet in the infirmary. Take your time, we won't disturb you."

Luca changed quickly—the infirmary was warm, but not as warm as the kitchen. Briefly, she looked around the room, counting seven beds. A screen had been put in front of one, obviously to give the patient in the bed some privacy. There was no sound to be heard; this patient was very fast asleep or unconscious. Either way, he or she wouldn't be able to see Luca getting changed, so she slipped out of her clothes, put the dry ones on, and rushed back into the kitchen.

Laure's eyes widened when she saw her. "By the sweet Lady," she said. "In these clothes, you look like one of my girls. Please, Luca, sit and eat. I won't bother you with any questions until you are finished."

The clothes—a wide skirt, a loose blouse, warm socks and wooden shoes—felt strange after the trousers and the jumper. But they were dry and warm enough too. That they had once belonged to someone else didn't bother Luca as much as she might have expected. After putting her own clothes on a second peg close to the fireplace, she sat down again and picked up the spoon. Hesitantly, she blew onto the stew, not sure she should really try to eat it.

Her child needed her to be strong and healthy. If she didn't eat, she would fall ill, not to mention being unable to search after Keiran.

"Let's give it a try," she told the stew and took a bite.

Delicious. And she said as much to Laure.

"Glad you like it. There are also some apples if you care for dessert."

It didn't take Luca long to empty the bowl, and she was more than a bit grateful that her body seemed to accept the food. She even ate an apple—it was less wrinkly than the one she had in her rucksack, but less sweet as well.

Her eyes dropped closed, and she might have fallen asleep on the kitchen table if a thought hadn't nagged at her the very moment her chin was about to drop onto her chest. She ripped her eyes open. "You said one of your novices looks a bit like me?"

Laure, who had been washing up her bowl, nodded. "Not just a bit. The resemblance is striking. Rebecca is thirteen. I would say you are about eighteen?"

"Sixteen," Luca replied absently. "Rebecca? Was she born in Windbrook?"

Now Laure turned around, drying her hands on her apron. "You know her?"

Luca paled. It wasn't often she thought of Lucius and what he had done when Rage had finally sought him out. Thinking of it made her physically sick, something she really didn't need in her state. But now she had to think of it. This was the nunnery where Rage had taken Rebecca after she had blinded Lucius. This was the place that had taken care of a girl who looked like her and who Lucius had raped on a constant basis.

"Yes, I know her," Luca said faintly. "She.... Let's say I know what happened to her. Is she still here? Is she well?"

"That depends," Laure said. "Do you plan to take her away from here? Do you intend to charge her for what she has done? Because I won't let that happen. She is in my charge. I won't allow you to do her harm."

Shocked at the sudden coldness in Laure's voice, Luca raised her hands in what she hoped was a peaceful gesture. "Nothing like that," she said. "Truly, I have no intention to drag her back home. Lucius was my... my father. I know what he did to Rebecca, and I know why he did it. He wanted me, but couldn't have me. I don't blame Rebecca for defending herself."

As quickly as Laure had become cold and angry, her mood changed again with Luca's words. "That's good to hear. Not what you said about your father, of course. It seems he is a horrible man. But that you won't take Rebecca away from here. She is.... Well. Calling her happy would be a lie. It took her weeks to get out of bed, not to talk about staying in a room on her own. She's tough, but she suffered a lot. Actually, I believe you couldn't take her away from here even if you wanted to. She'd die the moment she'd be dragged outside the gates." Moving through the kitchen with the dreamlike security of a woman who spent a lot of time between pots and pans, Laure took the boiling kettle and poured them two mugs of tea. Putting one of them in front of Luca, she asked, "How is your father?"

"He's dead."

Laure blinked. "Oh."

Luca wrapped her hands around the mug, breathing in the rich scent of the tea. "Long story," she said quietly. "Too long to be told, too cruel to be remembered. All that counts is that he is gone and that he won't come looking for Rebecca. Or me, for that matter." Sighing, she craned her neck. "I'm very tired, abbess. Would it be possible for me to go to bed now? I need to be on my way tomorrow."

"Why did you come here? I mean, if you care to tell me. Curiosity is one of my many flaws, I must admit." Laure took a sip of her tea, not really trying to hide how interested she was in the answer Luca might give.

Rage had been here before. Asking for him couldn't hurt. So she said, "I'm looking for the man who brought you Rebecca," and hoped not too much desperation showed in her words. "You didn't happen to see him lately, did you?"

Laure put the mug down. "Rage."

The way she sounded—not really surprised but suspicious and tense—caused hope to flare up in Luca's chest. "Has he been here? When? Please, don't tell me he was here only recently, and I have missed him by a day or two!"

Laure got up. Looking down at Luca, she said, "Rage…. He hasn't talked much, although I tried to get some answers. He hasn't eaten, either. Staying in the stables, staring at the walls was all he did."

Anticipation nearly choked Luca; it was hard to get the next words out. "When did he leave?"

Laure quietly opened the door to the infirmary, and she beckoned Luca closer. "Rage didn't leave," she said. "He's in the infirmary."

Stunned, Luca took a few steps toward the screen and the bed it was hiding. "What happened?" she asked. "I've seen him getting injured and I've seen him ill from wild magic, but he was always back on his feet in no time."

Laure looked at her oddly. "He is not ill, and what happened to him was no wild magic. A few days ago, he tried to kill himself. I doubt he'll survive the night."

CHAPTER
Three

THIS WAS wrong. Totally, completely wrong. She shouldn't sit here, in the middle of the night and in a nearly dark room. She should be in bed herself, sleeping peacefully.

She shouldn't be looking into Rage's deathly pale face. His wrists shouldn't be bandaged; the fabric shouldn't be soiled with his blood.

Involuntarily, she shuddered.

Laure, standing next to her, put a soothing hand to her shoulder. "There is no use wondering why he did it," she said in a low voice. "All that matters is whether he survives. As it is, he was lucky. Hadn't Rebecca paid him a visit in the stables ahead of dinner time, he would already be dead."

Absently, Luca pushed a strand of hair behind her ear, then reached out and touched Rage's face. He was unconscious and looked surprisingly small between the white sheets. Even his lips were white. He was drained of color, drained of life, and for a moment, Luca wanted to strangle him for trying to sneak away like that.

"I know why he did it," Luca said. "I just don't understand why he waited this long to do it."

Pulling a chair close, Laure sat down at the other side of the bed. Methodically, she changed the bandages on Rage's wrists. "He's lost a lot of blood. I must admit, I did not foresee this. I knew he was a broken man. He would have been starving to death sometime soon, but cutting his wrists… no." Gently, she wiped the sweat from his brow. Despite the fever, he was shivering underneath the thin blanket that covered his haggard body.

"You can stay here, if you like," Laure added. "I can also ask one of my sisters to sit with him. Your decision."

"I think I will stay for a while."

The silence increased once Laure had left the infirmary. No one was in the kitchen, and from outside no sound could be heard, either. The darkness beyond the small window next to Rage's bed was impenetrable. Luca couldn't even say whether or not it was still snowing.

The assassin's hand underneath hers was ice-cold. It was a clear sign the fever would rise further in the next few hours, which was a scary thought given he was almost dead already. Apart from the shivers, he didn't move, and when Luca touched his stubbly cheek, he didn't turn his head away like she'd half expected him to do. "I don't want you to die," she whispered in his ear, but he didn't respond. Of course he didn't.

"I won't let you die." Luca's voice sounded loud in the mostly empty room. "My chance to survive a journey to the mountains is next to zero without your help. My chance to find Keiran, be he alive or dead… well, it's so very small I won't even think about it."

Her eyes burned. Either because she was tired or because of the unshed tears behind her lids.

"Your hair's grown since I last saw you. I don't like your beard, either. And you're too thin. And too pale. Well, you've never had a tan, as far as I know, but this here is ridiculous. Keiran would scold you badly if he were to see you like that."

Keiran, who was calling for her even now, who was, she was convinced of it, waiting for her to get him out of that horrible abyss, Keiran who counted on her not to give up.

Letting Rage die would mean giving up.

Pushing her doubts and her fear aside, Luca put both her hands on Rage's chest. She could feel his heart, fluttering like a caged bird. She could hear his labored breath. She even thought she could sense his fear, buried deep inside him.

"Nonsense," she said, trying in vain to reassure herself she was doing the right thing. Then she closed her eyes and began to weave a powerful Healing spell.

At first, nothing happened. Luca could feel her magic seeping into Rage's body all right, but his body refused to react.

Her will to heal him seemed to hit a wall; it just bounced off without having any effect.

Frowning, she drew back. *This is odd*, she thought. *He's unconscious. How can he fight against me?*

For a moment, Luca didn't know what to do. She'd always used her magic whenever she needed it, and always successfully. The magic was strong in her, always had been, and not getting her way felt unfamiliar and embarrassing. Even more so as she knew Rage was unable to use his own magic. "You can't even light a candle without using matches," she hissed at the unconscious, silent figure in the bed. "So don't you dare die right under my nose only because your stupid magic thinks I want to do you harm and won't allow me to help you!"

Stubbornly, Luca put her hands back onto Rage's chest. She'd been in touch with his magic before so it should be easy to outwit it. His magic was wild, untamed, whereas she knew exactly what she wanted and how to get it. The only thing she needed to do was to keep his magic in check whilst she healed those wounds.

And afterward, she could try to deal with an assassin who would be damn angry at her interference.

Well. One task at the time.

"I know you," she told him sternly. "I've seen you asleep. I've seen you bleed. I once saved your life when your magic went wild and threatened to kill everyone close by and maybe even yourself. I deceived you. I lied to you. I know how you look naked and how you look when you come. I saw you cry. Truly, I can understand your decision to take your own life, but I can't accept it."

With every word, she calmed her nervous mind. With every truth she spoke, it became easier to reach inside him. She'd done it before, and in a way, it had been equally hard back then. She'd seduced him, and his magic and hers had reacted in a very bad way. He'd nearly died in Lindsay's attic room, but she'd found a way to deal with the wildness.

She could do it again. And she didn't see another way to save him.

Shedding her last doubts, she pushed on, broke through the barrier his magic had created, and searched for the raw, bloodied edges of the wounds his knife had cast.

Luca felt him tense and smiled—there was some life left in him after all, and some stubbornness. Hopefully there was enough of both to persuade him not to die.

There were the wounds, a dark red glow in an ocean of blackness. So easy to find but not that easy to heal. Rage had done a thorough job with his knife.

Luca sensed the stitches in Rage's flesh. They were professionally done, but by far not as good as even the most basic healing magic. Luca could do more than heal the wounds, she could heal the veins and arteries; she could mend the cut muscles and nerves. She could even tell Rage's body to compensate for the blood loss, and because she could do it, she just did it the moment she thought about it. In another few minutes he would be as good as—

Rage screamed. His body cramped, and ripped out of unconsciousness, the assassin's hands shot up. His fingers, much stronger than expected in his condition, closed around her throat. "Out… of my… head," he rasped, his voice hoarse from lack of use.

He tightened his grip.

Luca choked. Her initial, instinctive reaction was to bring her own hands to her throat, trying to pull his off. She also wanted nothing more than to get away from the bed, break the connection she had woven so very carefully. She wanted, needed, to get away….

But then she didn't. She had to finish what she had started. Fresh blood seeped through the bandages around Rage's wrists. He wasn't yet strong enough to be a threat to her life. So instead of fleeing his attack, she ignored it. Instead of jumping up, she leaned in. She put one hand across his throat, adding gentle pressure. With her left, she held his body down, her palm firmly pressed to his chest. "Quiet now," she said. "It's me. Luca. I don't mean you harm, and if you don't stop fighting against me, I swear this will become really unpleasant for the both of us. By the Lady, Rage, it's not that bad to have your life saved!"

Under different circumstances, he would have shaken her off like an annoying puppy. Tonight, he was confused, weak, and taken by surprise by her movement. It was easy to push him back into the pillows and hold him down whilst she finished her Healing magic. Luckily, there wasn't much left to do. The damage to the muscles and nerves was already undone, and only his flesh needed to be mended. A couple of minutes, no more.

She should have known Rage better than to believe he'd give up that easily. When she took a bit of the pressure off his throat to allow him to breathe a bit easier, he brought his elbow up and caught her squarely at her temple. She staggered, swayed; then her legs turned to jelly and she fell.

Rage was out of the bed in the blink of an eye. His breath came in labored gasps; his face was ashen even in the golden light of the candle, and his fists were balled. The bandages around both wrists were soaked with blood. Luca hoped what she had done was good enough because surely he wouldn't let her anywhere near him anytime soon.

"You."

"Yes, me," Luca snapped, getting up and half tumbling over the chair. "Who else would be daft enough to save your life? That's twice, just for the record. You owe me, husband. Now get back to bed before you collapse. And you're looking ridiculous in this nightshirt, by the way."

She'd just said it to distract him, to hopefully take the edge off his wrath.

Didn't work.

Visibly in pain, Rage took another step away from the bed. The nightshirt he wore was of soft gray linen and reached down to the floor; only his bare feet could be seen. They looked fragile, the bones pressing against the skin like they wanted to break through. Briefly, Luca wondered how he managed to stand on the tiles without noticing how cold they were.

She watched him scan the infirmary, taking in the high, small windows and that he was closer to the door than she was. She saw him calculate the distance and how fast he'd make it outside given his weakened condition, and she saw him glancing at his wrists.

A few drops of blood hit the floor.

"You had no right to interfere." Another step toward the door. He'd obviously decided to take it slowly, step by step, instead of running. Had he tried, he'd have collapsed. Luca was certain of it.

"I did what I had to. I need your help, and anyway, as your wife I have every right to interfere. You, on the other hand, had no right to take your life without consulting me first. I think we are even." Crossing her arms over her chest, Luca raised her chin and tried to stare Rage down.

Didn't work, either.

"I should have broken your neck whilst I had the chance," Rage bit out. He'd reached the door to the kitchen. Sweat was running down his temples. Leaning against the doorframe for support, Rage wiped his face dry—he'd need to sit down soon if he didn't want to end up unconscious again. Pushing the door open, he closed his eyes against the sudden brush of warmth, then took a seat on one of the benches.

Slowly and with her hands half raised so he could see she didn't hold any weapons and wasn't weaving secret magic, Luca followed him into the kitchen. She poured him a glass of water, which he drank greedily, but the hostility in his eyes didn't vanish.

She was just about to explain why she had saved his life when the main door to the kitchen opened and Laure stepped inside. In her hand she held a lamp, and instead of the blue dress and veil, she wore pajamas and a long woolen coat. Her mouth was set in a thin, angry line. "Pray tell me what is going on here," she said, putting the lamp down on the counter with a loud thump. "I heard noise from the infirmary. What happened?"

Then she saw Rage, and a smile spread across the abbess's face, which made her look younger and a lot less tired than she was. "Good to see you up," she said. Gently, she put her hand to his forehead; he didn't shy away from her as he'd shied away from Luca.

"You've still got a fever," Laure stated, dipped a cloth into a bucket of water, and wiped off the sweat on the assassin's face. "You should have stayed in bed."

"You should have let me die."

Laure laughed softly, not at all troubled by the fact that a man was sitting in her kitchen who had been dying only moments ago. "Ah, no, assassin. I definitely shouldn't have done that. And anyway, it was not my decision. Rebecca found you, and she acted fast and very efficiently. She is fond of you. Your death would have hit her hard, so I am glad you decided to live instead."

Rage lowered his head. Luca saw him close his eyes in despair at what the abbess had told him—she guessed the news of Rebecca having found him just in time was nothing he was happy about.

"Not my decision," he said, neither looking at Laure nor at Luca. He'd put his hands onto the table, palms down, fingers outstretched. They looked lifeless, very much like their owner.

Surprised, Laure sat down. "What do you mean, not your decision? You were dying when I went to bed. If not yours, whose was it?"

Rage jerked his head into Luca's direction.

"But that can't be," the abbess pointed out. "We tried to heal you with magic—it was not possible. The wall around your mind was too strong for your own good. Rebecca cried bitter tears seeing you out of our reach."

No comment from Rage, not even a reaction. He was staring at the table's surface, and Luca wasn't even sure he'd heard what the abbess had said.

"I'm familiar with his magic," Luca said with a sigh. This here was a mess, far worse than she'd expected. "I know how strong it is, and I also know he can't control it. But I can, and I did. I broke through the wall his magic had created and healed his wounds. Well. Most of them. The flesh is still damaged, and so are some smaller veins, or he'd have stopped bleeding by now. Besides, there's still the fever. I'm certain, though, that he will survive."

Silence filled the room, only interrupted by the crackling of the low-burning fire.

Luca's temple was throbbing from where Rage had hit her. She took the jug and his glass and poured herself some water when he looked up.

"Why?"

"Told you. I need you," Luca drank, but the headache throbbing behind her eyes refused to go away. "I went to Coldwell. Lindsay and Ben told me you'd been there before the midwinter fest. They weren't able to tell me where you'd gone. Finding you here was pure coincidence. Obviously, I took the opportunity to save you when I saw it was you lying in that bed. So sorry for having interfered with your plans, dear."

All right, a bit of sarcasm had slipped into her words. "I'm tired, Rage. The weather outside is lousy, I've been on the road for days, I've got a bagful of problems back home. All I want is that you show me the way into the mountains. Once I'm on my way, you can lie down and die for all I care."

Well, that was not completely truthful. She liked him, and seeing him unconscious had unnerved her more than she cared to admit. No reason to tell him that, though.

Before Rage could answer—if he would have answered at all—Laure put a spoon and a bowl filled with vegetable soup in front of him. "I want you to eat," she said. "But first, I want to look at your hands. The cuts were deep. It is likely you lost the movement in your fingers." Holding out her open palm, she waited for Rage to do what he'd been asked. In a way, she treated him like a child, giving orders more than asking for compliance.

Hmmm, Luca thought. *If it works, I'll have a try too.*

Rage held out his left arm to Laure. She took off the bandage, dropping it to the floor. Then her eyes widened. "This is… unexpected. Would you please move your fingers?"

Moving his fingers didn't seem to cause any problems.

"Exceptional. There doesn't seem to be any damage left other than bare flesh wounds. I didn't expect you to ever be able to move your fingers again, and now all you will have to face when this is completely healed are the scars. Your friend here must know you really well—and care for you a great deal, for that matter—to have been able to do this." Taking a fresh bandage, Laure treated first one, then the other hand of her patient, then pushed the spoon toward him. "Now eat."

Rage hadn't let Luca out of his sight. Admittedly, his stare made her uneasy. "You either talk to me, or you eat your soup," she said defiantly. "I'll drag you to the mountains if I have to, but I'd prefer you showing me the way voluntarily."

"Rage is not going any—" Laure began.

"He's dead," Rage stated flatly. "No use to go back up there." Visibly disgusted at the smell of the soup, he pushed the bowl away.

Luca took the bowl and pushed it back at him. "Let's say I want his body back. He deserves a decent funeral."

Quicker than she thought he could move, Rage took the bowl and threw it against the wall. The bowl broke, spraying soup and vegetables through half the kitchen. "He's *dead*, Luca. Whether you bury him or let him rot in that river, he's still dead. Nothing you do can change that, nothing, and I swear if you are still here by morning, I will kill you first before I kill myself." Thoughtfully, he flexed his hands. There were only a few drops of fresh blood on the bandages Laure had put on a few minutes ago. If she—or the abbess—could persuade him to eat, he might even manage to mount a horse without collapsing.

Who am I fooling? Luca thought desperately. *He's not coming anywhere with me no matter what I tell him.*

Telling him the truth—that she thought Keiran was still alive—didn't even occur to her. Too crazy, too risky if she was wrong. Too cruel.

"Rage," Laure said softly. "I accept you don't want to leave, but I need you to lie down again. You're as pale as snow, and you need to rest."

With visible effort, Rage pushed himself off the bench. He was taller than both women, and even without weapons, underfed, and suffering from the effects of his suicide attempt, he radiated danger. "I'll go now," he said. "Don't follow me."

Laure held him back, putting her hand to his arm. "I can't let you go, Rage. You're under my roof, you're my responsibility. Please—"

"He's able to break your arm, you know, even when barely able to stand on his legs," Luca warned her.

But Rage didn't break her arm. Instead, he brought both his hands to his head, crashed to his knees, and let out a low, harsh howl of pain.

Laure was beside him immediately, but Luca just stared in horror. For the first time since she'd seen Rage, she thought about Keiran's voice in her head. Only now it occurred to her it was nearly gone. A faint murmur was all she could make out, and if she hadn't looked for it, she wouldn't have even noticed it was there.

"By the sweet Lady," she whispered in horror as understanding dawned. "He isn't calling me, never did. He's calling you!"

Rage lifted his head. His eyes were bloodshot and wide with something very close to madness.

Luca dropped to her knees and took his face between her hands. "I heard his voice, Rage," she whispered. "It's gone now, but

I can see you still hear him. No wonder you tried to kill yourself. He was driving me crazy and only searching for you kept me going."

"What on earth are you talking about?" Laure asked, but neither Luca nor Rage paid any attention to her.

"He's dead," Rage rasped. The pain, which must be threatening to split his head in half, had made his voice rough and his words slow.

"I think he isn't," Luca said with as much confidence as she could muster. "I heard his voice, Rage. You hear his voice. I think he is alive and needs our help. This is why I was looking for you and why I saved your life. All you need to do is come with me and get him back!"

CHAPTER
Four

RAGE'S HAND locked around Luca's throat, and he pinned her to the wall, getting back on his feet in a swift movement that betrayed his fragile health.

He'll kill me, she thought. *Might have chosen my words more carefully.*

And then he let go of her. Staggering back, he sat on the bench and stared at her as if he were seeing her for the very first time.

"If you're going to attack me again, I'd like to be warned beforehand," Luca said weakly. Her knees felt like jelly. She sat next to him and pressed one hand to her belly, trying to calm herself, trying to reassure her unborn child that all would be well now.

"Explain yourself," Rage croaked. "Before my head explodes."

He sounded so very lost it made Luca want to cry. Not knowing how else to deal with him, she slipped an arm around his bony shoulders. Her fingertips touched his cheek. "I heard his voice," she whispered. "Before, I only dreamed of him. But a week ago, I heard him call for help. It sounded as if he were just in the next room."

"A week ago, Rage cut his wrists," Laure said.

"His voice was driving me crazy." Rage frowned and shook his head. "It *is* driving me crazy. Ever since he jumped, I hear him. Every moment, day and night. Every—" He stopped speaking, putting some distance between himself and Luca. Looking down at himself, he touched the fabric of the garment he was wearing. "This is a nightshirt," he stated, and Luca nearly laughed with relief—he sounded like himself, his voice a mixture of arrogant and cold. Right now, a great deal of indignation showed as well. "I don't wear nightshirts. I sleep in my clothes, or I sleep naked."

"As your clothes were soaked with blood, we took the liberty to wash them," Laure pointed out. "They are next to your bed, which is in the infirmary."

Rage's eyes darted from her to Luca and back. "Wait here," he said—ordered, rather—then added, "I'll be back," and went to the infirmary, firmly closing the door behind him.

IT TOOK Rage fifteen minutes to come back. All the while there was a somewhat awkward silence between Luca and the abbess. Occasionally, Luca wanted to say something to explain herself, why she had looked for Rage and how they were involved, but each time she opened her mouth, she closed it again at the last second. What could she say, anyway? That she had forced Rage into a marriage by pretending to be someone else, and male on top of it? Stupid idea. That she was pregnant and needed a father for her child but didn't even know who the actual father was? Equally stupid. The sisters of the Lady helped the ones who needed help, but would most likely throw her out into the night if she were to confess either sin.

Nor could she tell Laure about Keiran. This was a story too long and complicated to be told carelessly between two sips of tea. So she didn't say anything at all, stared at the closed door, and wondered whether Rage was about to hang himself whilst they were waiting for him.

Just when she became really scared, he came back into the kitchen, not only dressed in his usual clothes, but also shaved. The contrast between the paleness of his face and the blackness of his clothes was even more prominent now the stubble was gone. From the hollow of his cheeks and the sharp bridge of his nose, it was also much more obvious how thin he'd become in the past months. Luca, who'd seen him naked before and knew there had never been much flesh on him, guessed she would be able to count his ribs without any problems were he to take his shirt off.

Taking the place opposite Luca, Rage pushed back the sleeves of his shirt. He'd taken off the bandages. "Finish what you've began," he said, holding out his hands. "Then I will eat. And we will talk."

Grumbling, Luca took his larger hand into hers. "You make it sound as if it's my fault I had to stop halfway through the healing process! You nearly broke my skull. I still have a headache!"

"My apologies."

Luca couldn't help but grin at his dry reply as well as the stern look on his face. She could see that, at the moment, nothing but curiosity and hope held him. Probably, the smell of the soup was pure torture for him now that he had decided to eat, so Luca quickly put her hands on top of his, closed her eyes, and picked up the loose threads of her nearly finished magic. It was easy; there wasn't much left to do, and after just a few moments, the wounds closed, leaving nothing but thin red scars.

Rage didn't even bother to say thank you aloud; he just nodded once before pulling the sleeves over his wrists.

Laure put a new bowl of soup in front of him. She waited until he'd picked up the spoon, and said, "That's all you get for now. It's not much, but you haven't eaten in days. Your stomach needs time to adjust, and I really don't want you to throw up."

Again, Rage didn't answer. Hesitantly, he brought a spoonful of soup to his mouth and inhaled the faint scent of herbs and vegetables before finally eating it. "Can't remember when I've eaten something warm," he murmured. "Trying to deal with the voice in my head made everything else unimportant. And on top of it, I failed at dealing with it. Eventually, it became loud enough I needed to stop it at all cost."

Luca and Laure shared a brief glance at this casual admittance of despair.

"This voice," Laure asked, "does it belong to someone you know?"

The spoon stopped halfway to Rage's mouth. The bowl was about two thirds empty and if Rage had planned to finish it, he had just changed his mind. Putting the spoon down, he shoved his hands under his armpits. "Yes," he finally said. "Someone I believed to be dead until Luca told me otherwise. I saw him die, and I killed his killer. How he can still be alive is a mystery to me. Much more likely all of this is part of my madness. Much more likely I am dead already and this is hell, tormenting me with false hopes."

Luca wanted to say something, but Laure was faster. "Let's just assume—for the sake of the argument, shall we?—you are alive and not yet in hell. In this case, the question is how a dead person can be calling you. Was there magic involved in his death? And is the one who calls dear to you?"

When Rage didn't answer, Luca said, "Very dear," in his place. "And no magic. He jumped into an abyss. I have no idea how he might have survived the impact, but as you already said, a dead man cannot call for help. Hence he must be still alive, and hence we have to find him."

"Could it be someone else's voice? Not that I want to indicate either of you are imagining things, but—"

"No," both Rage and Luca said at the same time.

"But how do you know it is his voice? Over the distance, without actual sound, after such a long time—how can you be certain it is him?" Apparently, the abbess was a curious woman and if she wanted an answer, she wouldn't stop asking until she got it.

Rage looked at her. "Assume you wake up in the middle of the night, get to the window, and in the moonlight, you see one of your sisters walk across the yard. She is hooded, and she doesn't talk to you. Would you know who it is even if you hadn't seen her in a while?"

"Of course." Laure smiled. "By the way she moves, mostly, but also by her height, how the hood covers her face, the tilt of her head… that kind of thing."

Rage merely shrugged. Luca grinned and said, "Well, then, don't ask how we know it's Keiran. He has a way to communicate that is unique, and I am as certain it's him as if I were seeing him standing before me."

Laure's smile deepened, and she nodded.

"We were friends," Luca continued thoughtfully. "Good friends, ever since we were kids. Actually, until Rage came along, I was the one he would have called for, which is the reason why I never even considered I wasn't his main target."

Suddenly, she felt how tired she was. Healing Rage had been more strenuous than she'd thought at first. When she reached for the now cold tea, her hand was shaking.

Laure saw it and got up. After setting the kettle with soup aside, she hung up a smaller one, stirring its contents continuously. Silence claimed the kitchen; nothing but the wind outside and the crackling of the fire could be heard. Eventually, Laure put three mugs onto the table, each one steaming, each one definitely not filled with tea.

Rage sniffed. "Hot chocolate." He sounded as if she'd offended him by assuming he would drink something that sweet and usually reserved for children.

"You can do with the sugar," Laure replied cheerfully. "So, did I get that correctly—you were called by a dead man, it drove you crazy, and when you tried to kill yourself, when the voice could not find you anymore, it called Luca instead?" She frowned. "Say, are you two related somehow? However distantly?"

Luca sighed. She'd known it would come down to this eventually.

"Not related." Rage wrapped his hands around the mug and breathed in the sweet scent with half-closed eyes. "Married."

"Didn't think you'd tell her," Luca said wearily.

And then another thought hit her. The marriage—it was nothing compared to the bond the child she carried created between them. Whoever the father was, the child linked the three of them and must be the reason she could hear Keiran's voice.

Rage frowned. "Why shouldn't I? It's no secret. And it would explain… this." Absently, Rage rubbed along his wrists.

The abbess smiled. "A marriage vow would certainly tie you to your wife. She heard the echo, and it led straight to you. Luca didn't find my nunnery—and you—by accident. Neat, really. Glad I figured it out."

Luca closed her eyes, hoping the abbess wouldn't do some more figuring.

Rage's lips twitched, maybe at the sound of pride in the abbess's voice. "*Neat* isn't the first word that comes to mind."

Putting her hand over his, Luca caught his attention. "I'm heading for the monastery. Are you coming with me?"

Rage raised an eyebrow, which was such a typical thing for him to do that Luca could barely stop herself from jumping up and hugging him.

"It's a bad place," he pointed out. "But as I do not see another choice, yes, I will come with you."

"Well, neither of you is going anywhere before you both have a decent night of sleep and a really big breakfast," Laure objected.

"Rage, Luca, into the infirmary, both of you. There are enough beds. If either of you dares to sneak into the stables tonight, trying to get the horses for a nice midnight runaway, you'll be grounded for at least a week. Do I make myself clear?" Even without a veil and in her pajamas, she looked every inch the abbess she was, in command of the nunnery, her sisters, and her guests as well. "You'd fall off the horse in less than an hour if you tried to get on the road right now. And you"—she narrowed her eyes at Luca—"are also in desperate need of rest. My healer will take a look at both of you in the morning. If she declares you fit to ride, I will allow you to leave. Otherwise, you will stay until she changes her mind." Invitingly opening the door to the infirmary, she added, "I could tie you to the bed as well," with a sweet smile that betrayed the determination in her eyes.

This time, Rage grinned. "I give up," he said and held out his hand to Luca. "Let's go to bed, girl. The sooner we lie down, the sooner she will let us go."

BOTH RAGE and Luca slept through the day and the following night, undisturbed by the sisters talking and laughing in the kitchen, by a newcomer having lunch with them and telling them loudly about the unfairness of life in general and his wife in particular, by the change in the weather outside, or the distant voice calling for help in their heads. They were out, well and good, and if someone had tried to shake them awake it wouldn't have made any difference. Rage knew he wasn't mad and could embrace sleep without fearing a nightmare, even though Keiran's voice drifted through his dreams. Luca knew she was safe and that she wouldn't have to go to the monastery on her own, and slept deep and dreamless like a child. Occasionally, Laure or one of her sisters checked on them, and twice, healer Michelle made sure Rage hadn't died in his sleep.

Luca woke first, so when Rage opened his eyes to the day, the infirmary was empty apart from himself. It wasn't long past sunrise; he could hear a few lonely birds singing outside, and then it occurred to him how long it had been since he'd seen sunlight at all. He'd come here during a storm, and ever since, winter had had a firm grip on the world. Clouds, rain, hail, and even snow had hit the earth. No sunlight at all.

Until today. A bright patch of light lingered on the infirmary floor, a golden pool too unreal to be true. Rage sat up and dipped his foot into the light, expecting it to vanish instantly. It didn't. Instead, his foot was now golden too.

"I must be dreaming," Rage said, and his voice was as hoarse as he'd expected it to be. He hadn't talked in…. Well. He'd said a few words to Laure the night he'd knocked on her door. She'd recognized him; he remembered the shock on her face when she'd asked what had happened.

Frowning, Rage scratched his neck, his foot still bathing in the early sunlight. A look around confirmed where he was: in the infirmary with its small windows and many beds. Apart from his own bed, only one other seemed to have been occupied recently: the one next to his. The pillow had been beaten into shape, and the sheets were crumpled, the bedcover lying half on the floor.

"I should be dead."

Not entirely sure what he was doing here, Rage pushed back the sleeve of his shirt—at least he'd been sleeping in his clothes, as always. At least no one had put him in a nightshirt.

Then he saw the scar on his wrist, an angry red scar, and he sighed.

He should be dead, true. He'd stabbed his knife deep into his wrists, both of them, and he remembered the blood erupting from the wounds. He hadn't hesitated when he'd tried to kill himself; he'd done a thorough job.

Then why wasn't he dead?

"Maybe I am," he mused. "I died, and this is hell."

Strange way for hell to look. Hell, as his father had taught him, was colder than ice; hell was pitch black. The noise in hell was incredible, caused by the ones who cried for mercy. There were no beds in hell, no peace, and definitely no sunlight.

Slowly, gently, memories dripped into the darkness of his sleep-hazed mind. Impatient, cruel, wonderful memories.

Rage dug his hands into the mattress of his bed. The only sign of his refreshed grief were his widening eyes and a slight quickening of breath as in between two heartbeats, the past weeks became alive again. He remembered walking through the night, trying to deal with the pleading voice in his head, trying not to go mad and failing nevertheless. Food, water, human contact, everything had become more and more unimportant until he'd used his knife to end it.

He remembered Luca, tampering with fate by saving his life. And he remembered what she'd said: that she could hear Keiran's voice too.

He believed it. She'd touched him, and the voice in his head had dimmed down to a whisper. Without the shadow of a doubt, he knew she'd told the truth—Keiran was alive, under gruesome circumstances, maybe, but alive. If his voice hadn't flattened him, if his brain hadn't given up service weeks ago, he might have come to the same conclusion.

But he'd seen the boy fall. He must be dead.

"Let's find out once and for all," Rage said aloud, put on his socks and boots, and went to find Luca.

OF COURSE it was just his luck he bumped into Abbess Laure first thing after he left the house.

"Oh, good morning," Laure said. She carried a sack of potatoes. "Back on your feet again? Fine. You look good. Would you take this bag to the kitchen, please." It wasn't a question. Unceremoniously, she shoved the bag into his arms and walked past him, leading the way. Apparently, she didn't even consider the possibility of him dropping the potatoes; she didn't even look back to make sure he followed her.

"Sure," Rage murmured under his breath, keeping the sudden flash of anger in check. He wasn't used to being treated like a servant, and whoever had tried it so far had learned quickly how bad an idea it was not to show him respect. For a brief moment, he saw himself putting his knife to the nun's throat, nicking the flesh just enough to show her who he was.

Then his lips twitched when he realized his temper had nearly gotten the better of him. Hadn't happened in a very long time. Once he'd understood that control was much more effective, he only drew his knife if he wanted to eat or kill.

The bag of potatoes grew heavy, so Rage followed the abbess into the kitchen and put it onto the counter. "I was looking for the girl," he said, half expecting Laure to tell him Luca was already gone. The abbess was busy preparing breakfast for everyone, and after a moment's hesitation, Rage sat down and began peeling potatoes. His fingers seemed strangely dumb, the texture of the spud in his hand much more prominent than it really was. His knife was an equally unfamiliar shape. Now that he thought about it, he couldn't even remember when he'd used it last.

Laure asked, "Are you hungry? Porridge is ready." Not awaiting his answer, she filled a bowl and put it in front of him.

Putting the knife back in its sheath and the spud into the bowl, he was about to pick up the spoon when Laure took one of his hands. It was an unexpected move, and the warmth of her fingers came as a shock. His muscles tensed, and he very nearly pushed her away.

Laure must have sensed his uneasiness. Her grip tightened ever so slightly, and when she turned his hand so she could see his palm, she traced the lines with her fingertip. Even more gently, she touched the scar. "I saw you frown," she said. "Touching things feels strange, doesn't it? Or being touched?" Her fingertip wandered across the bones in his hand, a mixture between a stroke and a tickle. "It is because of what Luca did. Our healer says you will have full control over your hands in a matter of days, if not sooner. The more you use them, the faster they'll be back to normal. Give yourself some time to adjust." Gently, she let go of his hand. "Now eat," she ordered, an amused sparkle gleaming in her eyes. "Soon, my sisters will want their breakfast. I assume a bunch of nuns will be a bit too overwhelming for you that early in the morning. Luca is in the stables, grooming the horses. We weren't sure how long you would sleep. She will be happy to see you are as eager to leave as she is."

Unable to eat more than a few spoonfuls of porridge, Rage pushed the bowl away and drank a mug of strong black coffee the abbess had put in front of him. Then he picked up his knife again and continued peeling potatoes. "You saved my life," he said. "Why? I am an assassin. Aren't there rules which lives you should take care of and which ones you should let perish?"

Laure chuckled. "Of course there are rules. But I prefer to see them as mere guidelines with room for interpretation. My mother superior in the empress's city would have disapproved of my decision of taking you in. She would have argued that a man who makes a living by killing others isn't worthy to be saved. I couldn't have reasoned with her, but then, she wasn't here. And I like you. Rebecca is here because you showed mercy. She likes you too. And now you are on the way to find another lost soul, maybe once more saving a life instead of taking one. I think it was worth the risk of annoying my mother superior." Another smile, a bit lopsided, a bit cheeky. "Not that I will ever tell her, of course."

With every potato Rage peeled, his hands and fingers felt less strange and more like they really belonged to him instead of being useless attachments at the ends of his arms. "Usually, I avoid being in debt," he said thoughtfully, remembering Teddy, the thief who had sold him medicine and magic for a few coins and the promise of a goat. Although the man was dead, Rage still owed his wife and daughter the price for his life. If he weren't careful, debts would become an annoying habit.

"You aren't in my debt," Laure objected, surprise in her voice. "This is what the sisters of the Lady do: help the ones who need help. I do not know how I will live with the knowledge of having saved an assassin, especially should I learn you killed another innocent victim. But this is the price I was willing to pay when I took the veil. In any case, I don't expect to see you again, and I also expect you not to take on a job that orders you to kill one of my sisters. You can see it as payment, if you wish."

Snorting, Rage put the knife down and stretched his fingers, balled them to fists, unclenched them. "I have my own rules, abbess. Not killing children is the most important one, but other than that, I always look into a case before I take it. Killing a woman who serves the Lady... no one has ever asked me to do it, and even before I met you, I would have probably declined the job. And you will see me again. Not doing something isn't what I call evening a debt. I will think of an appropriate way to pay you."

He was about to get up and look for Luca when the door opened, and a small figure slipped into the kitchen. The girl—not much more than a child—didn't wear a veil, but she was dressed in the familiar blue clothes the sisters wore. Rage barely recognized her—it was Rebecca, and apart from her hair being cut short, the terror had vanished from her face. If there hadn't been faint scars on her face from where Lucius had beaten her, she would have looked like any other child.

Quickly, the girl put the basket of eggs she was carrying down, greeting Laure with a shy nod.

Then she saw Rage, and a smile lit up her face. "Good morning!" She sounded genuinely happy to see him, and without asking Laure whether she was needed elsewhere, she let the door behind her fall closed and stepped toward the table. She moved swiftly; nothing showed how badly she'd been beaten up some months back. When Rage had found her, she'd fallen unconscious on the way to the nunnery. He was more than glad to see her look like the young girl she was, not like the half-mad victim he remembered.

"Good morning," he replied gently. "And thank you. You were there when I needed help. I do thank you for this gift."

Rebecca blushed. "I shouldn't have come to the stables," she said, glancing at the abbess. "Sister Laure had forbidden us to disturb you. But I saw you were in trouble, so I broke my promise to leave you alone."

Rage raised an eyebrow. "You saw it?"

Rebecca nodded. "Occasionally, I know about things that have not happened yet. Sister Laure calls it 'seeing' things. I saw you, covered in blood. I became scared and ran to see if you were all right."

"And just in time," Laure said, putting a reassuring hand onto the girl's shoulder. Rebecca had gained some weight in the past months but was still as thin as a sparrow. For a brief moment, she leaned back, seeking warmth and reassurance in the abbess's touch. Then she put a small hand into a pocket and pulled out a wooden box. "I wanted you to have this," she said shyly. "I made it for you—I am the healer's apprentice, and she showed me how to do it properly." A smiled tugged at her lips. "At first, she didn't want to. But when I told her for whom I needed it, she agreed. It wasn't easy. Here." Between two fingers, she held the box out to him.

Carefully, Rage took it. The box was smaller than the span of his hand, it weighed next to nothing, and when he opened it, he found a glass phial inside it, filled with a clear liquid. "And what's this, then, Rebecca?" he asked, guessing by the red that crept into her checks that she was happy to hear him remembering—and using—her name.

"It's what the sisters gave me when I woke up in the infirmary," Rebecca said. "I was screaming, and I wanted to jump out of the window. I remembered everything, everything this man had done to me and to my sister, and I remembered what I had done to him. It was all so bright and vivid and horrible. I didn't want to live with those memories, but then healer Michelle gave me this to drink, and all was well. I can still remember what happened, but it doesn't hurt anymore. You will need it. That's the reason why I made it for you."

A distinct coldness ran down Rage's back when he heard her words. After taking the phial out of its wooden box, he uncorked it carefully, sniffed its content, and put the stopper back in. The liquid had a vaguely sweet fragrance, not unpleasant, but it nevertheless scared him to the core. "What do you mean, I will need it?" he asked, although he didn't really want to hear the answer.

Rebecca put one of her hands above the other as if she wanted to keep them still, hinder them from doing things she didn't want them to do. Her shoulders began to tremble; her eyelids fell half-closed until only the whites of her eyes could be seen. Simultaneously, her body sagged against the woman behind her. If the abbess hadn't been so close, Rebecca might have slipped to the floor.

"You'll need it," the girl repeated dreamily. "This is medicine. It will heal what is broken. What you hear is but an illusion. The voice in your head is not real. You will need something to mend the pieces lest your knife will be the only answer."

A shudder ran through her fragile body. Laure had both hands on Rebecca's shoulders, holding her upright as well as steadying her. Then, as quickly as it had begun, it was over. Rebecca opened her eyes, rubbing them with both hands as if she'd just woken from a deep sleep. She smiled sheepishly and licked her lips. "Sorry," she said. "I can't help the seeing. Could I have some water, please?" Yawning, she emptied the glass Laure handed her and was out the door a moment later.

Rage stared after her, speechless. The phial was on the table, looking innocent. He didn't object when the abbess put it back into the wooden box, but he didn't touch the small casket, either.

"I wish I could tell her she was speaking nonsense," Laure said quietly. "But from experience I know that what she says always comes true, one way or another. I am sorry."

Rage frowned. "She said… what exactly did she say? That I will want to kill myself again? I can live with that. That the boy is dead? I know that already. That the voice I hear—and which Luca hears too—is an illusion? Nothing new there either." He sighed. "I need to leave now. There is only so much time one can spend grooming a horse, and I have the strong suspicion that Luca is by now massively angry with me for lingering in the kitchen whilst she's doing all the work."

"Rage—" Laure began, but the assassin silenced her with a quick shake of his head.

"I am grateful for your hospitality, but there is no use in staying any longer. I need to see the boy's corpse myself before I believe any of what has been said in here, be it Luca's opinion or Rebecca's visions. I'll go back to the Forbidden Monastery. I'll climb into the abyss, and if there is anything to find down there, I will find it. If I survive, I will come back. If not, fine with me as well."

He got up and went to the door that led to the yard. Only at the last moment, he turned and picked up the box with the phial.

CHAPTER
Five

IT HAD been a lie, of course. Rebecca's words had cut deep, opening anew the wound the boy's death had ripped and which had ached less when Luca told him she believed Keiran was still alive.

You'll need it. The girl's words rang in his ears, loud and clear as if she were still talking to him. In his fist, he held the phial. The box's edges cut into his palm, and for a moment he considered crushing it. He didn't want his memories flattened; if he couldn't live with what he would find, so be it.

Gradually he tightened his grip. The box, though made of wood, wasn't strong enough to withstand him for long, and the phial inside was made of glass. It would be easy to destroy it; it would be easy to forget about Rebecca's vision and believe in what Luca had said. Believe that Keiran was alive, believe the past months had been nothing but a lousy dream.

Tightening his muscles hurt.

Rage thought of the past weeks and months. As he stood rooted to the spot between kitchen and stables, one hand was clutched around the box and the other hanging forgotten at his side. He felt lost and dreadfully vulnerable.

He was mad. Still.

"Ever since Keiran died," Rage murmured. That day, his brain had stopped working, and he'd acted on instinct only. How he'd managed to get down the mountains, he had no recollection; what had happened to his horse was a mystery to him. Vaguely, he remembered walking for hours, days, weeks. At one point, he'd visited Coldwell, had slept in the bed he'd shared with his love. Or had tried to—sleep had fled him as if his mind feared the nightmares that plagued him whenever his body was too exhausted to stay awake.

The night in Coldwell had pushed him further into madness. After he'd left, he'd stopped eating, not on purpose, but because he simply had forgotten about it. From then on, the voice in his head had become louder, more insistent, more demanding, and much more heartbreaking. Keiran's voice, begging him to save him. Which was impossible because the boy was dead.

Slowly, Rage unclenched his fist. Watching the small box that lay innocently on his palm as if expecting it to explode, he finally decided to keep it, just for a little while and just as long as it would take him to find out about the voice in his head and the secrets the abyss held. He wouldn't jump; he would take a rope and climb down until he reached the river. Once, the ghosts had scared him. Now, the only thing he was afraid of was the thought of finding nothing at all. And if he found nothing in the abyss, he would need the phial Rebecca had given him.

When he finally reached the stables, Luca was putting a saddle onto the back of a tall, lean horse. It wasn't young anymore, and it was ugly, but it looked as if it could walk for hours without tiring or needing more than a bit of water.

"About time you showed up," Luca said by way of greeting. "What have you been doing—chatting up the abbess?"

Taking the saddle out of her hands, Rage put it aside and placed a blanket onto the horse's back first. "Talking to Rebecca," he said. "She's here and looking much better than last time I saw her. Basically, she told me not to waste time searching for Keiran." Saddling the horse, he then filled a sack with oats and put it onto the horse's back, too. In a corner, the one he had chosen as shelter until he'd tried to commit suicide, he found his rucksack. Quickly and before Luca could see it, he slipped the box in.

In the meantime, Luca was saddling a second horse. "Doesn't matter what anyone says," she repeated coldly. "I know what I heard. His voice, calling for me. You've heard it too. The only question is, will you accompany me, or will you run away again?" A skin filled with water went to the horn of her saddle. Taking the reins, she led her horse outside.

Rage followed her. "I assume I'm stealing a horse? Because it's not mine."

"The abbess agreed to lend it to you. She expects it back, though. Which means you better not do anything stupid once we get near the abyss. Or beforehand." She swung her leg over the horse's back. "Are you coming?" she asked again, only this time, Rage could hear the desperation in her voice.

He got into the saddle. One of the sisters came around a corner, saw him, and smiled. "Have a safe journey," she called, went to the gate, and opened it. "I'll tell the abbess you will come back with our horse in a little while."

"I'll do my best," Rage murmured and rode out of the nunnery.

When he'd arrived at the nunnery, it had been winter. When Luca had arrived, a snowstorm had hit the world. And now, sudden as a twittering bird at dawn, spring had arrived. The snow had melted, and grass and leaves were growing everywhere. Snowdrops showed their tiny heads, and the sun, though barely up, shone warm on their backs. True, there was a chill in the air, and underneath the trees they could see a thin layer of frost. But the sun would melt it soon. Hopefully the weather would stay like this so their journey into the mountains would be a bit more pleasant than last time.

It took them several days to even get to the foot of the mountains. Rage couldn't ride as fast as he wanted to—his overall condition was feeble at best, he tired easily, and although he had walked for months, he wasn't used to spending hours and hours in the saddle. Often, he got off his horse and walked instead; often, they had a rest, something Luca welcomed as well. Riding made her sick, and pregnancy made her tired. Eating was as unpleasant as ever, and although she hid the truth from Rage out of fear he would leave her behind, she didn't insist to ride on when he considered it time to make camp.

Rage was silent most of the time. He'd never been a talkative man, and being in delicate health didn't improve his conversational skills. As soon as Luca lit the fire with a bit of magic, he went off hunting, often staying out long into the night. As it was early in the year, with spring just beginning, the game he brought back was as skinny as he was, barely more than fur and bones after a long, hard winter. In combination with the dried meat and the shriveled potatoes the abbess had given them, he managed to cook a decent meal most nights at least, and enough to last until breakfast. He ate slowly because he wasn't used to food anymore; Luca ate slowly to hide that she didn't want to eat at all.

Eventually they reached the mountains. Covered with snow, they looked forbidding and dangerous, even more so as there was green grass sprouting on the ground, and the first birds had begun building nests in some nearby trees. Going up there seemed wrong; not going up there was impossible.

"Looks worse than last time," Luca said. It was the first sentence she'd spoken in over a day.

Rage slipped off his horse, wiping the sweat off his brow. They'd ridden fast for the past hour or so. Luca guessed it was his way to prove he was up to this. Not that she'd ever doubted it—if Rage put his mind to something, she knew he would see it through. But despite the regular food, he was still weak, and despite his silence, she knew he sometimes would have liked to smash his head into the next tree. She could see on his face that he heard Keiran's call. It kept him awake at night, and it made his eyes hard and forbidding. Faintly, she could hear her friend calling too, and she would have bet the manor Rage heard his voice ten times louder.

Sometimes this hurt more than the thought that Keiran might be dead despite her hopes. That he loved Rage, not her. That when in danger, he called the assassin, not her. That when given the choice, he would always kiss him and never her.

Sometimes she wished she could turn her back on both of them, walk back to her life at the manor, and forget they both existed.

But when she saw the assassin take his rucksack and the bag with food along with the waterskin, when she saw him walking up the narrow path leading to the Forbidden Monastery, there was no question whether or not she would follow him. It didn't matter that Keiran didn't love her; she loved him. It didn't matter that he didn't call for her; it was still her sole wish to get him back, and for that she needed to stay with Rage. Afterward, she could turn her back on them. Once she'd found Keiran. Once she'd severely kicked him for his stupidity of jumping into the abyss.

Snapping out of her thoughts, she saw that Rage was out of sight. "Wait for me!" she called, breaking into a run and only vaguely wondering if the wolves would get their horses once night came.

After a few steps, she knew why Rage had left the horses behind. Unlike last year, the path was frozen, the ground slippery after a long and hard winter. Her feet lost touch, and she would have fallen if she hadn't caught hold of the stone wall. A horse would have no chance to get up here.

Rage was still out of sight. "He must be running," Luca grumbled, speeding up herself. It wasn't easy, but with every step, she got more used to the tricky ground. She also got out of breath quickly, and accompanied by a sickening rush of nausea, a piercing pain shot through her.

Gasping, she stopped, leaning against the rocks. With one hand, she steadied herself lest she would fall, and the other hand she pressed against her belly.

My baby.

The thought was crystal clear in her mind, new and fresh as if she'd found out only now that she was pregnant.

Another cramp caught her, twisted her stomach, and made her throw up lunch, which was a pity as she'd really enjoyed eating it.

"No," she whispered. "Please, no, please, don't go, please don't die, please—"

Rage slipped his arm around her and caught her just when her legs gave way. He steadied her, and with his sleeve, he wiped off the tears running down her face. Then he got a handful of snow and helped her clean out her mouth.

Gradually, the piercing, shocking pain subsided. Luca managed to draw in some deep, even breaths before pressing her face against Rage's shoulder.

"You should have told me you are with child," he said.

"You would have left me with the sisters."

Stroking her back, he replied, "Impossible. I can't do this on my own, not even if I were in a better condition than I am. I need your help and your magic. Telling me would have prevented such a situation. Telling me would have put your mind at rest."

Eating another mouthful of snow, Luca looked up at him. The sky above him was blue, which only highlighted the contrast to the white snow. They weren't high up in the mountains yet, and the snow would melt soon, but right now, it was still cold. Rage was as pale as always. In his eyes, she could see a spark of sympathy. "It might be your child," she whispered. "I didn't dare tell you. I didn't know how much I wanted it until a moment ago. And now… and now I'm afraid I will lose it."

More tears were running down her cheeks. Under different circumstances, this would have embarrassed her. At the moment, all she could do was beg, hope, and pray her child would decide to stay with her.

Unexpectedly, Rage put his hand over hers. "I guessed about as much," he said quietly. "When I saw you being sick in the mornings, when I saw your reaction to food and smell, I knew you were pregnant. There are no visible signs yet, but it was obvious you knew about your condition. The timeframe fits. My child or Keiran's."

Luca raised her chin just a fraction, just enough to show him she was not broken. "I could have taken someone else into my bed."

Faint amusement sparked up in Rage's eyes. "Unlikely. You're an arrogant little twat, but you don't jump from man to man. Now eat some of these, and then let's get on. I want to be at the monastery before nightfall." Holding out his hand, he waited until Luca took what he offered: a handful of hazelnuts, found in one of the various pockets of his rucksack.

Dubiously, Luca ate one of the nuts and then a second one. Not long, and the handful was gone. "My stomach—it's getting better," she said, eyebrows raised in surprise.

"Old household remedy." Rage grinned. Taking her hand, he held it a bit longer than she needed to get back on her feet. "You won't lose this child," he said. "You were running too fast, and you haven't eaten enough for such a strenuous task. From here on, we will take it slowly. After so much time, Keiran can wait for another few hours."

One step after another. One breath after another. No running anymore and no silent cursing. Luca concentrated on the slippery ground. She concentrated on Rage's back and copied his steady, silent rhythm. Not thinking about the task ahead calmed her; trying not to worry about her child was harder, but concentrating on Rage's statement that she wouldn't lose it made it possible.

The higher they got, the slower Rage walked. At first Luca thought it was solely because of her, and she was grateful. They rested, and whenever they did, Rage gave her some more hazelnuts, which magically kept her nausea under control. The air didn't get colder—it was above the freezing point, and under any other circumstances, she would have actually enjoyed it. She could see for miles, and high above her, swallows sailed through the sky, looking for places to build their nests.

With a somewhat content sigh, she leaned against Rage, seeking warmth as well as reassurance.

When she felt him tremble, she thought it was because of the cold. But it wasn't that cold; they'd walked themselves warm, and their clothes were cozy enough for the weather.

So his trembling must have come from a different origin.

"Are you all right?" she asked, putting her hand to his face so he had to turn his head toward her. He'd been watching the path, maybe thinking about a way down the abyss. He hadn't been looking at her.

Actually, he'd been ahead of her since they'd begun ascending. She'd seen his back, and that had been it. Until now.

She was shocked at how tired he looked. Deep lines around his mouth and eyes indicated that he was close to a breakdown. His cheeks were hollow, and he was breathing hard, although they'd been resting for at least fifteen minutes.

"You look horrible!" The words were out of her mouth before she knew she would say them.

"Fits. I feel horrible too." Rubbing his hands across his face, he was about to get going, but Luca took his hand and held him back. It was easy; there was barely any resistance on his side.

"Tell me what's wrong with you," she urged. "This cannot be simply because of your poor health. You were eating regularly these past few days, we were going at a fair pace, and my magic healed you properly. There is no reason for you to look like a corpse."

Humorlessly, Rage grinned at her. "Thanks," he said. "Just what I needed—the blatant truth. I just felt awful, but now I feel like I'm dead."

Luca frowned. "You won't reach the monastery like this, not to talk about the bottom of the abyss. You're shaking, with cold or exhaustion or both, it doesn't matter. Is there anything I can do?"

Rage shook his head. By now, he'd wrapped his arms around his body. His lips were pressed tightly into a small line.

"You can hear him, can't you?" Out of fear she'd jumped to random conclusions, worried that if she said nothing, he'd get up just like that, continue walking and drop dead after a few steps.

From the look on his face, she knew she'd hit a tender spot. "You can really hear him?" she asked, letting her hands drop to her sides. Ever since she'd brought Rage back from the brink of death, Keiran's voice in her head was gone. Silence was all she heard when she dreamed, and even when she went looking for his voice, it wasn't there. She'd assumed Rage couldn't hear him anymore either. Apparently she had been wrong, as Rage just nodded without further explanation.

"Shit."

There was something in his eyes she couldn't identify. Maybe it was fear; maybe it was just fatigue. But this something twisted her heart, and she felt the blood rush through her veins with sudden strength. "You're not… you're not planning to do anything stupid, are you?" No way not to ask this question. No way not to comment somehow on the fact that he looked like a living corpse, although the previous night, he'd seemed nearly his old self.

Rage was silent for a long time. Eventually he leaned against the wall behind him. "We'll stay here for the night. I know it's early, but I cannot walk another step, and we wouldn't have made it to the monastery during daylight anyway."

Wordlessly, Luca piled up a few stones, added magic, and had a makeshift oven that would keep them more or less warm during the night. In a tin cup, she melted snow, added some herbs, and handed the lukewarm tea to Rage. "Resting seems like a good idea," she mused. "Tomorrow things will look a lot better, and maybe you can even grab a decent night's sleep."

His hands wrapped around the cup, a blanket draped around his bony shoulders, Rage once more shook his head. "Unlikely. From the moment my feet touched the rocks, Keiran's voice screamed for me even louder than before. It's taking all the strength I've got left not to run headfirst into the next wall. It's worse than before I cut my wrists. I won't be able to fight against it much longer."

So much for her hope of a bit of sleep. With his words fresh in her mind, she'd be too scared to close her eyes for more than a moment.

Hesitantly, Luca got closer, took one of his arms, and pulled it around her shoulder until she was comfortably leaning against him. Half the blanket went around her body, and at least one thing hadn't changed: Rage was warm, and instantly she felt safe. Or at last safer than a moment ago. "You'll have to push me off your lap before you can do anything stupid," she said. "I'll sleep in your arms, if you don't mind."

By the Lady, it should be forbidden to be that haggard! She could feel his hip bone, his ribs, his elbow, and she could already feel bruises coming along. "You should eat something," she added.

"I think I will skip eating until this is over," he said, but he pulled her closer. "Food has lost its appeal, and I know I can't do anything about it until I've made it into the abyss."

"Problem is, you won't make it down there, given your condition." Sleep began creeping up on her; the thought of a night of peaceful dreaming was as appealing as it was scaring her. She might dream of lovely things, or she might have nightmares.

Most likely it would be the latter, this close to the Forbidden Monastery.

Anyway. She was tired, she was warm, and the hazelnuts were preventing her from becoming sick. She'd eaten enough to not be hungry, the hot stones warmed her, and most importantly, she didn't have to walk another step in the foreseeable future.

Rage's heart beat a steady rhythm into her ear. No matter how beaten he looked, he was alive and stubborn enough to see this through. At least so she forced herself to believe, because if she dared to give in to her doubts, she'd go crazy with fear.

Absently Rage stroked across her hair. "Don't worry," he said quietly, as if having read her thoughts. "You can sleep. We can ponder the rest tomorrow."

"Will you at least try and close your eyes?" From her angle—with her head on his shoulder—she couldn't see his face. But she felt him shake his head.

Different question, then. "Will you come back to Babylon Manor with me once this is over? My lovely neighbor wants to have me disowned for trying to run my home without a legal guardian. If he finds out I'm pregnant, he'll have a heart attack from pure joy. I need to present him with a husband, at least until my status as Lady Babylon is safe."

Feeling his surprise at the sudden change of subject, Luca smiled. Anything to keep him talking, anything to make him forget about tomorrow, at least for a few short minutes.

"Your lovely neighbor—what's his name?"

"Lord Barnard. Tight-assed bastard he is, with a nasty mouth and filthy fingers. Never smiles, and behind your back, he tells the most awful lies, whilst to your face, he is sickeningly friendly. Small, thin apart from his beer belly, sparse hair… and he wants Babylon Manor. Now that Lucius is gone, he spread the rumor I had him killed. I can't fight him on my own."

Rage was still stroking her hair. It seemed to calm him, and as it was a nice feeling, Luca didn't ask him to stop. No one had ever stroked her hair apart from her mum, who had died when she'd been little. On quiet nights between heartbeats, between wakefulness and sleep, she could remember her mother's fragrance and her hand on her head. Strange that here, so close to the Forbidden Monastery and the horrible memory it brought, Luca was able to remember her face as clearly as if she'd seen her yesterday, and only because of an exhausted assassin stroking her hair just like her mum had done.

Luca had to clear her throat before she could talk. "Barnard will take Babylon Manor, he will take my child once it is born and put it into an orphanage, he will have me taken to a nunnery… you name it."

"He might die," Rage said. "By accident. Or by an assassin's hand."

In despair, she shook her head, only a bit so he wouldn't stop stroking her hair. "He's got connections. There are rumors he even knows people in the empress's palace. If he drops dead, no matter the circumstances, I am certain everyone will point at me, accusing me of his murder. Although I have to admit, the idea of him lying in his grave has a charming appeal." She turned ever so slightly, snuggling up closer, if that was at all possible. "So will you help me out? Announce you are my husband. Scare the life out of him. Tell him to leave me alone, or you will cut him to pieces. Whatever. I need your help. If we survive tomorrow, that is."

Damn. She shouldn't have added that last bit!

Rage just put his hand onto her belly, and Luca's mouth sagged open in surprise. It wasn't a frightening gesture. Protective was the word that came to her mind.

"You could have got rid of it," Rage said. "This child—it means trouble for you with or without a husband. Suppose I came back with you; suppose I will be accepted as your husband. Suppose this child will be born with brown hair and amber eyes, growing up to be the spitting image of its real father. You might be safe now, but in a few years, it will become obvious you cheated on me and gave birth to another man's child. They will hang you."

Luca shuddered despite the warmth. "It's my child," she bit out. "No matter which of you fathered it, she is mine."

"She?"

"Yes, she. As in a girl. My child is a girl, she is mine, and neither you nor Lord Barnard nor the empress herself will take her away from me!"

Right, she was shouting. So what? This was not a subject she liked talking about, and anyway, a moment ago she'd been nicely tired. Now she was totally furious.

Rage pulled her back into his arms; after a short fight she might have even won, Luca gave in. After all, he was probably her daughter's father. She'd slept with him first, so her girl would have black hair most likely.

Or blond hair, if she was really lucky. No one would have reason to doubt Rage was the father if the child had blonde hair and sea green eyes.

"You see the problem," Luca finally managed. "Without a husband, I'm lost. Either you help me, or I will have to find someone else who agrees to play my husband. If you do this for me, I can arrange for you to have a nice, deathly accident. No one will ever find a corpse. You can go your way once you are declared dead. You could simply vanish, leaving me behind."

"You couldn't marry again if I did that," Rage argued, and suddenly, Luca had to laugh.

"This is ridiculous, you know that? I can't imagine I'll ever get home again. No need to worry about Lord Barnard or my child's future or a life spent at the nunnery. Definitely no need to think about a second marriage given what a mess my first one turned out to be."

Maybe she only laughed because otherwise she'd begin crying.

Rage wrapped his other arm around her. In a mixture of tenderness and hesitation, he kissed her temple. "Go to sleep now," he murmured into her ear. "And thanks for the distraction. I will try and think about your little problem tonight."

"Fine," Luca managed. And then she was asleep.

THE STONES were cold when she woke, and a pale morning light had chased the night away. Both moons were but thin scythes above the horizon; it would take another two months before they were full and round again.

Rage was up already, packing the blanket into his rucksack. When he saw that she was awake, he threw a snowball at her. Part of it got into her collar, and she gasped from the sudden rush of cold.

"Morning," he said.

"Idiot," she replied with a grin.

He didn't give her time to heat up water; wordlessly, he handed her some dried meat, a small chunk of bread, and a piece of cheese along with the last hazelnuts. She ate whilst walking, still half-asleep and glad she didn't have to do any thinking but munching and keeping up with him. Putting one foot in front of the other was enough challenge that early.

In the afternoon, they reached the bridge.

It was still daylight behind the mountains, but that close to the Forbidden Monastery, the sun was but a vague memory. The light was dim, the bright blue sky above them pure mockery. No birds were up that high, and it was eerily silent.

The bridge swung gently in the evening breeze, looking as harmless as a bridge could look, although it had been made out of blood and bones.

Even from ten feet away, Rage could hear the voices in the abyss calling for him. No gentle persuasion to join them—outraged screams, demanding him to jump, demanding him to kill Luca, demanding him to end his life and hers as quickly and cruelly as possible. The voices of the monks who'd died here so many years ago.

It was nothing compared to Keiran's pleas to save him. They were loud, barely allowing him to hear his own thoughts. They hummed through his body, set his bones to vibrating, made his nerves burn—silent torture, nothing less. Eventually the voice would liquefy his brain, and when that happened, he'd find a better and faster way to kill himself.

He'd made it through the night only because of the girl sleeping in his lap, her weight grounding him, her even breathing reminding him of the promise he'd given.

It might be the best idea to jump into the abyss right now, and the fastest too. Once his body hit the ground, his skull would explode, and the voice would be gone.

"Do you have a rope?"

Luca's words couldn't have come at a better time. His balance had been about to tip, and he was standing way too close to the edge without even knowing when he'd stepped there. The last time he'd looked, he'd been several feet away.

He turned and looked at her. In her face he could see her reaction to his obvious exhaustion; in her eyes he could see her fear of him jumping instead of climbing down.

"In my bag," he replied hoarsely. "It's not long enough to reach all the way down. I'll figure out how to continue once I've reached the end of it."

"And you expect me to wait up here until you come back? Are you crazy? No, hang on, stupid question. Actually, I think I should go down there. You can barely stand on your own legs, not to mention climbing into that abyss."

For a moment he stared at her, wondering if he should push her down first before jumping after her.

Instead, he forced his mind—or what was left of it—away from the abyss and went to his bag, rummaging through it whilst Luca bound the end of the rope to the underside of the bridge. She was right—he was exhausted and needed a little help to accomplish the task ahead. Luckily, there should be some drugs in his bag for just that occasion.

There. Under his fingertips, he felt the leather pouch that contained one small pill, purchased about half a year ago when he'd had enough money to afford this kind of drug. It was for emergencies only; he wouldn't have taken it had there been another choice.

His hands were trembling when he took out the pouch. His fingers fumbled at the strings, unable to open them. Rage wondered if it was possible to age for a hundred years in one single night—it was how he felt, like an ancient relic, a dried-out mummy unable to move without shriveling to dust.

Silently, Luca stepped next to him. She knelt, took the pouch out of his numb fingers, and opened it. The pill landed on her palm, small and white, a speck of dust about to be blown away by the breeze.

He was hallucinating. The pill was the size of a pea, and not even if he blew at it directly could he blow it off Luca's palm. Rage blinked repeatedly, trying to get his senses under control but making a lousy job of it. He was too exhausted, too far gone into madness to be able to keep control. So he just took the pill and put it into his mouth, kept it under his tongue until the bittersweet taste flooded through him, and finally bit it in half. Methodically, he chewed it, ignoring that bittersweet turned into foul, ignoring the voices in his head—from Keiran, the ghosts, the whole world apparently shouting at him—ignoring the stab of pain shooting through his heart. He'd only done this once before, and back then, he'd been in perfect health.

Back then, the strength of the drug had landed him in bed for a week after his task had been done. Today, he was sure he'd drop dead once it lost its effect.

But the voices drifted away, and he could take a deep breath for the first time in hours. His empty stomach was forgotten in a heartbeat, and his headache was dimmed down to a gentle, nearly pleasant humming.

Rage rolled his shoulders, his muscles relaxing, his body gathering strength. He smiled. "Good stuff, this," he said, got up, and stretched. Taking his knife, he flicked it several times, his hand as steady as ever.

Luca watched him closely before she asked, "What have you taken?"

Nearly no noise in his head now. "Anubis pill. Nothing I'd do voluntarily, but without it, I wouldn't be able to do more than *think* about getting down there. Provides me with strength. Keeps the pain at bay. Even mollifies Keiran's calls. Either I find him and manage to bring him up before the pill loses its power, or you will have to find your way back home on your own."

The rope looked good. Luca had done a perfect job with the knot. Rage sheathed his knife, took the rope, and swung himself out into the emptiness above the abyss and the river and the ghosts awaiting him below.

"Cut the rope when I pull twice," he said, feeling the drug rush through his blood, making him feel invulnerable, unbeatable, godlike.

Then he was gone, sliding down the rope like a spider before Luca could reply.

Seeing the bridge from below was a spectacular sight—he'd crossed it four times so far, twice toward the monastery, twice the other way. Each time he'd tried to get off it as fast as he could, as touching the bridge was and always had been a horrible experience. Through the wooden planks, through the ropes, the dead called, the ones who had died building the bridge, who had given their blood, whose bones had been broken during the process of spanning the river below.

From underneath, the bridge looked different, as did the walls building the abyss. From above, they looked solid, without cracks or places one could rest. Now that he was close to the rocks, Rage saw this image had been wrong. There were cracks, wide enough to serve as support for his feet, and there were places his hands could hold on to. With the help of the rope, he descended fast.

He was feeling better than he had in months, but it wouldn't last long, and he knew it.

When he reached the end of the rope, he pulled twice, and a moment later, it slid toward him, cut off by Luca. He was still a long way from the ground, so he retied it, pulling it around a root and hoping it would hold his weight. "Good thing I haven't eaten much lately," he said with a grin, knowing madness was held at bay only by a tiny little pill containing the most illegal drug a man could find. He needed to hurry.

The rocks cut his hands, but he didn't feel a thing. His muscles trembled with fatigue and overuse, but he didn't notice.

He shouldn't be able to concentrate on the rope and the rocks and the task of getting into the abyss. He shouldn't be able to think, to decide which way to go, which hold to use. Yet he was close to the ground now. Hearing the river, he also perceived the coldness welling up from the water rushing through the abyss. The spray wet his clothes, his hair, his face. The rope got slippery, and underneath his feet and fingers, he could feel moss.

Another fifteen feet to the ground, and the rope ended. Jumping would mean breaking his legs at the least and his neck more likely. And there was no one up there to cut off the rope a second time.

Without hesitation, Rage let go of the rope and clung to the rocks instead. Without the drug, he would have felt how icy they were and how sharp. He would have sensed his fingers freezing and his clothes getting soaked with the river's spray. He was dripping wet, the wind and the cold chilling his bones. But the drug was strong, and so he had no problem at all descending farther, leaving smears of blood on the rocks from where they cut his fingers, wrists, and legs. He jumped the last few feet, landing on the riverbank. His body was covered in bruises, but it was of as much importance to him right now as a mosquito's sting.

Above him, he could see the bridge, black against the sky. He guessed Luca was looking into the abyss, trying to make out where he'd gone, but she was too far up to be seen.

The river roared; it was louder even than his heartbeat drumming in his ears.

Help me!

Rage staggered when Keiran's voice thundered through his head. His feet lost track of the ground, and he landed knee-deep in the river, crashing through a layer of thin ice.

His hands flew to his head—his brain was burning, his eyes swimming in tears of sudden pain.

Help me. Help me! Help! Me!

Each time the voice became louder, if that was possible at all—Rage had the impression the words would bring down the mountains, dry out the river, make the sky fall. Impossible. The voice was everywhere. It was everything. Nothing else counted. He needed to find the source.

Blood began dripping from his nose and eyes.

Turning, Rage tried to see where the voice was coming from— if it was the boy, he must be nearby, and therefore easy to see. But all he could make out was the river, the rocks, and a few low bushes. No other human being apart from himself, not even an animal.

And the voice in his head was screaming.

Galloping heartbeat, tightening lungs. Rage was sweating despite his wet clothes and the fact that he was standing in a partly frozen river. "Where the hell are you?" he shouted. "I'm here. I'm here to help you!"

Help me! Please, please, help me!

Rage fell again, the impact of Keiran's scream bringing him down. Water embraced him; blinded, he reached out, found the riverbed, and grabbed hold of a root just before the drift could tear him away. Half-drowned, he managed to get back to his feet, but just before he could wade back to the shore, a large branch floating in the river hit him at the back of his knees and threw him over once more. Losing his grip on the root, he was prey to the stream, tumbling through the waves without the smallest chance to do anything about it. Nothing but sheer luck eventually landed him on the other side of the river, caught between the shore and a fallen tree. Some ribs cracked; more bruises to worry about should he ever get out of the abyss.

On all fours like a beaten dog, Rage crawled away from the river, collapsing on the stony ground with the waves still washing over his boots. Breathing hurt most, the pain barely dimmed by the drug. He guessed there wasn't much time left before it ceased working.

Help me! Please help me, please!

The words were more than enough motivation for Rage to get back to his feet. Swaying, he had to steady himself by leaning against the rocks. Blood from a cut on his forehead mixed with his still bleeding nose—if he were to find the boy, he was pretty sure Keiran would run away from him.

But Keiran wasn't here.

"Damn you," Rage rasped, wishing Luca hadn't saved him, wishing he was lying in his grave already. It would be nice and quiet there, he wouldn't ache, and hope wouldn't tear his heart apart. Because there was still hope. He heard Keiran's voice—how could he not hope to find the boy himself?

Actually, the pleas for help seemed stronger on this side of the river. Not louder—nothing could top the noise in his head—but stronger. More prominent, clearer, more insistent…. Rage couldn't quite put a finger on it, but when he moved to the left, he knew it was the wrong direction.

So to the right, then. Toward the rocks, and toward a small crack in the wall, no bigger than a child and just wide enough that he could squeeze through if he wanted to. Probably, there was a cave behind the crack; nothing Rage wanted to know about. It was bad enough out here.

When he caught movement at the corner of his eye, Rage whipped around. His cracked ribs protested, but he wasn't fast enough to catch whatever had caused the movement. He wasn't even sure if he'd really seen something or if his mind was playing tricks on him.

His mind was telling him to move on, toward the crack in the wall. Something was there, something he needed to see.

Not wanting to move, Rage took another step and another nevertheless. Like a puppet on strings, he was pulled forward, his boots slipping on the tricky ground. Finally he stood directly in front of the crack, his hands pressed to the rocks to steady himself as well as to be able to lean forward, to take a look inside.

Nothing but darkness. What had he expected—a fire and a cup of tea awaiting him?

"No one down here." His voice sounded strange in his ears, faint and foreign and far too weak. He was at the brink of unconsciousness, he realized; either he went back up again, or he would die down here.

When he turned, the screams in his head exploded, and he yelled in sudden agony. Nothing had ever been that bad; nothing had ever hurt so horrendously. He staggered, and his hands, frantically trying to find something to hold on, found a patch of moss.

They also found the small doll placed on the moss. Made of wood and carved by a madman, decorated with blood and a bit of brown hair, it was clear it hadn't been created as a toy.

Dumbstruck, Rage stared at the doll in his hand. Blood and water dripped onto the wood. Disbelieving, he touched the ridiculously large crotch Ethan had shaped three months before.

The doll called for him. *Help me!* it screamed, and Rage winced as it was Keiran's voice he heard. *Save me!*

What had Rebecca said? That the voice in his head was but an illusion?

She'd been right. Keiran wasn't here. Never had been. He was dead, had died by jumping into the abyss and washed away in the river in his attempt to save Rage and Luca.

Only the doll had survived.

There was no hope anymore. There was only the fact he'd been driven into madness by a piece of wood shaped by Keiran's murderer. And the doll was his way to have a last laugh.

Water, blood, and tears ran down his face, mingled, and dropped onto the ground.

Rage knew he wouldn't be able to climb up the wall again, so he didn't fight his failing knees and sunk to the ground, his hands clutched against the doll, his mind empty, his heart still as broken as it had been the moment the boy had died.

CHAPTER
Six

WHETHER HE sat with his back pressed against the rocks for minutes or hours, Rage couldn't have said. Minutes, more likely— but eventually the cold and the pain took its toll and he winced, shaking and feeling every single one of his ribs, cracked or not. The drug was losing its magic, and although it allowed him to take a few deep and steady breaths, its effect wouldn't last much longer.

Now what? he wondered, staring at the blood on his hands.

He should throw the doll away and climb back up to Luca, leaving the abyss behind and getting as far away from the mountains and the Forbidden Monastery as possible. Forget about the boy once and for all. Pick up the shards of his life; go with the girl, most likely, and help her deal with her problems.

What he would do, though, was remain seated until there was no trace of the drug in his blood anymore, until nightfall, until the temperature fell below the freezing point, killing him softly.

Coward.

"I know," he said, fully aware and not caring at all that he was talking to himself.

Luca needs you.

"I know!"

Keiran....

"The boy is dead. He died when he jumped. His corpse was washed away by the river months ago, and what called me was this damn fucking useless doll." Disgusted, Rage spat, still clutching the doll. In a sudden impulse, he broke it in half, the head snapping off with a dry little sound that made his hair stand up on his neck. He dropped the two halves and watched as they began smoldering. The wood blackened, then burst into flames. After a minute, nothing was left of it but two tiny piles of ash.

The screams in his head, the pleas for help, the endless whispers vanished. In between two heartbeats they were gone as if they'd never been there.

Rage's stomach cramped, and he would have vomited had he eaten anything.

"You shouldn't have done that," a voice said next to his ear.

At any other time, under any other circumstances, Rage would have jumped, outraged at the fact someone had been able to creep up on him. At any other time, under any other circumstances, no one would have been able to creep up on him no matter how badly he'd been injured, not whilst he was still conscious.

The ghost had done it easily, and for some reason, Rage wasn't even surprised. He'd known there were ghosts awaiting him. He'd heard them; everyone who crossed the bridge heard them. They were demanding, luring, threatening the ones seeking the shelter of the Forbidden Monastery. They promised peace or hell; they whispered or screamed depending on what hurt the traveler most.

This one had talked almost normally.

Pressing a steadying hand to his ribcage, Rage tore his eyes from the ash at his feet, turned his head, and raised an eyebrow. "Shouldn't I?" he asked, mild curiosity in his voice. "Why's that, then?"

The ghost didn't really look like a ghost. For one, it wasn't translucent, nor did it hover above the ground. Second, the rags it wore looked too damn real to be an illusion.

"You're a ghost?" It was probably best to just ask. And anyway, given he was seeing a ghost, he could also talk to him.

The... thing chuckled. For it was a thing rather than a ghost, one that had been male in life. It had large teeth, yellow and reaching down to his chin. Empty hollows as eyes, burned out or maybe ripped out with greedy nails. No ears, only lumps where they should be. The rags it wore stank of mold. Here and there, Rage saw moss growing on the thing's sagged, bluish skin.

"I'm what you'd call a ghost, yeah," the thing said. "Name's Ryan. Or was Ryan, whilst I was still up there, amongst the monks." He jerked his head upward, a small gesture, but incredibly hateful.

"They drained me, took everything I had to give to build their monastery. Took my daughter too. Luisa. Two days after she'd arrived, they raped her. Next thing, they cut her tongue out when she didn't stop screaming. One monk destroyed her eyes with his thumbs just because he didn't like their color."

He looked at Rage and grinned. "They were green, her eyes. Luisa. Beautiful girl. My girl. Wish I could have taken her bones down here with me, but the fuckers just kicked me into the abyss when I tried to get to her."

With the tip of his tongue, he licked his lips. It shot out of his mouth like a snake. It became longer, long enough to wrap around Rage's wrist. It tickled.

If the assassin hadn't been beyond fear, he might have tried to take a step backward.

Ryan grinned admiringly. "You're brave," he said. "Or mad. Or both. You're—"

His eyes widened. His tongue snapped back into his mouth, and instead, he grabbed Rage's neck. "It's you!" he breathed, blowing foul breath into the assassin's face. "You came to save the boy!"

Rage shook his head, more to get away from the stink than to deny facts. "The boy is dead."

Really, it wasn't that bad talking to a ghost. It surely occupied his raving mind, distracting him until he was dead.

Ryan came a little bit closer. His cold, clammy hands roamed over Rage's face, and his tongue, clearly having a will of its own, caressed his cheek. "You destroyed the doll," he whispered.

"Couldn't stand the screaming. Destroying it put an end to the noise."

"But he'll wake up now!" Ryan hissed, worry in his voice. "All the memories the doll kept from him will flood back inside him. He'll wake!"

"He's dead," Rage repeated patiently and decided he'd gone mad sometime in the past half hour. Talking to a ghost certainly wasn't anything a sane man did.

Ryan shook his head. It nearly came off. "Isn't. We caught him when he fell. We usually don't do that. We call out to the ones above, scaring them enough to make them jump. Doesn't always work—the really strong ones can withstand us, or the ones who become crazy instead—but when they jump, we have a feast on their broken corpses. The boy was a victim, though. Knew it because the doll came down first, radiating dark magic, radiating evil. It pulled him down. He didn't stand a chance. We couldn't let the boy die, so we caught him and saved him, and now he'll wake up, and he'll see us, and it will drive him crazy!"

With sudden force, Rage pushed the man—the ghost, the thing—away. "What the fuck are you talking about?" Hope, that damn hope was flaring up inside him like a bushfire. "The boy is *dead*. The rotten doll was calling for me. No one is alive down here. There's no corpse, not even his bones. I'm the one who's mad, and you don't even exist!"

And the voice in my head is gone, he thought and wasn't sure anymore whether he should be happy about it.

Ryan jumped, graceful like a dancer at the empress's court. Hands outstretched and tongue lashing out, he wrapped himself around Rage, clung to him like an overgrown tick. His nails dug holes in Rage's flesh, his breath made him sick, and because of the ghost's steel-like muscles, Rage had no chance to shake him off. Struggling to remain on his feet, he winced with pain when Ryan's arms tightened around his chest, sending agony through his already cracked ribs.

"We caught him!" Ryan hissed, his tongue licking Rage's neck. "Three of us. Unconscious he was, and so alive! Injured, tortured. But we caught him. Victim, he was. Carried him inside. There's magic in those mountains, lots of magic, dark magic, black and white and rainbow-colored magic. Turned us into what we are. Turned us into monsters, but a different kind of monsters than the fucking monks. They are up there, their voices woven into the bridge. We're down here, and we tamed the magic. We can use it, and we can exist as long as we stay here. We caught the boy, we carried him inside, we healed his injuries, but we couldn't heal his mind."

His grip tightened further. That Rage had a hard time breathing, that he swayed and desperately tried to get him off didn't seem to bother Ryan. "The boy's not dead," Ryan hissed into the assassin's ear. Like a slimy worm, his tongue accompanied the words. "He was linked to the doll, with his blood and hair stuck to it. We healed him. His last thoughts before he passed out—they went into the doll. Calls for help. Calls for you. Now you broke it, and there is no channel anymore for his voice. He will wake, he will see us, and it will be too much! He's not dead. Not yet. *You* broke the doll; *you* will be responsible for his death. Unless...." Suddenly, he relaxed his grip. "Unless you take him away from here."

As quickly as he'd attacked, Ryan let go of Rage, jumping toward the wall and clinging to it. His tongue was back in his mouth. The empty sockets of his eyes were wet from the spray. He looked like he was crying.

Rage collapsed, one hand pressed against his ribs, the other to the ground. One more minute, and the thing would have suffocated him.

The boy's not dead.

The words rang through his mind.

We caught him.

If that was true....

"Where is he?" The words nearly refused to leave his mouth. "If you weren't lying, if he's really alive, I want to see him."

"Thought you'd never ask," Ryan said with a grin, hopped down to the ground, and vanished through the crack in the wall.

Rage blinked. In a way, the pain in his ribs and lungs kept him grounded, prevented him from believing he was dreaming or dead already. A dreaming man couldn't feel pain without waking, and a dead man didn't feel anything at all.

Kneeling, Rage stared at the crack in the wall. There was nothing but darkness behind it, no movement, no sound, nothing. All he could hear was his own labored breathing, the river, and his heartbeat thundering in his chest.

"Are you coming?" Ryan called just when Rage had convinced himself he'd imagined the creature. His snakelike tongue shot through the crack, wrapped itself around Rage's wrist, and pulled him inside, stronger than a hand and a lot less gentle. Rage bumped his head against the rock, his shoulders getting stuck for a moment until the tongue pulled harder, forcing him through. The rocks tore his shirt apart and dragged several long gashes into his flesh.

As he was coming from light into darkness, he didn't see a thing. Nevertheless, he got the impression of being in a narrow chamber, or rather, a narrow path leading deeper into the mountain. Around his wrist was Ryan's tongue, pulling him on like a dog on a leash.

Gradually the darkness became less deep. One moment Rage wasn't able to see his own hand in front of his eyes, the next he made out Ryan ahead of him, hurrying along on all fours.

With a sudden jerk, Rage freed his hand. "Wait," he said, a harsh command in the total silence of the mountains.

The tongue had left raw skin and a slimy track. "What?" Ryan asked. "We're close. We've got to hurry. If the boy wakes before you are there, a human man, an alive man, his mind will snap. We're not a nice bunch to look at under the best of circumstances, but he's beyond weak. If he wakes before you're there, you can just as well leave him with us."

Unexpectedly, Rage's leg muscles cramped, and with a strangled cry, he clutched his thigh, trying to get back control.

Sympathetically, Ryan patted Rage's back, both with his hand and his tongue. "You might like to think about staying here too. You're kind of dead already, I say. At least you and the boy would be together. Although… you wouldn't have much fun with him down here. The mountain drains you worse than the monks did. Just as likely you'd kill him after a day or two."

"The light, where does the light come from?" Rage needed to say something to distract himself from the cramping muscles. Forcing himself to put weight on the leg, he was relieved it worked. The cramps ceased. For now.

"Worms," Ryan replied cheerfully. "They live here, and they glow. Near the entrance, it's too wet for them. Nice, isn't it?"

One step, and another. His leg held his weight. "Creepy. And what's the smell?" Rage became aware of the foul and rotten smell only now. Looking around, he saw something pushed into a niche in the wall.

Ryan pointed a finger at it. "That one was bad. Pity, but he came down here dead already. Bad man. Evil. Beaten to a pulp, and when he crashed into the river, the few unbroken bones in his body crumbled like sandstone." Somewhat hesitantly, his tongue danced across the corpse's clothes, covered in dried blood, dirt, piss and sweat. "Of course, we made sure he didn't recover from his death," he added somewhat proudly. "Didn't want his kind down here. Just like we didn't want the monks. They're all above. This one here is just dead, though."

Rage bared his teeth at the rotten corpse in the niche. It was an instinctive reaction, unplanned and uncontrollable.

Seeing it, Ryan stepped closer, putting his hand onto the assassin's shoulder. "You know the man?"

"I killed him." Breathing slowly, Rage tried to stay on his feet. Tried not to think about how it had felt to beat the life out of him. "Ethan. That I am here is because of what he'd set in motion many months ago."

Ryan's grip tightened. This time it wasn't unpleasant, just comforting. "You did well, killing him. We felt his presence. He's been at the monastery before, three, four times at least. We're not good with time, but we recognized him, and we feared he'd continue where the monks had stopped. Glad he's gone." His tongue dashed to the corpse's skull, or what was left of it. It sneaked into one of the eye sockets and came out through the mouth. "Bet he would have hated the thought of being displayed like this." He chuckled.

"Take me to the boy," Rage said.

THEY WALKED through the glowing darkness in silence. Occasionally, Rage thought he could hear voices echoing against the walls, but when he tried to listen closer, there was nothing there. Eventually, he began to fear Ryan was leading him deeper and deeper into the mountain without anywhere to go, leading him on until he dropped dead.

Worse even was the thought he was still sitting leaned against the outer wall, his dying mind providing him with pictures of hope.

He was about to halt his step when Ryan was suddenly gone. "Come in," his bodiless voice said, and Rage realized the ghost had walked around a corner.

When he followed, it took every bit of his willpower not to scream.

He'd stepped into what seemed to be a large cave, with many more tunnels leading in every direction from it. It was low; he wasn't able to stand straight. And the cave was filled with what once might have been people but what looked like a crowd of nightmares.

Ryan grinned, a disturbing sight given the length of his fangs. "Welcome to my home," he said and bowed. "We're honored someone is visiting us of his own free will, and someone alive on top of it. The boy is over there." Pointing to the far end of the cave, he waved away the approaching corpses, ghosts, and abominations.

Grumbling, they made way for them, Ryan going first, Rage following him and trying not to look to his left or right. But no matter how he tried, he couldn't help seeing former human beings with only half a head, missing arms, or split-in-half bodies. Many had faces that couldn't be called faces anymore, much worse than Ryan's.

"The boy's waking up."

One creature whispered the words, the others picked them up, repeated them, until they were thundering with hundreds of echoes through the cave.

A bony hand touched his, held him back. Rage had no choice but to look at its owner.

A skeleton. What a surprise.

"We care for him," the skeleton whispered. It wore a dress. Worms were crawling over its skull, making it glow eerily. "The boy. We made sure he didn't die. You're Rage, aren't you?"

"How do you know who I am?" Rage's voice sounded as weak and crazy as he felt.

The skeleton's hand touched his cheek. "We can hear him dream. Awful dreams of pain and fear. Dark dreams of a madman using him and his magic. Sometimes, he manages to dream of you. Not dark, just black. Not a madman, just an assassin. But your hands are gentle, and your kisses taste of summer and freedom and happiness." Briefly, the skeleton's skull came close enough to brush lips over Rage's neck, had it had lips and not only bare bones instead. "Be there when he wakes," it whispered. "Let him see you when he opens his eyes, not one of us." Pressing its hands into his back, the skeleton urged him on toward the bed the ghosts had made for Keiran.

The boy was resting on a layer of moss covered by all sorts of garments. Rage could make out part of a skirt, bright blue but torn apart. Trousers, nearly new. A sleeve, decorated with tiny flowers. And blankets, half a dozen of them, draped on top of him.

Keiran was anything but sleeping peacefully. Tossing and turning his head, it was obvious something scared him even when unconscious. His mouth worked as if he were trying to speak, and behind his closed lids, his eyes moved.

With one last, large step, Rage was beside him, pushing Ryan out of the way. Just before he took the boy's hand in his, he hesitated.

Silence spread through the cave. Every creature watched him swallow, ball his fists. Everyone watched him when he finally dared to place his hands on Keiran's chest, and everyone witnessed as their guest, their treasure, calmed under his touch.

For the first time since they had put him onto the makeshift bed, Keiran stopped fighting against the invisible chains the creatures had put on him to keep him unconscious Sighing, he relaxed, and with him, the crowd sighed too.

"He's the right one," a small ghost said, slipping a tentacle around the waist of a creature that looked more like a sponge than a human being.

Right one, he's the right one, he's the right, right, right one, the right one, the ghosts whispered.

"Of course he's the right one," Ryan snapped, shushing his comrades with a fierce gesture into silence. "We saw the boy's dreams, didn't we? We saw *him*." His tongue touched Rage. "And we know we have to let him go now."

The ghosts groaned. Clearly, parting with their treasure, with the only one amongst them who was still looking human, didn't go down well.

"We have to let him go! If he stays here, he'll become like us. He'll die without being dead. He'll go mad without knowing it." Ryan's words became demanding, accusing. "His flesh will fall off his bones, and he will grow extra limbs like most of us have."

"We don't want that," the skeleton woman said.

"We don't want that," the others agreed.

"Take him and get him away from here," Ryan told Rage, his empty eyes turned to the boy.

That was the moment when Keiran opened his eyes.

The crowd gasped in shock. "Oh no," the small ghost whispered, translucent tears running down his face. "Too late, too late now!"

Rage, his hands still on Keiran's chest, bent low over his lover's face, well aware of the dozens and dozens of eyes watching him. "You're safe," he said clearly, hoping the boy would hear him. "I'm here. I came for you. You are safe now."

Keiran's eyes widened. They darted from Rage's face to the low-hanging ceiling, covered with moss and worms, to Ryan's nightmarish fangs, to his own hands, which were white and thin and weak after months of an unnatural, magical sleep.

Then he screamed: a silent, but nevertheless most impressive scream full of panic, fear, and agony.

Without even thinking about what he was doing, Rage brought his elbow up and slammed it hard against the boy's temple. He hit the perfect spot with perfect strength: hard enough to knock Keiran out, but not hard enough to break his skull. Keiran's body became limp. Rage pulled him close until the boy was cradled safely in his arms.

"Fuck," he said wearily. "Ryan, I need to carry him out of here. Show me the way. Show me how to save him." And after a moment of thought, he added, "Please."

Ryan nodded. "I'll show you the way through the heart of the mountain. There are hundreds of paths through it. I can take you somewhere with a village nearby."

Rage picked Keiran up. A thought crossed his mind, a mad, impossible thought. "Is there a way of getting us near Dragon Spring? It's in the north. Going around the mountains it would cost me more than a week to get there, but—"

"We can reach the place in a few hours. It's easy. Let's go!" Pushing through the crowd, Ryan was already out of sight before he realized that Rage didn't follow him.

Ryan turned. "What's the problem? I can help you carry the boy. Actually—Fred, come with me. If we have to, we can carry you both."

"Luca is waiting for me."

Luca, Luca, Luca—like an echo, the name spread through the cave.

Rage took a few steps with Keiran in his arms. It was easier than he'd thought to carry him. "My friend. A young girl. She's waiting for me. Up there." He nodded toward the cave's ceiling. "I cannot abandon her."

Thoughtfully, Ryan looked at him, then had a whispered conversation with some of his friends. Finally, he shook his head. "No way back up. You probably wouldn't make it yourself, and you definitely couldn't carry your friend up the wall."

"I could go and get her," a child piped up eagerly. A boy, no more than five years old, and with more arms and legs than necessary. He resembled an overgrown spider apart from the sweet smile on his rosy lips and the peach-like texture of his skin. "I'd be up there in a minute. I could tell her we are all really nice, and wouldn't she want to meet us?"

The tall figure of a female ghost stepped up behind him, putting her long, slender hand on his shoulder. Wearing a bright red dress, she looked beautiful, although Rage could see the wall behind her. Through her. "Lovely idea, honeybunch," she whispered. Even her voice was ghostlike. "But this Luca—is she an adult woman? Children should not come down here."

"She's sixteen. And she would be scared of him."

The boy's eyes became wet with sudden tears. "Is it because of my arms? It's not my fault! They just grew. I wouldn't scare her, I promise!"

The ghost woman smiled at him. "You heard him, honeybunch. Tell you what, why not lead the way, and I come after you? Together, we will—"

"She's pregnant."

The ghost frowned. "That is a problem. Her child wouldn't survive down here." She stroked over the little boy's head. "So we will find her and, instead of bringing her down here, we'll take her the secret way, honeybunch, yes?"

"Sorted," Ryan said firmly, putting his tongue on Rage's shoulder. "Come along, assassin. Your friend will be safe with Elly and Bo. We need to hurry now."

DANGLING HER legs over the edge, Luca refused to admit how worried she was. For a while, she had felt Rage's weight on the rope. When he had given the signal, she had cut it off, and now it had been ages since he had vanished.

All she could do was wait and hope. That he had made it down there safely, that he hadn't fallen.

"He might have broken his neck," she mused, ignoring the cold dread creeping up and down her spine. "Maybe he's trapped, in need of help. And I'm sitting up here, lazily enjoying the peace."

She was well aware of the bitterness at her uselessness in her words.

Problem was, she was too afraid of heights to go after him. Not if someone paid or threatened her, not if a monster turned up behind her, not if the only other choice would be death could she force herself to climb into the abyss.

Shuddering, she looked down. That her legs were dangling over the edge was just bearable, mainly because a fog had occurred, creeping nearly up to the soles of her feet. It looked as if she was sitting just an inch above solid ground, and what her eyes told her was what her brain and her heart believed.

Hating herself for her weakness didn't really help, nor did wishing she would be braver or could jump over her shadow. "Just a bit of climbing," she told herself. "And anyway, if Rage found Keiran, he needs me to get him back up. He's at the brink of a breakdown. There's no way he will manage this on his own."

Tentatively, she put a hand to the underside of the bridge, where the rest of the rope was still dangling.

Fear nearly strangled her. Nothing could ever be as bad as the thought of nothing but emptiness beneath her body and the image of her tumbling through thin air.

A head appeared next to her feet, the head of a child with rosy cheeks and a sweet smile. A boy, and he seemed a bit out of breath. His hand found a root right next to Luca's feet. When he saw her, his face lit up with joy. "We're up, Elly!" he called into the fog. "I found her!"

Luca opened her mouth, but her brain refused to provide her with words she could speak.

The boy's second arm appeared, and a third, and a few more. A moment later he sat next to her, staring eagerly into the abyss as if awaiting someone else. "Hi," he said over his shoulder. "I'm Bo. You are Luca, yes?"

Had he mentioned someone called Elly?

Was there someone else hiding in the fog?

And did the boy really have so many arms and legs?

"Who're you?" Luca finally managed to croak.

The boy looked at her. "I told you. I'm Bo. Your friend sent me and Elly to find you. Look, that's Elly. Don't be afraid of her, right? She's nice. Just don't try touching her. She doesn't like it. Says it feels like someone walking over her grave." He grinned. "Silly, isn't it? Her bones are down there with her."

A second head floated up through the fog, the head of a woman. She was nowhere near the wall. Impossible she was clinging to the rocks; impossible she had been climbing up here.

Luca could see the bridge although the woman was right in front of it.

"I take it you are Elly?" Luca said weakly. "Pleased to meet you. I always wanted to meet a ghost. I'm Luca, and by the way, I've just gone mad."

The woman laughed, an eerie sound, high and faint. She stepped through the fog and put her foot onto the bridge, leaning over and staring into the abyss. "I haven't been up here in a long time," she whispered. "Maybe I should not have neglected my need to see the world above at least now and then." She turned to Luca. "Tell me, are the monks truly gone?"

It was probably not a good idea denying answers to a ghost, so Luca nodded. "As far as I know, they are all dead. Rage told me he killed the last ones over a decade ago. Rage being the one who should be down there somewhere. Have you seen him?"

Elly smiled. "All dead, yes? That is good news. Though their influence is still strong on people. Do you know Keiran, yes?"

Luca jumped up. Pebbles rushed into the abyss. "You have seen Keiran?"

Yes, she was truly mad. Talking to a ghost and a spiderlike boy who, somehow, had slipped one of his many hands into hers and honestly believing Keiran was somewhere down there, safe and sound, had to be madness.

"Keiran, and Rage as well." Languidly, the ghost woman stretched. The wind blew her form to bits and pieces, and it took a few moments before she was herself again. She shook her head. "Tsk. Now I remember why I don't come up here more often. Silly wind." She smiled. "Your friends are on their way out of the mountains, but I cannot guarantee they will make it. Keiran is unconscious, and if he wakes up whilst being in the heart of the mountain, he will die. Rage is way beyond his powers. If he stumbles, if his will to survive withers under the weight of the rocks, he will die as well. But you—you will live. If you follow me."

"I'll make sure you won't lose us," the little boy said, his hand tightening around her fingers. "It is an easy way, really, with many magical shortcuts. There are some inside the mountain as well, but not that many. Just hold my hand, and you'll be fine. You and the little one," he added shyly.

Immediately, Luca's hand flew to her belly. "How do you know? I don't show yet, so how do you know?"

Elly came closer. "Rage told us," she whispered. "He cares for you. We came to make sure you can leave this place. Awful place, full of black memories. You need to leave, or you will either die or end up like us. There is a path through the mountains, just across the bridge. Follow me, Luca, and hold on to Bo's hand all the time."

One glance into the abyss, covered by fog. One glance back to where she and Rage had come from. Neither way offered much hope of survival, not without Rage by her side.

But the bridge was bad, too.

"Well," Luca said, gripping the little boy's hand and setting one foot on the bridge. "Not that I think this is a good idea, but at the moment, I don't have a better one myself."

Elly was already at the other side of the bridge. Her long red dress billowed behind her. When her foot went through a skull lying close to the abyss, she halted. Frowning, she bent, letting her translucent hand wander across the smooth bone. "Hello, Luisa," she whispered. "Your father is looking for you, sweetie." Over her shoulder, she added, "Would you mind taking the skull with you, Luca? The man who is leading your friend would be very happy to have his daughter back."

CHAPTER
Seven

MILES? ETERNITY? Or just a few steps? It was impossible to tell. There was darkness around him, and his lungs were burning. There was the boy's weight in his arms, arms he had ceased to feel—how long ago? Had he ever possessed arms?

He couldn't remember.

Step by step, Rage made his way under the mountains. Somewhere ahead of him was a man whose name he couldn't remember. Somewhere behind him was a man called Fred, with silent steps and shoulders like a brick wall. His arms occasionally separated from his body, steadying the assassin, so he wouldn't fall.

Neither of them talked.

The burden in Rage's arms—who was it, anyway, and why was he carrying an unconscious body? Was he dead already? Rage couldn't tell. The body was cold and limp, and if it breathed, he couldn't see it. Probably there was a purpose to what he was doing—walking, carrying, trying to stay upright.

Or maybe not.

The Anubis pill had long lost its effect, his body running on its last reserves. Very soon, he would drop the boy and give in to his need to sleep. It would mean to die, but well, that was the least of his concerns.

Step by step; breath by breath. It was an endless walk through eternal darkness, and maybe it would have been bearable had he known why he had to do this. But he didn't. All he knew was that he had to continue walking and that he couldn't let go of the body in his arms.

Step by step, one at a time.

Breathing became hard, nearly impossible. Dizziness, washing though him with bitter, blinding strength, made him stagger, but someone, something, protected him from falling.

Eventually the darkness became less dark. Fresh, cold air hit his face, drying the sweat on his forehead and sending a shiver down his spine.

"We're here," someone said, and someone touched him. "We thought you wouldn't make it, but we're here now, and much faster than anticipated. You're a strong man, assassin, and very stubborn on top of it. I believe that you wouldn't have stopped walking even if you had died on the way."

The assassin looked at the creature standing in the golden evening light, looked at the fangs and the empty sockets, looked at the tongue that was wrapped around his own upper arm. Vaguely, he knew that tongues should not exist that far outside one's body, but then, what did he know.

Maybe he should say something, but he didn't know what, and he had forgotten how to talk anyway.

"Take the path to the right, and you will reach a small farm about a mile away."

Ryan, the man with the impossible tongue was called Ryan.

"We would accompany you. Really. But we can't get away from the mountains. You have to make that last mile without our help. See, the girl is here too. Elly took her across the top just as promised. Now stay alive for that last mile, Rage. And keep the boy alive, too."

Someone got up from a rock hidden in the mountain's shadows.

Luca. Blinking, Rage looked at her, too, saw that she seemed to have no extra limbs or see-through flesh, and thought it best to just do what she told him to do.

"I'll make sure we reach this place you were talking about, if I have to drag them there." Her eyes darted from Rage's face to Keiran's unconscious body.

Ryan beamed at her. In his hand, he held a skull Luca had handed him. "Good. How was your journey?"

"Strange." Luca's teeth began to chatter. "Each step felt as if I were making ten instead, each yard like a mile. Without little Bo's hand in mine, I would have been too scared to do it, but with his help, I made it."

The little boy grinned happily. "Come and visit us," he said invitingly. "You could stay overnight without growing any extra limbs. I think."

Luca gulped. "I need some rest first," she managed. "I'll think about it, if that's all right for you?"

"You need to rush," Elly cast in. Her red dress was glowing in the sunset. "You are all close to death. Get to the farm. Get to safety." Without further words, she went back into the mountains.

Luca reached out to touch Keiran's face.

Rage bared his teeth at her and took a step back. His shirt was drenched in sweat. Coughing once, he turned and walked away, cradling Keiran in his arms.

Ryan sighed. "He's beyond what a man can take. Been there myself. Unlike him, I died when my strength was taken up. He didn't. Wouldn't let us carry the boy. Fred occasionally steadied him, but that was about it. I believe he'll make it to the farm. Once the boy is safe, Rage will lie down and die."

"Fucking lousy, shitty day this is," Luca said, nodded good-bye to Ryan and ran after Rage.

"I've had worse." Ryan looked at his daughter's skull, a tear trickling down his cheeks. Cradling it to his chest, he kissed the bone right above the brow. "Come on, Luisa," he murmured. "So glad to have you back. Let's go home, sweetheart."

Luisa didn't say a thing. But if a skull could look happy, this one did.

IT DIDN'T take Luca long to catch up with Rage. He wasn't walking as much as staggering, his path not a straight line but marked by bends and sudden halts in between when exhaustion got the better of him.

In the distance, Luca could make out a low wall: surely this must be the outer bounds of the farm they were heading to. "What makes you think we are welcome there?" Luca asked, putting a hand on Rage's arm, partly to steady him, partly to make it clear she was talking to him.

He didn't answer, but at least he didn't shake off her hand, either.

"Look, this place could belong to anyone. And we are not exactly visitor material. The way we look, it would be the right of anyone who lives there to kill us first and ask questions later."

Rage didn't confirm that he'd even heard her. If anything, he sped up a bit. The path below his feet was muddy from molten snow and a long winter. His boots were splattered with dirt up to his knees, his trousers were ripped apart, his shirt hung off him in rags. There was blood on his hands and face.

The empty look in his eyes made Luca shudder. He'd looked like that when Keiran had jumped, shortly before he'd beaten Ethan to death. Luca wouldn't put it beyond him to try to kill the farm's owner in order to find a bed for Keiran.

"If Keiran saw you like this, he'd run from you," Luca shouted after him.

Rage stopped and blinked. "I know."

"Thank the Lady, he's talking to me again. Let's figure out how to do this, Rage. At least we should try and clean ourselves up a bit before knocking on that door."

"No knocking," Rage said and walked on.

"Damn you!" Luca had no choice but to run after him. In her experience, people reacted badly to strangers on their doorstep. They didn't offer help no matter how desperately help was needed. When she'd been small—too small to intervene—a woman had once knocked at the door of Babylon Manor, beaten by her husband. Her arm had been broken, and she'd asked for shelter and a sip of water.

Lucius had set the hounds on her.

Hugging her arms around herself, she went after Rage, shivering in the evening breeze. She longed for a bed and food and a bath, not necessarily in that order.

Shouldering Rage's bag, which Ryan had handed her, as well as her own, she took the path he had taken, hoping to survive by simply pleading for the landlord's mercy. "If the owner of this farm is anything like Lucius, we don't have to worry about dinner," she murmured to herself. "We'll be dog food before the sun is down."

The wall she'd seen from the distance was higher than she had thought at first, reaching above Rage's head and radiating magic. He wouldn't be able to climb it, and it was abundantly clear she wouldn't be able to find a way around the magical protection, not in her state, not with her head being light from hunger. Even putting her hand onto the stones was impossible; this was strong magic, expensive and expertly created to keep unwanted visitors out. There was no door in sight. There would be no door-knocking simply because they wouldn't be able to find the door in the first place.

Dread at the thought of sleeping outside with an unconscious Keiran and a three-quarter-mad assassin welled up inside her.

Rage just stood before the wall. His head was tilted as if he were listening to silent orders. Then he turned left, leaving her behind once more.

Great. He wasn't three-quarters mad, he was totally insane if he believed looking for the main gate was a good idea. Someone had spent a fortune to protect this place, making it impossible to get in for anyone who was not invited.

On the other hand, it was unlikely they'd survive the night outside, given the temperature was dropping dramatically that close to sunset. Twilight and an oncoming mist obscured their steps, and even Galadriel's pale green light didn't help to take the fear off her.

Against all odds, Luca could make out the main gate, hidden behind two willow trees. Briefly, she wondered how Rage had found it, but she was too tired to think about it properly. Gate or not, the magic would only acknowledge the farm's owner and the people living here.

"This is hopeless," Luca said. "Can't you feel it? If you touch the gate, the magic will lash out, hurting you, maybe even killing you. Whoever lives here doesn't want visitors. We have to find another place to sleep tonight."

Carefully, Rage let Keiran's feet slip to the ground, only holding him upright with his left arm. Keiran's head lolled against his shoulder.

"Didn't you hear what I just said?" Luca didn't dare to shout. "There's no way—"

Rage put his flat hand against the gate and closed his eyes.

"Oh shit!" Expecting an explosion, Luca jumped backward.

Silently and invitingly, the gate granted them entrance.

Luca's mouth sagged open. This was impossible; this was not happening, couldn't be happening! Even if Rage had his magic under control, which he hadn't, and even if he were at the height of his strength, which he wasn't, he didn't have the smallest chance to touch the door, not to mention opening it.

Only—he'd just done that.

Rage picked Keiran up and stepped through the gates.

Luca followed him. There was nothing else to do unless she wanted to stay outside and watch the gate close behind Rage's retreating figure.

No way.

In front of them was the house. It was small with only one floor, made of plain bricks and with a thatched roof. A few windows, but not enough to show off richness—glass was expensive, and only people with heaps of money could afford to have more than one window for each room. The door was made of wood and didn't bear any ornamental decoration, the veranda was clearly made by a skilled but nevertheless amateur carpenter, and the stable had places for two, maybe three horses at the most.

This place didn't look like what Luca had expected. The wall's magic was so advanced she'd believed she'd find a palace behind it.

Some chickens were searching for worms in the grass around the house. Pigs grunted in the pen. Apple trees, bare of leaves this time of the year, shook their branches at them.

Aside from the clucking chicks, it was very quiet.

Rage reached the front door. Not bothering to knock—hadn't she feared just that, damn him?—he kicked it open, staggering and nearly losing his balance as Keiran had chosen this moment to stir in his arms.

Luca rushed after them, having seen Keiran's movement and casting aside all fears of a possibly furious farm owner. Whoever lived here obviously couldn't be bothered to greet—or chase away—his guests. "He better not dare to show up right now," she murmured, steadying Rage and steering him toward the table standing in the middle of the room. "If he does...." Well, if the owner showed up, Luca planned to have a total breakdown right on the spot.

Rage dropped Keiran onto the table, barely able to keep himself upright. Both hands placed onto the wooden surface, he panted heavily. Even from where she stood, Luca could see his leg muscles tremble and his shoulders shake with the effort not to keel over.

Keiran turned his head, but his eyes stayed closed. Quickly, Luca was by his side, touching his face and searching for the pulse in his throat. He was, despite all odds, really and honestly alive.

For the moment. It seemed as if Keiran's body wondered if living was worth the effort.

"We need to find a bed for him, Rage." Behind Keiran's closed lids, his eyes made rapid movements as if seeing things they didn't want to see. Convulsively, his hands opened and closed. He tried to swallow, but clearly, his throat was too dry. "And a doctor. Soup for sustenance, and water, and—"

"Hello, cub," someone behind her said, and Luca jumped as she hadn't heard anyone entering the room. Whirling around, she had problems keeping up with the sudden turn of events. She saw a man standing near the door, but somehow, she couldn't figure out where he'd come from.

"You look like shit, cub," the man said, leaning against the doorframe in a most relaxed manner. "Like nearly always when you pay me a visit. Who are your guests? Care to introduce me?"

Luca blinked, hoping he would vanish. *Who is this?* she thought, and *Cub?*

The man was around sixty judging by the wrinkles around his eyes. When he pushed himself off the doorframe, taking a step, there was a clinking sound on the planks: the telltale swaying walk and his stick indicated a wooden leg. Broad shouldered, with strong legs and more muscles than she'd expected on a man his age, he reminded her of the blacksmith tending her horses back home. Long gray hair fell down his back, a three-day stubble showed on his face, and his one eye was of a piercing blue. Where his other eye had been, a patch obscured the socket.

"Lost the leg through a poisoned arrow some years ago," the man said, winking at Luca. "I'm Jack." He turned his attention back to Rage. "What's wrong this time, cub? You haven't been home in over five years. Must be serious if you chose to arrive out of the blue."

Home?

Rage didn't move, just stood with his hands on the table, staring down at Keiran, who was still fighting with whatever was going on behind his closed eyes.

Luca raised a shaking hand. When Jack looked at her questioningly, she stammered, "Are you telling me…. Are you saying Rage lives here?"

Jack's lip twitched. "Hard to believe, isn't it? But yes, he does. Sometimes. I tricked a customer into giving me the land, Rage called in a favor from a magician he once hadn't killed, and we both built the house with our own hands. Bet you wondered why the magic let him in, eh?"

Luca managed a nod.

Jack was next to her within the blink of an eye, pushing her onto one of the chairs. How had he managed to move without her seeing it?

"Sit, girl. I want some answers. What's wrong with the boy, for example, and where do you come from, looking like this?"

And from where did he get the cup of water, and why was he helping her drink it?

Ah, yes, because if he hadn't, she would have dropped the cup.

Wearily, Luca watched as the man—did he say Rage had built this house?—leaned his cane to the wall and put his ear to Keiran's chest.

We need help, Luca wanted to say, but the words wouldn't come out of her mouth. Her tongue was made of lead, and her body belonged to someone else. At least it didn't obey her orders anymore. She could only watch Jack sigh and turn to Rage. She could only watch as Rage sagged and Jack caught him. She could only watch when the old man picked him up and carried him like a child into one of the rooms, no matter his limp and no matter Rage must be half a head taller.

Should follow them, she thought or dreamed, and Keiran was still lying on the table, pale and unconscious, and maybe she *was* dreaming. Maybe she was still sitting at the abyss, waiting for Rage to come up again.

A door opened and closed, and a plate of food appeared in front of her eyes. Fresh bread, butter, honey. Not much, but just what she needed.

Was that really her hand, stuffing bread into her mouth? Was that her tongue, licking honey off the table's surface?

Was someone laughing at her? Well, if so, she didn't care.

Warmth surged through her, partly because of the food, partly because of the tea someone had poured for her. Her hands were wrapped around a steaming cup, and slowly, sound came back and feeling, and her brain felt as if it could do a little more thinking before it would demand sleep.

Jack sat opposite her, the table and some empty plates between them. A glass of wine stood in front of him, the red liquid dark in the light of the candles someone had lit.

"'S Keiran?" she managed, glad her voice was working again, though considerably slower than usual.

"The boy? Marit poured a bath for him. She's also making sure he won't drown. He's only half-awake, and he's refused to eat anything so far, but I think he will be fine. Eventually." Lazily, he leaned back, rolling the glass's stem between his fingers as if awaiting her next question.

"Rage?"

"You know who he is. Just his name or his profession as well?"

Luca swallowed. "He's—well. It's complicated. He is my friend, and Keiran is my friend, too. Rage saved Keiran's life, I think. You're an assassin as well?"

Jack grinned. "What gave me away? Eye or leg or the color of my clothes or maybe something equally unpleasant?"

She couldn't help it—Luca grinned back. "It was an educated guess. And I can see the tattoo underneath your necktie."

Jack nodded. "I was an assassin until I lost my leg. Raised him"—he pointed at a closed door—"and showed him how to survive. He's in bed now. I doubt he will survive the night, though, if you don't tell me what happened to him."

Luca grabbed herself a chunk of cheese and told Jack everything that had happened from the moment she'd first met Rage.

Her host listened silently, without interrupting her once. Outside, the moons rose high in the sky, and the stars came out. Inside, the candles burned low when Jack finally got up and took his walking stick with a smooth, long-trained movement. Faster than a man with only one and a half legs should be able to move, he was at the door behind which Rage was resting. "Come along," he said over his shoulder and turned the handle.

Silently, he entered the room.

Luca followed him in, only partly noticing the rugs on the floor and the fireplace, the high-backed chair, the bookshelves along the walls, the old, worm-eaten wardrobe and a table one could write or eat or work on. It was a peaceful room, and much to her surprise, she found it fit Rage quite well.

Jack looked down at the man who lay in the bed as if dead already. "She told me what you went through, cub. She cares for you. Dying would be a coward's way out of the mess you're in."

Luca, who had sat on the edge of the bed, was relieved to see Rage's chest rising steadily under the blanket Jack had put over him. "Cub?" she asked, hoping with all her might Rage would survive so she could tease him about this nickname.

Jack sat too. "I was paid to kill him when he was fourteen," he said, a small smile tugging at his lips. "The people of a village near his were afraid he'd—" He stopped himself midsentence. "But if you know him as well as you claim, you know what happened when he was a boy."

Of course she knew. A story like that she'd never forget, especially not when remembering the circumstances under which Rage had told her what had happened. "He killed the people in his village. By accident, I should add."

Now was there some fondness creeping into the old assassin's one blue eye?

"When I found him, he attacked me, a stone in his hand, with bare feet and bloody hands. He'd buried his kin, and he thought he had to protect their graves. Was a pitiful sight, my cub, nothing but a scrawny boy far too young to be killed by an assassin. I don't kill children. Only took the job because the villagers had told me he was as big as a tree and as strong as a hurricane and even more dangerous than death itself. Figured they'd lied when I saw the boy, half-starved, trembling and crying and ready to attack again should I come too close to the graves."

Ever since Luca had met Rage, she had wondered if she would ever learn more about his background, what had happened after his magic had killed his family and his love. Now that she knew, she wished Jack hadn't told her.

"Took him with me," Jack continued, brushing the hair out of Rage's pale face. "Fed him and put clothes on him and told him death wasn't the end. Taught him a lot over the years, although I never intended him to become an assassin. Was quite a surprise, that, but then, he's good. Precise and determined, so I taught him my rules and hoped he would manage to stay out of trouble."

"That would be the rules about not killing children?"

"No children. No one who is deeply loved. Kill as painlessly as possible. Take a job only if it is pays well and if you trust your customer. As far as I know, he always stuck to the rules." Jack sighed. "He should have woken by now. You would have told me if he had taken anything, wouldn't you? Drugs? Magic?"

The question made Luca frown.

She had, hadn't she? Of course she had; she'd told Jack everything. "I told you," she said firmly and with only a small quiver in her voice. "Right before he went into the abyss, he took a pill. Small, round… can't remember the name…."

Jack's hand locked around her wrist. "You haven't told me. How small was the pill? What color? Did he name it? Come on, girl. Talk to me, or I'll beat it out of you."

His fingers hurt. They would leave bruises.

Had he just threatened her?

"White. The pill was white and about the size of my thumbnail. He said, he said…. Anubis pill! That's the one!" Luca nearly laughed with relief now this last riddle was solved. She must have been too tired to tell Jack before. "Ryan—that's one of the ghosts living in the river, he's not really a ghost and his tongue is far too long and too cheeky—he said Rage is acting on borrowed strength and that he thinks Rage would die the moment Keiran was safe. But he is wrong, isn't he? We arrived here hours ago, and Rage is still alive. He… he will stay alive, won't he?"

Jack put both his hands on her shoulders, shaking her. "When?" he asked. "When did he take the pill?"

It seemed to Luca as if he was shaking all her remaining thoughts out of her head, tumbling them onto the floor where she had the task of finding the one matching his question. When had Rage taken the pill—good question, that was. The journey over the mountains had messed with her sense of time. Occasionally, she had believed she'd been walking for days, weeks even; occasionally, she'd known it had been mere seconds, barely more than she needed to take two breaths in a row. "I… don't… know," she stuttered. "We were at the foot of the mountains. We needed the day to get up, and we took a rest overnight. The next morning, Rage took the pill. I don't know how much time has passed since because of the ghosts taking me over and him and Keiran through the mountains!"

Instantly, Jack let go of her. "More than twelve hours in any case." He rushed to a small cabinet, pressed a secret latch, and opened a drawer. "Thanks to the Lady you always make sure you don't run out of drugs, cub," he muttered, back at the bed with a pouch in his hands. Putting its content onto his palm, he bent low and let the powderlike substance drizzle into Rage's mouth.

Seeing Luca's face, he said, "He's always had an interest in drugs, and he created this one years ago, after he'd taken the Anubis pill for the first time. Killed some monks, back then. Never told me what had happened up in the mountains, but like tonight, he came back to me half-dead. He was younger then, and stronger. He survived. Said afterwards that should he ever have to take the pill again, he needed a remedy to cure the side effects. Guess we'll find out tonight if it works."

"Great," Luca said, or maybe she only thought she'd said it. Fatigue got the better of her, and she sank down next to Rage, asleep before her head hit the pillow.

CHAPTER
Eight

RAGE WAS in hell and wondered why he didn't mind.

Hell wasn't that bad at all. Right, it was chilly, but by no means as cold as he'd expected. It wasn't as dark, either, the cave enlightened by an eerie glow whose source he didn't want to examine any further. What counted was that he could see and that he wasn't in pain.

Well. That was a lie. His bones ached, his head was pounding, his mouth was dry—but real pain felt different, and there wasn't any of that.

And the… people—condemned—ghosts—whatever… they looked pretty bad, though not at all as if they were about to rip him to pieces anytime soon.

Vaguely, Rage wondered if this kind of hell would have been approved by the priests who were telling people it was a place worse than their worst nightmares. This place wasn't exactly what he called nice; still, it was a place where one could stay if one had to.

IN THE world outside of his dream, Rage tossed restlessly on the bed. Jack sat in a chair by the fireplace, watching him and waiting for him to wake up, and remembering the day they'd met.

The boy had fought him. Bit and scratched, screamed, and never stopped crying. It had cost all of Jack's strength to get the better of a boy less than half his age, and he clearly remembered his surprise at that. A farmer's son, true, working hard all day and with not much time for personal pleasures. But a boy nevertheless, and on top of it a murderer, a cold-hearted killer who'd erased a whole village.

Jack hadn't bought it for one moment once he'd seen the child guarding the graves.

Eventually, exhaustion had felled him. The people who'd paid Jack for the assassination had also told him the murders had happened a week ago, and if that was true it meant the boy had been without food for a long time.

It also meant he'd buried all the people he'd killed. Deathly accidents were bad enough. Burying the people whose death one had caused inadvertently was much worse.

He'd decided to take the boy with him. Presenting an unnamed corpse he'd dug up to the people who'd paid him, Jack had thrown the boy over the back of his horse and taken him to an inn where he bathed him, fed him, and put him to bed, never getting any reaction out of him.

Jack had seen Rage fighting with nightmares before, but somehow it was worse now that his boy had turned into a man.

Silently, Jack got up and limped to the bed, leaving his walking stick behind. "Time to wake up, cub," he murmured, brushing sweaty strands out of Rage's face. "You've slept long enough. You didn't die. Marit healed your wounds, there is a bath waiting for you—believe me, you need one—and food. The girl is frantic with worry. Keiran wanders about the house like a ghost. You're needed."

The fire crackled, sending warmth toward them. Rage was sensitive to cold, always had been. That first night in the inn, he'd been shaking, his skin clammy, his fingernails turning blue. Jack had seen no other way to keep the boy warm than to get into bed himself and wrap his arms around the thin body until the boy finally stopped shivering.

It had taken Jack another six months to get the first word out of him and a year before he would tell him what had happened the day his family and his village had died. By then, the boy named himself Rage and refused to tell anyone the name his mother had given him. He'd accepted Jack as the one who provided for food, shelter, and money.

Until today, Jack wasn't sure if Rage had ever accepted him as a friend.

He rarely came for a visit, no matter that this was the only house that was something like a home for him. Mostly, he did so when he was injured or needed a place to hide.

Never had Rage brought others with him. As far as Jack knew, he'd never had anyone he cared for, anyone who knew him, anyone he allowed to come close.

And now there were those kids, sixteen and nineteen years old, beautiful and nevertheless both injured in their own way. The girl either babbled like a waterfall or refused to answer the simplest questions, barely ate what Marit cooked—which drove Marit crazy—and often sat outside, staring at the mountains. The boy, mute as he was, refused to communicate at all and had a strange fear of darkness and sleep.

With a jolt, Rage sat up in bed.

"About time, cub." Jack went back to his chair. "You've been out like a light for five days. You're home."

Panting, Rage stared at him. He was still wearing his dirty clothes, and dried blood was still on his skin.

Briefly, he closed his eyes and swallowed hard.

The pain was gone. He felt weak like a kitten but alive. He was hungry and shaky but strong enough to swing his legs out of bed. Experimentally, he rolled his shoulders and took a deep breath. "The boy." Rage swayed when he stood up. "I need to see him."

Jack shook his head. "The boy is asleep. Marit gave him a draught that knocked him out. Bad idea, trying to wake him now. Besides, you stink. Take a bath before you go outside."

If there hadn't been a mirror next to the door, if Rage had needed more than one step to take a look at himself, he would have stormed out of the room anyway. But there was a mirror, and there was enough candlelight to have a clear vision. What Rage saw made him pull a face in disgust. "Good idea," he managed, allowing Jack to help him sit on a chair. "Surprised Marit didn't throw a bucket of water on me whilst I was in bed."

Jack grinned. "She tried, the old bat. Didn't let her. But she dragged the tub in here days ago. Take a bath, cub, or she'll try drowning you in the river."

Lifting his hands, Rage saw they were trembling. "Guess I can forget shaving," he murmured, turning his hands so the palms could be seen. "Been like this even before I climbed into the sodding abyss. Remind me to never take an Anubis pill again no matter how good the idea might sound at the time."

Behind him, Jack dropped a small stone into the tub, similar to Rage's rainstone, only this one didn't provide water, it heated it up. "Quarter hour, and you can have your bath. Enough time for me to shave you." He pulled his knife and went to get a bowl filled with creamy soap. Swiftly, he scooped up a handful and rubbed it onto Rage's cheeks. "The trembling is just an aftereffect. It will cease once you've eaten."

"Might be." Rage closed his eyes, allowing Jack to scrape off the stubble on his face. For some minutes, only the bursting of the logs could be heard until Jack sheathed his knife and handed Rage a towel to clean off the remaining soap.

"The boy. You care for him?"

"Wouldn't have climbed into the damn abyss for someone I didn't care for."

"So you've got a heart after all. Doubted it more than once. Sit still." Now the knife cut off thick strands of black hair. Like charcoal black snowflakes, they sailed to the ground.

Rage turned, looking at Jack, who nearly cut his temple. "Would have done it for you as well, old man, so don't complain."

Jack frowned. "Good to know. I hate ghosts."

When Rage's hair was as short as it had been before winter began, Jack put the knife aside. "Now get into the bath, cub."

Rage's rags were thrown into the fire and burned to ashes whilst warm water embraced his body. Dark clouds of dirt and blood blossomed around him and sank to the bottom of the tub. Jack handed him the soap, watching Rage as he scrubbed himself until his skin was pink. When he leaned against the back of the tub, exhausted, Jack took one of his wrists, turned it, and traced the thin scar with his fingertip.

"Tell me."

Rage opened one eye briefly. "Nothing to tell. I tried to kill myself. Didn't work. Luca insisted I had to help her find Keiran, so I did that instead of dying. Simple."

Jack snorted, not letting go of Rage's wrist. "Nothing is simple with you, cub. Committing suicide is not in you, or you'd have killed yourself after what happened when you were fourteen. Why now?"

"When I was fourteen, I didn't know how to kill myself, or I would have done it. Back then, the magic had slashed me but left me alive. This time, Keiran's magic called for me, and it drove me crazy. I wasn't myself. I heard his voice in my head, begging me to save him, but as I had seen him die, I figured I was mad. When the voice became too loud, I tried to end it."

"I see."

Jack was quiet for a long time. Then he said, "Get out and lay on the table. I'll take care of the sore muscles."

It was kind of soothing, being ordered around. Putting a towel around his waist, Rage stretched out on the workbench. His muscles were sore, true enough. And he was bruised all over.

"How come the boy has magic although he's mute?" Jack asked, kneading Rage's back muscles. "No one crippled in whichever way can do magic. You know that. And Luca told me that boy of yours has been mute from the day he was born."

Content, Rage allowed Jack to massage his stiff muscles back to life. The warmth of the water had loosened them, but Jack's hands in combination with the salve he used at just such occasions worked miracles. "I think Ethan—did Luca tell you about him?"

"She told me everything, cub."

"Somehow, Ethan learned how to steal people's magic by cracking them like eggs. He drained his uncle until I killed the old man. He drained Keiran." He groaned when Jack hit a tender spot high up between his shoulder blades.

"He cracked Keiran so he could use his magic?"

"Yes. And with the doll he made to trap us, he created a link between the doll and the boy. It continued working even after Ethan was dead and Keiran unconscious. The doll called for me because calling for me had been the last thing Keiran did before jumping into the abyss."

Jack stopped for a moment. "You say there is magic leaking out of the boy?"

"He cannot use it himself, but it must be there. I can see no other explanation."

Jack stopped kneading, his hands resting on Rage's back. "If he has magic, you cannot be with him."

Much faster than when he'd got up from bed, Rage swung his legs off the workbench. Taking the shirt and trousers Jack handed him, he got dressed, his now short hair standing up in spikes and his heart hammering with unnamed emotions.

"I know."

RAGE CHECKED on Keiran first, finding the boy lying on the bed, eyes closed and breathing evenly. Not daring to get closer out of fear of waking him, he closed the door and decided to have a late-evening dinner with Jack.

Marit had set up the table for them, and she had cooked the spicy stew Rage was very fond of. He'd never found out which herbs the old woman used, so he'd never been able to cook it himself.

Sometimes it was a good thing to come home.

Last year's apples and yesterday's bread, watery beer, the stew, butter, and a jar of marmalade—it was a feast, and he enjoyed every bite he took.

"Seems you haven't eaten on a regular basis." Jack handed him another slice of bread. "You've always been lean, but the way you look is way beyond that. Not enough food where you've been?"

"Not enough willpower left to force anything down."

The apple tasted delicious. All of the stew was gone, and the beer was a welcome way to quench his thirst. It was too weak to have any effect on him, but then this was fine. He'd been out of his mind long enough. He had no intention of getting drunk in the foreseeable future.

"The girl told me about you and the boy," Jack said, stretching out his legs and making sure the wooden one didn't get too close to the fire. "You should have seen the horrified look on her face when she realized it might not have been a good idea to do so."

Rage frowned. "I don't understand."

Jack grinned. "She began stammering and finally asked if we'd been lovers and if I might get jealous."

Rage barked out a laugh. "She has silly ideas, Luca. I hope you told her you prefer your bed partners with more chest and less years."

"The widow I am seeing at the moment would agree with you. She's half my age, and her breasts are to die for."

Rage grinned. Sudden happiness claimed him, unexpected and overwhelming. Maybe Keiran wasn't yet completely healed, but he was sure it was only a matter of days before he'd come round. They were safe, all of them.

A door creaked, and on silent soles, Luca marched toward them. She wore a nightshirt that had once belonged to Jack, a blanket around her shoulders, and thick socks she must have nicked from Jack. Her hair was tousled, her eyes half-closed—she'd obviously been asleep.

"How nice that you two are having fun," she mumbled, and then her eyes widened. "Rage! You're awake, you're up, you're eating, you've shaved and bathed and—" Clearly out of more words she could add, she rushed over and hugged him.

Rage hugged her back, much to Jack's amusement and surprise.

"You are—are you well again?" Luca asked, pulling a chair close and looking Rage up and down. "You look passably well. Have you seen Keiran?"

"He's asleep." For some reason, Rage had never been able to keep up with Luca's hopping mind. It was easiest to just answer her questions and see where she was heading.

Thoughtfully, Luca took the bread, tore off a small piece, and began chewing it. "You might think he's asleep, but probably, he's just pretending. He doesn't sleep much. I really hope now you are up and about, he'll get better. The way he acts—he's freaking me out." After dipping a finger into the marmalade, she licked the sweet drops off and then added a generous amount to the rest of the bread. "Didn't know how hungry I was," she muttered between bites. "Jack, why haven't you told me you've got bramble jam? And—are these olives?"

"Filled with anchovies," Jack said, staring at her in horror as she put an olive onto the marmalade. "You can't eat this, missy. You'll get sick."

"Phew. I've been sick for months. I'm sick of being sick and decided to eat what I want to eat and ignore my stomach. Seems to work. And maybe eating will persuade Marit not to club me next time she puts a tray in front of me."

Halfway back to her room again with the bread and the jar of olives in her hand, she turned around once more. "You will take care of Keiran, won't you, Rage?" All flippancy was gone from her voice; she sounded very worried and very young. "Because I can't. He doesn't let me get anywhere near him."

Rage took the last sip of his beer. "I didn't carry him away from a bunch of crazy ghosts to allow him to misbehave as soon as he is safe. Go back to bed, Luca. In the morning, things will look better. And don't get sick," he added.

"Idiot," Luca said cheerfully before taking another big bite. Silently, both men watched her disappearing into her room.

"Is it true? Keiran's not well? I hoped once he was out of the mountains...." Rage's voice trailed off.

"He did wake up. Doesn't mean he's well." Clearing the table, Jack kept himself busy before finally continuing. "Something is wrong with the boy. He doesn't get up unless he has to, he doesn't eat, and he's visibly scared of everything here in the house. If he had a voice, he'd scream." He put his hand to Rage's shoulder, squeezing him briefly. "Go and see what you can do, cub. Maybe if he sees you, he'll understand he's not surrounded by ghosts any longer."

And now the house was quiet. Jack as well as Luca were in bed, and Rage sat in Keiran's room and wished Jack were still here so he could ask him what to do.

Keiran wasn't asleep. The moment he saw Rage enter the room, his eyes widened in horror, and he slipped off the bed, hiding behind it.

"It's me," Rage said, trying to believe Keiran had mistaken him for Marit. The old woman could be terrifying, especially if someone added more work to her daily tasks. As Keiran refused to come for meals, she'd been forced to take a tray to him three times a day only to see it come back untouched.

As unthreateningly as possible, Rage put a three-armed candelabra onto the windowsill.

Keiran cowered in the corner of the room, the bed between him and Rage. His amber eyes darted to the door like nervous flies, calculating his escape route.

"It is me," Rage said again, barely able to keep the urge in check that told him to grab the boy and shake some sense into him. "I won't hurt you. No need to be afraid of me."

Keiran tried to shove the bed at him. It was a heavy bed, made out of a dead pear tree. His muscles began to tremble, and sweat built up on his face, but the bed wouldn't move.

Very swiftly, Keiran slid underneath the bed, taking the blanket with him. As Rage knelt, he heard the boy move; when he looked, he saw nothing but a dark heap of wool.

His initial urge was to grab hold of Keiran's arm—or a leg, if necessary—and pull him out. Last year, before he'd faced Ethan, the Forbidden Monastery, and the holes in his own soul, he might have even done it.

As it was, he simply couldn't bring himself to use force on Keiran. Vaguely, he remembered the nuns taking care of him after he'd stabbed the knife into his wrists. They'd helped him stay alive, although he hadn't wanted to stay alive. They'd ignored his wish to die; they had forced him to breathe, and it had been horrible.

He couldn't do this to Keiran.

So all that was left was to try to talk him out of this.

He wasn't that good at talking, never had been. Arguing, right. About a price, a target, a task he wanted to get done. But talking to someone he cared for? No.

But if he didn't talk….

Sitting next to the bed, Rage put one hand to the floor, casually and not too close to the breathing blanket. "I found you. I heard your call." Rage leaned his head against the bedframe. Remembering the voice in his head, remembering his despair. "You were lonely and scared. You needed me to help you, to find you, but I was deaf. Or—not deaf. Stupid. I heard you but didn't believe it could be true. I saw you die. You couldn't call."

Silence crept out from under the bed.

"Luca persuaded me to find you. When I tried to kill myself, she began to hear you too. You know how insistent she can be. She wanted to go back to the Forbidden Monastery, she wanted me to come with her, and so I did. I climbed into the abyss. I found the doll and broke it. I saw Ethan's body, what was left of it, crammed into a hole. He's dead and will stay dead. Unlike you. You are alive, Keiran, and safe."

Nothing but silence.

"I found the ghosts, or rather, they found me. When you woke up, you saw Ryan with his fangs and the tongue and those empty eye sockets. No wonder you panicked. That's why I knocked you out."

A sound emerged from under the bed, more distinct this time: a deep sigh, although it was unclear whether it was a sigh of relief or a sigh of defeat.

"The ghosts caught you when you fell. They protected you, kept you safe, healed your wounds. And they showed us the way to

Jack's farm. This here is home, Keiran. And all you have to do is to believe that you really are safe. I miss you. And as I'm still black and blue all over from the too many bruises I got by bringing you here, I'd prefer you coming out from under the bed rather than me having to creep underneath it."

Silence stretched, and Keiran made no attempt to get out of his hiding place.

Damn.

Then a hand caught his. Keiran's hand, squeezing hard.

Rage looked under the bed. Where there had been nothing but a blanket, he now saw Keiran's face, a shadow amongst shadows and his eyes like two sparkling stars.

The boy was crying.

"You don't believe I am real, do you?" Rage kept his voice low. "You think you are dreaming this, and you are afraid to wake up and see nothing but rocks and ghosts and creatures with endless tongues."

There must be a way to solve this problem. If only he knew which one.

Then he remembered Rebecca and knew the contents of the phial in his bag were meant not for himself but for the boy, so he could deal with the months he'd spent underneath a mountain, dreaming hopeless dreams and waiting for someone who didn't come.

His bag was in his room, and at first Rage thought he'd lost the wooden box and its precious contents when he couldn't find it in the mess. He'd wrapped it in his shirt, but his shirt was gone, and then he found the box on his desk, the lid half-open, and he knew that Jack had found it and kept it safe.

He carried the phial back into Keiran's room and knelt in front of the bed, holding his hand out once more. "Come out of there."

Maybe if he'd been less patient, Keiran wouldn't have taken his hand. But Rage had learned a lot about patience in his life, and so he kept holding out his hand until his arm began to hurt, and when Keiran finally took it, he didn't pull him up but waited until the boy made the first move himself. Inch by inch, Keiran left the bed behind until he sat next to Rage on the floor, head low and trying not to run away.

"Drink this," Rage said, holding out the uncorked phial.

And Keiran did.

CHAPTER
Nine

KEIRAN DIDN'T open his eyes—he'd done so before, and it had always made his heart stop and his mind scream with terror.

Better keep his eyes closed.

I should panic, he thought dreamily.

He didn't.

I should be dead.

You aren't.

I am not?

Strange. For a moment, he believed he heard Rage.

Stretching carefully, Keiran found out that no rocky walls surrounded him. It seemed as if he were lying in a bed, covered by a blanket.

A steady heartbeat beneath his ear. Arms hugging him.

He smiled. *Impossible. I'm dreaming this.*

You aren't.

At least it was a nice dream. His other dreams were awful because in his other dreams, he died. At first, there was always pain and fear. In his dreams, someone hurt him, took his strength and his will away and turned him into a mindless doll.

Keiran knew he was dead. He'd been dragged into the abyss, and no one could survive such a fall. Only he had continued dreaming, of hope and rescue and light and warmth.

No one had found him. No one had saved or warmed him. Of course not—he was dead.

Warm skin under his fingertips. His hand had slipped under a shirt, and yes, this seemed to be an excellent dream.

Really, I should panic, he thought again. *Why don't I?*

No reason for panic. I found you. You're safe.

Only once had he heard Rage's voice so very clearly in his head. His lover had been drunk and stoned, had opened his mind and his soul, and of course this couldn't be real.

But here—wherever here was—were candles. Keiran could smell them, feel their flicker teasing his lids, trying to persuade him to open his eyes.

His fingertips went exploring although the dead didn't have fingers they could move. He found buttons and opened them. He found a pulse, steady and strong. He rubbed the fabric of a shirt, and then his nose woke up completely and inhaled that scent, that fragrance he connected with Rage, wild and free and yes, definitely, overlaid by a faint hint of soap.

Maybe I should open my eyes, Keiran thought. *Maybe this is real. Could I dream a fragrance?*

If you open your eyes, I promise you breakfast.

And now there were lips under his fingertips, and high cheekbones, and the flutter of eyelashes against his open palms.

Rage?

"Yes."

Can't be you. I'm dead. Better to insist on that point lest he be disappointed when it turned out he was right.

"You were never dead. Caught in a nightmare, but not dead."

Right. It was time to open his eyes if only to quench his curiosity.

"Good morning," Rage said.

Good morning, Keiran managed, staring at him, at the room, and at the graying sky outside the window. Sunrise wasn't that far away.

Slightly disbelieving and shaky in equal amounts, Keiran put his hand to Rage's face, brushing his thumb over his lover's lips and his palm across his hair.

How long?

"Since Ethan tried to kill you? More than three months. Winter is over. This place here is called Dragon Spring Farm."

Keiran blinked. Three months—now that was an awful long time to be dreaming, especially if the dreams were so very nasty.

But somehow, the nightmares didn't bother him anymore. The fear was gone, the pain….

Could it be he was really alive?

You can hear me.

"I always could."

And—you can answer me.

If I choose to. It feels odd.

Keiran grinned, which felt odd as well.

Then another thought drifted through his mind, and he frowned. *Why come after me? Why get me out of there?*

"You called for me. Through the doll smeared with your blood. Your voice filled my head until nothing else wanted to be in there, not even my own self. I didn't have much of a choice."

Keiran, not knowing yet what Rage had gone through in the past months, pondered upon this. *You could have ignored my call. You don't care for me, you said so. Had the killer not kidnapped me, you would have left me behind without second thoughts.*

"Probably." Gently, Rage brushed his hand across Keiran's sleep-tousled hair. "Only when I saw you jump I realized you mean much more to me than anyone else. Your death...." He hesitated.

Patiently, Keiran waited for him to continue.

"Your death broke me. Losing you was worse than anything else that's happened to me in a very long time."

With sudden fierceness, Keiran's stomach began to growl.

"Breakfast?" Rage asked.

Good idea.

LUCA AS well as Marit were still asleep. Jack wasn't in his room, so maybe he had chosen to visit his lover's house, or he was out hunting. So it was Rage who made coffee and set up the table, closely watched by Keiran, who tried to wrap his mind around the idea that he was alive, well, and safe.

The coffee was hot and black and sweet. Bread, butter, and honey were just what his stomach needed. Apart from eating, they didn't do anything else but occasionally share a glance. Rage gave a relaxed impression, something Keiran wasn't used to. He knew the assassin as being alert even when drunk or injured, always watching their surroundings, always expecting the worst. Here, in this house, he sat with his back to the door, something Keiran would have sworn to be impossible, and when they heard a noise Keiran identified only after some moments as the groans of an old woman getting up, Rage didn't even turn his head.

You have been here before.

Rage nodded. "I built the house, together with Jack. Remember him? Strong guy, long gray hair, eye patch and walking stick. An assassin, like me, but retired some years ago."

Very vaguely, a picture formed before Keiran's inner eye. A single blue eye, hair bound by a leather thong. Someone telling him to eat lest he would be forced.

I remember him. He's... nice?

"Not exactly what I would call him. Reliable. Ruthless. Thorough. But nice? Only if bribed."

Keiran felt a smile tug at his lips. It very nearly made him frown because not that long ago, he had forgotten how to smile.

Rage was watching him, head slightly tilted as if as unsure about the situation as Keiran himself.

To hell with it. Keiran allowed the smile to claim his face, and Rage smiled back at him. *You say this is your home and that you built this place?*

"Yes."

Then you have a room here?

"Yes."

Keiran grinned. It was that special grin that could make a straight guy turn and look him all over, seriously questioning his sexual preferences. Combined with a sparkle in his eyes, he just knew—and saw—it went straight to Rage's groin.

Briefly, Rage closed his eyes. The same moment, Keiran saw his jaw muscles tighten as if he were making a really hard decision.

Keiran's smile faltered. It had never been hard to seduce Rage, not from the first moment on. He'd welcomed the first kiss Keiran had given him, laced with smoke. He'd welcomed his touch, hadn't minded that he'd taken the initiative, and had groaned with joy when Keiran had fucked him that night under the waterfall. Ever since, it had never taken more than this special smile, and often even less than that.

Right now, Rage leaned back in his chair, crossed his arms over his chest, and lowered his head.

There couldn't be a clearer sign of his unwillingness concerning seduction.

And then he said, "I can't," in a voice that betrayed his pose. There was sorrow as well as regret in those two words, longing and bitterness and… something else. Something strong, something hard, something that made Keiran's heart flip.

Something like love, maybe, but if there was love, where was the problem?

Maybe… was he still dreaming this? Had he dreamed he'd woken up in Rage's arms and with the past pleasantly far away? And now was this dream about to turn into a nightmare, just as they always did?

Rage must have seen the horror creeping up his face because he reached out and—

Just before he would have touched Keiran, he stopped himself. Flat and limp, the assassin's hand dropped to the table. It looked as dead as his eyes.

"I can't. I wish I could touch you. I wish I could take you to my room and back to bed. But I cannot. Never again."

Keiran blinked. He didn't have the strength nor the willpower to do anything else.

Eventually Rage turned his hand palm up. "Put your hand into mine," he said.

If Keiran had expected anything dramatic to happen, he'd been wrong. There was just that: two hands touching, one warm, one cool. Two pairs of eyes looking at the hands, then looking at each other.

I don't understand.

"There's magic in you," Rage said calmly, but Keiran could hear the edge in his voice.

Keiran's grin flickered back to life. *No, there isn't. I'm mute, remember? Disabled. No magic.*

Rage didn't smile back. He tightened his grip on Keiran's hand and with his right, pulled the sleeve away from his wrist. It was the one he wore his bracelet on, the black bracelet that told him if someone was ill, or injured, or disguised by a glamour. If someone had magic.

It should be black.

It wasn't. It gleamed a deep, dangerous red.

Disbelieving, Keiran touched the bracelet. He knew what the color meant. Rage had explained it to him months ago. Black meant all was well. Yellow meant poisoning.

And red meant magic was at work, interfering with the barrier Rage had built around himself to keep his own wild magic in check.

"Last night, when you fell asleep in my arms, I watched the bracelet getting red." Rage did not let go of Keiran's hand. "I knew it would happen and still hoped I was wrong. I thought it was the lack of light or that my eyes were tired. Soon, it was too obviously red to be taken for anything else. It is the reason why we cannot go into my room, why I didn't kiss you, why I cannot touch you beyond this." He nodded to their hands. "Were I to do otherwise, my magic would lash out like always when I am with someone who's got magic himself. It happened twice already, and it was only because Luca reacted fast and managed to keep my magic in check that no one died the second time."

Keiran traced the bracelet from wrist bone to pulse. In its wake, he left dark red sparks.

But... this cannot be true.

Rage cast him a thin smile. "I know. No man and no woman disabled in whichever way has magic. You didn't, as we both know. But you have magic now."

With sudden fierceness, Keiran shook his head. *How?* he demanded to know, as if an explanation would change facts. Just to make sure Rage wouldn't jump up and leave right now, he put his other hand on top of his lover's.

The red gleam didn't vanish, no matter how badly he wished it would.

"Because of what happened to you in the mountains. Because of something Ethan did. It's my best guess, but whatever happened, whether I am right or not, does not change the facts."

Instantly and without warning, Keiran was back on that cursed bridge, dragged across it with a rope around his neck. As if he weren't sitting on a chair, as if there were no walls around him, he felt the cold of the nearing winter getting at him and tasted his own fear bitter on his tongue.

And he felt weak and dizzy. Whenever Ethan had been near him, thinking had become impossible. He'd lost his will to fight, to flee, and even to live.

Ethan. First he'd kidnapped him. Then he'd forced him to jump. And now—

You will leave.

Rage raised an eyebrow. "Would you rather I stayed and there could be nothing but holding hands?"

The fire became too warm, and the walls seemed to move closer. Keiran had to get up, now, and he did, tumbling over the chair. With a few long strides, he was at the door and pushed it open. Outside, the gray light had turned into a pale blue.

He stepped into the new, fresh morning and breathed in deeply. Last time he'd been outside—and remembered it—it had been winter. Around him there had been rocks, behind him there had been a table and ropes and terrible memories. He'd been beaten, broken.

He'd had the chance to push the killer into the abyss and had helped him instead because Ethan had willed him to do so.

He'd jumped into the abyss himself because Ethan had made a doll from his hair and blood, a doll that had as effectively killed him as a knife stabbed into his heart. Only because of the ghosts had he survived the fall.

Rage had carried him out of there.

He wants me. He cares for me.

That was good, wasn't it?

I can't even kiss him.

Not so good. Really bad, actually.

He turned, looking at the assassin who still sat at the table. *Can I go for a walk? Stretch my legs a bit?*

"Sure. Head east. The river is about a mile away, and there is a hot spring well worth paying a visit."

Will you come with me?

Rage hesitated, but eventually he got up and joined Keiran. "Sure," he said again.

ACHING LEGS, as usual that early in the morning. Aching back as well, damn the Lady, and a headache although Marit hadn't had anything to drink for at least a month.

Shit life.

Someone had got up before her and made a mess of her kitchen. Probably that awful girl. Not only blonde, no. She had to be beautiful as well, and smart on top of it. Worst of all, she was young. Could move without her knees cracking. Could sit down without supporting herself at the table. Could even run if she wanted to, unlike other and more valuable members of this household.

Phew.

But the girl preferred to sleep in.

The boy, then. Keri-something. The silent one.

The boy scared the shit out of her. His eyes were empty, and when he slept, he had black dreams. She could taste them. Foul. Bah.

Magic had its disadvantages.

The master had gone out really early. Probably staying with one of his toys. All beautiful, with big breasts and large bums. All younger than himself, but not too young. One day he'd die whilst getting ridden by one of those hussies, she was sure of it. Though hopefully not too soon. Serving him was easy. He often cooked for himself, old Jack, he never let her tidy up his room, he took care of the animals and the house, and only the magical tasks he didn't do himself.

Guess I can live with him screwing whatever gorgeous thing he finds if it allows me to stay here for a little while longer, she thought with a sour smirk.

So—as the old master was out and the girl still in bed and with two plates and two cups on the table, it meant not only the boy was up but the young master as well.

Hmm.

Now the young master was a different matter. She hadn't seen him in years, and last time he'd showed up on her doorstep, he'd been in a terrible state, although considerably less terrible than this time.

"Make that old Jack's doorstep," Marit grumbled to herself. "Silly old fool is fond of the young master. As if I didn't know, he nearly had a heart attack when Rage turned up looking like a ghost, with this girl at his side and the half-dead boy in his arms. Nasty thing to do that to old Jack. I should tell him. Might do as well."

Crumbs to the floor so the sparrows could pick them up later. Plates and mugs to the sink. Bread… could stay on the table. And the jar with marmalade. The girl liked her bread, especially when there was something sweet to go with it. Ah, her bramble marmalade. Yeah, that had been a good day, when she'd made that.

And that was…. No! Not the olives! Someone had stolen her olives! The pot had been full when she'd gone to bed and now it was not full anymore. "Old Jack doesn't eat my olives." She shuffled back to the table, sat on one of the chairs, and stared in the pot. Five, maybe six olives were missing. The good ones, filled with anchovies.

Bramble marmalade and olives. And wasn't there a glow around the girl, that special kind of—

Ah.

Triumphantly, because she'd solved the riddle of what was wrong with the little brat, Marit finished tidying up her kitchen.

Old Jack's kitchen. She was just the housemaid.

House… spinster.

Housegranny.

"Wonder where the young master has gone. And with the boy as well. Kir-thingy. Awful name. No decent person can remember a name like that."

A sparrow landed on the table, flown in through the open window. She always opened the windows in the morning unless it was raining. Today it promised to be a warm day.

Probably the young master had taken his lover to the spring. Although both of them had had a bath only recently.

She shuddered at the thought of water. Unhealthy habit, bathing too often. Made the skin thin. Invited illnesses. Fine, Rage had been in dire need of a bath given the amount of dirt and blood he'd been covered with. His clothes had to be burned, rotten rags they'd been. And the boy—Jack had seen he'd been clean before he'd put him into bed.

"Bet they've gone to the hot well," she murmured. "Bet they're naked already, kissing and rubbing against each other in the water. Dirty habit, this. Should do it in a bed, not outside where everyone could see them."

Not that anyone could get past the wall, mind her. But she might have to take the long and painful walk down to the spring. She might stumble over them. Certainly, it would give her a heart attack, seeing two men… doing things.

She grinned, half-toothless and very amused. Wouldn't have been the first time she'd spied on her masters. For their own good, of course. And hers. One needed to know what masters were up to, or one might be left in really deep shit.

Clean kitchen. Good. She'd tidy up master Rage's room now that he was outside enjoying himself. The bathtub needed to go back into the spare room, the sheets needed to get changed—by the Lady's sore feet, the young master had been filthy, and old Jack had put him to bed like that, clothes and blood and all. Probably best if she burned the sheets, just in case he'd brought back some bugs from wherever he'd been.

She was on her way to Rage's room when she heard the knock on the gate.

Now that was impossible. No one could knock on the gate simply because no one could find the gate. It was hidden behind layers and layers of magic. Only someone who knew where it was could find it, and even then wouldn't be able to touch it.

Another knock, louder this time and demanding and very impatient.

Probably best to ignore it. The masters could come and go as they pleased, so it couldn't be them. The girl was in bed—until lunchtime, she would bet on it.

If the mute boy wasn't with master Rage, though… if he'd been daft enough to open the gate….

Could be. He'd be able to see it, to touch it, and to knock. The gate would recognize him but wouldn't let him back in.

And now she had to walk all the way up to the gate only because the boy with the name she couldn't remember had locked himself out instead of doing the decent thing and staying in bed as well.

When the third knock came, she put the towel and the last plate down and shuffled out of the door toward the main gate. Muttering nasty swearwords under her breath, she made her way through the morning dew slowly. Rushing things were never good, and especially not for an old woman like her. "Should have sent that insufferable girl. Should have thrown her out of bed. Would've served her right, staying up half the night and nicking my olives, and who does the boy think he is, making me walk that far? Nasty things, children are. No idea why master Rage is so fond of the boy. If it weren't for him, I would let him wait for another few hours."

Knock.

"Yes, yes, I'm on my way. Patience is something you still have to learn, lad. Will find a nice task for you to do once you are back inside. Muck out the stables, maybe. Doesn't matter that old Jack likes to do that himself. He's with his mistress and won't be back before dinnertime. Wonder where he gets the stamina, I do. If he weren't such a good master and paid me more than the bit of dusting and magicing is worth, I'd find a decent man to work for, one who had no teeth left and stayed in his room all day and behaved like a proper old man. Not like Jack. Far too lively for my taste."

There was the gate, and now the knocks came faster as if the boy outside tried to break through the wood. Stupid idea, of course. No one could break through the main gate.

She, on the other hand, only needed to wave it open.

"By the Lady's rotten teeth," she began when the gate swung open. "Do you thin—"

Then she saw the horses and frowned. "Where did you get the—?"

And then she saw the soldiers and gulped. She didn't like soldiers, and old Jack didn't like soldiers, and master Rage was positively not fond of soldiers at all. Which was only normal given that both Jack and Rage were assassins. Soldiers and assassins were mutual enemies, so to speak.

She shouldn't have opened the gate. She should have gone looking for the young master and let him deal with the knocks. But over the years, Marit had begun to see this place as her own, and when there was a knock on the gate, she opened up and dealt with whoever was outside. Once it had been one of Jack's mistresses telling her he'd managed to get himself into a fight with a bull, and although he'd won, had broken his one good leg. Once it had been a beggar, and as he'd been close to starving, the magic had informed her someone was dying outside the wall. He hadn't been able to see the gate, that beggar, and had died in the guest room a day later, but well, that had been that.

And now those soldiers.

"Yes?" she snapped, her eyes scanning for old Jack's face. He had to be with them, hadn't he, or they wouldn't have found the gate.

He wasn't there. Only five soldiers and one lord, and she knew none of them. One of the soldiers had two spare horses in tow.

Odd.

The lord thrust a piece of parchment at her. "Read this, woman, if you can read. Search warrant, signed by the empress herself. Let us in, or the horses will trample you down."

Now this one was definitely an asshole.

Marit snatched the parchment out of his hands. When she touched it, she felt magic surge through her, and she knew this letter had made them able to see the gate and to knock as well. No magic could keep the empress out.

Slower than necessary, she opened the scroll, having a close look at the seal and the signature. The morning sun shone right into her eyes so it was a bit tricky to read the text. Word for word, she mumbled through it, occasionally eyeing the soldiers as well as the lord.

"I'm losing my patience," the lord snarled. Apparently, his name was Lord Barnard, and he was looking for someone called Lucinda of Babylon. "Get out of the way, woman."

"No one here with this name," she snarled back. When it came to snarling, no one was better than her.

"We'll take a look ourselves," the lord replied icily. "Found her horse at the other side of the mountain. Found a path she might have taken, although I didn't know her magic is that strong. Been to dozens of villages so far, and even more farms, looking for her. She's a murderess. Killed her father, Lucius of Babylon. Fishermen found his severed head, and a magician confirmed his identity. Do you wish to live with a killer under one roof, woman?"

Now that would have made her smile if she hadn't got rid of that nasty habit years ago. She'd spent most of her life living with a killer—and sometimes even two—under one roof. One more wouldn't have made a difference.

So they were talking about the girl, then. "Killed her papa, eh?" she mused, stepping aside. "Interesting."

The lord and his soldiers hadn't heard her. They were galloping toward the house already. She couldn't have stopped them. Now since she knew the young master was fond of the girl, she could only hope she wasn't who they were looking for.

Stupid. Of course it was her. Arrogant manners, hands that had never seen hard work, a habit of stealing olives—if the little chit wasn't a lord's daughter she'd eat hen shit for lunch.

"Damn the Lady," she grumbled. "Old Jack won't like this. Rage and the boy will go all higgledy-piggledy with worry. Killed her papa, did she? Wonder what he did to her."

The soldiers were in the house, and now Marit heard shouting. One was the girl's voice; she sounded very, very angry.

And scared.

Well, the girl was pregnant. "Brambles and olives, sure sign," Marit cackled and watched as the soldiers dragged the girl outside, her hands bound. They forced her onto one of the spare horses. She was still wearing her nightshirt, her long hair flowing unkempt down her back.

"I better go and find master Rage." Marit sighed as Lord Barnard, the soldiers, and the girl galloped out of the yard and out of the main gate. "Think he might want her back no matter he's after the boy. Strange creatures, men. Really strange creatures."

CHAPTER
Ten

IF SHE wanted to—which didn't happen often—Marit could walk fast. Not as fast as a young girl, no, not that fast, but fast enough to make the distance from house to river in a decently short amount of time. Her knees cracked with every step, she got out of breath, and she hated the soldiers and that uppity lord for making her do this.

Briefly, she'd considered going back to the kitchen and having breakfast first, just to state where her priorities were. But then she'd considered the possibility of Rage and Jack finding out she'd kept such important information to herself and decided otherwise. And anyway, a pregnant woman shouldn't stay in prison, no matter how arrogant she was and not even when she'd been born as a lord's daughter.

There was the river. It gleamed in the morning light, and it whispered to her and tried to persuade her to have a rest, put her aching feet into its cool waves.

"No time," Marit barked and hurried on. Of course master Rage wasn't here. The water was too cold that far up the river. He'd gone to the spring, where the water left the earth hot enough to make you gasp.

A voice. Not loud, but loud enough to make out it was Rage. And since Rage wasn't a talker if he could help it, she guessed the boy was with him.

Yeah. She could see them now through the trees. Both of them. Good.

They were just talking, it seemed, or at least Rage was, and the boy listened. No gasping, no groans and moans. Apparently they hadn't been in the mood for lovemaking.

Marit wasn't sure if this was good or not. She didn't mind the occasional peek, be it on old Jack on the rare occasions he brought home one of his mistresses, or on the young master. It had been a while since she'd seen two men together. It certainly would have made her morning.

On the other hand, it was better they were both dressed. She needed to interrupt them, and interrupting horny men always led to angry shouting and embarrassed looks. She wasn't in the mood for either.

They heard her anyway. When Marit emerged from the trees surrounding the well, both Rage and the boy were looking at her, Rage's hand on the hilt of his knife.

"Just me," Marit snapped. She disliked knives, and she very much disliked the suspicious, alert look on Master Rage's face. She'd healed his wounds when he'd been barely more than a teenager, she'd taken vigils at his bedside when he'd been too ill to recognize her, she'd seen him naked, scared, and in pain. How dare he as much as think about pulling his knife in her presence!

The moment he saw it was her, he relaxed.

"Lucky you, young man. Manners, Master Rage. I think I tried beating some manners into you from the moment we met. At that time, you didn't know how to shave yourself, not to talk about how to treat a lady. At least you are presentable. Wouldn't have wanted to see the two of you rolling over the ground stark naked."

Rage opened his mouth, most likely to give her an acid reply, thought better of it, and asked instead, "What can I do for you, Marit?" in a nearly respectful voice.

Marit's birdlike eyes dashed from man to man, judging their position, their expressions, the tension between them and the fact that they sat at least five feet apart, backs pressed to different trees. She knew for sure the boy—damn, but she couldn't remember his name. Kay-thing-bram?—had the hots for Master Rage simply by the way his whole body used to tense whenever he saw the assassin. She knew Master Rage had the hots for the boy simply by the way he looked at him, his gaze caressing the brown locks, admiring the soft cheeks, trailing along the long, slender limbs. Still, she hadn't interrupted anything here. Strange.

"The girl's been kidnapped," Marit stated and ordered the boy to get up. "What's your name again?"

"Keiran," Rage answered for him.

"Ah. Yes. Will forget it in another moment, but well, my brain's got more holes than cheese from the Southlands. You look different, boy. Yesterday you gave me the shivers. Dead eyes, dead soul. And you didn't eat my roast potatoes. Bad thing, that. Offensive."

Keiran shot a panicked look at Rage, who just grinned. "She won't hurt you. Much. What do you mean, someone kidnapped the girl? No one can find the gate, never mind enter without mine or Jack's permission."

"Something happened," Marit murmured, momentarily forgetting about the girl and focusing on the boy instead. "There's life in you, heart and a working brain. Can you hear me?"

Keiran nodded.

"Strange. Yesterday you didn't even know I existed. What have you done to him?" Her eyes pierced Rage.

"I gave him something that helped him deal with what happened. Marit, who kidnapped Luca?"

"Soldiers, young master. They knocked at the gate, and they could do that because they had a search warrant signed by the empress. Took the girl with them. Thought you might like to know." Turning back to Keiran, she patted his cheek, satisfied to see he had to suppress his urge to step back and out of her reach. Always good if the kids were a tad terrified of her, and she had the strong feeling she would see more of this specific kid in the future no matter how much the boy and Rage might pretend not to be interested in each other.

Pity young master Rage was able to move so very fast and silently. Nasty habit, that, always causing her half a heart attack when he did it, standing next to her although he should still be several feet away. This time, he'd even grabbed her and spun her around as if she were a silly little maid and not the woman who actually ran this place.

"Oy!" she exclaimed, slapping him across the face.

He didn't care. Seemed the girl meant a lot to him. Maybe it was his child she carried?

Nonsense. Master Rage wouldn't touch a girl when someone as gorgeous as the boy was at hand.

"When did they leave?" he urged. "And what did they accuse her of?"

Marit freed her shoulder. "Accused her of having killed Lucius of Babylon." He would begin shaking her if she didn't come up with the full story. "His head has been found. Guess they're taking her to the city. Guess it won't be good for her and the baby if she ends up in prison. Or the gallows."

Rage paled, and so did the boy. They looked at each other, and it seemed as if they were having a silent conversation.

Interesting.

"Let's go," Rage said flatly. "I don't know if we can catch up with them, but I won't leave her in the hands of soldiers."

"Not only soldiers." Marit put her hand to Rage's elbow, remembering the man who'd been in charge. "One Lord Barnard was very eager to get her into custody."

Without another word, Rage signaled the boy to come with him. Together, they ran back to the house, faster than she'd ever been able to.

"Finally time for breakfast," Marit muttered, and went back to the house as well. Of course, Rage and the boy were gone by the time she arrived. The door stood ajar, and one of the chickens had found its way into the kitchen. It sat on the table, clucking accusingly when Marit entered.

Jack had taken his horse when visiting his mistress. It was a good one, but it was also the only one.

"Guess old Jack won't be able to resist the temptation of hunting down soldiers. Guess I'll have the house to myself for the next couple of days." After putting the kettle on the fire, Marit sat down and stretched her legs. "Good. Peace at last. Nasty habit, all that running around and worrying and bleeding. Makes a mess of the sheets, bleeding. They're better off in the city. Find the girl, get her back, fix their own problems.... Shush, chicken. Get off the table, or you'll end up as lunch."

LANGUIDLY, JACK pondered the problem of whether he should get up and make himself some coffee or stay in bed and nick another half an hour of sleep, *or* search for soft flesh and warm lips and willingly spread legs before considering either of the two other options.

Not an easy problem. Worth thinking about for a little while longer, ideally without moving and without waking up completely. This time of the day was too perfect to be rushed, especially as no Marit was pottering around, making noise, and letting him know it was high time to muck out the stables.

Jack grinned a lazy smile and snuggled up a bit closer to the woman next to him.

Then the door was kicked in, and Rage stood in the bedroom. "I need your horse, and I need you to organize me a second one. Now. Get up, old man." He picked up Jack's trousers and threw them onto the bed.

"You ruined the door," Jack said, sitting up in bed and not at all surprised—as an assassin, even when retired, one became used to unexpected events happening at any given time. "And you ripped me out of a lovely, quiet morning pondering about what to do with this beautiful day."

"My pleasure. Now—"

A head came up from the pillow. Short brown hair, big blue eyes, lustrous lips, and a frown. "Who's that, Jack?" the woman asked. She had turned twenty-five the previous week. "He's scary."

"He's just a nuisance, and he'll be gone in a minute."

A hand became visible from under the blanket, searched for the pillow, found Jack's shoulder instead, and hesitated. It was a female hand, long and slender, with delicate nails and a ring clearly showing the woman attached to the hand was married. Also, it wasn't the hand of a young woman. This hand was seasoned, had seen many summers as well as hard work.

"You ruined my door," said the woman who owned the hand once she'd emerged from the blankets. Dark locks streaked with gray flowed down her back. The blanket had slipped down to her waist and revealed large, ripe breasts and a belly that had clearly seen childbirth. A beautiful woman, no question, but as different from the other one as one could possibly imagine. She slipped out of bed and stood before Rage, looked at him, then at the other woman in bed, and finally at Jack.

"And I thought you'd grow up one day," Rage muttered, just loud enough for Jack to hear it.

"Get out." The older woman shook her head at Rage. "This is my house, and you are not invited. And you owe me a door."

With a sigh, Jack strapped on his wooden leg and then pulled on his trousers. "Belinda, my love, I fear this morning has ended prematurely. Whatever it is that bothers him, it clearly cannot wait. I'll repair the door once I know what's wrong. And since this seems urgent, may I borrow the horses in your stable?"

Belinda hesitated for but a moment. Then she nodded.

Jack kissed the young woman. "Henny, I apologize for this. Once I am done with whatever task he wishes me to accomplish, I will be back and make up for it. Would that be acceptable?"

Henny gave him a sunny smile, kissed him, and fell back into the pillows with a deep, satisfied sigh.

Picking up the door and leaning it against the frame so the morning chill was at least partly blocked, Rage earned himself a brisk nod from Belinda, who now calmly wrapped a shawl around herself.

"Soldiers took Luca. They're on the way to the city. They're accusing her of her father's death. Judging from experience, I guess she'll be hanged before new moon."

Jack put on his boot, then the shirt. "Any idea how they found her?"

Rage shrugged. "Doesn't matter. I need to get her back before they reach the city."

"What makes you think she won't get a fair trial? She told me about her father and how he died. She had nothing to do with it." With practiced hands, Jack forced his gray hair into a braid and even managed to kiss Belinda whilst doing so.

"The man who took her is Lord Barnard. He's her neighbor, and he wants her land and the manor. The chance for a fair trial is next to nil."

Keiran's head showed in the doorframe. Impatiently, he slammed his hand against the door.

"Saddle the horses. They are in the larger barn behind the house," Jack told him.

Rage and Jack went outside, leaving the ladies behind. Effortlessly, Jack slipped through the gap, then closed the door as best he could. "Henny is a guest in Belinda's house whilst their husbands are away hunting." One longing glance went back to the house. "And anyway, Belinda is strong. She can move the door easily. She will have it repaired by lunchtime."

"Old fool," Rage said with a grin. "Two women at once? You must be crazy."

"Says the man who lusts after a boy he cannot have and risks his life for a girl less than half his age."

"She's pregnant. And she's my wife."

Jack spun around, nearly losing his balance, a rare thing for a man who was used to the disabilities of his body. "Pregnant. Married. You might have wanted to share this information over a beer, cub, and a bit sooner than now."

Rage sighed. "You are right. I should have told you. My apologies, Jack. For now, all I can say is that I want her back. You know the city much better than I do. Compared with what I went through to get Keiran, this should be easy."

"With you, nothing is ever easy. But I haven't been in the city for ages. Besides, I don't like my guests getting kidnapped, especially if those guests are dear to the one person in the world who is as close to me as a son." Effortlessly, he swung himself into the saddle. His wooden leg went into a specially designed hoop that allowed him to ride fast but wouldn't hinder him from jumping down if necessary. "Come along. By the Lady, I bet Marit is having a fit at the prospect of looking after the farm on her own."

They rode fast, not bothering to look for tracks as they knew where the soldiers were heading. Occasionally, they found a broken branch or the outline of a hoof in wet ground; enough to prove the soldier hadn't chosen another direction suddenly, but not enough to ensure they were getting closer.

Before nightfall, they reached the woods surrounding the empress's city. Their horses were tired, they were tired, and they didn't speak.

They hadn't been fast enough. The soldiers and Luca had already reached the city's main gate. Getting Luca back before the trial was out of the question now.

At least getting into the city was no problem. Even assassins were allowed inside, although the minute they passed the gates word spread that not only one, but two killers had arrived. There would be job offers soon; most likely, the city guard would pay them a visit should they decide to stay longer than a few days.

Rage and Jack had no intention of staying more than a day and a night. They went to an inn along the road, a large and loud place ideal for mingling with the crowd. Every day, dozens of people came and went. If necessary, they could vanish, and no city guard would ever know where they'd gone.

They got a small room near the kitchen, and they made sure it had a window large enough to get through. Rage organized dinner whilst Keiran took care of their horses, and Jack persuaded the landlord not to put any other guests in with them. It would have been normal to do so—at least two more would have fit into the room—but tonight, they preferred not to have company.

Plans needed to be made.

"She arrived two hours ago," Rage reported when he was back, carrying a tray with bread and cheese and a bottle of wine. "One of the guests told me. It's not often someone that young arrives here bound to the back of a horse and accusing the empress's soldiers of kidnapping her. Didn't know where they were taking her, though. We'll have to find out tomorrow."

"You might find out by staying in the bar for a while," Jack suggested. With easy, precise movements he cut bread and cheese. The wine they drank from the bottle, sitting on the floor, keeping an eye on door and window.

KEIRAN STOOD aside, watching them and wondering how he fit into this. Throughout the day, he'd followed them. In the city, he'd trusted them to find a place to stay. He'd listened to their dealing with the situation and pondered on the riddle of how Lord Barnard had managed to find Luca.

Most of all he thought about what Jack had said: that Luca was pregnant.

If it was true....

They'd both been with her. Rage could be the father of her child. Or he could.

Weren't things complicated enough?

Not really tasting cheese or bread, Keiran ate methodically and more to keep his hands busy than because he was hungry. Rage and Jack were finished already and were discussing the possibilities of breaking into a prison—whichever of the five prisons in the city it might be—and getting Luca out alive and unharmed.

Rage, who couldn't touch him beyond a friendly slap on the shoulder. Rage, who had kept his distance ever since this morning, since he'd told him about the magic and that as much as kissing him would mean killing him and anyone nearby.

Thoughtfully, Keiran rubbed his fingertips together. He didn't feel any different. The magic inside him—if it was really there—seemed to hide well enough to make him believe it wasn't there at all.

Well, that was a lie. Keiran could feel it, or rather, see it whenever he closed his eyes. It was one more flame burning inside him, alongside Rage's black flame and Luca's golden one.

If he focused on the magic's flame, he couldn't find it, but when he looked elsewhere, it was present in a hesitant way. Fire magic, the most basic magic one could perform, didn't work if he tried it, but yesterday, when they had arrived in town, he'd thought people had looked the other way simply because he wished them to do so.

Nonsense.

The mere possibility that it could be true scared him as much as it was exciting.

Whilst Rage and Jack were busy planning Luca's escape, Keiran worked on a way to corner this new ability that had been forced upon him. Obviously it was useless to push it or to try to use it the common way. But gently nudging it, asking it politely to maybe help him achieve a set goal… that might work.

He hoped.

Not that he planned to ever use magic. It had ruined what had been growing between him and Rage. It hindered him from as much as kissing the man he loved, not to talk about fucking him senseless, or getting fucked, or even sleeping in the same bed because sleeping in the same bed would mean too much temptation. This morning, when they'd been at the hot spring, he would have loved to take a bath but hadn't dared for fear Rage would take it the wrong way. There was a hunger in his lover's eyes, a need so deep it seemed impossible to quench.

No need to add more pain.

There must be a way around this problem, Keiran thought. Absently, he watched a small spark emerge from his fingertips— nothing he'd wanted to do but had happened anyway. *Either I kill the magic inside me or lock it in or whatever. Or Rage learns to control his magic.*

Neither option seemed very likely.

He hadn't been listening to what Rage and Jack had been talking about, so Keiran was surprised when Rage opened the door and stepped into the corridor. He was even more surprised when the assassin looked at him and asked, "Are you coming?"

Where to?

"Gathering information. A bar is always a good place to learn things. Like where young girls accused of a crime will be held in prison nowadays. They wouldn't take her to the North Prison. It's reserved for minor crimes. The empress's dungeon is where you end up if you are accused of plotting crimes against her and her family. Leaves three prisons and an uncountable number of other places they could lock her in until her trial. As she's so very young, people will talk. If we are lucky, we will know where she's held by midnight."

And you want me to come? Keiran couldn't hide his surprise— he'd have sworn an oath he was a burden for the two assassins.

Rage grinned, and the crow's feet around his eyes deepened, but the smile made him also look much younger than he was. "Always more fun to go to a bar when in company. Besides, you've got that look of innocence we have to get rid of if you want to survive in the city. Nothing better for that than spending some time with people earning their bread and butter in those streets."

THE TAVERN was crowded, as expected. Rage found a table near the back entrance. He sat with his back to the wall, a glass of cider in front of him and occasionally eating from the bowl of baked potatoes the landlord had put on the table before leaving them alone.

It was fascinating to see the reactions to Rage's presence. The moment he'd entered the room, it had become quiet; everyone had sensed he was there. People moved out of his way, even men three times his weight and with forearms strong enough to break the assassin in half. Women took one look and then turned away, visibly glad to be here with someone less dangerous even if that someone hit them on a daily basis. One whore looked at him calculatingly, shuddered, and went for an easier target.

The table near the back entrance was suddenly empty although every other table was packed with people. The landlord hurried along to clean the surface of crumbs and spilled beer. No one made a comment; no one tried to talk to them. Once Rage and Keiran had taken their seats, a sigh of relief seemed to rush through the crowd.

They fear you. The concept of being afraid of Rage puzzled Keiran. When he'd met the assassin, he had seen his black clothes and the tattoo. He had sensed an air of danger around Rage, but for some reason, he hadn't been afraid of him. Attracted, yes, and aroused too. But not afraid. Seeing those people paying him respect simply because they feared him more than they might fear the guards, the soldiers, or even a madman, was strange.

Rage and Keiran didn't talk; they only listened. People around them had heated discussions about their employers, the guards, money, the fight for power between the empress and her daughter, the guards, the girl who'd been taken to Well Prison, worries about a war if the empress and her daughter couldn't solve their problems, and the guards. Snippets of information, gathered over a period of more than three hours in a noisy, crowded, stinking place.

Keiran could have stayed for many more hours given that he was with Rage. They didn't touch, not even their elbows or knees. They didn't share looks or smiles. No flirting, no innuendo for seduction. Keiran was sure that even had Rage been able to touch him, nothing like that would have happened. This here was work, and it was serious. And Rage was a professional. He'd taken Keiran because four ears heard more than two, because he was less intimidating when in company, and because it was easier to hide if someone was there to block him from view if necessary.

Keiran tried to look as if what he heard didn't shock him too much, but he knew he wasn't very good at pretending. More than once, he felt the color rise in his cheeks, and equally often, his mouth sagged open at the open hostility people treated each other with. Several fights happened during the time they were in the bar, and whilst one ended with no more than a cut-off ear, another one was broken up too late, the challenger lying dead in a pool of blood. It had happened so fast, so casually, and once the dead man had been carried outside, life continued as usual.

Looking at Rage, Keiran didn't even need to say what he felt: that he hated this place, the city, the people. That he wanted to go home and wished Rage would come with him.

"As soon as we get Luca back," Rage said, speaking his first words since ordering the cider. "Never liked the city. Lived here for years, though, right before Jack and I parted ways." He took a sip. His glass was still nearly full, but the landlord didn't boss him into buying another one as he did with every other guest in the room.

Ignoring a heated discussion about the empress's daughter and the riddle of why she didn't take over and have her mother imprisoned, Keiran leaned forward, a question in his eyes.

"Assassins rarely work as a team," Rage answered quietly, always watching the crowd. "We also—usually—do not have families. But Jack has a soft heart, and so he not only spared my life, he also raised me. At seventeen I decided to become an assassin, not to please him but because I knew I would be good at it. I have a knack for opening doors and finding the best way into any given place. When he was sure I truly wanted to learn, he taught me as well as used my abilities to build up his reputation of being able to get every job done no matter where the victim hid. We were a good team, and eventually, we had more and more jobs in the city. Jack liked living here; I didn't. After a few years, I had enough. I took a job I shouldn't have taken—killing the monks at the Forbidden Monastery. Afterwards, it was impossible to come back to the city. Too crowded, too loud. I chose a life of traveling around."

At the door, someone began to argue. Apparently a customer wasn't allowed in, and apparently, this didn't go over well with the customer in question.

Rage briefly glanced at the door, then continued. "Years later, Jack was set up. He lost his eye, his leg, and nearly his life. If not for Marit, who used her magic to find me, he would have died in prison."

You got him out.

"Of course I got him out. Marit made sure he survived. When he was healed, he decided to leave the city. Together, we built the farm and the wall around it. Surprisingly enough, farm life suits him, mainly because of the many lovely ladies he likes to visit on a regular basis. He doesn't take on jobs anymore, but occasionally, he misses the city. He also misses pulling the strings, knowing what's going on and acting accordingly." Another sip. His full attention was at the door now where the unwilling customer still demanded entrance and the landlord still tried to deny it.

"Jack has a lot of connections here. Getting Luca back shouldn't be a problem now that we know she is in Well Prison."

The landlord was losing the argument. Annoyed and frustrated, he threw his arms up and turned his back to the man who refused to leave although this place was clearly not a place for the likes of him. "Do as you wish," the landlord shouted. "I'll blame you for any broken furniture and every smashed glass. Last time you blessed me with your presence, I had to renovate the damn place!"

"No swearing, if you please," said the man, smiling gently.

Rage's eyes widened ever so slightly. If Keiran hadn't been watching him—and if he hadn't known him so well—he would have missed it.

The new customer was small, no bigger than a ten-year-old child. The light reflected on his completely bald head. His beardless face was smooth, but his childlike and mostly toothless smile betrayed his age: close to eighty, if not more. He wore a cowl, sandals, and around his waist he'd bound a rope. Friendly eyes twinkled behind a pair of round, gold-rimmed glasses, matching the golden necklace seen just underneath the collar of his cowl.

Rage leaned back in his chair and gave Keiran a sign to get up and stand behind him. He did as asked but wondered what was so special about the man that Rage wanted him out of his way.

Together, they watched the tiny monk walk through the crowd; together, they watched as people made way for him, a mixed expression of amusement, disgust, and pity on most faces. Only very few preferred not to laugh at the monk. Rage was amongst them.

Finally, the monk stood before their table—the first to do so apart from the landlord, who'd served them nervously and had left them alone afterward.

The monk held no such restrictions. Smiling broadly, he'd walked straight up to the assassin, his hands pushing people out of the way if they weren't moving fast enough. He was alone, a rare thing for a monk and surely madness for such an old and small man.

"I truly hoped you'd died by now," Rage said when the monk smiled at him.

"My dear, dear boy!" Quicker than expected, the monk snatched Rage's hand and shook it enthusiastically. "How wonderfully nice to see you again! The guards came running into my cell the moment you'd entered town. Of course I had to see you. Silly Timothy here wanted to persuade me to go back home. He didn't know we are old friends. Or maybe he was afraid I could destroy his lovely tavern once more." Still shaking Rage's hand, the old monk suddenly lost his stamina and sunk to the chair Keiran had vacated only moments ago.

Rage freed his hand from the old monk's grip. "Wulfric. Still annoying. Still dangerous. How come no one has killed you yet?"

The monk snorted. "I once offered you an exceptional job, my dear boy, and you were intelligent and brave enough to take it. I'm not that annoying at all. And people tend to laugh about me rather than trying to end my life. Timothy, old friend, please be so kind and prepare a cup of really strong tea for me. No milk, two sugars, if you please."

The landlord, who'd lingered in the background, rolled his eyes and vanished behind his bar.

Keiran, standing behind Rage, sensed his lover's tension and wondered why a tiny, ancient monk could make the assassin that nervous. Out of instinct, he put his hand on Rage's shoulder, realizing only then how close his lover had been to jumping up.

And to his surprise, Rage didn't shrug his hand off but put his own on top of it.

The monk giggled. "I see you found a mate? How lovely. Last time we met you were so full of restless, bitter energy. It is still there, the energy. And still restless. But the bitterness is gone. Or— no. It's just changed into something different. Despair, maybe? Well. He's the one, then, yes? He's—Oh!" The monk's face was a picture of pure joy. Jumping up, he was around the table in a heartbeat, taking Rage's face between his hands and totally ignoring the knife Rage put to his throat.

"Step back," Rage hissed.

"Yes, sure, in a second," the monk said, careless even in the face of certain death. "Don't kill me right now, if you please. I can sense the magic inside you, dear boy. It is as exceptionally strong as last time, maybe even stronger. You've used it, haven't you? Yes, of course you have, though I bet you needed help to control it. Magic that strong cannot be used without help, and you've never been trained. Was it him?" Questioningly, Wulfric peeked up at Keiran, brushed his fingertips across his face, and smiled. "Ah, no. Mute, are you? Impossible for you to help Rage control his magic, I'm afraid to say. Though—it's strange. There's magic in you too. Extraordinary. Wonderful. By the sweet Lady, I am so glad I found you!" With a sigh of relief, the monk sat down again, muttering something about aching bones and yelling only a moment later for his still missing tea.

Rage's knife vanished once the monk had freed his face. In his eyes burned cold anger, and Keiran could feel the muscles in his lover's back tighten, ready to strike.

Brother Wulfric beamed at him. "I don't make much sense, do I? So sorry, my dear boy. The age, you know. Twenty years ago, I nearly went with you to the Forbidden Monastery. Only because my beloved empress Deoris ordered me to stay by her side did I reconsider. You did a splendid job back then, by the way. Anyway, what I wanted to say. Erm…. Ah. Yes. I've got a job for you. Nice and easy, done in five minutes. Interested?"

Rage took the time to breathe in deeply before answering. "No." From the way he said it, Keiran knew his answer was final.

Delighted, Wulfric clapped his hands. "I knew it! Perfect. I love a good negotiation. Fine. You do what I ask of you, and I will help you with your little problem. How does that sound?"

Keiran tightened his hand on Rage's shoulder. The little monk, ridiculous and harmless as he might appear, had a core of steel hidden underneath fragile bones and behind twinkling eyes.

"What problem?"

Brother Wulfric tilted his head. "Oh, the sexual problem at hand, of course. I thought you knew. Well, let me explain, then. Your magic, dear boy, lashes out when touching someone else's magic, meaning you cannot have… I mean… you cannot lay… I mean—by the Lady, you know what I mean. Be with anyone like yourself. Someone with magic, I mean to say. No tender kisses with the lovely young man behind you, and certainly no way of sharing… intimacy with him. The magic inside him has been woken up by force, and it cannot be undone. Easy to know if someone—me, for example—knows what to look for. Someone cracked him. Someone tried to feed on his strength, his buried magic. Ah, dear, I wonder how it must be for people not to be as smart as me. Dreadful idea." Proudly, he brushed his hand across his bald head. "Anyway, I can help you. There's a way you can learn to control your magic even at the height of passion. Quite easy, actually, the learning process, although not really pleasant. Take the job I've got for you, and I'll teach you without charge. It's a good offer. You won't get a better one tonight."

Slowly, Rage got up, for the first time not really watching the crowd. Only Keiran saw how people took a step back and focused elsewhere, anywhere but the assassin and the mad monk.

"How do you know what happened?"

Wulfric got up too. It didn't make much of a difference. "I thought you knew? Didn't you? No, obviously not. Well, dear boy, remember it was I who sent you to kill the last remaining monks in the Forbidden Monastery? Remember I told you how to get across the bridge—not trying it at nighttime—and how to enter the monastery and where to find the monks and how to kill them?"

"I didn't forget."

"Didn't you wonder how I knew about their secrets?" Wulfric giggled. He looked positively delighted. "I was one of them, my dear boy. I built the monastery, together with my brothers. I learned how to drain others, how to set their hidden magic free and how to steal it from them afterwards. Did you know that there are ghosts living in the river?"

Rage's muscles hardened under Keiran's hand.

"I am responsible for many of them. That's why I know what happened to your young friend here. Someone drained him, but not entirely. He didn't die in the process, and he didn't become a ghost, either. His strength has come back, and now it is roaming freely, so to speak. Amazing. Happens once in a lifetime, maybe. Or less. Never met anyone like him. The boy is alive and well, the magic is awake, and you, dear Rage, cannot touch him. Pity, really."

Smoothly, Rage's hand closed around the small monk's throat. "You sent me to kill the last remaining monks. I thought I had succeeded. I was wrong. Time to finish what you paid me for all those years ago."

Like a sparrow, Wulfric hung at the end of Rage's arm, his face turning reddish and his eyes becoming big. His smile, though, never faltered.

Eventually, Rage let go of him. Sinking back onto the chair, the old monk coughed, smoothed out his cowl, and took a generous sip from Rage's still nearly full glass of cider.

Then he coughed again, longer and louder this time. "Uh, strong stuff, this," he wheezed. "Truly, Timothy is lazy tonight, not having served my tea yet. Anyway, dear boy, it was a good decision not to kill me. Obviously, I am not one of the forbidden monks anymore. Unlike my dear brothers, I saw the errors of our way long before we met, and I left. I realized their doings were against the good Lady's will and so on and so forth, blah-blah. You know what I mean. I serve the empress now, have done so for decades. It was she who decided my brothers needed to be put to rest. I chose you as my weapon. However, there is no need to kill me. Well, you might want to before the night is over, but then that cannot be helped. If you are willing to take on the job and learn what I have to teach you, come with me. I promise you won't regret it. Much."

For a long moment, Rage looked at the monk. Keiran wanted to shake him, to make him turn away from Wulfric and come back with him to their room.

Useless.

"Tell Jack what happened and that Luca is held in Well Prison. I'll be back before sunrise," Rage said and got up.

He didn't wait for Keiran to reply. Whilst the little monk made his way through the crowd, Rage slipped out the back door and was swallowed by the night before anyone had noticed he'd even moved.

CHAPTER
Eleven

JACK WAS sharpening one of his knives when Keiran rushed into the room. He was about to make a joke when he saw the boy's face. "What happened?" he asked, already knowing that whatever it was, it wasn't good.

Keiran went to his bag, rummaged through it until he'd found a piece of chalk, then dropped to the floor and began writing.

Jack stepped behind him.

Rage took on a job.

"He wouldn't." Jack shook his head. "Not here, and not tonight."

He's gone. A monk, Wulfric, he offered, and Rage agreed.

That made Jack slam his stick hard to the floor. "Brother Wulfric? Small monk, looks friendly enough, bald as a table leg?"

Keiran nodded.

"Fuck. He's mad as a banshee, that one. They have issues, those two. Wulfric offered him a job before, and it was a bad thing for Rage to take it. He wouldn't kick the monk if he lay in the gutter. Why the hell would he go with him? What could Wulfric possibly pay that Rage would agree to working for him?"

Keiran sat back on his heels, pointing at himself.

It took Jack a moment to understand. "You? Wulfric is— Oh fuck."

Keiran hung his head.

Throwing his stick into a corner, Jack grabbed him by the collar and forced him to look up again. "Rage has fallen for you, boy. Before you came along, he was never letting anyone get close—never shared his thoughts or opened his heart. It's impossible to know what he thinks unless he cares to tell you, and impossible to make him talk if he doesn't want to. There's been a wall around his soul since I found him, and over the years, it began to imprison him. I saw it. I could do nothing to change it. Now you're there and he's changed. And I would have said that's a good thing, only you tell me that because of you, Rage once more has walked into Wulfric's trap."

Keiran just looked at him, a deep furrow between his brows. Then he pointed to the words on the ground and questioningly raised his eyebrows.

Jack let go of him. "Madman or not, this time Rage knows who he is dealing with." Reassuringly, he patted Keiran's shoulder. "Whatever the job, he'll be back in the morning. Did you find out where Luca is held?"

Well Prison, Keiran wrote on the floor.

A wide grin spread across Jack's face. "Good news at last. It's where they keep the rich folks. Well protected but clean and less crowded than the other prisons. We'll wait until Rage is back and then get the girl out."

Trying to look reassured, Keiran nodded. It wasn't much of a plan, but it was better than nothing.

GALADRIEL AND Arwen hung low above the empress's city when Rage caught up with Wulfric. The little monk was idly strolling through the deserted streets as if he were walking down a church aisle and not through one of the more dangerous areas of the city. From distant bars, laughter and shouts could be heard, occasionally someone screamed, and one might have assumed an old monk would be a bit nervous. But he wasn't, and when Rage stepped next to him, he didn't even blink.

"How lovely you could join me so quickly. It is always a bit boring, walking through the city without company. I do enjoy intelligent conversation, my dear boy. And I am curious. Would you mind terribly telling me how exactly you killed my brothers? You never came back to give me your final report. I mean, it's about twenty years too late for that now, but late is better than never. Wouldn't you agree?"

Rage, no more than a shadow against the night's darkness, adjusted his long stride to the little man's hops. "They are dead. That's all that counts."

Wulfric giggled. "Ah, no, it isn't! Those last three were dear to me, you understand? We shared many wonderful memories, we figured out how to best lure cattle to the monastery—oh, sorry, I should say victims, shouldn't I?—and especially Artise was gifted when it came to draining them. Such a surprise it was to find out everyone is born with magic. Such a success to pierce them, to free their hidden forces, to use them for our own necessities. It made us drunk with power. And maybe drunk with madness, too."

An extra little hop; an additional, happy giggle.

"Then I'm surprised you left the monastery," Rage said. "You're nearly dribbling with excitement at the memory of past pleasures."

"Of course I am! Fabulous times. I was young back then, not even seventy years old. Eager to learn and even more eager to unravel all the secrets concerning magic." Coming to a sudden halt, Wulfric took Rage's arm. "But when I realized that I would never be able to even scratch the surface and when I saw one victim after the other end up in the abyss, I thought it best to leave. You need strong people with strong magic to make a difference. And strong magic is hard to come by. Why do you think I sent you to kill them? Because I knew your magic is strong, caged or not. I know you would be able to cross the bridge where others would have gone mad at the first step. I also knew my brothers did not stand a chance against you, simply because you not only cannot wield magic, you are also basically immune to the magic others want to use on you."

He patted Rage's cheek. "But even back in the city, the ghosts were whispering in my mind at night, calling me, persuading me to come back. I hoped by sending you to kill my brothers, to close this chapter of my past for good, they would stop." He tilted his head thoughtfully. "Although, now that I think about it, I still can hear them, on moonless nights."

"They hate you. If they could, they would come after you, but the mountain's magic won't let them leave. You are safe, little monk. If ever you decide to go back there, though, give them my regards before they rip you to pieces."

Wulfric's eyes widened. "You spoke to the ghosts? And survived? You are truly extraordinary, my dear boy, but in the Lady's name, what did you do it for?"

"They had something that belongs to me." Rage looked down at him. "Tell me about the job you have for me, monk."

Sighing, Brother Wulfric locked arms with Rage, leaning against him for support. "It is getting late, dear boy," he muttered, sounding tired. "Be so kind and steady my step, will you? Fine. Very nice of you. I knew it was a good idea to get you here. From the moment I met you, I knew you were the one. The only man who might survive a night at the Forbidden Monastery without being part of the group. The only one whose magic is strong enough to withstand the dark magic my brothers would raise against him. And I was right, wasn't I? You survived, and they are dead. Had to order their death, grieving as it was. They were crazy. A little longer, and they would have found a way to drain the mountains themselves, and then our world would have ceased to exist. That's why I left, really. We became megalomaniacs, I think, is the right word. Ridiculously hungry for power. Had to be stopped."

Enduring the little monk's touch and making sure he wouldn't fall, Rage slowed his step, leading the monk along the quiet streets. They were heading for the palace.

Rage didn't like this at all, but for the moment decided to go along with it. "You didn't bring me here, monk. I came to the city because a friend of mine is in trouble." He was scanning the area for guards out of habit.

With every step, Wulfric leaned heavier on him. "Didn't I?" He wheezed. If the Lady was in a really lousy mood, the monk would drop dead right at Rage's feet, which would guarantee a lot of trouble.

"Lucinda of Babylon, that's your friend, isn't she?" Out of breath, Wulfric stopped. Galadriel's green light made him look dead already. "Lovely young girl. Accused of having killed her father, if I am correct. One Lord Barnard came to the city a little while ago, seeking help in finding the young woman in question." With a shaky hand, he wiped the sweat off his brow. "Shouldn't have eaten this duck for dinner. Bad things, ducks, especially when filled with oranges."

Rage closed in on him. For the second time in less than an hour, the little monk had the assassin's knife at his throat.

It didn't seem to bother him much. If anything, it made him smile. The wheezing stopped, and if he had looked ill only moments ago, Wulfric now seemed nothing but slightly amused. "I like to pull the strings, my dear boy," he said with a smile, all fatigue gone from his voice. "When Lord Barnard wailed about his nasty neighbor owning all that beautiful land and how much he would like to get the little chit out of the way, I thought I might be of help. He had some items belonging to her—a hairbrush, if I remember correctly, and a skirt. Had them stolen, I'm certain, from her home. Anyway, it was easy to track her down. Barnard found her horse and another one at the foot of the mountains, but they couldn't find her. Sad, sad thing, if a man wants to find a woman and fails."

Rage's knife didn't waver, but it didn't cut deeper, either. He wanted to hear the rest of this. "We were busy dealing with the ghosts. Barnard couldn't follow us once they took the lead."

Wulfric's smile didn't waver, either. "And I was so surprised when I sensed you being with the very person Lord Barnard wanted to find. You see, I am a bit like your young, mute friend. I can find people. He can find you, can't he? I knew the moment I saw him. Well, I can find extraordinary people. Like… you, for example. You are very extraordinary. Your magic is so very strong, and so uncontrollable. Unexpectedly, I not only knew where young Lucinda was hiding, I also knew where *you* were hiding. So I pointed the good lord in the right direction and provided him with a search warrant."

A single drop of blood soiled the monk's cowl.

"I know, I know. He failed to take you into custody, as he should have done. Too focused on the girl, and frankly, dumb as shit. Luckily, she means enough to you for you to follow her. You are here. I found you. And now you will come into the palace with me so the empress can explain what sort of job she wishes you to do."

WALKING THROUGH the corridors of the royal palace was an extraordinary experience even for Rage, who had done a lot of extraordinary things in his life, not the least of them talking his lover out of the hands of a bunch of ghosts only recently. Out of curiosity, he had once broken into the palace only to realize that staying there for longer than it took to risk a glance was suicide.

No professional assassin would ever kill a member of the royal family. It was an agreement as old as mankind, figured out and vouched for by the first emperor. He had considered that sometimes there was a need for professional killers—for example, if an emperor needed a trusted man to get rid of an opponent in a quiet, quick way. He needed cold-blooded men who knew what they were doing and had no emotional reasons to swing the knife. He had also figured that men of such a profession needed a certain kind of royal protection. The first emperor foresaw their use, and everyone knew about the unwritten contract between the royal family and the assassins: they were allowed to do business, even enter the city and accept jobs if they agreed never to kill any of the emperor's kin.

As far as Rage knew, none of his trade had ever tried.

Like the streets outside, the palace's corridors were deserted. Silently, Rage followed Brother Wulfric, whose cowl brushed over the carpets and who refused to tell him any more about the task that needed to be done. He'd tried to get some more information; Wulfric had just smiled his annoying little smile and walked on. As if the palace belonged to him, he opened a door that led into the inner yard. From there, he proceeded to the private rooms of the royal family.

Even Rage hadn't been here before.

Vaguely, he wondered if the empress would ask him to kill her only daughter. They didn't get on well; that much he'd overheard in the tavern. The old woman refused to hand over the crown. It was said she had lost her last marbles but stubbornly held on to the throne just out of habit. The old empress was loved, and Princess Kayla didn't have many followers inside the palace. The people considered her not strong enough to reign, too focused on the welfare of her children and not interested enough in politics.

I should get out of here, Rage thought. *Whatever happens tonight, it will be bad.*

But he didn't turn, and he didn't leave. The moment the old monk had said there was a solution for his problem had been the moment Rage had known he would at least hear him out if the reward was the chance to learn how to keep his magic in check.

Terrifying, really, how much the boy meant to him.

Wulfric sped up, a sheer miracle for a man his age and given he'd been pretty fast from the moment they'd sneaked into the palace. The little monk pushed open a gate barely bigger than him. Rage needed to go down to his knees to crawl through.

No one awaited them on the other side.

"We're late," Wulfric said with a frown. "Empress Deoris will not be pleased. Not good, that, her being not pleased. Could you hurry up a bit, my dear boy, please?" Vanishing around a corner, he was gone when Rage followed, only to reappear from a hidden door. "In here," Wulfric hissed. "And behave yourself. I guess it is the first time you meet the empress? Lovely. She won't expect you to bow, but try not to be intimidated by the fact that we meet her in her bedroom. No one must know about this meeting."

It was too late for second thoughts now. This here was so obviously a trap it would have made Rage laugh had someone told him the story over a glass of beer. But he was here, and although he had no idea why Wulfric would go to such great measures to lure him into town and into the palace, he had every intention of finding out who was really waiting behind the curtains of the big bed that dominated the room.

Silently, he pulled his knife, ignoring Wulfric's annoyed intake of breath. He wouldn't go down without a fight.

Wulfric bent his head and pushed his elbow into Rage's side, indicating he was supposed to do the same. "Bad idea, threatening the empress," he hissed.

Sidestepping him, Rage was about to pull the curtain aside when there was movement on the bed. Naked feet appeared, old and fragile and slipping into worn slippers. Certainly not the feet of a soldier. Not even the feet of a man.

Rage didn't care. He'd been attacked by women before, and if anything, they were more dangerous and lethal than men because they put a wrath into their attack that always managed to surprise him.

Rage pulled back the curtains.

The old, fragile feet belonged to an old, fragile woman sitting on the bed. Wrapped in a gold-embroidered dressing gown, her feet in said old slippers, she stared at the knife in Rage's hand, then at him, and said, "Good evening. I expected you earlier. Wulfric, didn't you tell him I dislike knives?"

The monk, pressing Rage's hand with the knife down, looked crestfallen. "I did, Your Highness, I did indeed. But he tends not to listen to me, mainly, I think, because he believes I am totally crazy."

"Which you are, Wulfric. Sometimes, anyway." Getting up, the empress pressed her hand flat against her lower back. "I hate being old." She sighed. "Makes life harder than it is already. Wulfric, did you explain to him what I need him to do?"

Wulfric, about the same age as the empress, pulled back a chair for her and lent her a hand when she sat down. "No, Your Highness. I thought it best you do that yourself. He wouldn't have believed me anyway, and you have a talent for persuading people into doing what you want them to do even if they are reluctant."

The empress frowned. "He is an assassin, Wulfric. A paid killer. No matter the rules, won't he do whatever I ask him to do?"

With a sigh, Rage sheathed his knife. He disliked being talked about, and even more so as he was in the same room as the ones who did the talking. On the other hand, getting treated like a piece of furniture had its positive aspects as well—he learned more in a matter of moments than he would have had he insisted in partaking in the conversation.

Wulfric cast him a glance. "He is special, Your Highness. That's why I chose him. And because I know him, of course. He killed the monks at the Forbidden Monastery, surviving himself, which I certainly didn't expect. Not many could have accomplished this task. No one else could have crossed the bridge twice and got back home relatively unharmed. He certainly is the man you need tonight, Highness. Treat him kindly. For some peculiar reason, he responds a lot better to orders when asked nicely."

"I see. Well, I expect you to pay him generously. That should help sweeten the deal."

Wulfric smiled somewhat ruefully. "Payment is not the problem here, Highness. I found out what he wants, really, really wants, so that part is sorted. Problem is, what you want him to do is not only against the assassins' rules, it is also against his personal rules. You will have to persuade him."

As this seemed to be becoming a longer conversation, Rage sat down. It was only shortly after midnight; he could be back by morning easily, assuming those two came to an agreement about how to tell him about the task at hand anytime soon.

With a sigh, Empress Deoris looked at him. "Rules? What sort of rules can an assassin have apart from the main one? And how do I persuade him to break them?"

Wulfric shrugged. "Just ask him, Your Highness. If he refuses, and he will, you need to find the right words to make him do it anyway."

A shiver went through the old woman, and she pulled her dressing gown tighter around her body. It wasn't cold in the bedroom, but her lips were blue, her fingertips white as if she'd spent hours in the frost. "Persuade him," she murmured to herself. "How can I persuade anyone to do what I wish didn't need to happen myself?"

Now Rage became curious. And somewhat uneasy.

"Fine," the old woman finally said, changing her posture by only a fraction and turning from old to powerful within the blink of an eye. "Assassin, you are here to help my grandson find his way from life to death. It is my will he dies tonight. Do you understand what is asked of you, and do you agree to the terms of this contract, entailing you killing my grandson Leon, son of my daughter Kayla, in exchange for the payment Brother Wulfric offered you?"

Rage had suspected something bad, but this was ridiculous. "Which of your daughter's children are we talking about?"

"Leon is the youngest boy," Wulfric said quietly as if to protect the empress from having to give the answer herself. "He turned eight this winter."

"I don't kill children. You know this, monk." He was at the door before either of them knew he had moved.

His hand was on the handle when the empress spoke.

"I did not allow you to leave," she said, and Rage turned around at the threat she put into the words. "And I do not accept your declination. I have my reasons for asking you to kill my grandson. I expect you to act accordingly."

"Your Highness," Wulfric said with a sigh. "This won't really change his mind."

With a few steps, Rage was back in the room, towering over the empress who was still sitting on the chair. "What sort of woman wants to kill an eight-year-old kid?" he asked, not even trying to keep the disgust out of his voice. "I haven't been in the city for years, and I am not interested in politics. I don't know what happened between you and your daughter. You seem to hate her enough that killing one of her children seems to be a good idea, but frankly, as much as I would like to kill you for your offer, your wrath with your daughter is your problem, not mine. I refuse to kill your grandson, lady. I will never kill a child no matter what you offer or threaten me with."

Wulfric's hand shot out and caught Rage by the wrist before he could turn around a second time. "Your Highness," he urged, "do not let him walk out of here! If you want this job done properly, give him an explanation, I beg of you!"

Surprisingly fast for a woman her age, Empress Deoris got up. "Come with me," she said. "I cannot explain why I want Leon dead, but maybe, he can."

JUST AFTER sunrise, Jack and Keiran left the inn and went to Well Prison. On the way, they bought some bread and milk for breakfast. "Wouldn't be good if we stole food and get caught us for such a minor offense," as Jack put it. "Never did anything illegal in this town and have no plans to start now." Then he reconsidered. "Well. I did business here for years. Killing people is not exactly what one might call following the law. And I'll break out the girl in another hour or so. Guess that could be called illegal, too. But then, I don't live here anymore. And the city owes me a leg since it was a guardsman who shot a poisoned arrow at me." Grinning at Keiran, he maneuvered them through the market, avoiding the women trying to sell vegetables or flowers, the men proclaiming the quality of their fish and weapons, the thieves trying to cut their purses, and the guards looking for criminals.

"They will put her on trial first thing this morning unless they have changed their working pattern, something I highly doubt." Jack waved away a child selling combs. "And if Rage was right, it won't be a fair trial. The most likely thing to happen is they sentence her to death without hearing witnesses. After the trial, they will put her back into her cell, and that's where I will be waiting. She'll be free before lunchtime."

Rage hadn't been back by sunrise. Jack was worried but didn't say so. The boy looked worried enough without him making futile guesses as to what might have happened. Rage could look after himself. It would have been easier doing this together with Rage, but since there was no use waiting any longer, Jack put on his easy grin and said, "He'll catch up with us. Let's get the girl out of prison."

Keiran had agreed to that mainly, so Jack guessed, because there was no other choice. He didn't know the city; he didn't know how to hide and stay out of trouble himself. Luca needed their help. Although Jack could practically see how torn the boy was between his urge to find and free Luca and his need to find Rage, Keiran trotted after Jack like a dog on a leash.

When the clock struck eight, they reached the main entrance of Well Prison. Luckily, Babylon Manor was miles away from the city. A girl no one had ever seen might have killed a man no one had ever heard of wasn't worth gossiping about, so only a handful of people were here.

Pulling the cap of his cloak deep over his face, Jack limped up to one of the guards, making sure everyone saw he was armed only with a walking stick. "Hello, luv," he said, putting a lot of charm into the words. "I take it this is an open trial? Any chance you'll let us past although we're not really high society?"

The guard, until a moment ago busy rummaging through an elderly woman's bag, waved her onward and then lowered her lance at Jack. "No common folk allowed in Well Prison." The helmet she wore covered her nose and nearly touched her upper lip. The tip of her lance pointed directly at Jack's heart.

Jack tilted his still-covered head. "Come on, luv. I won't tell anyone."

The lance connected with his throat; he didn't retreat. Behind him, a couple squeezed past, trying not to stare openly at them.

"Step back," the guard said lazily, "or I will put that lance through you. Not a nice start to the day, neither for me nor for you."

"You gonna kill an unarmed man?"

"Easily."

Jack soothingly raised the hand that didn't hold the stick. "No offense meant." Then he raised his head, just a tad. "Say, Penny, do you still sleep naked?"

Behind her helmet, the guard narrowed her eyes. "You're dead, stranger." The well-cultivated laziness was gone from her voice. "You don't know it yet, but you are very definitely very dead."

Jack shrugged. "Many people have tried to kill me." His walking stick was tapping a cheerful rhythm against his wooden leg. "But you, Penny my dear, were not amongst them—at least not as long as I fed you with strawberries."

Very slowly, the guard lowered her lance. "Show your face. One wrong move—"

"And I am dead. You said so." Brushing off his hood and always keeping an eye on the second guard who was just about to become suspicious, Jack was enjoying this encounter.

"You're so damn dead," the guard said again, only this time, a smile accompanied the threat. "By the Lady's tits, Jack. How dare you scare the shit out of me!" She lowered her lance and nodded at her friend. "It's all right, Kate. I know him."

"You better take him aside if there's some serious talking taking place now," the other guard, Kate, said. "I can manage here on my own. It's not as if the place is getting flooded today."

Nodding her thanks, Penny pushed Jack into a small room next to the main entrance. "Heard you were killed during a job," she said, looking him up and down. "Seems rumors were wrong and only a few parts didn't make it out alive. What the hell are you doing here?" She pulled her helmet off, a ridiculous mop of brown curls springing up around her face. She was neither young nor beautiful, her nose having been broken several times, and there was more than one scar on her face. Still, there was something about her that made men look at her twice if she didn't wear her uniform.

Jack took one of the curls and twisted it around his finger. "Long story, luv. Gotta tell you over a mug of wine, or preferably in bed." He grinned.

Penny grinned back, grabbed his coat, and smacked a kiss onto his lips. "Missed you, old rascal. Wine and bed accepted. Now tell me what I can do for you and how much you are willing to pay."

"Straight down to business, just as in old times." Leaning his walking stick against the wall, Jack fished out a pouch and threw it into Penny's waiting hands. "Ten Talents. Not much, but all I can afford right now. All I ask is for you to take a break once the trial is over. The girl to be questioned and blamed for her father's death is precious to a friend of mine. If I haven't lost my gut feeling, they'll sentence her to death. Can't let that happen. If you like, I can knock you unconscious so no one will get suspicious."

Penny weighed the pouch in her hand. "Serious stuff, breaking out a prisoner. And you don't have friends. So what's really going on?"

Casually, Jack slipped his arm around her waist. "Does it matter? I want her, and you can help me get her. You won't do it for free, I pay you—problem solved." His lips found her neck. Tenderly, he trailed some kisses up to her ear.

Penny had her knife under his chin before he'd reached her mouth. "I can be bribed," she whispered into his hair. "But I want an explanation nevertheless. Who's this ominous friend of yours, and why is she so important to him? More interesting, why doesn't he come to get her himself?" The knife slipped down to the top of his shirt where it cut off a button.

"You're just too clever for me," Jack said after a moment. One last kiss to Penny's cheek, and he limped to get his stick. "Rage grew fond of the girl sometime last year. For whatever reason. He wants her back. And he cannot come himself because he's still half-dead from his last adventure. Besides, the girl didn't kill her father. It was Rage. Proper contract, and none of the city's business. Look away for half an hour, luv. I'll be in and out before you know it."

The coins in the pouch clinked when Penny fondled the leather. "'Kay," she said. "Around two, they'll be done with her. Be here at one o'clock. And don't hit me too hard. Don't want to wake up with a broken skull."

"Knew it," Jack said. "We'll get out of your way until it's time to kidnap the girl."

"We?" Penny had opened the door. Apart from her colleague, the hall was empty.

Jack stepped to her side. Keiran was nowhere to be seen. "Damn the boy," he muttered. "Should have known. Stupid little idiot will end up dead before noon."

Penny rammed her helmet back onto her head and took up her lance. "Kate, have you seen where the guy went who came in with Jack?"

"The young one? He wandered off the moment you two disappeared. Problem?"

Penny questioningly tilted her head.

"No problem," the old assassin answered. "Just more complications. Thank you for a pleasant morning, Pen."

"Thank you for dropping by," the guard replied, the pouch safely stored in the inner pocket of her coat.

CHAPTER
Twelve

SUNRISE WAS still hours away when Rage followed the old empress to her grandson's quarters. He expected guards protecting the doors, but there weren't any. He watched out for signs of a trap but couldn't see anything suspicious. There was just the empress, slowly making her way past dusty tapestries, ancient vases, over fading carpets and creaking floorboards. Her nightgown brushed over the floor, scaring dust kitties—this part of the palace was not well tended. Rage doubted it had seen a maid or a bucket of water in a while.

Which was odd as it was well known how adamant the empress was to keep up the high standards her father had set. Even the prisons and dungeons got inspected on a regular basis for cleanliness. Once, Rage had taken on the job of killing a woman who'd been imprisoned for trying to poison her best friend. According to her husband, she was innocent. According to the law, she had been sentenced to torture so she would confess to her crime. The husband had paid generously for Rage to kill his wife before she could get tortured, and Rage had broken into North Prison only to find he'd been too late. The woman was barely alive by the time he had found her and had confessed to every crime in the past hundred years.

Rage had killed her quickly and had left without taking too close a look at his surroundings, but he still remembered how clean her cell had been, the straw new and dry, the walls washed of the blood that had been shed.

That there were unwashed curtains in the middle of the palace could only mean the empress didn't want this part to be cleaned.

Odd.

No use watching out for guards, anyway. Impossible to get out of here alive if this was a trap. So Rage just followed, cursing himself for his overwhelming urge to find out whether Wulfric's promised payment would actually work.

Keeping his magic in check, always, whatever happened and under whichever circumstances. The simple thought was overwhelming. No need to check anymore whether his bed partner was of magical abilities. No fear he might forget to check his bracelet. It wouldn't even matter if someone tricked him as Luca had tricked him.

Who do I try to fool? Rage wondered. *I do this because of the boy and only because of him. I do this because I fell for him, because I want him, and because I am too weak to leave him. I risk my life for a fuck.*

Pathetic.

Nevertheless, it was true, and Rage had long ago stopped lying to himself. Keiran was important to him—fact. He didn't want to lose the boy—fact. He'd agree to do nearly anything to be with him. Also a fact. No use moaning because he was the man he was and because he knew what he desired.

Still, he wouldn't kill a child, not for any reward in the world.

Then why am I still here?

"Here we are," Wulfric said, slipping a key into the hole and unlocking a plain old door. It opened slowly, as if reluctant to let in the visitors.

And then the small hairs at the back of Rage's neck stood up when the smell hit his nose: a sweet, heavy, sticky fragrance. The smell of rot and decay.

The smell of sickness and looming death.

Wulfric managed to open the door wide enough for the empress, Rage, and himself to slip in. "We haven't used this passage in ages," he whispered. "Usually, we take the main door, but well, that's guarded, and the empress doesn't want anyone to know we are here. Princess Kayla will know anyway, of course. But not before it is too late."

The room was lit with dozens and dozens of candles. No shadows were able to hide under tables or behind bookshelves, the curtains were drawn open as if to let in sunshine, and toys were scattered across the floor. No tapestries showing frightening scenes of men slaying dragons or enemies were in here. Instead, there were pictures of knights in armor, smiling at the observer and patting huge greyhounds instead of wielding their swords.

A child's room. A place where a little boy could spend hours and hours having fun.

Only this little boy wasn't playing anymore. This little boy, youngest son of Princess Kayla, was quite obviously too sick to even get out of bed, not to talk about playing with his toys.

Quietly, the empress walked to a chair where a woman was fast asleep. Gently, she brushed her fingertips over her cheek. "When did you give her the sleeping draught, Wulfric?" She sounded tired herself. "Not too long ago, I hope. We will need some time here, and I do not want her to wake up before we are done."

Wulfric bowed his head. "Two hours ago, Your Highness. She won't wake up before morning. Rage, dear boy, would you be so kind and put Princess Kayla on the sofa over there?"

"Do you know how surreal this is?" Rage murmured, but did as asked. The woman—the princess, he reminded himself—didn't weigh much although her features indicated that not too long ago, she was used to three meals a day and more. Her skin was sallow; the candles cruelly outlined the wrinkles around her eyes, making her look older than her mother. On her breath he could smell the herbs Wulfric had laced her tea with. She wouldn't wake up anytime soon.

She didn't stir when Rage carried her to the sofa. Probably, she would prefer to sleep forever, given her youngest son was so very sick. Sick enough for her to sit by his bedside day and night; sick enough to fear the worst and have all visits prevented and all dusting and cleaning around her son's rooms forbidden so he wouldn't be disturbed.

The bed was too big for the child, Rage observed when he stepped next to the empress. The little boy looked lost and forlorn between mountains of pillows, even more so because he was a small child. Hectic red spots flushed his otherwise pale face, and beads of sweat trickled down his temples. His hands, clawlike above the bedcover, clenched and unclenched constantly as if he were trying to dig his way out of the bed, out of his body, and maybe even out of his life.

"Hello, honeypie," the empress said, and the little boy opened his eyes.

"'Lo, Gramma," he whispered. "Where've you been? Missed you!"

The empress smiled. Rage, who'd moved to the other side of the bed, watched her as well and saw tears building up in her eyes.

"I was busy, beloved. But now I am here. And I found a doctor who will help you go to sleep." She put her hands on top of the boy's. His face tightened with pain, but he was clearly too happy for her presence to ask her not to touch, not to hurt him.

With visible effort, the boy turned his head to Rage. "Hi," he piped, and that was all he could say because he was out of breath.

"Hi," Rage replied quietly. "I hear you have trouble sleeping, and I see you are in pain. What happened to you, little one?"

Damn, but he always had had a soft spot for the very small and innocent. This might very well not turn out as planned. He watched the boy lick his lips, trying to come up with an answer. Instead, his head dropped to the side, his eyes rolled back, and he slipped into what seemed to be a mixture between fever, sleep, and unconsciousness.

"He's very ill," the empress said. "Always been small, always been sickly. But he prospered, in his own way. Bright boy, my little Leon is. Charming and absolutely adorable. I love him more than I can say."

Wulfric pulled Rage away from the bed so the boy wouldn't hear what else there was to tell. "Last autumn, he fell off his pony and broke his leg. Nothing serious, really, but ever since, he's been in bed. The leg doesn't heal, he cannot keep food down, and he has horrible nightmares. It's the one thing he wishes for—sleep without dreams." He sighed, standing on his tiptoes and pulling Rage down at the same time so he could whisper into the assassin's ear. "He's dying. His mother, Princess Kayla, is convinced he's been poisoned and blames the empress—you must have heard of their quarrel concerning the throne. You've heard the rumors in the bar. People know something is wrong in the palace. Mother and daughter are fighting against each other, the nobles are taking sides, and if this isn't solved soon, there will be war. Only the empress hasn't poisoned little Leon. The boy is in death's realms, but Princess Kayla refuses to see it. She keeps him alive with sheer willpower, sitting at his bedside every minute of the day and during the night as well. She doesn't allow her mother or anyone else to visit him. So I slipped the princess a sleeping draught and brought you here, and now it is up to you to do your job."

The boy in the bed coughed, accompanied by small gasps of pain, and at that, Rage turned back to the bed.

"Why me?" he asked. "Why now? This could have been done days, weeks ago. Waiting this long was cruel. No sense plotting complicated plans to lure me into town just to end his misery when all it needs is a pillow over his face."

He knew his words were cruel, but he also knew that in a situation like this, clear words were needed to cut through the grief.

The empress pecked a kiss onto her grandson's cheek. He was restless. Through cracked lips, he called for his mum, his toy horse, and someone to make him feel better.

The empress bit her lips. Twice, she tried to answer and failed. But she found the requested horse and gently pushed it into the boy's scrawny arms.

"At first, there was hope he would recover," Wulfric finally explained when it became clear the old woman wouldn't. "The doctors declared they'd found a way to heal him. They gave him magic-laced medicine, and for a little while, the pain lessened. The prince could even eat, sparsely, but enough to make his mother believe the worst was over. She was wrong, but can you blame her for hoping?"

Rage, knowing a lot about hope himself, didn't comment on that.

"The medicine didn't help." Wulfric looked at the boy in the bed. "The leg became worse. By then, it was impossible to get near the child. Nothing gets to Leon's lips that Princess Kayla hasn't tasted first. And the boy doesn't touch anything given to him by anyone but his mother."

"You could have given her the sleeping draught the moment it was clear the boy wouldn't live. You could have sneaked in here and ended his pain, either of you." Rage's voice was cold.

Briefly, the empress closed her eyes. No tears slid down her cheeks. When she spoke, her voice was cold, too. "I cannot harm him. I thought that to be obvious. And Wulfric? I asked him, and he denied his service, for the first time ever since I've known him. He was with Kayla when Leon was born." Taking a deep breath, she looked at Rage. "There is no one I can trust. *No one.* Do you think I could send a soldier in here to slaughter my grandson or, as you put it, press a pillow over his face? I promised Leon to find a doctor who can heal him. Leon believes you are this doctor. He believes you are gentle and competent and will stop the pain for good."

"I'm an assassin, not a doctor, and I am bound by the rules. No assassin is allowed to kill a member of the royal family. My own rules state not to kill a child. Why me?"

Wulfric patted his shoulder, or tried to—the man was tiny and managed to get as high as Rage's elbow. "Because you managed to keep your heart and your soul, dear boy. You've got your own rules. You follow them regardless of the consequences. You won't let a child suffer." Oddly gently, Wulfric pushed Rage back to the bed.

The boy's big, sad eyes fluttered open. "What's an assassin, Gramma?" he mumbled. In his arm was the toy horse, soft and big and wrought bald by the prince's small hands.

"It is another name for doctor, love," his grandmother answered without hesitation.

Rage sat on the bed. The stench of illness was nauseating, and because he needed to know what exactly he was dealing with, he pulled the bedcovers, damp from sweat, aside.

The empress tried to stop him, but the look he gave her made her stay her hand.

The stench of illness intensified. Thin limbs, fragile bones, next to no flesh—it was a pitiful sight that greeted him, and the heavy cast around the boy's left leg made the rest of his body look even more vulnerable. Leon shivered in his fever-induced state, and his hands clawed at the bed sheets.

Rage put his hand onto the boy's chest.

Leon looked at him. His gaze was confused, as if he'd forgotten he'd seen Rage before, and in his chest, his heartbeat sped up. With fear? With hope?

Then a smile flickered across his lips.

He didn't scream, and he didn't try to get away from the hand that held him down.

"Will you—" the empress began, but Rage cut her off.

"I want you to leave," he said, not taking his eyes off the boy. "Now. Take Wulfric with you."

Obviously, the empress was not used to being ordered around. Her features, softened by her grandson's presence, became stern. Maybe she would have argued, would have considered throwing Rage into the dungeons for his insolence if the boy's hand hadn't wrapped around Rage's fingers. "I'm so tired, Gramma," Leon whispered. "Can I go to sleep now, please?"

The empress swallowed. Very lightly, she brushed a strand of hair out of Leon's face and kissed him. "Yes, love, you can sleep now. I wish you the sweetest dreams, and I promise there will be no more pain once you close your eyes."

"I'd like that," Leon said dreamily. His eyes dropped closed once more. He didn't see the fresh tears running down his grandmother's face.

Rage didn't watch them leave as it was unimportant, really. They could linger in a dark corner for all he cared—he just wanted them out of the boy's eyesight so Leon could concentrate on him as long as he was able to concentrate at all.

"I'm so cold," Leon whispered. His face was burning with fever. Rage pulled the bedcover up to his chin. It didn't matter anymore whether his temperature would rise another little bit. In another minute, the boy would be dead.

I don't kill children, his brain told him.

You will kill this one, his heart replied.

And it was as simple as that. He would kill this little boy because otherwise, this little boy would continue to suffer. His mother could have killed him more gently, so could his grandmother, or even Wulfric. None of them could have done it, though.

A knife in his heart; a pillow over his face. Neither was an option. Leon would feel death's grip, and it would scare him. He would struggle, weak as he was, and he would try to scream.

Poison might have worked, but unless injected—against which the boy would have fought, Rage was sure—even the best death draughts had a horrible taste. Leon would have thrown it up immediately.

Besides, he didn't have any poison.

And I don't kill children.

Jack had wanted to teach him that lesson long ago, but Rage had already known that part. He'd killed everyone he'd loved at the age of fourteen. He'd buried his parents, the people he'd grown up with, and he'd buried his sister.

He'd buried his friends, boys and girls his own age and younger. Not that many people, if one would have counted. He had lived in a very, very small village containing only a few houses.

Yet he still remembered how awfully still and heavy the corpses had been when he'd lifted them into their graves.

No children, never again.

Only this here was different. This here was a child who needed to die tonight.

Now.

"Are you a magician?" Leon's voice was scratchy, his breath light, and his heartbeat feeble. Rage guessed he would need another month to die. Longer even if his mother could talk him into allowing her to inject him with strengthening medicines.

"I'm not a magician," Rage answered. "Which is a good thing because you are afraid of magicians, aren't you?"

A long shot, but Rage had seen how anxious Leon had been when Wulfric came too close to his bed.

"They are scary. They always try to make me eat, but I don't like their food."

Rage bent a bit lower. "I won't make you eat anything," he assured the boy. "I will make you go to sleep."

Leon sighed. "Will it hurt? I want my mommy."

His mommy was fast asleep on the couch. Pity she couldn't say good-bye to her son.

Couldn't be helped. She'd slaughter Rage with her bare hands if she knew what he was up to.

"The sleep I bring doesn't hurt. It is a warm sleep, soft and cozy and safe. Your mommy is on the sofa, taking a nap. I can wake her, if you like."

Risky. After all, Leon was a small boy, he was alone in the company of a man he'd never seen before, and it was late—he might insist on having his mother by his side.

But Leon wasn't an ordinary boy, not anymore. "She yawned, just before you came, and then she dozed off." He had to wait for a moment, catching his breath, before he could continue. "Mommy doesn't sleep that often." His fingers tightened around Rage's hand, his other arm around his horse.

"I think I can go to sleep without her," he finally decided.

"Then close your eyes," Rage said. "Yes, just like that. Think of someplace nice. Can you do that?"

"The stables!" Leon said immediately. "My pony is there, Buttercup. I fell, but it wasn't her fault."

"The stables, then. Buttercup is there, some dogs, and it smells of hay. The sun is out. It is still early. Can you hear the birds singing in the trees?"

With his left, Rage held the boy's hand. His right brushed down the bedcover just enough to reveal the boy's throat. The pulse beat slowly beneath the soft skin.

I'm about to kill a child.

It wasn't a pleasant thought, but it wasn't as disturbing as it had been a few minutes ago.

He wasn't doing this for payment. Not for love, not for money, and certainly not because the boy's grandmother had ordered him to. He was doing this because it was the right thing to do.

The only thing to do.

The boy's mother would hunt him mercilessly should she ever find out his name.

Rage's fingers found the pulse. At first, he barely touched this feeble beat of life, just caressed it, treasured it, feeling how fragile it was. A life could be taken so easily. A knife pulled across the throat. A bolt in the neck. A string, cutting off the breathing. Broken bones, if he'd been paid to make death painful. There were so many ways to kill, some fast, some slow, all cruel.

All but one when talking about taking a life with one's own hands. When seeking out the pulse, when interrupting the connection between heart and brain, the victim could breathe easily whilst the brain slowly went to sleep. Rage had killed like that before, rarely, but every now and then and always when the one who'd paid him didn't want the victim to suffer. Once, he'd killed an old man like that. George had hired him, had paid him, and had also been his victim. It had been an easy death, and it hadn't been George's fault that everything afterward had turned into a nightmare.

Hopefully, the death of this child, though as easy and painless as George's, wouldn't end up just as catastrophic.

"Sleepy," Leon whispered, maybe a bit surprised at the fingers touching his throat with gentle pressure, but not scared at all. "Warm."

"How about taking a ride on your pony? See, one of the stable boys is already bringing the saddle."

Was his own voice a bit hoarse? Maybe.

Just a little more pressure. There was not much life left in the boy. His pulse stuttered.

"Mom—" Leon said, and then his heart stopped, deprived of the brain's order to beat and relieved it could finally let go.

For many minutes, Rage kept his gentle grip on the boy's throat, something he had never done before. He knew the boy was dead, but he couldn't bring himself to let go. The boy's hand was still clutching his, the small body still warm, the last breath still fresh on the bluish lips. Nearly alive; not asleep.

Impossible to be woken up ever again.

His mother would be devastated upon waking up.

His mother would go through hell and back to bring down her son's killer. And she would know it—after all, she had been drugged, and upon waking, she would taste the herbs on her tongue.

And no matter how gentle he had been, killing someone left marks. She would see them, and she would draw the right conclusions. That her son hadn't died a natural death.

"Sleep well, little one," Rage said, knowing the boy couldn't hear him anymore. Without haste, he freed his hand from Leon's. Time to leave. Time to get back to Jack and Keiran. It was hours until sunrise: more than enough time to plan Luca's escape.

Silently, he closed the door behind him, getting out the same way he'd gotten in. As expected, the corridor was empty apart from Wulfric, who'd been waiting patiently outside.

"Is he dead?" the monk asked.

Rage nodded.

"Then all that needs to be done is sort out your payment. Excellent. I am very proud of you, dear boy. I feared little Leon would begin to scream once his grandmother was out of sight, but as expected, you managed to do and say just the right things."

"You spied on me?" Rage was not really surprised. Now that his job was done, he was nervous—the palace was a bad place for an assassin, and anyway, if he hurried up, he might catch a few hours of sleep before it was time to get to Well Prison.

Brother Wulfric grinned happily. "The empress went back to her rooms. I assume she is crying her eyes out, poor old thing. Understandable, of course. She loved the boy. Anyway, yes, of course I spied on you. There is a peephole in the wall. I needed to know if my trust in your skills was rightful, didn't I? The empress can tell if I lie. Unnerving gift, I can assure you. If I told her you killed the boy gently and that he wasn't afraid without actually knowing it happened that way, she'd have me beheaded before sunrise." Chuckling, he rubbed his hands together as if having plotted and completed an especially complicated bargain.

With sudden force, Rage became aware of the palace walls all around him. "I need to go now." And he was tired, too. "Get me out of here, monk. We can talk about my payment anywhere else but the palace."

"Ah," Wulfric said ruefully. "Payment. I think I told you you wouldn't like it too much, didn't I? Frankly spoken, dear boy, I might have put it a bit too mildly that way."

Three guards stepped around the corner, swords raised.

No use pulling his knife. He was in the middle of the empress's palace, he'd just killed the empress's grandson, and as Wulfric had just betrayed him, he would end up in the dungeons with or without knife raised.

The little monk patted his arm. "Don't you worry, dear boy. I've planned this well. There are no flaws, although you might be of a different opinion quite soon. Guards, put shackles on this man, will you? He just killed Prince Leon. I caught him red-handed, and I want him in the dungeons immediately."

A trap, just as expected.

Fuck.

He could have tried to fight his way out. He might have succeeded, but it was very unlikely. So Rage decided not to fight and not to get beaten. If he made it out of this part of the palace relatively unharmed now, there might be a better chance to escape later, once the guards thought they'd captured him well and good. Had worked before. It might work again tonight.

A fourth guard, one that had been hiding in the shadows, knocked Rage over the head with a club.

"Don't kill him, if you please," Rage heard Brother Wulfric say. "Maybe later, if necessary, but not quite now. And don't torture him before I'm there to supervise."

His feet refused to carry him, so the guards dragged Rage away, downstairs, until the carpets gave way to stone steps, and the walls weren't decorated with tapestries anymore but with hooks and axes.

Pulling his knife—or fighting—really wouldn't have made any difference at all.

THE MOMENT Jack began weaving his charm to woo the guard, Keiran realized this was the wrong place for him to be. This was Jack's game, not his, and he couldn't do a thing to help him get Luca out of prison. The old assassin was enjoying this. Keiran only wished he had followed his initial instinct to search for Rage.

Penny pulled Jack into a small room. The door closed behind them, and the other guard—Kate?—flashed him a small grin as if asking for his understanding. *They won't be long*, the grin said. *All is well.*

Nothing was well. As much as Keiran wished Luca would be free and safe, he couldn't suppress his worries about Rage.

Rage's flame, the black flame and that so far had always led him to his lover, was nothing but a flickering, feeble shadow. Dwindling. Dying.

Was he worried? No. He was close to a panic, to put it precisely.

Jack would be better off without him. He knew what he was doing, but Keiran had no idea how to behave in town, how to hold a sword, how to fight. If Luca had a chance to get out of Well Prison at all, it would be Jack, and Jack alone, who could make sure she got out safely. So Keiran decided to trust Jack with Luca's life no matter how badly he felt about it, then turned and left Well Prison. He went back the way they had come, cursing the time he'd wasted already.

The market was buzzing by now. The sun was high in the sky, most of the goods were sold, and the fish caught before dawn began to stink. It was much harder to get through the crowd now, partly because there were more people, but mainly because Keiran didn't possess Jack's natural arrogance and the air of an assassin. No one made way for him, and more than once, a market woman didn't give a damn he was walking past and threw waste from her stall right at his feet.

It would take him ages to get to the other side.

Briefly, Keiran considered turning around, to go back to Jack, only to find it didn't matter where he headed—he was locked in between a woman selling scones, a cheese monger, a couple selling weapons, and about half the city's population. All he could do was wait until the crowd allowed him through.

So he stood and waited, and after an eternity, he began to listen to the people.

"Heard it?"

"Did you hear what happened?"

"Got the news?"

"A guard told me little Prince Leon's dead."

"Did you hear?"

"Killed last night."

"Yeah, found dead in his bed by his mom."

"Princess Kayla, you know, it's said she's gone mad with grief."

Goosebumps showed on Keiran's arms although it was not a cool morning.

The cheese monger cut a chunk off a big wheel, wrapped it in paper, and handed it to his customer with the words, "They caught the bastard who did it. Bet he's dead by now, hanged or slaughtered or whatever. Earned it, know what I mean? Killing an innocent little boy. Disgusting."

The customer paid for his cheese, looking anxiously over his shoulder. "Think this means war, then?"

His words shocked everyone around him into silence, at least for as long as a heartbeat or two. "War?" the man selling weapons asked. "Don't give me a fucking heart attack, man! Why would there be war now?"

The cheese monger snorted. "War's been in the air for months now, idiot. And rumor says the old empress hired the assassin who killed little Leon. After she paid another one to poison him. Princess Kayla is bound to lash out now, isn't she? Held back for the sake of her kids so far, but now the youngest one is dead she has no choice but to react. Which means war." He cut off another piece of cheese and ate it, chewing methodically as if chewing cheese was all that was left to do.

Assassin.

Impossible.

"But if the guy who killed Leon is caught...."

"He's just the weapon, isn't he? Kayla will want her mother's head for her boy's death. Can't blame her, really. And the old empress has enough followers left—and the city guard by her side— to make this fucking war a damn bloody one." As if he'd proved his point, the cheese monger nodded several times. "Damn bloody war," he repeated. "Damn fucking bloody war."

Rage wouldn't kill a child.

"But why did that guy kill a child, say?" the fisher woman asked. "Tiny little Leon. Saw him last harvest feast. Harmless, really, and not even the heir. Why him?"

Rage would not kill a child, for no reason whatsoever.

"Guess it was a great way to add the final spark," a woman eyeing the mussels cast in. "Easy thing, killing a kid. And anyway, they say the killer is a professional. Assassin, you know? They do everything as long as you pay them. How much for the blue ones, dear?"

The cheese monger rolled out his last cheddar. "Funny thing the old bitch found an assassin at all. Not many in town nowadays. And there's the rule. Never kill a member of the royal family. There's a reason why the lot is somewhat respected, y'know? They've got rules. Two are around from what I hear. And one has retired end of last year."

"You thinking about the woman, what's-her-name. She couldn't have done it. Out in the bars by lunch, pissed by sunset. And the boy was killed during the night, they say."

"Which leaves an outsider," the fisher woman spat. "Hate them. Everyone not born here shouldn't be allowed in the city."

Now that talk was about to take a nasty turn. As quietly as possible, Keiran took a few steps back, knowing that if someone really looked at him, it would be obvious he was born and raised in the countryside simply by checking out his clothes.

Another thought began bothering him. At first, he tried to ignore it, but it became loud and insistent and eventually he had no choice but to actually think it.

Maybe Rage did it because of what Wulfric had to offer. Maybe he killed that child because of me.

It truly wasn't a chilly morning, but Keiran felt his hands and feet go cold nevertheless. When they had met Wulfric, when the little monk had offered to show Rage how to control his magic....

He wouldn't kill a child!

"Wonder what prize they paid him," the fat baker mused. "Can't have been cheap."

"Doesn't matter 'cause he's dead or will be pretty soon. Dungeons, eh? They'll cut him to pieces." The cheese monger chuckled, and the agreeing murmur from everyone around him didn't help Keiran to feel any better.

And finally it occurred to him that those people had answered every one of his unspoken questions during the past minutes.

His heartbeat sped up just a tad. Rage had said there was magic in him. Worth a try to use it.

Keiran thought, *Where is Leon's killer?* leaned against the baker's stall, and waited.

Customers came and bought and left, the fisher woman hit some other woman with—what a surprise—a fish, and the cheesemonger could have sold his entire wheel if he hadn't denied the customer a tidbit to chew on. For a few brief minutes, talk was entirely about food, the market, and awful foreigners.

Then someone asked, "Where have they taken him? North Prison?" and Keiran just knew he was able to use his magic in a way he definitely hadn't expected. He'd known there was something new inside him, something he couldn't tag or name or even find. Just… something. But this? Never.

"North Prison?" The baker snorted. "No way. Too easygoing."

"Well Prison, maybe? Nah, unlikely. That one's for the high society." The weapon seller's wife pulled a face.

"Probably the Main Dungeons," a new customer chimed in. He had a small voice, which perfectly fit his small body. "Right underneath the palace would be the place for such a monster. Killing poor Leon, really. What a horrendous thing to do. A slab of that cheese, if you please, Master Winfried."

The fisher woman beamed at the monk. "Brother Wulfric!" she screamed. "Lovely to see you. Any more gossip you can part with?" Swiftly, she packed two mackerels and handed them over, denying any payment Wulfric might have offered. Clearly, the little monk was much better liked at the market than in the tavern where Keiran had first seen him.

Keiran took another step back. He was hiding behind the baker's stall, certain the monk hadn't seen him and eager to hear what he had to say.

"Gossip, dear woman, is against our good Lady's wishes," Wulfric said, but there was a twinkle in his eyes that belied his words. His glasses were missing, though, and he blinked repeatedly as if the sun was too bright for him. "Now I don't know anything about last night's horrible events, of course, having been in bed by sunset."

Liar. You left a tavern at ten, taking Rage with you.

"But well, I hear others talk, naturally. And I might have heard the man who killed Prince Leon wasn't from the city. An assassin, of course. Tall, black hair, black eyes. Killed the little prince in cold blood." Wulfric leaned forward a bit. Everyone around him leaned forward as well to be sure to catch each and every of his words.

"It is said he's already been tortured half to death," the monk whispered. "In the Main Dungeons. And that soon he will be hanged."

Wulfric smiled, his strangely ageless face a harsh contrast to his bald head, the crow's feet around his eyes and his smile only highlighting the cruelty hiding in the wrinkles around his lips.

Keiran stared at him. *This cannot be true*, he thought, desperately trying to wrap his mind around what the monk had just said. *It isn't true, and why is he here, and how can I save Rage?*

The little monk looked up, ignoring his audience and their muttered agreement to the assassin's fate. Wulfric looked straight at Keiran instead. His smile deepened; then he winked his eye, took his mackerels and cheese, and vanished in the crowd as suddenly as he'd appeared.

MAIN DUNGEONS?

"Down the street, sweetie, then turn left, left again, and then ask for further directions."

It was as easy as that. Although he'd never been able to make himself understood without the help of his hands, his expression, and often a piece of paper and a pen, Keiran only had to think about the question he needed an answer to, and he got it, provided he was close to the person and managed to keep other thoughts out of his mind. To him, it felt like yelling, and to his immense relief, his normal thoughts seemed as safe and secret as ever. Rage probably would be able to pick up some of them, given he'd always been able to understand Keiran, but that was something he could worry about later—he didn't want to be an open book, not even to his lover.

Keiran took the second turn left, having no clue where he was. This part of the city was a maze of small streets surrounded by high, narrow houses with high, narrow windows. Occasionally, a bucket of waste was emptied before or behind him, dumped right onto the stones. The stink was bad, increased by the warm day; Keiran couldn't imagine being here in the summer and fully understood Rage's decision to leave the city behind. Although the stink most likely didn't have anything to do with it. The crowd, yes, and the constant background noise. Rage was a man who liked open spaces, silence, and the smell of hay.

Country boy, Keiran thought with the flicker of a grin.

The assassin's flame flickered too, just like it had in the past hours. Rage wasn't dead no matter what people gossiped, but he wasn't well, either.

No one staying at the Main Dungeons of the empress's city would be anywhere near well, Keiran guessed, although he had only a very vague idea what exactly dungeons were. At home, there wasn't even a prison. Anyone committing a crime was locked up in the cellar of Babylon Manor, awaiting judgment by the lord or the lady in charge. Lucius often had forgotten about the suspects—unless it had been a young girl—and more than once, Keiran had let them out after a month or so. After all, stealing a sheep or dodging tax wasn't a major offense. Only if someone got seriously hurt, had there been a trial. Lucius had made sure his punishment was brutal but fair, knowing that an unfair lord was prey to revolt.

Keiran wondered how Luca would handle the job as Lady of Babylon and experienced an unexpected, painful jolt of guilt at the thought of his friend. He'd left her behind, with only Jack to take care of her well-being. A man he didn't know; a man with only one leg and one eye and the Lady knew what reputation or skills.

I should have freed her first. The thought was bright and precise.

Ruthlessly, Keiran pushed it into the back of his head. Rage trusted Jack; Keiran would have to trust him too were he to find Rage.

No time to get distracted, not even by Luca, given he was about to break into the dungeons. By now, he'd learned it was the darkest prison in town, reserved for the worst crimes and the lowest criminals. Rapists, child abusers, murderers—they all ended up there no matter their social status. You could find a lord getting tortured in one cell whilst in the next, a washerwoman pleaded for mercy. And no one ever got out alive unless it was proven beyond doubt he or she was innocent. At least everyone got three meals a day—if one was in the condition to eat meals. Everyone had a cell and a bucket to himself, each bucket was emptied regularly, and each cell was swept clean once a day or after torture. The empress had witnessed the outbreak of typhus as a child, killing three-quarters of the city's population and her younger sisters as well as the heir, her older brother. Typhus was now also known as gaols fever. It lingered in the prisons and dungeons, and when it spread out, it was deadly.

One of her first verdicts as empress had been to keep the cells clean and the prisoners healthy so gaols fever didn't have a chance to break out again, at least not as long as she lived.

Keiran's idea of the Main Dungeons was that of a cellar slightly larger than the one at home, with only one or two prisoners held. Right, as this was a city, maybe four or five.

He had to ask two more people for directions, but eventually, he reached the Main Dungeons, or rather, the south side of the palace the dungeons were placed underneath. He was just about to walk up to the entrance and ask permission to see a prisoner when he actually saw the entrance. Stopping dead in his tracks, he just had time to duck behind a cart before the guards protecting the gate could see him.

Not two guards, as in Well Prison. Five guards.

Not a normal gate; no people going in and out. Clearly, to this prison, no court was attached. Which was only logical, as the people held in the Main Dungeons didn't get a formal trial like every other prisoner in every other of the city's prisons. Suspects held here got tortured. If—or rather, *when*—they confessed, they got killed for the crime they'd committed. If they didn't confess, they died of their injuries. And on the rare occasions someone didn't confess and didn't die, it was up to the empress herself to judge.

Five guards, one small gate wide enough for a cart or two guards dragging a prisoner to get in, high enough for a tall man not to bump his head, the arch made of stone and the door encrusted with iron hinges, iron lock, and iron bars.

No one could walk in or out unseen. The sheer thought of asking for permission to see a prisoner was ridiculous.

Anyone who wanted to get in had to be a guard, a prisoner, or the empress.

There weren't many people on the street, so hiding was tricky, but Keiran managed just barely by risking opening a door left ajar and slipping inside, hoping not to scare the life out of some old folks thinking him a burglar. Luckily, the house was empty, and abandoned on top of it. No furniture, only a broken chair in the fireplace. Dirty windows, partly covered by paper to keep the wind out where they were shattered. And no footsteps from the first floor, either.

Perfect place to hide and think about his next steps.

Not that there was much to think about. He needed to get into the dungeons, and as he couldn't see another way, he needed to get in through the front gate.

I could kill one of the guards.

Nice idea, only it wouldn't work. He could handle a scythe or a bat, and he knew how to fight with a quarterstaff, but he couldn't handle a sword and wouldn't be able to survive a fight with a soldier.

Impersonating the empress was an equally daft idea, but at least it made him grin for a heartbeat.

I could... maybe....

Yes. That might actually work.

CHAPTER
Thirteen

IT WAS barely past sunrise when she knocked on the door of her prisoner's cell, carefully like a little service girl asking for permission to enter. Not that she had to knock—after all, this was a prison, not a palace, and she wasn't actually a servant girl but a guard. A very young guard, true, but a guard nevertheless, complete with armor, helmet, heavy boots, sword, and lance.

Which she left outside simply because she couldn't carry the tray and the lance at the same time.

She wasn't that little, either.

Her name was Anika; she was eighteen years old and a member of the guard for two years. She could kill a man, if the man didn't fight back too hard, she could play cards, she knew how to drink with her companions, and she would go to war soon should the empress and her daughter fail to find a way to put aside their grudges.

And she was terribly afraid of her prisoner.

"Good morning," Anika murmured, looking everywhere but at the prisoner on the bed.

"Is it? Are you sure? Because I think it is a lousy morning. Could be the day I get hanged for a crime I didn't commit. Could be the day I get flogged, if I'm lucky and Lord Barnard is in a merciful mood. Did you find out who the judge will be for my trial?" Getting up from the narrow, hard bed and dropping the rough blanket to the floor, Lucinda of Babylon strolled to the table, eyed bread and tea suspiciously, and folded her arms over her chest. Anika saw that her hair was loose but clean and kempt, her eyes sharp and hard. She must have woken up a while ago, washed herself from head to toe although the water was cold, and wore the prison clothes as if it were a royal garment and not the plain linen dress every prisoner had to wear.

Picking up the bread, Lucinda sniffed it and dropped it again. Flicking off the lid of the teapot, she peeked inside, wrinkled her nose, and turned her back to Anika.

Anika sighed silently. So far, this had gone well. If she were extremely lucky, she'd be out of here before her prisoner decided it was time for a lengthy discussion about torture, death, injustice, or Lord Barnard.

Usually, the people held in charge at Well Prison were older than Lucinda of Babylon. Matrons who'd cheated money out of their husbands; old men guilty of not paying their taxes. Couples were put into Well Prison also, or neighbors, the former because only in Well Prison were the cells large enough to comfortably hold two people, the latter mainly because of disputes over land. So far, no prisoner had ever given Anika a hard time or, for example, tried to strangle her.

She couldn't suppress a slight shudder. Lucinda of Babylon wasn't old, she wasn't scared although she didn't have relatives looking after her, she was here although technically, she didn't belong here—and she knew how to launch an attack. Definitely, she wasn't the average rich, spoiled girl too terrified to speak her mind and overwhelmed by the prison routine or the weapons or the fact she couldn't go where she pleased. This prisoner had a filthy mouth and quick hands. This prisoner had attacked Anika only an hour after her arrival and very nearly had managed to escape. Only because Kate had been with her, Lucinda hadn't succeeded.

Involuntarily, Anika rubbed her throat. A rich girl shouldn't have such strong hands, and a rich girl shouldn't know where to put her thumbs to do as much damage as possible. A rich girl like her, so beautiful and slender and gifted with everything a girl like Anika could only dream of should wait for her prince to marry her, not be put into prison.

On the other hand, Lucinda of Babylon was charged with having killed her father, and only because she was sixteen years old was she in Well Prison at all. Normally, for a crime like that, even rich people were put in North Prison or, more likely, into the Main Dungeons.

Sixteen. Anika shook her head in disbelief. *She's younger than I am, and she looks as if she's gone through a lot more than I ever will.*

"The judge's name?" Luca snapped. "Come on, girl, did the cat eat your tongue?"

"Federico of Allis House will judge you, miss," Anika mumbled obediently. Her eyes dashed to Luca's hair, wishing she would braid it and tame it so it wouldn't look that wild and unladylike, and anyway, what rich girl ever left her hair unbraided? It was rude to do so, inviting anyone to stroke it, to let the golden strands run through her fingers and *really, I need to get my thoughts under control!*

Blushing, Anika realized she'd been staring, something a guard didn't do and definitely something Lucinda would have rewarded with an acid comment had she seen it. Anika's prisoner was so very quick with her tongue, she always saw things she wasn't supposed to see, and she never let an opportunity pass by to deliver an insult. Anika should have been used to it, having grown up with three brothers and a drunkard as mother plus having been a member of the guard for two years—but if Lucinda made an acid remark about the quality of the food, it nearly brought her to tears although she hadn't even cooked the damn stuff!

Actually, Lucinda didn't have to say anything. One raised eyebrow, one disgusted look was all that was needed to make Anika feel like a piece of dirt, worth less than a pile of dog shit. She'd have given a lot to be able to counter her, to master that look. But she couldn't, and so she feared each moment she had to spend in Lucinda of Babylon's presence.

At least it would be over soon. "You'll be judged today, miss," she added, slightly belated. "Judge Federico will arrive late morning. He'll want to eat lunch first, so you can expect your trial to be set for early afternoon."

Swiftly, her prisoner turned, her long hair waving in an arch behind her. It looked... fabulous.

Anika gulped.

"He's having several hours of lunch break?" Luca sounded incredulous. "What is he, a man or a pig?"

Anika hadn't expected this—for the first time, her prisoner had a go at someone else besides her. She grinned, relief washing through her. "Judge Federico is a hungry man," she said carefully. It wasn't a good idea to insult a man who was able to order her hands chopped off for insolent words. "He is large, though shorter than you, miss. And he likes his lunch."

Luca shrugged. "More time for me to imagine how I will die. Maybe they'll drown me. What do you think?"

That wiped the grin off Anika's face. That was why she dreaded her encounters with her prisoner most—because her prisoner was accused of murder and because dying was what would happen to her.

And Anika didn't want her to die. How could anyone be so cruel and kill such a beautiful person? Fine, maybe she had killed her father, and yes, she was practically unbearable, but still….

"Or starve me to death? Given the state of this so-called breakfast, they've already started."

Anika decided it was time to change the subject. "Miss, you need to get presentable for the judge," she said, hoping it wouldn't earn her another of those dreaded looks. "Judge Federico doesn't hold with prisoners looking like… like…."

"A common whore? No, I can understand that. Well, it is what he'll have to live with. Maybe if I open my shirt a bit wider and have him take a good look at my décolleté, he'll consider fucking me rather than killing me."

Anika had to swallow hard so as not to gasp—it was the first time ever she'd heard a rich girl use such filthy language, and only the good Lady knew what décolleté might mean. Probably it was an exceptionally awful swearword.

"Wouldn't work, miss," Anika eventually managed. "Nothing but food interests Judge Federico. The more the better. He'll eat during the trial, he'll tell you the sentence with his mouth full, and if the food isn't to his liking, the verdict will be harsher than otherwise."

Her reward was the first smile on her prisoner's face.

And how she hated to call her that. Prisoner. A nasty word, implicating *the prisoner* was truly guilty and not only a suspect, someone who might not have done what she'd been accused of. And an ugly word as well, erasing the beauty of the… person… woman… now staring back at her openly and with a frown on her face, and finally Anika realized *she* was staring, her eyes roaming hungrily over that perfect body and the gold of Lucinda's hair and *How might it feel to run my hands through it?*

Quickly, Anika lowered her gaze. "Sorry, miss," she whispered, hoping her prisoner wouldn't call Kate and tell her what she'd done.

Staring. Making it obvious how much she wished they weren't in a prison cell, there wouldn't be a murder verdict, and she wasn't so fat and ugly.

Head down and not thinking for a single moment Lucinda could try to attack her again, Anika waited for her to say something, do something, even if it was to laugh at her dreadfully obvious desire.

"Eats, does he?" Lucinda asked, pouring herself a cup of now cold tea. She didn't drink it, just held the cup between her hands, turned it, caressing it. "And he's fat? Good to know. However, how will he judge me?"

Damn, but she could have run out of the room any time, Anika thought, snapping out of her guilt and instantly moving to the door, guarding it as she should have done all the time. *I guess the only reason she didn't is because she knows Kate is out there somewhere.*

"Judge Federico? The verdict?" Lucinda said, sounding only slightly impatient.

Easy answer. Judge Federico wanted food, and whoever needed to could bribe him easily. A goose, fresh fish, scallops, two dozen eggs—he'd judge accordingly. And Lord Barnard, as Anika knew, not only had enough money but also engaged excellent cooks. "He'll judge guilty," Anika replied without hesitation. "No matter if you did what they accuse you of, no matter how you argue, you're already guilty. If you're lucky, the judge will order you to stay in Well Prison until the verdict will be executed. If his lunch is really, really good, he'll sentence you to a quick death. Depends on what Lord Barnard wants to happen. Miss."

Lucinda put the cup down with a hard *clink*. "Damn the bastard," she hissed, and Anika flinched. Her prisoner was definitely too beautiful to use such filthy language.

"He'll have me killed. I can't believe it, but he'll truly have me killed, and I can't do anything to stop him." Restlessly, Lucinda began pacing from wall to wall, which was a pretty fruitless thing to do as the room was really small.

"You could—" Anika began, and reined herself in just in time. *Prisoner*, she reminded herself. *Don't tell her how to get out of here.*

Too late. She'd already said too much.

"I could what?"

Anika sighed. "If you know someone in the city, someone who's got money, you could try to find a better cook. And offer Judge Federico better food. Bribe him. Simple, and it would probably work if you did it fast enough."

The second smile in one day! She'd done the right thing, telling Lucinda what to do.

Only Lucinda didn't seem too enthusiastic about it. She'd stopped pacing. "In this city there are only three people I know who would risk bribing a judge, and none of them has much money to spare. It would be a lot easier if you'd just let me walk out of here."

Then she tilted her head and looked at Anika in a way that made her legs weak.

Later that day—after sunset, and after a couple of beers and a few more gins, Anika confessed to herself she would have let her walk, just like that and without any payment at all. She would have opened the door, and she would have protected Lucinda from the other guards. She would have smuggled her out of Well Prison and that evening, crying into her gin, Anika didn't know whether she should be glad or sad it hadn't happened.

"I would've let 'er walk," Anika mumbled, late at night and with no one sitting next to her. Not even Kate, who often agreed to go for a drink after work. So no one heard her confession, and no one heard her telling the glass of gin about Lord Barnard and how he had prevented her just in time from becoming a criminal herself.

"DAMN GOOD idea of you to come back a bit earlier than planned." Catlike, Penny arched her back and rolled her shoulders. Most of her clothes lay discarded at her feet. Only her boots she hadn't kicked off nor the knife that was hidden in the shaft.

Jack, fishing his shirt off a rack with swords, flashed her a grin. "Lunch wasn't that good, and I didn't find the boy, either. No use wandering aimlessly through town any longer." After lacing up his trousers, he began hunting down his walking stick. It had rolled under the rack, and Penny had to get down on all fours to retrieve it.

Jack lightly slapped her naked bum. "You wriggle that ass for another moment, and we'll have to repeat our little party."

Penny handed him the stick. Jack wore his trousers but hadn't put his shirt on yet. He was barefoot; playfully, she bit his ankle. "No time, old man. Got to be back at work in ten minutes."

"I can be quick," Jack replied, still grinning. "I'm good at quick."

"You're lousy at quick, Jack. With you, it takes all night what could be done in seconds."

"Do you complain?" Closing the last buttons of his shirt, Jack opened the door, peeking out into an empty corridor. Good thing the weapons chamber only held a small number of swords, and was located in the farthest corner of the prison's cellar. "Because if you do, I'll have to punish you. Badly." He let the door fall closed, pulled her into his arms, placed a tentative kiss on her shoulder, and let his hand begin to wander. "Very, very badly," he murmured into her hair.

Briefly, she hugged him, responded to his caresses before pushing him away. Quickly, she got dressed. "Tonight, when I'm off duty," she said. Her lance leaned next to the door; she took it and stepped out into the corridor. "You need to get into the courtroom now anyway, old man. Truly, I have no idea how you manage to do it twice in half an hour when my ex-husband couldn't get it up once a month. Tonight at eight?"

Jack stepped next to her, his walking stick not making a sound and his clothes not at all looking as if they'd been ripped off his body only thirty minutes ago. "Depends. Now that the boy's gone missing, I cannot guarantee I will be free tonight. He's bound to get into trouble. And the girl—by the Lady, I'm too old for this shit."

Penny laughed. "You won't be too old in another twenty years, Jack. You love the city. You love the plotting and the planning and the excitement of breaking out a prisoner. You love to have a kneetrembler between jobs, and I cannot imagine either a job or a fuck happens too regularly in the countryside. How the hell did you manage without all of this?"

At the staircase, they stopped. Penny had to go downstairs whereas the courtroom was one flight up. Jack shrunk back into the shadows until only the end of his stick could be seen, and two people passed him without noticing he was there. When they were out of sight, Jack said, "That question needs more time to answer than I have right now, luv. See you tonight, if possible. If not, I'll catch up with you as soon as I can. Deal?"

Penny grabbed his neck and kissed him. "Deal," she replied, then put her helmet back on and went downstairs where Kate was waiting for her turn to have a break.

When she was out of sight, Jack remembered he'd wanted to ask her who would sit court over Luca, but, of course, he couldn't run after her. Her colleague had seen him twice already today and had grinned widely when he'd picked Penny up for lunch. *Not that there'd been time to eat*, he thought, satisfied with the outcome of their break. She'd always been a wild lover, rough and demanding and insatiable in her lust, and nothing had changed since he'd seen her last. He was looking forward to seeing her again—if he managed to bring this other business to a good end.

Knowing beforehand who Luca's judge was would have been valuable information, but then, he could also find out himself.

The courtroom was at the end of the corridor on the first floor, surprisingly large given it was in a prison, with high windows that let in the noon sun. Bright patches were scattered across the tiles, moved by the trees outside and the wind rustling through the first spring leaves. It was very clearly a courtroom where rich people were judged, not the poor folks who had to do with their cells if they were lucky enough to get a hearing at all. Only the empress's courtroom was bigger; only the most important cases were held there, and mostly for political crimes or if the suspect was somehow related to the royal family. In theory, Luca could be glad to be held and judged here. In fact, it didn't matter as Jack was sure the judge had been bribed. It was how it was done—bribe the judge and get the verdict you want no matter what crime had been committed or whether the suspect was guilty or not. As Barnard had gone to such great lengths to get Luca in his hands, he would not risk a fair trial.

Not many people were in the room when he sneaked in. The elderly couple Jack had seen this morning sat in the first row, a basket with food next to them. The man was pouring his wife a glass of wine whilst she chatted to her neighbor about the case that had just been finished. Twenty people all in all, Jack guessed, choosing a place in the last row, close to a window as well as the entrance.

It had been more than ten years since he'd been in this room. Back then, he'd attended the judgment of one of his clients, a man who'd offered to pay him five hundred Talents if he killed his wife's son. The child had been conceived out of marriage, and the man couldn't bear the thought that his wealth would go to an heir who was not his flesh and blood. Too cowardly to do it himself—and too afraid of his wife if he did—he'd tried to find an assassin to help him out. When he'd found Jack, and after Jack had declined to do the job, the man had hired a drunkard who'd beaten the child to death, and when Jack had learned of it, he'd dropped Penny a quiet hint, and the man had been arrested.

He had also bribed the judge, just to be on the safe side. Directly from the courtroom, the man had been escorted to the gallows and hanged no matter how loud he'd screamed.

Not much had changed since. The floor was maybe a bit cleaner, and some of the benches looked new. Other than that, it was the same room with the same stale, slightly bitter smell, the same half-excited, half-bored audience, and the same tree in front of the window.

Somewhat surprised, Jack realized he missed his home, quiet as it was. He'd loved the city and only rudimentarily understood Rage's decision to leave. He would have never moved to Dragon Spring if he hadn't lost his eye and leg.

"Must be Marit," he murmured, rubbing his thigh. Sometimes, when he overdid it, the muscles cramped. Which was the reason why kneetremblers were not something he did on a regular basis nowadays. "I am missing her lovely personality. And her stews."

A smile curved his lips. He might not move back into town, but maybe he could stay for another week once Luca was free.

A man came through the door, his huge belly serving as a tray for the mug of ale he held in his fleshy hands. Flopping onto the seat next to Jack, he took a deep gulp, belched, and wiped his mouth clean. "Lovely day, isn't it?" he said, or rumbled, rather. His voice sounded like stones rolling about in an empty barrel. "Should've stayed in bed today. Can't stand the sun."

He stank of beer. His shirt was covered with various stains in various colors.

Jack recognized him immediately. "You've become fat, Federico. Fatter than I remember you, anyway." Holding out his hand, he waited until the man had put his mug down on the bench and wobbled his girth around enough to face him.

The blank expression changed once the fat man had taken Jack in from head to toe. "Thought you were dead," he said, and took Jack's hand, shaking it. His grip was firm, but his hand sweaty. "Didn't someone cut you in half?"

Jack stomped his wooden leg lightly on the floor. "Not in half. Lost my leg and moved to the countryside. Nice and pleasant out there. Lots of willing widows, farmers' wives, barmaids…. You should visit me, Federico. Would get you away from all the food the city's offering."

The judge picked up his mug again. "Nothing else to do but eat," he said, clear disgust in his voice. He belched again. Equally clear was his being miles away from sobriety. "Can't do my job properly because everyone bribes me. Can't find a whore who's willing to fuck me, mind my language. Couldn't get it up anyway, though, so probably not the worst thing the whores stay clear of me." He frowned. "Life fell apart when Thanit died and our daughter with her. Never found the one who killed them." He stared at the mug in his hand as if he'd never seen it before.

"You got bribed for the upcoming case?" Jack asked, not sure if he could expect a coherent answer.

He'd underestimated the judge. From a thin folder Jack hadn't seen as it had been hidden by Federico's size, the fat man took out a few sheets of paper and studied them with concentration. "Yes," he finally said. "Can't remember a case where I had to judge from my own knowledge and experience instead of other people's wallets. Lucinda of Babylon. Age sixteen. Daughter of Lucius of Babylon, deceased. Suspected of murder, first grade, out of lewd reasons. His severed head had been found by… hang on." His greasy fingers left stains on the paper when he turned the sheet. "Ah. Yes. A fisherman. Bad luck, that. Without the head, there wouldn't be a case. Pity. I hate sentencing such a young girl to death."

Jack frowned. "Death? That not a bit exaggerated?"

Federico snorted. "'Course it is. No proof she killed the man. Unlikely she killed him at home, where the servants found blood on the carpets, and then cut his head off, taking it miles away to an inn no girl of her breeding would ever set foot in."

"Then why the death sentence for her?" Jack knew the answer, but he wanted to find out how much Federico would let on.

"Because it's what the lord wants, that's why. He's bribed me well, that man. Stupid git he is, but he ordered a decent cook to prepare my breakfast, lunch, and dinner for three days now. Once the girl is out of the way, he'll find a way to get his fingers on her property. He's aiming to get a seat in the royal court, Jack. He'd do much more than get rid of a little girl too young to run her dead father's estates."

As if agreeing, Jack nodded. "Still, seems unfair," he mused. "The girl's too young for the gallows. You could sentence her to a life in a nunnery and the result for the lord would be the same."

"The guy's paying for my roast duck. He gets whatever sentence he wants."

Not knowing why he argued—he would get Luca out of her cell before nightfall no matter what sentence was spoken—Jack decided to challenge the judge. "You could have refused," he said, throwing an arm over the back of his bench and putting his wooden leg on the seat before him. "There was a time when you spoke law, Federico, and anyone who tried to bribe you ended up in the Main Dungeons."

Grunting and with cracking joints, Federico heaved himself into a standing position. He emptied his mug and belched. "Can't remember those times," he murmured. "Was before my wife died and my daughter. Did I tell you I had refused a generous bribe just the day before they were both run over by a riderless carriage? My wife was dead immediately. My daughter lived for another three days, screaming all the time and begging me to heal her. Never refused any offer since, Jack. I've got a sister, and I've got two nephews. My father is still alive too. I don't care for law anymore as long as my family is safe."

Step by step—and slowly, for he was a heavy man—the judge got up and made his way through the benches, pushing some out of his way where his girth wouldn't get through. Groaning, he went to his chair behind the one table in the room, poured himself a fresh mug of ale, sniffed at the plate a servant had put in front of him, and began to eat.

Jack didn't move. He waited for the trial to begin, glad he knew Penny and that she had agreed already to look the other direction when he'd smuggle Luca out of the prison. "Death sentence," he murmured. "Greedy bastard. Guess I have to pay Lord Barnard a visit once this is over."

NOT BOTHERING to knock—this was a damn prison, by the Lady's tits!—Lord Barnard burst into Luca's cell, and from the look the girl gave him he pretty well guessed she would have tried to strangle him if the guard hadn't stood between her and him.

"Good day," she said, her voice alone making the small hairs at Barnard's neck stand up. Her smile was false, her words dripping with venom. "How thoughtful of you to visit me. I heard you bribed the judge. Pray tell, will I get beheaded or hanged tonight?"

It wasn't often Lord Barnard was taken by surprise, but Luca's words caught him totally off guard or he would have been able to school his expression in time. As it was, his mouth went slack and he said, "How do you—" before reining himself in.

His left hand went straight to the dagger at his side. "Damn little bitch," he hissed. "You. Guard. Get out of here. I've got some private matters to discuss with that b—the lady."

Anika took a step backward. The moment Lord Barnard had busted into the room, she'd grabbed her lance. Now she lowered it, a slight, but clear warning to Barnard not to come closer. "Can't do that, lord. The prisoner is my responsibility. You can only talk to her in my presence."

One of the first things every guard learned was how to bully people, and Barnard was well aware of that. The guard at hand was young, but she was also big, and he guessed she'd had her share of insults since she was fat and ugly on top of it. He guessed that bullying people into what she wanted them to do instead of accepting their jokes about her looks and her figure and her lack of intelligence had come quite naturally to her, judging by her dangerous looks and the way she held the lance.

He decided not to risk pulling his dagger.

"I've got the right to talk to her in private," he bit out. "Before the trial. It's a simple enough request."

The guard glanced at Lucinda. "Do you wish to speak to Lord Barnard alone, miss?"

"Only if you bind him and then stab him with your lance. Through his heart, preferably."

The guard shrugged. "I take that as a no. Sorry, lord."

"You'll be dead by sunset," Lord Barnard hissed. "I just came to see if there was anything I could do for you. Inform friends of your misfortune, relatives… anyone?"

"You know I do not have relatives, and very few friends. You came here to see me broken, to have me beg for my life. You wanted to dwell in my fear and you know what? Fuck off. The sight of you makes me sick."

"Dead. By sunset, you're dead, and I will get your land and your cattle, and I will sleep in your bed and eat what's been stored in your cellars. I might make you sick, but it is me who will win." Spittle flew from Barnard's lips and landed in the damn bitch's face.

Served her right, only she didn't even twitch.

He stared at her and then, without another word, turned and stormed out of the room.

The last word he heard was when she called, "Asshole" after him.

She would hang. Tonight, he would watch her die, and then he would celebrate, and then he would claim her body, take it home, and burn it.

"CASE THREE of today's cases. Lord Barnard accusing Lucinda of Babylon of having murdered her father, Lucius of Babylon. How do you plead?" Pen ready, the scribe focused on the prisoner.

"Not guilty," the prisoner said, and the scribe wrote down her words.

Judge Federico stopped chewing. Not much was left of the roast duck he'd had for lunch, but chewing took his mind off the task at hand. "Not guilty, eh? What a surprise. Can you prove you're not guilty of killing the man?"

Federico sighed. No one was ever able to prove not having done something. Gave him the perfect reason to sentence them as he'd been bribed to.

This prisoner didn't get intimidated that easily. Maybe it was because she was so young and thus unaware of what he could do to her. Maybe it was because she wasn't from the city and hoped there was something like honesty and respect or even honor left in the judge.

Most likely, she was just stupid.

Whatever she was, the prisoner stood up a little straighter, looked at him evenly, and replied, "When my father was killed, I wasn't anywhere near Babylon Manor. I have two witnesses to this fact. If you'd allow me—"

Federico silenced her with a wave of his hand. His fingers left greasy stains on the parchment when he leafed through the documents of her file. "There's nothing about any witnesses."

"Because no one asked me my side of the story before now. Of course you don't know about them!"

Federico disliked getting shouted at. But he only sighed and took a sip of beer. "Can you present those witnesses?" he asked, causing several people in the audience, including Lord Barnard, to gasp.

"Not at the moment. If you'd allow me—"

"No witnesses present. Anything else that might prove your absence from the manor at the time of the victim's death?"

"Look, you fat cockroach, if you think you can sentence me to death only because that ratty little ferret has bribed you with a duck, and if you think I will let you do it without telling you what really happened, you're totally mistaken."

After a few shocked gasps, a bit of an outraged murmur by the elderly couple, and a few giggles, only Federico's breathing could be heard in the room. About to nibble on a bone with a bit of flesh left, he dropped it onto the desk and wiped his fingers on his robe. "Fat cockroach, eh? Interesting point. Haven't had a look in a mirror in some years, but I guess you're right."

His daughter would be just a little younger than this girl, had she lived.

"Anyway, as you can't prove anything apart from being impolite, I'll hereby judge you to death for murdering your father, Lucius of Babylon."

Luca rolled her eyes. "You can't do that. Not without proof I have done it. Not just because someone bribed you to do it. This here"—she gestured at him, the audience, and the guards—"is ridiculous."

Again, Federico sighed. "Ridiculous or not, I can do what I please, young lady. Any requests concerning time or method of death?" Expectantly, Federico looked at Lord Barnard, who stood up in a smooth move. He had an uneasy feeling somewhere deep down in his guts, but then, it was probably just the duck. Or the pancakes.

"Immediate death," Barnard said smugly. "And as there are no living relatives and I am the nearest neighbor, I request her house and land to go into my possession the moment she dies."

Luca shot up from her seat. "In your dreams, you bastard! My house and land will go to the sisters of the Lady, namely one Sister Laure and her nunnery. You won't lay a hand on anything that belongs to me!"

"She is a minor and cannot make decisions on manor or land. She should be taken to the gallows directly, I say." Barnard sat, chin raised, eyes blinking frantically.

Federico looked out the window, wishing he was anywhere but this courtroom. Today's last case got on his nerves, he had to admit. Maybe it was because he'd talked to that old rascal Jack and had been reminded of how old and disgusting he'd become. Maybe it was because he was thinking of his daughter, who had been just as blonde as the young girl standing to be sentenced. There was fire hidden behind her quite nice features.

But right now, he could see fear in her expression, for the first time since she'd entered his courtroom. As he was the only one sitting higher than the prisoners, he was the only one who could see over the chest-high barrier that surrounded her. It was for her protection as well as for the audience's. It didn't happen often, but in the past, a convict occasionally had a go at the one who'd brought him to court or a relative tried to attack the convict.

Fear. Interesting.

Federico took another gulp of beer. It wasn't often he got surprised nowadays, being usually just drunk enough to make it through the trial before waddling back home and surrendering to sleep. Today, he hadn't drunk that much, though, and he'd seen what surely no one had been supposed to see. But she'd reacted on instinct at Lord Barnard's request of immediate execution, her fear and her youth taking over for one brief moment. The mask of arrogance had dropped.

And her hands had flown to her belly.

Thoughtfully, Federico wiped the beer foam off his upper lip. "Granted," he said, and belched. "House and land are to become the property of Lord Barnard after the execution of Lucinda of Babylon."

"They're to go to the sisters of the Lady!"

Federico shook his head. "You're not of age yet. Thus, you cannot have a will, at least not one that would stand legal attention. Get a grip, girl. Does it matter who gets your stuff once you're dead?"

Barnard grinned from ear to ear. It made him want to vomit, preferably right on the little ferret's greasy head.

For the third time, the judge sighed. The taste of beer in his mouth turned foul, and the roast duck along with the sprouts lay heavy as stone in his stomach. He'd seen so many prisoners, had sentenced so many to death that he could read the minds of most of them like an open book. He knew when they were lying, he knew when they were hiding their true motivations, and he always knew when they were fearing for someone else but themselves.

The girl told the truth, of course. She hadn't killed her father, and she was genuinely angry at him for him not being willing to judge fairly. Someone, probably one of the guards, had told her about the bribery. It was no secret; it was why his verdicts were never a surprise.

This girl knew she would die, she fought for her rights—not that she had any—and at Barnard's request to have her hanged right now, her eyes had dashed to the audience, pleading for help.

Her hands on her belly. A telltale sign for anyone smart enough to look. She was with child.

Knowing he'd sent an underage, pregnant girl to the gallows… now that would surely be reason to drink himself to death.

Chewing on a bit of meat he'd found stuck between his teeth, Federico put his double chin to his hand and looked at the girl, wracking his mind for how to do something honorable for a change and still keep his family safe. His daughter had been killed, and his wife had been killed because he'd refused to take a bribe. Barnard had bribed him. He'd accepted it.

Now what?

In the background of the room, he saw a shadow. And he knew what to do. It was easy. All he had to do was get the girl back into her cell. For truly, why else would Jack be here if not for the girl?

Apparently, his brain wasn't totally dead yet. In a way, Federico was even proud of his conclusion. "Now let's see," he continued, only dimly aware he'd pondered for several minutes on the problem at hand. "Immediate execution. The gallows. Hmmm. Tricky." He flicked through the sheets lying in front of him. "Hanging is out of the question. Booked out until end of year. Beheading… maybe…. No. Too many criminals, too many death sentences, and not enough help with the more dirty deeds of jurisdiction. Ah. Here. We'll burn you to death, I think."

Lord Barnard rubbed his hands. He was practically dribbling with excitement.

The girl's color changed from merely pale to an unhealthy gray-green.

"Burning is a nasty death," Federico clarified, focusing his sunken eyes on the girl. "It is well deserved for someone who's killed one's own father, even if this someone is as young as you are. Anyway, and as much as I would have liked to grant Lord Barnard's second request as well, the fulfillment of the verdict has to wait until Corporal Teneras can fit you in. So you'll be held in Well Prison for another three days, then taken to the marketplace, bound to the stake, and left there until your body has turned to ashes."

Briefly, the scribe looked up. A drop of ink hit the parchment. Federico knew what he was thinking: that it was unheard of for judge Federico not to do what he'd been asked. If he ordered someone hanged immediately, it was done immediately no matter what the executioner's time schedule said.

"No!" Lord Barnard shouted. "She's got to be hanged today! Now!"

"She'll be burned when we have the time and the resources to burn her," Federico said icily. "Shut your mouth, lord, if you don't want to spend a fortnight in the Main Dungeons for insulting a judge. I am certain you can wait for another three days."

Lord Barnard didn't seem to know when to stop. "She called you a fat cockroach, and you want to sentence *me* for insulting you?"

"Ten Talents fine for insolent speech."

Barnard opened his mouth to object—and then he stopped himself. "Three more days," he bit out. "Fine."

Federico waved to one of the guards to bring him a new jug of beer. Satisfied, he stroked his hands across his massive stomach and flashed Luca a quick, barely recognizable smile.

A heartbeat passed; then she smiled back.

TIME TO leave. The guard was already taking Luca's arm, about to take her back to the cell. Jack got his stick and was already halfway to the door when something unexpected happened.

A monk entered the courtroom, carrying a roll of parchment. He would have looked like a messenger boy if not for his age.

"Wulfric," Jack hissed under his breath; his hand tightened around the stick's head.

The small monk hopped to the judge's desk and placed the parchment next to the plate that held the duck's remains. "Just a wee little moment, if you please," he piped up, and Judge Federico had to get up to as much as see him.

"What d'you want? Trial's over. Verdict's spoken. Whatever it is, you're too late. Guards, take the prisoner back to the cell."

"Ah, no," Wulfric said. "See, I have new information on the girl. I need to ask her a few questions. Won't take long. And in case you intend to decline my request, this parchment here bears Princess Kayla's signature, permitting me to overrule your judgment and your verdict as well if necessary."

Heavily, Judge Federico fell back into his chair. "Princess Kayla? What in the Lady's name would she want with the girl? She's no one."

Brother Wulfric giggled. "I hoped you'd ask. See, this girl, this Lucinda of Babylon, is not as innocent as she looks. We've learned she's married. Is that not true?" He spun around, looking at Luca. When she didn't answer, he giggled some more. "No use denying it. Smart move, not to mention your husband to the court. He is, after all, a known assassin and you, if I remember correctly, are accused of murder. He might have helped you?" Nodding several times, he continued, "Anyway. Your husband confessed practically everything, even what I didn't want to know. You are married to one Brian of Wivenhoe, better known as Rage. You also carry his child. The man has been accused of killing Prince Leon last night. Maybe you had a hand in planning this crime. You need to be questioned more thoroughly. Can you follow?" Expectantly, Wulfric looked around the courtroom, seeing nothing but shocked faces.

"Fine. I'll take her with me now. Brought my own guards. Don't worry, Federico. This young girl here will get judged by Princess Kayla herself. The original verdict is hereby postponed. Young lady, please step down so you can be taken away."

Cheerfully, he clapped his hands, looking like a misbuilt child about to kill his favorite pet.

Two guards grabbed Luca's arms and pulled her down from her pedestal. It spoke of her shock that she looked up to Judge Federico for help.

He just lifted his shoulders. There was nothing he could do, not when a member of the royal family had decided to overrule him.

"Damn," Jack murmured. In a matter of moments, the day had turned from slightly awkward to utterly horrible. Luca was about to be taken to the princess. There was no way he would be able to get anywhere near her.

Jack gritted his teeth, the knuckles of the hand holding his walking stick turning white. Rage wouldn't kill a child. His cub had taken on a job, and he'd been tricked. And caught. Given the information the little monk had spilled so carelessly, Rage had been tortured as well.

Maybe he was already dead.

Jack watched as Federico waddled out of the courtroom, and he watched as the monk's two guards escorted Luca out. One by one, the audience disappeared until no one was left but him.

Leaning on his walking stick, Jack watched the shadows getting chased by the sun and wondered what he should do now and who to save first.

CHAPTER
Fourteen

A BIT more than twelve hours before Luca was escorted out of Well Prison, Rage was being dragged to the Main Dungeons underneath the palace. Limply, he hung between the guards, partly because of the blow he'd received to his head, partly to make clear how very harmless he was.

He waited for an opportunity to escape.

But there wasn't one, and even if there had been, Wulfric was close at their heels, making sure his prisoner didn't vanish from under his guards' noses.

The carpets and the tapestries were replaced first by wooden planks and dusty pictures and eventually by stones. Torches lit the way downstairs, and the smell of water and blood became more and more dominant. Water from the nearby river; blood from the nearby prisoners.

Last time Rage had been down here, it had been of his own accord and because he'd been paid a good amount of money. It had taken him more than two days to find a way in and less than half an hour to get out once his task had been completed. Back then, no one had seen him or even suspected his target's death was anything but natural.

This time, it was unlikely he would get out at all.

When the guards threw him into a cell, he forced himself not to slow his fall and landed hard on his knees and left shoulder, his face scratching across the stones. He wanted them to turn and leave without chaining his hands to the block in the middle—were he bound, the chances of escaping would sink to zero.

Neither guard moved to get chains. They just stood there, waiting, whilst Rage lay on the ground, also waiting.

In the next cell, someone groaned with pain.

"If you'd let me pass, please," Wulfric said, waiting until the guards stepped aside from the door so he didn't have to squeeze through. "I need a word with him before we begin."

The small monk crouched next to Rage, patting his shoulder as if to get his attention. "So sorry for this, dear boy," he said, not sounding sorry at all. Excited, yes, and expectant. But not sorry. "You see, what we need is for you to confess you killed Prince Leon. If you do that, you can spare yourself the torture."

Rage rolled over, pushing himself into a half-sitting position. "I killed Prince Leon," he said. "As you know. You're part of this, Wulfric. And you're a liar."

A hurt look crossed the monk's face. "Ah, how nasty of you to come up with such horrible lies. I rarely lie, and if I do, then only for good reasons." He sighed. "It seems we have to torture you. Pity. The poor wards will have to clean up this cell afterwards. It is always such a nuisance, scrubbing the blood off the stones, and they dislike doing it so much." To the guards, he said, "You'll be needing the whip and a jug of water, please. Hopefully, this won't take us too long. For a man my age, getting to bed after midnight is sheer agony. I beg you to wake me up if I happen to doze off. Sleeping on stones is even worse than not sleeping at all." He got up, his knees cracking when he stretched.

Rage made his move the moment Wulfric turned to the guards. He'd hoped to have more time. If they'd left him alone for a few hours, and if they'd believed him too far gone to chain him, it would have been easy to break out of the cell and the dungeons. But Wulfric was too eager to end this and clearly unwilling to wait even until morning. Trying something, anything now was Rage's only chance. If he didn't use it, if he didn't make it out now, he would be dead.

At least they'd left the door open.

Straw and sawdust covered the stones; Rage got a good grip, jumped up, and threw two fistfuls of dirt at the guards. Both were hit directly, coughed, and swore. By the time they'd wiped their faces, Rage was already out of the cell.

Compared to North Prison and even Well Prison, the Main Dungeons were small. The cells were arranged around a single square room, two cells at each side counting up to eight cells in all. The main room held a table and some chairs for the guards to sit, eat and drink, and take a rest between jobs. A narrow stairway led to the privy; a second one led upstairs where suspects got dragged in and the dead carried out.

Rage was at the door to the stairway leading outside in just a few steps. It wasn't locked—after all, the guards had dragged him downstairs only minutes ago—and the stairs were steep and slippery. The torches were flickering, shedding only feeble light. It didn't bother him since he knew where to go and where the loose step was, the one that would make a man trip and fall were he to stand on it with his full weight. Last time he'd been here, he had paid attention to the details.

He'd get out of here alive, after all.

More curses behind him as he scurried upstairs. The guards were at his heels, but they were too far behind to be able to catch him. And the ones at the other end wouldn't expect someone to burst through the door at full speed. He'd be out of here in another few moments.

Stop!

The silent order hit him right beneath his shoulder blades, turned his spine to cobwebs and his legs to jelly. In between steps, he lost control of his body, stumbled, and fell downstairs, a disturbing and painful experience, even more so as he couldn't even move his arms to slow his crash. Twice, he hit his head against the walls. The old bruises along his ribcage weren't healed yet; when Rage hit the bottom of the staircase, it felt as if he'd broken the same set of ribs that got cracked in the mountains.

Footsteps: two sets in heavy boots, one in sandals. Rage got a close look at old leather, expecting a blow to his face or stomach at any moment. He tasted blood on his tongue mixed with sawdust. Back where he'd started. And he'd been so close to the upper door.

Wulfric bent to pat his shoulder. "So sorry, my dear boy. I am, of course, aware of how badly you want to get out of here. But I couldn't let it happen, could I? Of course not. Chain him to the block, please, will you? He'll try to escape again or fight alternatively. I won't have either. Not until I am done with him, anyway."

The guards took his arms and took him back into the cell.

Even lifting his head was impossible. As if his body didn't belong to him anymore, Rage had to watch helplessly as his feet dragged across the floor, as his hands got chained, as the guards stepped aside and let the little monk step in.

He tried to talk, but couldn't.

"The effect of my little magic will cease in another minute or so," Wulfric said as if he'd read his thoughts. Probably, Rage's bewilderment was written all over his face.

Conspiratorially, Wulfric whispered, "A bit of black magic, you know," and suddenly, Rage could move again. Jerking his head up, he tried to free his hands, a futile attempt but one born out of instinct. He had to try, or rather his body had to make sure he could get up at least in theory if only the chains hadn't held him down.

Wulfric held his fingers right in front of Rage's nose. Rubbing them, he said, "See, your blood is on my fingertips. A few drops from a small wound on your face. I agree that it is not much blood but certainly enough."

Wulfric's fingers were only inches away from his eyes.

"Blood magic," Wulfric whispered. "Bad, bad magic. I use it only in emergencies. Of course, I'm not supposed to do it, and the empress would be very cross with me if she knew, but well, I won't tell her, and you won't either."

"Bastard," Rage croaked, mainly to test his voice. Kneeling in front of the wooden block with his hands chained to the ring on top wasn't the most comfortable position, and the prospect of what lay ahead didn't really lighten his spirits. He wasn't fond of torture, neither the giving and definitely not the receiving part.

Movement behind him. When Rage turned his head, he saw one of the guards had taken a whip from the wall. Other instruments hung there too—knives, swords, an ax. A bucket with water stood on the floor, and in the corner, there was a chair.

Seemed this would become a long night.

"Now what?" he croaked. As long as Wulfric talked, the whip might stay in the guard's hand, unused.

Wulfric took the chair, dragged it a bit closer to the block in the middle of the cell, and sat down. He folded his hands; he crossed his feet at the ankles. He looked like a polite old lady waiting to be served a cup of tea.

"You'll tell me why you killed the little prince," he said and smiled.

Rage raised an eyebrow. "I killed him because the empress asked me to do it. You know that. You were there."

Wulfric laughed. "I know everything. Well. Most things. But that is not the point. Asking questions is part of the game. I ask, and you refuse to answer. My wonderful guards will inflict pain. Eventually, your resistance will break, and you will tell me the few things I don't know yet."

Rage forced his lips into a friendly smile. "No need for that, monk. I'm quite sick of being in pain already. Ask, and I will answer."

The whip in the guard's hand unfolded. Its tip brushed the floor.

Sadly, Wulfric shook his head. "It doesn't work that way. Pain is an immanent part of this. So tell me: why did you kill the little prince?"

Rage's muscles tightened when he heard the guard change position, stepping behind him. The other one was at the cell's exit, closing and locking the door.

No way out of here anymore.

"He was tired of living," Rage said, trying to brace himself, trying to anticipate how hard the first blow would be but failing. He always failed. The pain was always worse than he thought it could possibly be, his body was always shocked at the fact it just had to endure it, and his mind always screamed at him to find a way to safety.

With a wet slap, the whip connected with his back, slashing the fabric of his shirt and leaving a bloody welt in his flesh.

It was a good whip, and wielded by a professional. Another few blows and he'd scream. But not yet.

More quickly than a man his age should be able to move, the little monk was up from his chair and next to Rage. He touched his shoulder; he dipped a finger into the fresh wound. "Wonderful. I'm always fascinated by how easily human flesh can be destroyed. From my time in the Forbidden Monastery, I remember a girl, quite young and kind of pretty. Her eyes were marvelous, a deep green one doesn't see often. Of course, my stupid brothers had nothing better to do than destroy her the moment she came to us instead of using her magic to strengthen our home. Benjamin especially hated the way she cried, and so he pressed his thumbs into her eyes, crushing them like grapes. One moment, she was gorgeous, the next, she was blind. So feeble humans are. Like butterflies, helpless and weak."

"Her name was Luisa," Rage said, shifting his shoulders to get away from Wulfric's fingers still stroking his back. In vain. The pain hummed through him; he knew it was only the beginning. "Met her father. You're a well-hated man, Wulfric."

"Oh yes, definitely." The little monk nodded eagerly. Then he frowned. "What do you mean, you met her father?"

The second and third slap landed on Rage's back, unexpected and harder than the first. He had to grit his teeth to prevent a groan. "Ryan," he bit out. "Expect him to come after you one day, monk."

Rage didn't see if Wulfric nodded again, but he felt the whip on his back, blow after blow. A steady rhythm; precise movements.

He began screaming when his back turned to a mass of bloodied flesh. Slumping over the block, he embraced the wood as best as he could with his chained hands—it helped him to keep control; it helped him not to lose his mind. At least not yet.

It wasn't the first time he'd been in pain, not by far. It wasn't even the first time he'd been imprisoned. But torture he had managed to avoid so far. Only once before had he been bound, caught by a bunch of outlaws who'd wanted him to tell them where his treasure was hidden. Explaining to them there was no treasure had been useless and killing them a dirty mess given there had been five of them. Still, he'd managed to survive, and he'd managed it before they'd decided what to do with him.

He'd survive this here too.

The whipping stopped as suddenly as it had started. Rage's last scream hung in the air, ringing in his own ears, and he felt blood trickling down his sides and seeping into the fabric of his trousers. *Need new clothes. Again,* he thought and, *Jack will be angry.*

"Tell me your name," Wulfric said into his ear. "Your real name, dear boy, not the name you've adopted. Will you tell me your name?"

"No," Rage rasped. Talking was strenuous, and he needed his strength to withstand the pain.

"But I want to know it!" Wulfric seemed genuinely offended by his refusal.

"Rage."

"No, no, no. Your mother didn't name you Rage, did she? Silly name for a newborn."

The whip whispered across the floor, disturbing the sawdust. Rage saw his blood soiling the floor; the sight made him sick. There would be more blood soon, and if he was unlucky, body parts as well.

He would have thought meeting one sadistic bastard in his life was enough, but two? Meeting two of them in less than half a year was utterly unfair.

Rage tried to suppress the cough that wanted to escape him and failed. Coughing tore at the wounds on his back; his knuckles went white when his fingers clutched at the chain.

Wulfric dropped to his knees right in front of him. His eyes behind his glasses were big and eager, and he looked so friendly and concerned Rage felt hope blossoming up inside him. Surely Wulfric wouldn't cause him any more pain?

He hated himself for his treacherous emotions, wishing the chain was long enough to wind it around Wulfric's birdlike neck and strangle him to death.

"Please tell me your name," the little monk whispered, putting his hands above Rage's. Squeezing; soothing. "It's important!"

"No."

"Ah, dear boy, you don't make this easy for me. Would you believe this is even harder for me—and more painful—than it is for you?"

Wulfric's hands were warm and comforting; so were his words.

When Rage didn't answer, Wulfric sighed. "Fine. Remember, you asked for this."

His grip tightened. His face was only inches away from Rage's, close enough for a kiss, close enough for Rage to catch the scent of the monk's skin: dry, pale, harmless.

Involuntarily, Rage relaxed, only a bit and only for a heartbeat—the pain was bearable, the guard had taken a step back, and he could breathe without fear of another blow.

It was a mistake. Touching Rage's cheek once more, a drop of blood, tiny and clotted, on his fingertip, Wulfric stepped inside his mind as easily as if he were stepping through an open door.

It hurt worse than the whipping; it hurt worse than anything Rage had ever experienced, and on top of it, the feeling of a strange awareness amidst his own thoughts was so deeply disgusting it made him retch.

Wrong. Intrusion. Danger. Run! his mind screamed.

"Too late, dear boy," Wulfric murmured. "Now let's find your name, shall we? It's always best, starting with the name."

Rage tried to fight but didn't know how. This was beyond anything he'd ever experienced, and he couldn't have described it had he been asked. All he could do was try to jerk his head out of Wulfric's grip.

The guard stepped behind him and put his hands to Rage's temples, holding him in position. Compared to the foreign mind inside his head, the guard's touch was tender.

Wulfric murmured constantly, his fingertips brushing over Rage's lips, his cheeks, eyes, his hair and throat. Inside his head, Rage could feel the monk, touching his thoughts, brushing over emotions, fears, hopes only to finally scan through his memories as easily as leafing through a book.

Disgust. Hate. Panic.

"Brian? That you, dear boy? Yes, that's how your mother named you. And Rage… I see your big sister came up with it. Cute. It fits you perfectly."

Just a bit of space to move his hands, and only about an inch or two. Wulfric had loosened his grip on his hands, so Rage took the opportunity to grab the monk's collar. "Get out… of my head," he rasped, and then his hands cramped, his body cramped, and he buckled over, retching and bleeding. Wulfric let go of him, jumping back when he spat into the straw again, nothing but a bit of blood and a bit of spittle because—what a surprise—there wasn't enough in his stomach to throw it up.

The cramps held him in their grip for a minute or more, and all the while the three men in the cell watched him trying to regain control. They were silent; they didn't do anything, but at least they didn't hit him, nor did Wulfric invade his mind again.

"Feeling better?" the little monk finally asked when Rage hung over the block, exhausted and wishing he'd gone home with Keiran whilst he'd still had the chance. He was still kneeling, his hands folded neatly in his lap.

The question wasn't worth an answer. And anyway, he didn't have the breath for it.

"Born in Wivenhoe, raised by a blacksmith and a midwife. One sister. Did you kill them all?"

He didn't want to answer, but the alternative was Wulfric touching him again. So Rage nodded.

"I see. You know, had you been trained back then, had your parents bothered to send you to the city, to a proper school, you could have become one of the most powerful magicians in our world. More powerful than me, definitely. What a pity. You might have become one of the monks in the Forbidden Monastery, dear boy!"

Rage spat directly into his face.

"Oh my, maybe not, then," Wulfric said, wiping his face clean with the sleeve of his robe. "It is too late now, anyway. You're too old, and no school would as much as think about teaching someone as strong as you."

One guard to his left, one to his right, holding the whip. His hands chained to the block, his body weakened. His mind in agony, and all he could think about was escape.

"Something else I learned when I was inside your head," Wulfric continued cheerfully. "The boy—what's-his-name?—you do care for him. And you fear he will find you and come for you and get killed trying. I wonder, what makes you think he could do such an extraordinary thing? Finding you, that is. I mean, he doesn't know what's happening here. How could he even choose the right direction, never mind getting in here, especially"—and here he came close to Rage again for the first time since he'd broken contact—"especially, dear boy, after I have warded this cell with magic, keeping us inside and every prying eye or mind or ear outside? You need not worry. Not about your lover, anyway."

There was a heavily faked sadness in the monk's voice, mixed with barely concealed joy.

Rage coughed; blood spattered to the ground. "Been through worse," he said hoarsely.

Brother Wulfric shook a finger at him. "Liar. True, you've suffered pain before. But—*but*, dear boy!—you've never been tortured before, not by city guards, not by anyone who knows what he's doing. This here is new to you, and your magic, trapped inside you, doesn't like it. And what happens when magic cannot cope with a new situation? It tries to break free. You'll lose control, and your magic will lash out. Wild, powerful magic. Ah, you have no idea how much I am looking forward to this!"

"If that happens, you'll be dead." Back to talking. Better than getting whipped, and much better than having his mind raped by that fucking little bastard.

Brother Wulfric, lifting his cowl a bit so as not to get the hem soiled by blood, patted Rage's shoulder. "Don't you worry, dear boy. It will happen. You keep control over your magic, usually. Not in bed, but then, this is not bed. It is, though, an extreme situation. And extreme situations… well, they are special."

Get closer, and I'll break your neck, Rage thought.

But Wulfric stepped out of reach again. "I think we are done with whipping," he said, slumping onto the chair again. "It was but a test, nothing more than warming up for the subject. Let's see. What else do I want to know? What else could I ask?"

One guard put his hand on Rage's shoulder, awaiting orders. The other one took a shovel and swiped up the soiled straw around the block, spreading out fresh sawdust and new stalks. All clean. All ready for the next round.

For the first time since they'd dragged him into the cell, Rage considered the possibility of getting killed down here. It was an unfamiliar thought. Death happened to other people. Death was what he brought, not received.

I won't let that bastard win.

Something to hang on to. Good. He could think about dying later.

Wulfric, fingering his nose as if he needed to confirm it was still sitting in the middle of his face, looked at him. His eyes were twinkling, and he smiled. "Tell me about the girl, dear boy. Lucinda. Luca, as you call her. What is she to you?"

"She killed her father. I like her for obvious reasons."

"She hasn't killed anyone, I think. Of course, I haven't met her, so I don't know for sure, but Lord Barnard is greedy, he's nasty, and he'd accuse his own mother of murder if it would earn him her jewelry. The girl. Why do you travel with her?"

The guard's hands locked around his throat—he couldn't answer although he desperately wanted to. Anything was better than—

Wulfric nodded his approval, and the man's grip tightened. Simultaneously, the little monk put a fingertip to Rage's nose, playfully, mockingly, and intruded into his mind even more easily than the first time.

It was like cold slime filling his brain, bringing with it pain, panic, and humiliation. Tears streamed down Rage's cheeks, but he was only dimly aware of them—impossible to say which was worse, suffocating or the monk rummaging inside his head as if it were an old trunk filled with worthless trinkets.

Weakly, Rage struggled; triumphantly, Wulfric smiled. The guard dug his finger deeper into Rage's throat whilst his colleague put a lance between Rage's shoulder blades, preventing him from as much as trying to get up.

Air!

"Married? Dear boy, how fascinating!"

Enough!

Close to unconsciousness and filled with the panic brought on by near death, Rage brought his hands up, breaking the chains in the process. The lance's head cut deep into his flesh, but it was unimportant. He was dying, he needed to breathe, and so his magic lashed out just as predicted by Wulfric. The lance broke. The wooden block broke, and Rage slammed into the sawdust, half-blinded by blood and tears and gasping for breath. He badly wished he could roll up and clutch at his head, trying to protect what little was left of his mind.

Instead, he jumped, grabbed Wulfric with his still chained hands, and took him down.

Rage screamed, harsh and deep, whilst feeling his magic slip out of control. To the whip wounds on his back were added fresh ones, slashed by the power surging through his already beaten body. Like before, his magic harmed not only the ones around him, it also harmed its owner.

Wild magic roared. The guard who'd been about to kill him crumpled to the floor whilst the other one stood rooted to the spot, staring at his broken lance.

Rage didn't think, he just acted, following his magic's orders. *Kill him*, it said. *Kill him and then get out of here.*

Wulfric's glasses slipped off his nose, fell, and broke. His eyes bulged, both from surprise and lack of air.

Pity Rage's magic was uncontrollable, or he might have managed to flee the prison. It was too strong to be handled, too unpredictable, and it let him down the very moment he needed it most. Instead of keeping Rage in its grip, directing his movements, it first wavered, then exploded into a million pieces.

He'd die first, then the guards, then Wulfric. Eventually, everyone in the prison would die, people who lived close to the palace, the empress and her daughter and the hundreds of servants sleeping in their beds above the dungeons.

So what? Rage thought, about to break Wulfric's neck. Blood dropped from his eyes into the little monk's face.

Wulfric's lips moved, but no sound came out. His hand, small as a child's, swayed into Rage's range of vision.

Then Wulfric *touched* him. Not his face, not the tip of his nose. Not even his mind; he touched his soul, weaving a net, and he caught the assassin's magic like a fisherman catches a school of fish. It was still not caged; it was still dangerous. But it was not free, either.

It felt like being touched by frozen fire, burning him and freezing him at the same time.

"See how easy it is?" Wulfric whispered into his ear, and only then Rage realized he'd loosened his grip despite his plan to kill the monk. His palms, sweaty and soiled with his own blood, were pressed flat to the stone floor, to the left and right of Brother Wulfric's head.

Wulfric wriggled out from underneath him, patted the dust off his clothes, and sighed. "That's how it's done. That's how you keep your magic in check under any circumstances." He waggled a finger before Rage's eyes. "Try it!" Wulfric urged, "Try it yourself, dear boy!"

What? Rage wanted to ask, but Wulfric just showed him, somehow, in this impossible, too personal, too intimate way that was so much like rape and still so awfully tender. The monk took his soul and guided it, he showed him how to hold the net and how to pull, and then Rage understood, and he put his outraged, unwilling, uncontrollable magic in its cage and locked the door.

Just like that.

The contact broke. Wulfric let go of him, stepped back, and smiled. Rage was alone in his head again, and wondered why his face was wet and why he sat on the chair instead of hanging across the block.

His hands were bound, but with ropes. The chains lay on a heap on the ground, looking as if molten.

And the block was broken neatly in two. No one would get bound to it ever again. The only use it had was for firing the oven.

The guards stared at him somewhat uneasily. He must have done something to scare them, although he couldn't remember what it was.

"Extraordinary." Wulfric shuddered, a remarkable sight to anyone who knew him. "Here, drink something. You managed this a lot faster than I had anticipated. A few more inflictions of pain, and you'll be able to control your magic without help."

Rage blinked. "What?"

The little monk took a copper cup from the guard and held it to Rage's lips. The water was warm and stale, but it tasted like heaven.

Wulfric refilled the cup. This time, Rage kept the water in his mouth, rolling it about with his tongue and checking for loose teeth in the process. It was just one sip; the cup was small. He guessed it would be all he'd get for a while.

Folding his hands, pretending patience, Wulfric said, "If I asked you again about your relationship with the girl, would you answer me?"

"If I said no, would you get into my head again?" It was good to sit. His knees ached, and his back protested at the thought of swapping chair for floor. So a bit more talking, a bit more time, and hopefully, a few answers.

A faint expression of disgust crossed Wulfric's face. "Your head, dear boy, is not a pleasant place to visit. So… raw. Disorganized. Chaotic, one might call it. Usually, I learn everything there is to learn within a few seconds. I know all there is to know about the person's life, his past, even his future. Your head…." His voice trailed off, and he shuddered again. "I think I will stay out of it, at least for now. And I already know you are married to the girl. What I don't know is what she means to you. Why did you follow her into the city?"

"She saved my life. I owe her."

"Currently, she is in Well Prison, but I think you know that. In the morning, your friends will try and free her. I hope you won't be too angry with me if I prevent that from happening?" Idly, Wulfric turned the cup in his hands before throwing it away. One of the guards caught it, putting it back onto the shelf above the door. Neither he nor his colleague had said a single word so far. Either of them would kill him without hesitation if Wulfric ordered it.

"She's pregnant, isn't she? There was a hint of it hidden quite deep inside you. I just want to be sure."

The question came too quickly. Rage hadn't anticipated it, and so the monk could read from his narrowing eyes it was true.

"What just happened?" Rage asked, trying badly to change the subject. "You did something in my head. What and why?"

The taller guard picked up his broken lance. The other one, smaller but with wide shoulders and arms the size of barrels, was behind Rage in two steps.

Wulfric sighed. "I'm getting too old for this," he murmured. "I should have gone to bed hours ago. Hopefully, I will make it to Well Prison in time."

The guard smelled of unwashed clothes, beer, and sweat. His hands, larger than average, landed on Rage's neck.

Wulfric obviously wasn't in the mood for answering questions. "Break his shoulder," he said. "Slowly, if possible."

And again the little monk had managed to catch him by surprise. "Why—" Rage began, but Wulfric turned away, and the guard put pressure to his shoulder, pushed with one hand whilst pulling with his other and twisting his arm, and of course Rage screamed, pain roaring through his body, agony killing any words he might have wanted to say.

And his magic flared up.

Rage's heart raced along, pumping blood into his lungs and his brain so there would be enough oxygen for his muscles should he try to break free and for his brain to come up with a plan. Short, desperate intakes of breath between roars, his feet kicking, his hands trying to wring their way out of the ropes around his wrists

More pressure. More pain. Rage could hear the joint crack.

Too much pain.

Rage's shoulder broke with a dry little sound, loud even above his screams. His magic roared.

The net. The fishing net, he thought, and then Wulfric was next to him, whispering into his ear.

"I predicted you wouldn't like it, did I not?" he said, and his voice sounded so sad Rage wanted to laugh if only he'd have the strength for it. If only he wouldn't be busy with screaming.

"Did you believe me at the time? Of course you didn't. And now look at you. Alive, only marginally harmed, with this extraordinarily strong magic of yours tamed, and still I bet you hate me. You know, all I did was pay you as we agreed upon."

Nothing made sense and then—it was over because there was only so much pain a human could take. Rage passed out, his muscles becoming limp, his body slipping off the chair. He didn't feel it as he hit the ground, which was just as well because he hit it with his injured shoulder first.

CHAPTER
Fifteen

KEIRAN WATCHED the changing of the guards, trying to figure out how to lure one of them over so he could knock him out and steal his clothes. He needed boots and a coat. He needed a guard's sword and one of their helmets. He needed to look like them so they wouldn't notice him being a stranger, so he could get into the dungeons. Rage was down there, which meant *he* needed to get down there.

For more than an hour, he'd been pacing the small room. It felt as if he'd break through the planks soon given how badly they creaked. He was tired and hungry and nervous. Rage's flame in his mind was feeble and flickering, as if he was about to die any moment.

He wasn't dead, though. Not yet.

A plan. An idea. Anything, Keiran thought, slamming his palm against the doorframe.

The new set of guards didn't look any different from the ones before. Heavily armed, strong and alert. Experienced and deadly. None of them looked younger than thirty, and when Keiran observed that detail, he knew it would be impossible to just steal a sword and march in there simply because he was too young.

From the corner of his eye, he noticed that one man from the first shift was talking to a guard who seemed to be commander of the second shift. Occasionally, the commander nodded; once, she laughed. Eventually, the man said good-bye, and out of an impulse—and out of desperation—Keiran decided to follow him. After all, there was nothing he could do here but wait and pace and curse and not accomplish anything at all.

As casually as he could manage, Keiran stepped out the door, trying to look as if he'd merely inspected the house like someone who might be looking for a new home. Then he went in the same direction as the guard who had just turned the corner. It was easy—the man didn't look back, didn't walk fast, and as there weren't that many people around, Keiran could keep his distance without losing him.

Until the guard was gone, that was. One moment, he was there, but the next the street was empty apart from a few children playing with a three-legged dog.

Checking whether there was an open door somewhere or a street he'd overlooked, Keiran was just about to believe he'd messed this up when a hand grabbed him, pushing him against the house wall. The tip of a sword was aimed at his throat, and right there was the guard, a look of mild curiosity on his face. "You've been following me," he said. "Don't like it. Tell me your name, boy."

Keiran. I'm harmless.

The guard grinned. "I'm Lee. You didn't think you could rob me, did you?" He lowered his sword and relaxed, clearly believing Keiran was harmless.

Maybe he could be manipulated just as the people in the market had been.

"What do you want from me? You've got no sword. You are not from the city—why seek out a guard? You in trouble?" Sheathing his sword, the guard gestured Keiran to come along.

You're thirsty. It was a shot in the blue, but Keiran needed more time, and with a beer in front of him, the guard might be more willing to listen to him.

The guard frowned. "Fancy a beer? If there's something you wanna tell me, I need a drink first. Been on duty all night. Come with me. I know just the place."

He really believed the drink was his idea. Fascinating. Vaguely, Keiran wondered what else he could do with his new ability only to shy away from the thought. It was magic, after all. He wasn't used to using magic. Much more likely he'd truly mess this up if he weren't careful. So he followed the guard without any further suggestion, sat opposite him when they'd found a small bar, and took a generous sip from the beer the man placed in front of him. Anything to keep him happy and unsuspicious, although the beer was bitter and stale.

"So. Keiran. What do you want?" The guard wiped the foam off his lip, leaned back in his chair, and stretched out his legs. His ankle touched Keiran's; after a long moment, the guard grinned.

A rush of emotions—*desire. An offer; a question. Too many lonely nights. Admiration*—overwhelmed Keiran, originating from the guard and transferred through the brief contact. The man wasn't aware of it. It had happened subconsciously, it had happened fast, and suddenly Keiran knew how to get inside the prison.

Ever so slightly, he shifted his position. Not much, just enough to suggest interest.

I need a job. I've got no money. I've got no friends in the city. Any idea how to earn myself a bed and a meal?

The guard—Lee—half emptied his glass in one big gulp. He wasn't in the slightest surprised at the silence of his guest, nor that he managed to phrase his words without moving his lips. Maybe this ability was more common in the city. Or he just hadn't noticed yet.

"A job," Lee mused. "Not easy, nowadays. With war looming, people tend to save up as much money as they can, so it will be hard to find anyone willing to hire. You could sell your ass, I guess. Beautiful boy like you won't have any trouble finding customers. You'd be a rich man in a few weeks."

Careful now. It was all right if the guard believed him open for a bit of adventure, but also, he needed to make it clear working as a whore wasn't an option. Keiran put his glass down, shock on his face. Then he shook his head and placed his hand on the guard's arm to emphasize he could never sell himself.

I like you, he added, not directly this time as he'd asked about the job, but on a lower level, one the guard would feel rather than hear. It was terrifying how easy it was.

"On the other hand, it would be a pity to see you on the streets," Lee said. "Getting fucked a dozen times each day breaks you in a few months, at least here in the city where people can be brutal. Sometimes quicker." He didn't pull his arm away. His foot still touched Keiran's ankle. "Where you from? You any good at fighting? 'Cause the empress always needs soldiers."

I can handle a sword. A blatant lie, but what the hell. *Guarded my master's home and any prisoners he put in the cellar. Wouldn't have left if he hadn't died last winter.* Nearly the truth. *Being a soldier would be beyond my skills, I fear.*

There. Now the ball was in Lee's field, and hopefully he'd come to the right conclusion.

Maybe a little encouragement would be good.

Even if I found a job today, I'd still need a place to sleep. Keiran shrugged, his special smile suggesting he wouldn't mind sharing a bed.

Lee leaned across the table and put his hand on Keiran's neck, his thumb briefly touching his lips. "We can always do with guards in the dungeons." He sounded interested rather than doubtful. "Not a pleasant job, especially not when you're new. People scream a lot, and then they die. A newbie has to do all the cleaning and dispose of the corpses. Think you could do that?"

Yes.

Keiran could smell the beer on Lee's breath. The man wasn't bad looking, with strong hands and legs, wide shoulders, and the missing front tooth along with the scar from his chin down to his throat gave him an air of danger. He was demanding without being bullying, he was offering a job and a bed in exchange for a fuck, and if Keiran had been looking for real, he would have taken it without second thoughts.

Right now, he had to persuade the man he was really as desperate as he'd said so he wouldn't become suspicious. And he had to make sure Lee didn't try to drag him to bed immediately.

Keiran met the guard's eyes. He saw the invitation to leave the tavern—and smiled.

I'm hungry. And I want to work for my bread and bed. It was an answer as well as a subconscious suggestion.

As hoped, Lee nodded. "Fair enough. Come along, then. I'll take you to the guards' quarters, find some gear for you, and I'm sure there's some leftover breakfast. Last guy who applied was gone before the shift was over. Threw up the moment he saw a whipping. Hope you'll last longer."

There it was—suspicion. Subtle, and Keiran doubted Lee was aware of it yet, but it was there nevertheless.

Quickly, Keiran put some coins onto the table, the last ones he had and hopefully enough for the beer. *My treat. It is rare for someone to be so friendly to a stranger. Thank you. For the job, and for the bed. I won't disappoint you.* Casually, he leaned across the table and kissed the man, only briefly but with the promise of more. *You can trust me. I'm the one you were looking for.*

Lee stiffened but accepted the kiss. He pulled Keiran up, hugging him roughly, grabbing his ass and squeezing it once before letting him go. Keiran felt the kiss and the hug had made Lee half-hard. The promise in Keiran's eyes and the money on the table had wiped away any suspiciousness that might have been growing inside him. "Guess you'll do just fine," Lee said with a grin, and together, they left the bar and went back to the Main Dungeons.

LUNCHTIME WAS long gone before Keiran got anywhere near the cells, and then he did so with a bucket in his hand and the order to clean the cells. He'd got a sword, boots, and a coat, he'd got the helmet although he didn't have to wear it inside, he'd got bread and ham, and he'd got more attention than he needed. When Lee had introduced him, five guards had been in the room, three of them female and all grinning from ear to ear when he'd nodded hello. "Found yourself a toy, Lee?" one of the women asked.

One of the men added, "If he's too hairy for you, boy, I'll be glad to help you out. My bed's bigger than his, and so is my cock."

"Shut up, all of you." Lee grinned, clearly enjoying the bickering. "He's in need of a job. Kenny, go fetch him a sword and boots and a uniform. Can't go downstairs in what he's wearing. Ellen, tell him what to expect."

Ellen, a thin woman with short, spiky hair, patted the bench beside her. "Sit with me, gorgeous. I don't bite."

Keiran sat, accepted a mug with water and a piece of bread.

"Well, we've got the worst down here. The child killers, the rapists, the cold-blooded murderers. Scum, no matter their status within the city. Right now, we've got a baron who killed eight old ladies in five years. Took us a while to get the truth out of him, but eventually, he confessed."

"After you'd cut off his hands," Tam said, and they all laughed.

"The baron will get hanged tomorrow, so you'll need to take him his food and make sure he doesn't die tonight. And you'll have to clean his cell. Other than that, there's a woman who killed her two children so she could be with her lover, two brothers who used to rape the whores in East Corner Street and then beat the shit out of them, and… who else, Lee?"

Lee placed a casual hand on Keiran's shoulder. "The assassin. Killed Prince Leon last night. But you don't need to bother with him. The assassin has his own guards. Stay away from the first cell to the left, and all will be well. Only the baron looks a bit messed up, and maybe the brothers. They've been flogged. Gotta change the straw in their cells. Now finish your lunch, and Tam here will tell you about our routines and show you the privy as well as the dungeons. Any questions?"

Keiran lifted his shoulders. There was nothing he needed to ask now that he knew where Rage was.

"You're of the silent sort, eh?" Tam said, licking his lips. "I like that in a guy. Until it comes to screaming, of course."

"You can make a man scream only if he's bound and bleeding and you with a bat in your hand," Ellen said. "Come with me, Keiran. I'm sure he'd try to corner you the moment you're alone with him, and I don't want to hear him whine he's been rebuked again."

"Bitch!" Tam called after them, and there was laughter again and Lee's voice, and then the door fell shut, and Keiran and Ellen were on the staircase leading into the dungeons.

"He's a good man, Lee," she said. "But in case you're not only interested in guys, I'd like to invite you for a drink after shift. What do you say?"

They were just crossing the point where Rage had fallen some hours ago, stopped by brother Wulfric's silent command. Keiran didn't know that; however, when he trod on the stair, the hairs on his arm raised. Rage was near.

"Hey, you all right?" Ellen's eyes gleamed catlike in the candlelit darkness. "I know first time down here can be a bit shocking. You'll get used to it, promise. So what do you say to a drink after shift?"

Keiran nodded. If everything went as planned, he would be out of the city before sunset.

Ellen beamed, her long face lighting up. "Great."

At the bottom of the staircase, she took a key ring from her belt. One large and seven small keys; she took out one and opened the first cell to the right. "Our first customer," she said. "Woman, age thirty-one, name Penelope. Married for four years. Until a week ago, she had two children, a boy aged three and a newborn girl, five weeks old. No one knows why, but she killed them both by drowning them in the kitchen sink. Her husband thinks she's been having an affair and that the kids were in the way. He called the guards. We didn't have to torture her. She confessed the moment she saw the cells. All you have to do is clean her bucket, bring her food and water, and don't get moved by her tears."

A quick peek into the cell showed him a woman looking much older than her age. Tears were running down her face. She'd wrapped her arms around her middle and was rocking herself.

"She's faking," Ellen said and shut the door. "Guess she'll die a slow death once a judge sees her. Killing kids isn't something judges like here in the city."

Keiran just nodded. Ellen seemed keen on talking, so he decided to listen.

Ellen pointed to the cell opposite Penelope's. "That one is the cell of the assassin. The big key opens it, but you stay the hell out of there, understand? It's a special cell, warded by magic. We rarely use it. And the assassin is dangerous, although by now he's nothing but a bleeding mess."

Keiran went over to Rage's cell, drawn to it as if it were magnetic and he made out of metal. Pressing his hands to the cell's door, he listened, with his ears and his heart and his soul, hoping to get at least a small sign, something, anything…. But there was nothing. The cell could be empty for all he could tell.

Rage!

He didn't get an answer.

"What do you think you're doing there?"

Keiran spun round, seeing Ellen standing right behind him, hand on her sword's hilt, brow furrowed. "I told you to stay away from that cell. Now—"

Keiran touched her. Her sword was out of its sheath and halfway up to his throat when he told her, *Do not hurt me*—and it worked.

Ellen's face went blank. The sword wavered, but her arm didn't move, hanging forgotten between them.

I didn't go near that cell. Keiran closed his fingers around her wrist. The contact was intense, scary, and intimate to the level of becoming unpleasant.

"Let's take a look at the baron," Ellen said flatly. Her eyes looked right through him. "Glad you didn't go anywhere near the assassin's cell."

Sheath your sword.

She did as ordered, though slowly. She blinked once, stared at her empty hands, and frowned.

Take the keys and open the next cell.

Again, Ellen did as Keiran told her, and that was the moment he realized two things: he hated to give orders, and her obeying him just like that scared the shit out of him. This… ability, this new skill that had been forced on him had become strong within days and gotten out of hand in a matter of hours. And he had no idea what to do about it. This woman he'd never seen before today was like a puppet in his hands, and she didn't even try to fight.

He would have to think about this later. After Rage was safe. Until then, he would use his magic whenever he needed to.

Keiran took a step back, breaking contact with Ellen. He felt dizzy. Sweat was building up on his temples as if he'd done half a day of hard labor.

Ellen sneezed and dropped the key ring. "Damn," she muttered. "Must've caught a cold somehow. Right. Where was I?"

The baron.

However, once this was over he'd have to do some serious thinking about this. Maybe talk to someone who knew about magic.

Ellen picked up the keys and opened the baron's cell.

Keiran's stomach heaved at the sight inside, and he nearly threw up at the smell of illness. Soiled straw covered the floor. There was one torch shedding light onto the man chained to the wall. He didn't move when they came in, and he didn't flinch when Ellen knelt beside him.

"He's unconscious," she said after a moment. "Clean up in here, Keiran. Empty the bucket, spread out fresh straw, change the dressings. I've got to check on the brothers. The baron won't wake up, so you won't get any trouble from him."

Without awaiting an answer, she left the cell. Keiran noticed she kept her distance from him. She might have forgotten what had happened, but in a way, she didn't want to be near him anymore.

Keiran doubted she'd remind him about the drink.

Keiran saw no way he could get into Rage's cell without making her uneasiness worse. For now, she needed to believe he was harmless and eager, so he swept up the dirty straw and cleaned the floor and emptied the bucket. He even put a mug of water on the ground next to the unconscious man before he realized that the prisoner had no hands left to grab it.

Finally, he heard Ellen come back in, keys jangling in her hand. "You done here?" she asked, and he was relieved he couldn't hear any mistrust in her voice anymore.

Ten more minutes? He had yet to wash the blood off the walls.

"Can't wait that long. Not enough guards in today. Otherwise, I would send down someone to help you. Think you can manage on your own for a while?"

When Keiran couldn't keep the look of utter surprise from his face, Ellen grinned. Apparently, her suspicions were completely forgotten. "There's not much you can do wrong down here. All cells are locked apart from this one, and the baron wouldn't make it out of here even if his ankle chain became unlocked. All you have to do is finish the cleaning, then sit at the table over there and wait for the next shift. Two hours. What do you say?"

It was what Keiran had been hoping. Not nodding too eagerly was all he could muster so as not to make Ellen rethink her decision.

"Good. See you on the morrow."

Leave the keys on the table.

Keiran was breaking a sweat at the risk he was taking. Ellen sooner rather than later would wonder why the keys weren't on her belt; she might remember that there was something strange about the newbie; she might notice that he was fiddling with her mind and decide to kill him—but he did not have a choice if he wanted to save Rage.

Absently, Ellen dropped the keys on the table. A moment later, Keiran heard her steps on the stairs, fast, nearly running, and knew she was glad to be out of the dungeons and away from him.

CHAPTER
Sixteen

THE MOMENT Ellen was out of sight, Keiran snatched the keys and rushed to Rage's door. He rammed the key into the lock, turned it, and slammed his shoulder into it when it didn't open voluntarily.

Ellen would be halfway up the stairs by now.

Three, maybe four minutes. At the most.

The door gave in, opening with a creak. Leaving the key in the lock, Keiran stumbled inside.

Darkness greeted him. He hadn't brought a torch, so he had to push the door wide open, allowing the light from outside to stream in. It didn't reach the corners; it did, though, show him the heap on the stone floor, chained to the wall.

Rage.

Nothing but a whisper, mind to mind. Only there was no answer.

Rage didn't move. A blanket had been thrown over him. Keiran could make out a hand and half an arm, part of the shoulder and a foot.

Keiran knelt down next to his lover and touched him, expecting, fearing the coldness of a corpse would greet him.

Warmth, and breathing.

Rage! Urgent this time, and accompanied by a rough shake. Ellen would discover the missing keys any moment now.

Keys. They were still in the lock, although he needed to open the chains.

Keiran was about to jump up and get the keys when a hand locked around his wrist and an arm around his throat. It had happened too fast for him to as much as twitch; it also was proof Rage was neither unconscious nor dead.

Nor asleep, for that matter.

"Who—" Rage began, and then Keiran felt him tense. "Keiran?"

We need to get out of here before Ellen comes back. Keiran, searching for Rage's face, leaned his forehead against his lover's. Just briefly, not even as long as a heartbeat.

He'd found him. And he was alive.

Rage sat up. His eyes gleamed feverishly and his hands shook when he pointed at the hilt of Keiran's sword. "You're a guard nowadays?" His voice was hoarse. "Lovely. You've got keys for the chain?"

Keiran jumped up and got the keys. He could practically feel Ellen looking for them, checking the pockets of her coat and wondering where she'd left them. Hopefully, she hadn't yet realized she'd put them on the table down in the dungeons.

The ankle chain clicked when the lock opened. Getting up slowly, Rage swayed, leaning heavily on Keiran.

How badly are you injured?

It was an easy enough question. However, Rage had some trouble answering it. "I don't know," he finally said. "I got whipped, not too long ago. I was bleeding. Someone broke my shoulder. Seems—" He frowned, rolled his neck, carefully raised his arms. "Seems the shoulder is not broken anymore."

Can you walk? We need to be out of here before Ellen gets back. I've stolen her keys.

He saw the white of Rage's teeth when he grinned. "We can't get upstairs, then, with her on the way down. There is another way out. Lock the cell and open—"

Footsteps, not too fast, as if their owner were checking the stairs for something lost. They had some seconds left, not more. Keiran helped Rage to get out of the cell and locked the door, his hands sweaty and fear building up in him that he'd drop the keys and Ellen would hear the sound and come storming in with her sword drawn.

From somewhere came muffled sounds—someone was begging for water. Through Penelope's door, they heard muttering. And the baron's cell was as open as Keiran had left it, a half-full bucket of water and bloodied walls waiting for his attention.

"Keiran?"

It was Ellen's voice.

Keiran didn't think, he just acted. *Come with me.* Hoping Rage wouldn't fall the moment he let go of him, he jumped to the child murderess's cell and opened it. The woman inside, Penelope, didn't even look up, kneeling on the floor with her hands folded, praying to the Lady.

Rage followed him. He was limping, he was pale, and there was blood on his clothes, but he could walk.

Hide in here and let me deal with Ellen! Keiran shoved Rage into the cell, quietly closing, but not locking the door behind him. He needed to get back to scrubbing the baron's cell, pretending he'd been busy with the stains.

At the last moment, Keiran threw the keys onto the table. A heartbeat later, he was on his knees, a wet cloth between his hands.

Seconds later, he heard Ellen snatch the keys from the table. "For fuck's sake," she yelled. "I never leave my keys behind. Never! Keiran, where are you?" Furious, she went to the baron's cell, slamming the door into the wall hard enough to make the bars rattle.

Arms up to the elbows in wash water, Keiran looked up from the floor where he was scrubbing at a large stain of blood.

"My keys were on the table," Ellen bit out through gritted teeth. "Why didn't you come after me to tell me I'd forgotten them?"

Keiran frowned and shook his head. His gaze drifted meaningfully over the cell, the bucket, and his wet hands. *Been scrubbing. Didn't see any keys.*

Innocent. Harmless. Trustworthy.

Ellen's fist, the one not holding the key ring, opened and closed repeatedly.

Nothing happened. All is well.

Gradually, if not reluctantly, she relaxed but looking as if she were fighting her own growing feeling of relief.

She turned, looked at the table, the cells.

"I've been gone for just a few minutes," she murmured. "Boy can't have done anything stupid."

Briefly, she glanced toward Rage's cell.

Shook her head. Her shoulders slumped, and she sighed deeply.

Finally, she cast him a crooked grin. "Sorry for the shouting," she grumbled. "It's just that Lee would go apeshit if he found out I left the keys behind."

Keiran shrugged and continued to scrub. *Shall I do the other cells when I'm done with this one?*

Ellen grinned. "Eager to stay down here for a little longer, ain't you?" she teased, and Keiran's heart flipped with fear.

"Most newbies are revolted at first, but a few have a knack for this here. They like the thought of being in charge, of keeping the scum off the streets, and they always offer to do the dirtiest work if it keeps them in the loop. You're one of those. I can see that. Finish this cell. Wait for the next shift to open another one for you. Two hours alone down here—guess it'll be heaven for you."

Before she left, she blew him a kiss. "Don't forget about our drink," she called, and Keiran cringed at that—she hadn't forgotten, she trusted him enough to recall his promise, and somehow he felt bad about getting her in trouble. She'd been nice and helpful, and he'd played her, manipulated her, stolen her keys to free one of her prisoners.

Couldn't be helped.

And it was time to get out of here.

Keiran dragged the table to the door that led upstairs and blocked it. Rage had said there was another way out, so blocking the only other entrance might buy them a few minutes should Ellen or someone else decide to come back before his two hours were over.

Rage was sitting on the floor, legs pulled up to his chest, head down, when Keiran pushed open the door. Hooking an arm under his lover's, Keiran helped him up.

"What time is it?" Rage asked, sounding tired.

The monk offered you the job last night. It is late afternoon now.

"Wulfric had me dragged down here just past midnight. It feels longer." He sighed, then shuddered briefly.

Ellen said she heard you scream.

"Wulfric has an interesting concept when it comes to conversations. I am glad you found me before the monk came back for a second round."

Rage stood close to him and made no attempt to move. He just stared at the wall, lost in thought.

Keiran wrapped his arms around his lover's waist, trying to comfort him.

If that was even possible.

Rage stiffened, then relaxed. Eventually, Rage hugged him back, lightly at first, but with increasing strength with every breath he took until it was more than just a hug. Rage clung to him until Keiran thought he'd break some bones.

The moment didn't last long enough—had they had hours, it wouldn't have been long enough, but as it was, time was crucial, and they both knew it. Rage loosened his hug, but still leaned on Keiran for support. "I'm as weak as a child, and every bone hurts. Are there any open wounds on my back?" He half turned, casting a glance to the praying woman on the floor.

Rage's shirt was shredded, encrusted with dried blood. In the light of the torches, his skin appeared less pale. Keiran brushed the threads out of the way and placed his hand on Rage's neck, running his fingers down his back. Rage tensed at the touch as if expecting pain.

You were whipped, but the wounds have been healed.

He kept his hands a moment longer than necessary on Rage's bare skin before snatching them away. It was just—it was so good to touch him, to see him and hear him talk and be close enough to him for a kiss.

Not that it was possible. But temptation was there.

Rolling his shoulders and craning his neck, Rage left Penelope's cell. Taking a look around the guards' room, he saw the table and the waterskin, the blocked door, and the bag with bread and cheese Keiran had been given. He took it and the waterskin as well, then went to the cell where the rapist brothers were kept. The door was locked.

Ellen took the keys with her.

Moving slower than usual, Rage placed his hands onto the wall right next to the cell. He knelt, his fingers whispering across the stones. "I've been here before. We don't need Ellen's keys to get into the cell."

He closed his eyes. His fingers cast dancing shadows in the flickering candlelight. "Ah."

Keiran, standing at the blocked door listening for anyone coming down, tried to figure out what Rage had found. It seemed to be a loose stone, its grooves disguised with mud and dirt. As it took Rage a while to pry it out of its cavity, it seemed fair to assume no one had removed the stone in some months, if not years.

"Never had a use for it before," Rage said, setting the stone aside and reaching into the hole underneath. "I hope… yes. Still there. Good old Jack."

On the flat of his palm was a single key, smeared with dirt, blackened by age, and not as rusty as Keiran would have expected.

"Master key to the cells." Rage reached out his hand so Keiran could help him up. "When we first moved to the city, Jack made it his duty to learn as much about all the prisons as he could. Back then, Peter of Lisben House was in charge of this one. Big man, good officer, lousy husband. Jack seduced his wife and found out what there was to find out about the Main Dungeons. She even told him about the master key between dinner and bed."

The key creaked in the lock when Rage opened the door to the cell. "The master key is kept down here for emergencies. A fire; a riot. No one wants to get locked up, especially not the guards. It's their way to safety. Wish I'd had the time to use the damn key before Wulfric had his chat with me. Would have saved me a lot of pain."

The cell Rage had opened was larger than the others Keiran had seen. There was enough space for several suspects. Right now, two men were held in it, both chained to the walls, both badly beaten. One hung limply from his wrist cuffs, unconscious. The other one croaked for water.

"Problem," Rage muttered when he went into the cell and the man's eyes, bloodshot and wide with madness, focused on him.

"Water," he begged. His nose was broken, and several of his teeth were missing. "They were just bitches. Useless, dirty whores. Deserved what they got. Water. Please!"

"Give him water," Rage whispered, his mouth only an inch away from Keiran's ear. "But first put the key back where it was."

Keiran put the key back into its hiding place, making sure to fill the hole neatly so no one would see it had been used. Then he filled a cup with water and took it back to the cell, helping the man drink.

"Who're you?" he croaked once he'd emptied the cup. "You're new. What man does a job like that? What man wants to torture a neighbor? Bastard." Gasping for breath, he spat at Keiran, missing him by inches.

Rage didn't pay any notice. His hands were steady, but every now and then, he stretched and rolled his shoulders, and once, he put his hand to the joint as if to ease out a constant pain.

Then the man in chains said, "And that guy over there isn't a guard at all," and began to scream. "Guards! Strangers down here! Gu—"

Keiran punched him, two quick blows to chin and stomach. The man went limp, his breath coming in wheezed gulps, but he wasn't unconscious, and he was grinning. "You know a way out of here," he managed. "Take me…. Take me with you. I don't want to die down here. They were only whores, and I didn't even kill them!"

"No keys to the chains," Rage said over his shoulder. "I am an assassin. I don't bring death unless I get paid. I might make an exception for you, though."

"You take me with you, or the guards will know exactly where you've gone," the man rasped. "I'll yell. The guards will hear me, and I'll tell them, and they'll catch you and torture you."

Rage grinned humorlessly. "Wulfric did that already."

The man's eyes widened. "The monk tortured you? Damn but you must be important."

Again, Rage put his hand to his shoulder, kneading it. Keiran was pretty sure he wasn't fully aware of the gesture, and a moment later, Rage continued touching each stone in the wall opposite the prisoner.

Suddenly, the color of his bracelet flared up, only once, but brightly enough to make Keiran close his eyes. When he opened them again, the light was gone.

Rage had both hands pressed to the stone. "*Open,*" he said, and just like that a door opened, melting into existence as silently and unspectacularly as if Rage had put down a handle.

"Fuck the Lady," the man in chains said, too loud and too demanding. "Fuck the damn bitch, if only I'd known about the door I would have been out of here days ago!"

"You're still chained to the wall." Rage didn't look around. "Keiran, let's go."

"Guards!" the man called, not overly loud, but with a nasty grin on his beaten face. "Find a way to get me out of here. It's that, or you'll have followers in a matter of minutes."

Rage sighed. Then he crossed the distance to the man in a few long strides, pulled his knife Wulfric had never bothered to take off him, and killed him with a precise stab into his heart.

Keiran felt his mouth drop open. Disbelieving, he looked from the now dead man dangling limply from his chains to Rage and the knife in his hand. Blood dropped from its tip to the floor.

Rage looked at him. "No choice," he said, wiping his knife clean and sheathing it. "You know anything about the whores he was talking about?"

He raped them and beat them to death afterward. Both he and his brother.

"They'd have put him to the wheel. Long, slow, painful death. Now let's go. The door stays open for only a few minutes." Taking a torch from the wall, he stepped through the gap.

Keiran, though, went over to the dead man, dug his hands into his hair, and pulled his head up.

He'd given him a cup of water; he'd helped him drink it. He'd felt the man's hot skin, riddled by fever; he'd smelled the blood on his clothes and his fear; he'd heard him breathe and talk.

What he'd said about the whores and that they'd earned what they'd got.

Rage did you a favor, he thought. *You should have died on the wheel.* Then he went after his lover.

THE PASSAGE was narrow and steep, but Keiran didn't need long to catch up with Rage simply because he'd sat down a few steps up the stairs. The torch he'd put into a crack in the wall. Grime and scale covered the ancient stones, and the temperature was lower than in the dungeons.

Rage had his arms wrapped around himself, and his head was resting on his knees. When Keiran sat down behind him, he leaned against his legs, exhaling an exhausted sigh.

"You shouldn't have seen that." He sounded tired to his bones.

I know what you are. Carefully so as not to hurt him, Keiran placed his hands on Rage's shoulders. *And what he said was worse than what you did.* After a moment's hesitation, he added gentle pressure as if to ask permission to continue, then began to massage the hard, knotted muscles. At first, Rage stiffened, involuntarily trying to get away from him, but then he relaxed into the kneading hands.

A few feet below, the door vanished, hiding them safely behind the walls.

What happened last night?

Rage shuddered under his touch. "A lot. In the end, I was locked up in the cell you found me in. Damn little monk brought me to my knees in no time. At one point, he had the guards break my shoulder. I passed out after that."

Keiran stopped kneading.

"My whole body aches. Again. I'm sick of this, really." With a sigh, he sunk against Keiran. "Any news about Luca?"

Jack met someone, a guard. Penny. I think he will get Luca out, or has already.

He felt Rage breathe out a quiet laugh. "Penny. Yeah, she would help him with anything he asks of her. At least that problem is solved."

Where do the stairs go?

Rage took a deep drink from the waterskin, then took out the bread and devoured it along with the cheese. "Up into the palace," he said between bites. "Near the stables. Should be easy to get out unseen."

He didn't move, though.

"I killed a child last night. Thought you should know."

The prince? It's all over the city. I did not believe it.

And he would have sworn an oath Rage would never touch a child.

Why? He had to ask. *Because of the price the monk promised you? Because of me?*

Rage turned in his arms. "No, not because of you."

But Jack's rules—your rules....

"The rules did not apply here. The child was dying. For once, I killed out of mercy."

Keiran stopped massaging his shoulders. Instead, he bent down and pressed his cheek against Rage's.

Very lightly, Rage kissed him. It was nothing more than the quick touch of their lips, but it left Keiran dizzy with love, need, and hope.

Rage's bracelet flared up. Immediately, Keiran tried to put some distance between them.

Rage put his hand behind his neck. "A lot happened last night, and most of it I don't understand. I killed a little boy because he was in pain and beyond saving. Wulfric, the empress, Princess Kayla—the political dimensions behind this must be immense. Right now, I don't care about any of them. All I want is to get back home."

Any chance for another kiss? Keiran wanted to ask but he didn't. It would have been cruel, untimely, unnecessary—dozens of reasons, each one more important than the last.

To hell with it, he decided, grabbed Rage, and pressed his lips to his lover's. Not lightly; hard and demanding. Not tenderly; forceful, longing, and greedy.

Not caring for the consequences. What could be better than to die in his lover's arms, right now and here and especially because the chances of getting out of the city alive were scarce no matter what Rage had said?

He expected Rage to push him away, to hit him even, but instead, his lover kissed him back.

There wasn't much space on the staircase. The torch's smoke made breathing harder by the minute. At one end were the dungeons and at the other probably a bunch of guards awaiting them. Still, there was nothing more important than this one kiss right now. Nothing mattered but their bodies touching and their hearts beating in sync, just like the very first time they had kissed. It was the kiss Keiran had wanted from the moment he'd woken in Rage's arms after three months amongst ghosts, and he just knew it was also the kiss Rage had wanted ever since he'd seen Keiran fall.

A lot had changed between them.

The kiss couldn't last. They both knew that, just as they knew this kiss was of the kind that led to more no matter the place, the time, and the attached risks. Still, they clung to each other, dwelling in each other's warmth, relishing the sudden, unexpected emotional high.

Keiran expected wild magic to flare up. But the staircase stayed dark and quiet, and when Rage spoke, there was surprise in his voice.

"I think I will have a word with Wulfric before I break his useless neck." Rage brushed his fingertips over Keiran's cheek. Then he got up and took the torch. "He did something last night. I remember him being in my head. I remember my magic breaking free. There was something he showed me. And although we just kissed, I am still alive, and so are you. Before we leave the city, I need to have a word with him."

Together, they went farther upstairs. The last few steps were slippery, and also the flame began to flicker. Air rushed in from somewhere—they must be close to the exit. Handing the torch to Keiran, Rage pressed his ear to the wall, listening, before pushing hard.

The door burst open. Keiran had his sword and Rage his knife pulled in case the corridor wasn't empty.

There were no guards awaiting them, just Jack, leaning casually against the wall as if he had every right to be in the palace. "About time you two turned up," he said. "Been waiting for a while now, hoping you'd be smart enough to remember the secret passageway. And you, cub, better have a damn good explanation for the rumors about an assassin having killed Princess Kayla's youngest son and you looking as if you'd been tortured all night for having committed the crime."

CHAPTER
Seventeen

PRINCESS KAYLA had once been a strong woman. Not massively beautiful—plain, boring, as one of her nannies had called her when Kayla had been not older than ten—and stubborn, she'd always preferred the stables to the throne room and the kitchen to the more formal dining hall. She was tall, her shoulders broad, and her nose crooked. Her dark hair refused to be put in any kind of fashionable cut, and so she wore it in a practical ponytail whenever possible.

At twenty-three, she hadn't been married but was with child nevertheless. At forty-three, she was mother to one daughter and two sons, the youngest one named after her grandfather, King Leonard. No one knew who had fathered her children, and no one had ever dared to ask. Princess Kayla could handle a sword far better than half the guards, and she often trained with them if her duties allowed it.

Or used to. She didn't anymore, not since her youngest son had fallen ill.

Or to be precise, since her mother had tried to kill him.

Kayla knew Leon was not a healthy child. He was sickly and weak, often ill, but sparkled with humor and intelligence. He was the only one of her children who could make her laugh even when she felt bad, and he never failed to show her the treasures he'd found when outside. A flower, a stone, an empty bird's nest—he had an open eye for the wonders of the world, and she couldn't bring herself to keep him inside despite knowing she should do just that. When he scratched himself, he bled for days, and when he caught a cold he was in bed for weeks. His stomach reacted badly to unfamiliar food. Her other two children—May and Marek—were strong, May being her firstborn and heir to the kingdom and Marek longing to become a soldier as soon as he was of age. Which wouldn't be much longer—he was sixteen already, much older than his younger brother, and fond of him in the way a man is fond of a toy he's outgrown long ago. Marek didn't understand why his mother loved his younger brother so deeply, but he didn't mind, either.

Staring at her hands, Kayla wondered when they had turned into claws, thin and pale and as ugly as the rest of her. She had always had strong hands. Now she doubted she could lift a knife, let alone a sword.

She had no use for a sword anyway. There was no one to kill because there was no one to protect anymore. For Leon, she had neglected her duties as the empress's heir, and when her mother had first scolded, then openly criticized her for her decision to stay at her youngest son's side rather than bother with politics, Kayla had turned her back and walked away to look over him.

In vain.

Her gaze flickered to the bed. She'd never thought it could be such an utterly horrible sight.

Tears dropped onto the bedcover and her hands. Steadily, endlessly. She'd been crying since this morning, ever since she'd discovered upon waking that Leon had stopped breathing.

She shouldn't have fallen asleep. Staying at Leon's side during the night when he tried to find his way into dreamland but barely managed to stay asleep for longer than half an hour was her duty.

She had failed. She'd dozed off, and whilst she had been sleeping, her son had died.

He looked so peaceful. And the hollow stone that once had been her heart broke at the sight of him lying in his too large bed, the empty shell of a small boy crushed by her mother's wrath.

He still held his toy horse in his arms.

She must have yelled because the maids had stormed in, although she'd forbidden them to enter. This room, this whole part of the palace was off-limits to everyone but the doctors and Brother Wulfric, her only consort, the only one she trusted.

Only then had she tasted that awful taste on her tongue. When she had asked him, Wulfric had frowned and then said he believed she had been drugged.

She had woken up on the sofa. But when she had dozed off, she had been sitting at the table, the teacup warming her icy hands. She hadn't wanted to spill tea on the linen, and she had left Leon's side only long enough to take a few sips.

There were people in the room now, two, three of them, and they touched her, although she ordered them not to, and they dragged her away, although she screamed and demanded to be brought back to the bed and her son because he needed her. He was so small and so ill, and he would begin to cry should he wake and not see her at his bedside.

Bruises on his throat, clear like ink on snow.

Soothing hands and a liquid running down her throat. Wulfric was there, concern written all over his wrinkled, wise old face, concern and grief. "You need to drink this, Princess," he murmured and persuaded her to swallow, but it was a bad idea to swallow the medicine he'd given her. It made her calm; it dulled her pain.

She didn't want her pain to be dulled. She wanted it to roar and to blaze because how else could she fight and kill her mother? Because it had been her who had killed her son. So she would come back to her side, so she would pick up her duties again, so she would be the good daughter she ought to be.

The medicine worked fast. Disinterested, she allowed Wulfric to lead her to the sofa she'd been asleep on, sat, and watched the maids pulling back the bedcovers from her son's body.

He'll be cold, she wanted to say, but her mouth wouldn't open.

They took her Leon away, a nameless woman cradling him in her arms and carrying him away, out of the room and out of her life. His toy horse dropped from his limp fingers. Soundlessly, it fell to the ground. The woman stealing her child didn't notice, and why wasn't she able to call after her and tell her Leon needed the horse because without it, he wasn't able to sleep?

Wulfric sat down next to her, taking her hand in his. He must surely see her pain, and he followed her gaze. Swiftly, he got up and picked up the toy, placing it in her lap.

Where had the woman gone? Where was her son?

Her hand found the horse. Clutching it to her heart, Kayla noticed tears streaming down her face and wondered why she was crying.

The horse smelled of her son. He told all of his secrets to the little horse, never let it out of his sight. She'd made it herself, this silly little thing, although she had two left hands when it came to stitching. She'd pricked her fingers dozens of times, she'd had to undo the seams at least twice, and at first, she couldn't figure out how to attach the tail and the ears. Stupidly enough, she had even been nervous when giving it to Leon—he wasn't a child fond of toys, always much more interested in the outside world, the stables, the meadows, the trees he was never allowed to climb. What would he do with an ugly, misshaped horse?

But he'd loved it at first sight. Still loved it, always fell asleep with it, and why did she have it and not him?

"Where's my son?" she asked, her voice muffled by the horse's thin fur.

Wulfric placed a blanket around her shoulders. "The sisters of the Lady are taking care of him," he said.

"They need to be careful. He's injured. His leg hurts. If they are not careful, they will hurt him."

"They will be very gentle, Princess, I promise."

What would she do without Wulfric? Always there when she needed him, always giving advice, forever trustworthy.

She turned to him. His face was blurred, but that was because of the tears still streaming down her face. "Why did he die? He shouldn't have died. He is so young. He can survive. It is only a broken leg!"

But he had been killed. She knew it. She could still taste the proof on her tongue, and she could still see the proof on his small, pale throat.

Bruises, made by cruel fingers.

Very nearly, she would have ripped Leon's toy horse apart. She had to be careful because he would be asking for it once the sisters were done with him.

A look of grieved concern crossed Brother Wulfric's face. "Prince Leon didn't just die," he said, confirming what she knew already. "He was killed. The assassin was caught, though. Would you like to talk to him before he is executed?"

JACK WAS wearing a guard's uniform, just like Keiran, though he had an air of power around him that Keiran lacked.

"Penny must have been happy to see you if she organized the uniform for you," Rage said, checking the corridor for unwanted bystanders.

"She was very happy." Smoothly, Jack put his walking stick to Rage's throat and pushed him against the wall. "Now tell me about these rumors, cub. And tell the truth."

Rage didn't wipe the stick away. Neither did he lower his eyes. Looking straight at the man who'd raised him, he said, "I killed the prince. Long story, Jack, and this is not the place to tell it. I had a rough night. Let's get out of the castle, let me get some rest, and I'll tell you everything you want to know."

Jack narrowed his eyes and increased the pressure on Rage's throat. Not much, not enough to really hurt him. But enough for Keiran. The sword practically jumped into his hand, and now they formed a triangle with Keiran's sword pointing at Jack's chest, Jack's stick pressed to Rage's throat, and Rage's hand around Keiran's wrist.

"You don't want to have a row with me, boy," Jack bit out, the words meant for Keiran but his eyes never leaving Rage's face. "Drop it. This is between me and the man who's forgotten everything I have ever taught him."

For a long moment, nothing happened. Maybe Jack increased the pressure for a fraction; maybe Keiran raised his sword half an inch. But when Rage didn't even try to fight, when Keiran let the sword sink, Jack finally lowered his stick.

"You killed a child?" The old man sounded more confused and hurt than outraged. "And a member of the royal family on top of it? Are you crazy?"

Never kill a child. Rage remembered those words as if Jack had said them yesterday. He'd taken them to heart, and he'd lived by them—until last night. The rules were more to him than just empty words, and he'd added his own bits and pieces over the years. Rage knew he'd lived up to Jack's expectations.

Until today.

Given the look on the old man's face, he was about to break the bond between them if Rage couldn't find the words to explain why he had done what he had done. Jack might decide to hand him over to the first real guard who came along. Which might be soon even though this part of the palace was rarely visited by guards as it was far away from the royal family's quarters.

But Rage wasn't good with words. And luckily, Jack knew it. "Did you do it for the payment Wulfric offered?" he asked, his gaze flicking to Keiran. "He offered you the boy as a price. Tell me you didn't let him buy you."

Rage grinned tiredly. "I'm an assassin, old man. It's the sole meaning of my job that people can buy me."

Jack growled deep in his throat, like a wild dog ready to attack. Rage was fairly sure he'd feel the stick across his head if he gave another flippant answer.

He sighed. "You should know me better, Jack. You saved me. You saw me cry and scream for my family. You held me although I tried to beat you away. You know my limits better than I know them myself. You *know* what I am capable of. Killing a child is where I draw the line, and still I did as the empress asked. *You* tell me why, old man. If you know me at all, you tell me why I did it." Tightly controlled aggression laced his words, and although he'd been almost whispering, it had felt like shouting.

For a long moment, the young and old assassin stared at each other. Then Jack relaxed. "You look like shit, cub. Again. What is it with you that I can't leave you out of my sight for more than a minute? You always get hurt, and I wonder if you do it on purpose or just to annoy me."

The tension between them was gone as quickly as it had flared.

"Didn't I tell you?" Rage raised his hand to his shoulder, kneading it. "I like getting beaten. And whipped. And having my bones broken."

"Broken bones?" Jack looked Rage over. "Frankly, cub, I can't see much under all the dirt and dried-up blood, but you don't look like you have broken bones anywhere in your body. Still, you look bad. Wulfric had a go at you?"

"Fucking little monk. The man is a chameleon, he is dangerous, and he is mad. It was he who pulled the strings regarding the little prince's death, and it was he who had me put into prison for having done as agreed upon. He has a knack for torture, that's for sure. No idea what would have happened if Keiran hadn't gotten me out of that cell."

Jack closed his eyes, looking as if he wanted to say something but thought better of it. Then he threw a bundle at Rage. "Tell me the rest of the story once we are out of here. These are guard's clothes. Got them from Penny. Find yourself an empty room, clean yourself, and get dressed." At his feet was Rage's bag; he pushed it across the floor with his stick. "We can't go after Luca with you looking like you just escaped from the dungeons."

Silently, Keiran put a hand to Jack's arm.

Jack shook his head. "No, I didn't manage to get her out of Well Prison. Wulfric intervened. Come on, boys, hurry. We don't have all day."

Taking the clothes as well as his bag, Rage peeked round the corner—no one else in sight and empty rooms in abundance down the corridor. Once, there had been more people serving in the palace. Nowadays, the rumors of war drew people back home to their families or into the army. Fewer stable boys, fewer gardeners, not as many servants as there were just three months ago. The rooms were abandoned, and no one would notice if one was occupied for half an hour just as no one had stopped a one-legged guard walking straight into the palace.

Rage opened the first door that was unlocked. "Care to tell me why I need a guard's uniform? We could be out of here by now already, Jack."

Jack's jaw muscles tightened. He hated the palace, he hated being here, and it showed on his face. "I told you Wulfric intervened. The girl is in the palace. The monk snatched her out from under my nose, so to speak. If you still want to free her, our best chance is now, whilst we are all here."

I can find her.

Rage looked at him, then nodded. "Do it. The faster the better. Wulfric asked questions about Luca last night. I'm afraid he got all the answers off me he wanted. Only the Lady knows what he wants with her."

"As I said, get clean and get dressed." Jack pushed Rage into the room and, after a moment of consideration, Keiran after him.

"Check him for injuries. I don't want him to collapse in the middle of this. I'll watch out until you're done," he said, and then the door closed, and Rage and Keiran were alone.

THE ROOM was cold. Why was it cold in this room? She never let the fire go out because Leon always shivered no matter how well she covered him.

But there was a maid cleaning out the fireplace. She hummed, obviously enjoying what she was doing, or maybe she was looking forward to meeting her boyfriend after work.

Were there really people who weren't broken with grief, who didn't care that her son was dead?

Kayla, clutching her child's toy horse, feared she'd strangle the kneeling woman. Or maybe she would jump out of the window and break her skull on the stones below. Death would bring peace, and her mother would be happy. No more quarrels; no more fights.

She couldn't even remember what the fights were all about.

Once, she and her mother had been on good terms. Kayla was an only child, her twin brother stillborn. Her mother had been there for her no matter how pressing politics were. She'd always made sure to have breakfast and dinner with her daughter, she'd read her good-night stories, and occasionally, Kayla had been allowed to sit on the throne, only briefly but long enough to feel the power emerging from that ancient place. In the throne room, lives were decided upon, war and peace, pain and happiness.

For a long time, Kayla had believed her mother was a good person, ruling fairly and never overly cruel. There hadn't been a war in decades. The city prospered, and visitors frequented the kingdom. Kayla could have married a prince or a lord's son at sixteen had she wanted to, but when she'd refused, her mother hadn't forced her.

When Kayla became pregnant, her mother didn't ask who the father was. It was unusual for a princess to have a child without a husband, but it had happened before. It wasn't forbidden, and as the empress seemed to be fine with it, no one else had dared to say a word.

Once, her mother had loved her. Kayla was certain of it. When had it changed? When had her mother begun to look at her oddly, keep secrets from her? When had she forbidden Kayla to enter the throne room whilst she judged and ruled her kingdom?

"She killed my son," Kayla muttered, the toy horse damp with her tears. "My mother killed my son, and for that, I will kill her."

"You mustn't say that, Princess." Wulfric sat next to her, patting her hand. Hadn't he been gone for a while? She couldn't remember.

Her gaze flickered to the bed. It was so big, and it was so very empty. Her son should be in that bed, healing, sleeping. His leg should be better by now. Soon, he would get up and tell her he'd go and find her some daffodils.

"She killed my son," Kayla repeated, her voice like an open wound. "I don't know why. I don't know how. But she won't be alive by the end of the day if I have to strangle her with my bare hands."

"An assassin killed Prince Leon," Wulfric objected quietly. "He's in the dungeons. As soon as you give the order, he will be executed. Unless you want to talk to him first?"

Kayla looked up from the toy horse. Leon had named it Buttercup, like the pony that had broken his leg. Maybe because the fur had a yellow shimmer; maybe because he loved buttercups.

She stroked the horse. No one else would be doing it anymore.

"Why would I want to talk to the man who murdered my child?" she asked, genuinely surprised. "I want him to suffer. I want him tortured. Don't have him executed, Wulfric. Keep him alive, and should he die, bring him back from the dead and torture him some more. He will never suffer as badly as I do, but he shall know pain."

"That can be arranged, princess." Wulfric nodded solemnly. "In fact, he has been tortured already. I supervised it myself. He is still alive, though. I thought that maybe you would like to question him. It might bring you peace if you knew why he took such a gruesome job?"

Kayla blinked and her fingers tightened. "A... job? Are you saying that... murdering my child, my sunshine, was nothing but a *job* for him?" Hate crept into her voice, outrageous, uncontrollable hate.

The maid finished cleaning the fireplace. Kayla watched her when she began to undress the bed. She knew it was filthy—Leon's broken leg had been oozing pus constantly.

The maid looked up and saw the princess watching her. Something must have shown on Kayla's face because after a moment, the maid decided to do another task first.

Briefly, as if reading it in an open book, Kayla had been able to read the maid's thoughts: that the assassin had done the little prince a favor by killing him. If Wulfric had not put his hand on her arm, she would have thrown herself at the maid, beating her until such horrible thoughts left her mind.

When the maid was gone—she practically fled the room— Wulfric pulled the bedcovers back over the sheets, covering the stains and the imprint on mattress and pillow Leon had left by being in that bed for so long. "I do not know the assassin's reasons for killing the prince," he said. "I just thought… I am sorry. It seems I did not think at all. Of course you do not want to talk to him. I will see your wishes concerning him are fulfilled."

Swaying slightly, Kayla got up as well. She went to the bed, touched the cover, the pillow, the frame.

It should not be empty!

"I want him to suffer," she said again, in case Wulfric hadn't heard her the first time. "Badly. Forever."

"What about his wife? Currently, she is in court. A young woman, barely of age. Should I arrange for her to be imprisoned as well?" Putting a steadying hand to Kayla's arm, Wulfric helped her sit down on the bed.

Kayla nodded. Then she shook her head. "Whose wife?" she asked.

"The assassin's wife. One Lucinda of Babylon. Apparently, she's been accused of having murdered her father, but there are considerable doubts about it. Much more likely Lord Barnard simply wants her land. So depending on Judge Federico's verdict, the young woman might walk free by the end of day. In case you would like me to prevent it…."

Kayla's hands smoothed out the bedcovers. For but a moment, her son's unique scent was in her nose.

She missed him so much already. How would she manage to live a whole life without him?

"Who would marry a killer?" she mused. "Is she stupid? Were there dire circumstances that didn't leave her another choice, and if so, why didn't she dispose of him the first chance she had?"

"They married last autumn, Princess, and she was not forced. It is all I know."

Leon, she hoped, would be treated gently by the sisters of the Lady. Kayla had time enough to take care of the killer and his wife. "Bring her here," she told Wulfric. "Yes, bring her to me. I want to ask her why she didn't prevent my son's death, why she didn't kill her husband on her wedding night. I want to ask her if she knows why he did it. And then she will burn, and I will watch her scream."

SOFTLY, THE door closed behind them. After only a small moment of hesitation, Rage put some distance between him and Keiran. Where they had touched, his skin was hot and longing for more.

Not good. Merely being in the same room was dangerous. And this room was quiet, it was locked, and it was guarded. Jack wouldn't allow anyone to disturb them no matter how long it would take him to get showered and changed.

Shower. Wrong line of thought.

But they had kissed, and nothing had happened. Rage had felt his magic stir, and somehow, had managed to keep it under control.

It had only been a kiss.

Still. Nothing had happened. Only, his desire had been stoked, and now Keiran was at arm's length, he was about to get naked, and so what? He wanted him, no surprise there. He couldn't have him, and even if he could, this wasn't the time to try.

You kissed.

Betraying, treacherous thoughts. Tempting, dark wishes.

Rage let the torn shirt slip off his shoulders. Fingers encrusted with dirt and blood, he first took off his boots, then opened his trousers and kicked them off. Naked, he searched for his rainstone in the bag Jack had given him.

Small and round, the stone lay in his hand, cool and gray and promising. The water would be cold—it was only spring, and even at the height of summer, the rainstone's water was lukewarm at best.

The cold water might freeze his desire.

Or so he hoped.

Lightly, he blew on the stone, his hands getting wet instantly. The stone's magic began splashing water upon him as if he were standing under a cloud made just for him. A puddle formed on the floor; shivers ran down his spine when the first cold drops hit his skin.

Keiran handed him the soap.

Flakes of blood and dirt washed off him. Dark streaks showed on his pale skin, and when he put the soap to his hair, the foam went from white to black instantly.

"Didn't know it was that bad," he muttered, holding his face into the spray. "Guess I can be glad there's no mirror nearby."

I can tell you how you look.

Keiran stepped behind him and put his hands on Rage's hips.

A kiss to his shoulder. *Tall and lean. Pale skin; long legs.*

Another kiss. When Rage half turned his head, he saw Keiran was still fully dressed, the fabric of his uniform already soaked by the water.

Strong shoulders. Gentle hands. And no open wounds. Just fresh scars.

Keiran didn't move. His grip might have tightened a bit, though.

I missed you, Keiran's mind whispered. *I love you.*

Rage was well aware that he should push Keiran away, or better even, out of the room. But he didn't. Water running down his body, he closed his eyes and enjoyed his lover's hands on his naked skin, and he didn't object when Keiran's fingers whispered upward, tracing the new scars on his back.

Why did he do that? This monk, Wulfric, he hired you, and you did what he wanted. Why torture you for doing your job?

"I don't know," Rage replied, ever so slightly leaning against Keiran.

His lover took the soap from his hands. Rage was far from being clean yet, and when Keiran began to lather him, Rage sighed with delight.

His magic stirred, but he kept it in check without even noticing.

Only his shoulder hurt.

Hands and foam and cold water. A warm body behind him. Arms embracing him. Kisses on his skin. Keiran, cupping his balls, massaging his cock into full hardness.

Why not just kill you so you couldn't tell anyone what happened and who ordered it? Why beat you so badly? Why cause so much pain? And why heal you afterward?

I don't know, Rage wanted to answer, but then the pain in his shoulder flared up, and he realized with sudden, blinding clarity that he did know. Wulfric had told him, between getting out the whip, invading his mind, and breaking his shoulder. Finally, he understood.

"It was my price for killing the prince. He'd even warned me it would hurt."

Rage turned in Keiran's arms, facing him, wrapping his arms around the younger man. His cock brushed over rough, wet fabric and it only made him harder. "By torturing me, he showed me how to control my magic."

Remembering the pain and his own screams and how Wulfric had reached inside him, touched him, woven the net—it was a nasty memory, but it also helped him remember that he could keep his magic in check if he had to.

When they had kissed, he'd kept control.

He could do it again.

Rage lowered his brow to Keiran's, exhaling slowly, tiredly. He closed his eyes. "He invaded my mind, and he did something I didn't understand at the time. I don't fully understand it now, either."

Carefully, he wrapped his arms around Keiran. "I should not do this. Staying so close to you. Allowing you to touch me. If it worked, I could make love to you. If not, I am about to kill you, Jack, half the city, and all of the royal family in one go."

The shirt was in the way, so Rage undid the buttons and peeled it off Keiran's body. The sword clattered to the floor, followed by the belt. This time, it was he who initiated the kiss, and this time, he didn't stop his hands from roaming over Keiran's skin. It was what he had longed to do: touching Keiran, kissing him, tasting his skin and inhaling his scent, feeling his breath in his ear and seeing the need in his eyes, reflecting his own.

His shoulder hurt; briefly, he remembered how it had felt when it broke.

He also remembered—or thought he did—that he'd kept his magic in check although it had been about to lash out.

Kept it in check without Wulfric's help.

"I shouldn't do this," he murmured, dropping to his knees.

Kisses to the insides of Keiran's thighs, always a good start for more.

But if he didn't do this now, he wouldn't ever dare to try again.

Keiran's hands were in his hair, urging him on. His lover's cock slipped into Rage's mouth, hard and sweet, and that silent moan told him how much Keiran loved to get sucked off.

There was no time for foreplay. He didn't want foreplay. Rage wanted to fuck. He needed to find out if what the monk had showed him would work even now. Pain was so much different from lust.

Would it work?

The bracelet burned a bright blue: impossible to overlook it. And his magic roared with hunger, wild and about to break free.

He wouldn't let it happen.

Keiran would spill if he went on sucking his cock, so Rage got up and pushed the younger man against the nearest wall, out of the water's spray. Keiran's hands were on his ass, his lips on his mouth, and with the wall supporting him, he now slung his legs around Rage's waist.

Loudly, his magic roared. It wanted to get out, it wanted to bite and to kill, and Rage froze, distracted and worried only to have Keiran's tongue part his teeth and slip into his mouth, so he had to get a grip on his magic, or his lover would have died on the spot.

Caged; angry. But the net Wulfric had woven, that Rage had learned to handle while bleeding onto the dungeon's floor, held.

Fast and hard, Rage pushed into Keiran's tight hole, his arms wrapped around him so they wouldn't lose balance. One of Keiran's hands was on his neck, the other spread out clutching the window frame.

Short thrusts; he would come soon, and so would Keiran. In his mind, Rage could hear his lover's moans, his gasps, his begs to fuck him harder and deeper. On his neck, he could feel Keiran's fingers tighten with pleasure.

He could also feel the little monk's touch when he'd showed him how to control his magic, and momentarily, his whole body screamed with pain. A cry formed deep inside him, and his lips left Keiran's mouth.

His magic fought. It was about to break free.

No, Keiran said. *No, it won't. Not now. Not ever while you are with me.*

Opening his eyes, Rage looked into Keiran's face. There was no doubt.

Another push, slower this time, more careful. Intense, erotic, beyond what he'd ever hoped for. This was not some nameless whore, this was Keiran, and Rage could hear him loud and clear in his mind, or rather not his voice anymore, just raw emotions, his need to come—and his love.

His magic didn't stand a chance against love. Its roaring died, and it calmed whilst Rage kissed and touched and stroked his lover. It didn't stir when Keiran came and the blue bracelet exploded with a magical light, and only when he was close to his own orgasm a heartbeat after Keiran had spilled his seed did it make one last attempt to get out of the net.

Ragged breathing; pounding heart. Rage stopped thrusting into Keiran and just held him, watched Keiran's amber eyes flutter open and focus on him. His fingers brushed over Rage's throat; then he moved, pushing himself off the wall just enough to make his whole body tighten.

When Rage came, he came hard, his face buried at Keiran's neck and the net around his magic somehow strangling him as well so the shout of relief was unable to escape his mouth.

No one had died.

For what felt like an eternity, Rage and Keiran stood against the wall, embracing each other, breathing in each other's scents. They didn't talk; they didn't even think. At some point, Keiran unwrapped his legs from around Rage's waist and stood on the floor. At some point, they got back under the spray, found the soap, and washed again.

No wounds showed on Rage's skin, no slashed flesh, no fresh blood.

He would kill Wulfric the moment he saw him. But maybe he would say thanks beforehand.

A KNOCK on the door. Princess Kayla snapped out of her thoughts and saw Wulfric granting entrance to a guard and a young girl.

She didn't want visitors. She didn't want to see anyone, talk to anyone. She only wanted to sit at her son's bed and hold his hand and see him smile in his sleep.

Only her son was dead. She'd never hold his hand again, and she would never again be blessed by seeing him smile.

He hadn't smiled for a long time. He'd been too much in pain.

The tears dried on her face. She was empty, hollow, her grief turned hard and cruel. No more tears. This visitor was important. This girl knew the man who had taken her son from her and must have had good reasons to marry a monster.

"Come closer," Kayla said. "Come into the light where I can see you. What's your name?"

The girl raised her chin. "You had me dragged here. Introduce yourself first."

Clearly, this was not a common girl despite the shabby clothes, the heavy boots, and the untidy plait her hair was bound into.

The guard slapped her hard across the back of her head and hissed, "That's the Princess Kayla, girl. Now bend your knee!"

Rewarding to see the girl struggle with that information, her pride, and her underlying fear. For afraid she was.

Eventually, the prisoner tilted her head ever so slightly. "My honor, Princess," she said tightly. "I am Lucinda of Babylon, I did not murder my father, and the judge who sentenced me to death was bribed. Anything else you would like to know?"

"You will die at the stake," Kayla said. The toy horse sat in her lap, giving her strength.

"I know."

The girl's answer came as a surprise for Kayla. "You know? How can you know how I will punish you? Or are you saying Judge Federico sentenced you to burn? Who hates you so much to have him pronounce such a gruesome verdict?"

The girl sighed. "Barnard, probably, although he would have preferred to see me hang tonight rather than seeing me burn in a few days. He wants my land. He's greedy. You should go after him, not me."

"Aren't you interested in why I want you dead?" Kayla was puzzled. The girl intrigued her. She was afraid, but not as much as she should be, and she radiated a strength not many youths possessed.

Luca shrugged. "Does it matter? You don't know me, and I have done you no harm. If you care to tell me, though, I will listen."

Wulfric, looking back and forth between them, lifted his hand. "Princess, if I may give a suggestion? Release the guard. She is bound and no danger to you. Talking to the girl will be easier and her answers more honest if she is not threatened by his presence."

Kayla thought about it, then nodded.

When the guard was gone, Kayla sighed once more. "It is true that you did me no harm and that I do not know you. But your husband killed my son Leon, and that is why you will die today. You are here because I want to know why you didn't end his life—stab him whilst he was asleep, put a pillow over his face, anything—while you had the chance."

Luca's mouth sagged open; then she closed it with an audible click. "You're lying. Rage wouldn't kill a child. It's against his code."

Kayla slapped her. She hadn't known she would do it—couldn't even remember how she'd jumped up—until her hand connected with the girl's face. It stunned Kayla how good it felt to see the girl struggle for balance, and the red imprint form on her fair skin.

"My son is *dead*," Kayla hissed. "Right now, the sisters of the Lady prepare him for his burial. I am not interested in knowing about his murderer's codex or his reasons to break it. I want to know how you could marry a monster!"

"He's not a monster."

"He killed my son!"

"He didn't." Putting her hand to her face and rubbing it, Luca raised her chin. "Rage is an assassin, but he has rules, and he sticks to them. Moreover, he saved my life more than once. He saved my friend's life. He is a gentle man, most times. He is neither cruel nor unfair, and if you knew him, you would know I'm telling the truth. I cannot imagine him killing a child. In any case, killing me won't bring back your son. It will only turn you into a killer yourself, and a double one, for that matter. I'm pregnant, Princess. Do you really want to honor your son's life by killing my unborn baby along with me?"

Kayla staggered back, falling onto the bed and staring at Luca in horror. "She's pregnant with a killer's child?" she whispered in horror, staring at Wulfric. "Did you know about this?"

The little monk shook his head sadly. "I did, Princess. I was able to pry this information out of the assassin, but I did not think it a good idea to share it with you given the circumstances. I am very sorry this stupid girl told you anyway."

Luca whipped around. "What do you mean, pry it out of him? Is he here? And I am not stupid!"

"He's in the dungeons, dear girl. I have tortured him personally when he wasn't willing to part with what I wanted to know. Did I not tell you he was caught? Right after he came out of Prince Leon's room—this room—we caught him. There is no doubt he killed the boy."

"IMPOSSIBLE."

Keiran, untangling his wet clothes, looked up from the ground.

"We can't do it the way Jack has planned it. Not all three of us." Rage, still naked and with a guard's trousers in his hands, began pacing the small room. "Two guards are no problem, even if one is hobbling on a wooden leg. Three guards—unlikely. They show up in pairs or in troops. Palace rule. Besides, your uniform is soaked, and mine won't fit. Too wide. Not much, but enough to make an already suspicious man draw his sword."

Taking the trousers out of Rage's hands, Keiran held them to his lover's waist and saw what he meant. The trousers had been made for a man less tall than Rage but heavier in build. Given the bruises on Rage's face, his limp, and his gaunt expression, it would be obvious at first sight he was only disguised as a guard.

Got an idea.

"Which would be?"

I take the dry uniform. You put on your dirty clothes. Jack and I will escort you through the palace, pretending to take you... somewhere. To the empress or the gallows or whatever. No one will get suspicious. The uniform fitted him much better than Rage. When he picked up his sword, he looked every inch a guard and not a gardener's son anymore.

Rage, though, was still naked. And he grinned. "Bad idea, getting back in uniform," he said, looking Keiran up and down with a raised eyebrow.

Keiran laughed, silently, wholeheartedly.

Reaching out and pulling him close, Rage kissed him before turning to the shards of his clothes. "I hoped I would not have to put them on again. But your idea will work." Reluctantly, he first stepped into his blood-soaked trousers, then put on what was left of his shirt.

"Let's find Luca, then. If we are lucky, we will get out of the city sometime this spring, unless she manages to get herself in even more trouble."

CHAPTER
Eighteen

THE PALACE resembled a beehive in more than one way, but what counted most for Rage right then was that once you were inside, the guards seldom bothered to look at you twice, assuming that whoever had made it that far couldn't be an enemy. Twice they met guards, and twice there was just a brief exchange of nods. Once, a scribe hurried past them, and they saw more chambermaids than actual rooms. Each time, Rage let himself slump against Keiran, who dragged him along as if he really were a prisoner. Each time, Jack made it clear he was in charge, no matter that he walked with a stick, and no one dared to ask them their business.

Keiran told them Luca was to the east of them.

Rage knew it was where the royal family resided.

It was a long way from the lower parts of the palace to the higher floors. It cost them a good hour to get there, and here, they earned their first skeptical glances.

"Might not work," Jack murmured when a guard came on to them, hand on the hilt of his sword.

"Your name," the guard demanded. "And your pass. Who's the prisoner?"

We're expected. The princess wants to see us. You believe us.

Keiran hadn't even thought about doing it, nor did he know why he mentioned the princess. Only that it felt right. And that Luca's flame in his mind burned brighter with every step they took.

The guard's eyes became slightly glassy, and his hand dropped to his side. "Princess Kayla is in Prince Leon's room," he said, his voice slurry. "Down the corridor and first to the left."

He swayed. Swallowing hard, he wiped his brow, then turned away quickly.

The first to the left led them into another corridor, large and highly decorated but looking abandoned nevertheless.

"Been here before," Rage murmured. "Last night. Keiran, are you sure this is where they hold Luca?"

Keiran nodded.

Before they reached the door that led into the prince's chamber, another guard ran toward them. "You," he snapped, pointing a fleshy finger at Rage. "The empress said to look out for you. Told me to find you and that you are to wait for her."

Rage shared a glance with Jack. This was beyond fishy, but now that they were here, so close to Luca, it didn't make sense to back off just because of a guard.

Jack shook his head; Rage agreed with a short nod. They wouldn't kill the guard but wait instead.

The guard pulled his knife. "The empress said you'd be bound most likely and that I should cut you free," he explained with a shrug. "Can't say I like freeing an assassin, but then it's none of my business what my empress wants. I just obey her orders."

The ropes from Rage's hands fell to the ground. Neither Keiran nor Jack stopped him from cutting them off.

"Strange," Jack said, and the guard snorted.

"Tell me about it. Damn strange day it's been. And here's the empress." He dropped to one knee, head bowed.

An old woman stepped through the door opposite the prince's room. She didn't wear a crown, nor did she hold the scepter as she did when sitting on her throne. A wide, soft dress fell from her shoulders, her hair was tied into a bun, and the only jewelry she wore was a necklace made of emeralds. It sparkled in the light, though it could not disguise the sadness in her eyes.

"Thank you, Gabriel," she said to the kneeling guard. "You shall be rewarded for your trust. Now leave us alone, if you please. I have to talk to them in private."

The guard looked uneasily between his empress and the three men. "I don't like the idea, ma'am," he said.

The empress sighed. "Nor do I, Gabriel. It has to be done nevertheless. Thank you for your concern. Now leave."

A quick salute, and the guard was gone without further argument.

"My grandson's killer," the empress said, taking in Rage from head to toes. "You look different, assassin. Dreadful, one could argue. I can see your night has been rough. But you are not beaten. It appears as if Wulfric did a good job."

"You planned this."

The empress frowned. "No, actually. Not entirely myself, anyway. Wulfric was the main force behind this. And I had no idea you would play a part. The most crucial part, I might say. But yes, there was a plan, complicated and bound to fail, but a plan nevertheless. It was he who told me you would come up here and that you wouldn't be alone. Your wife is with my daughter, assassin. I have been told you would like to free her, so come along."

The corridor's air was stale. Noticing the dusty floor and the covered windows, Rage—not for the first time—wished he were elsewhere. But Luca was behind that door, and even if they hadn't a shared history, he wouldn't let anyone stay in that room with a grief-ridden mother seeking revenge for her dead son.

"I did what you asked me to do," Rage said, rubbing his wrists. "And I was paid for it. I want to leave, and I want to take my friends with me. Jack and Keiran. Luca. Send her out, and we will be gone. No one will ever know you are behind this."

The empress's fragile blue-veined hand pushed open the door. "You don't understand," she said. "You are part of the plan, and I am not done with you yet. You want your wife back? Then come inside and explain to my daughter why you killed my grandson and that it was me who hired you."

IT WASN'T easy not to strangle the little monk the moment Rage saw him. Instead, he went straight to Luca and gathered her into his arms, having seen the fear in her eyes and the doubt and the too many sleepless nights since Barnard's men had abducted her.

"About time you came to the rescue," she mumbled into his shoulder, her arms wrapped hard around him. "What happened? Was there someone else you had to rescue first?"

"Myself, girl. I spent the night in the dungeons."

"Right. Good point."

Rage felt her tighten her arms even harder, pressing herself to him as if she feared she'd drown otherwise. For a few moments, no one else existed, no one else counted. He felt her tremble, smelled the faintly sweet scent of her hair, and was surprised at how much she meant to him nowadays.

Maybe he felt a tear drop onto his skin, but maybe he was mistaken as she instantly shrugged, stepped away from him, and wiped her sleeve over her nose. "I caught a cold, I think. My cell was icy."

Rage grinned. It wasn't easy to subdue this girl; certainly neither Wulfric nor the princess had managed it.

Then she saw Keiran, and her face lit up. She slipped past Rage and flew into the boy's arms, this time not trying to hide her tears. "You're well! You're alive! You're up and about and what are you doing here? I thought you'd be still at Dragon Spring Farm, and why are you wearing a guard's uniform and honestly, Kei, if you do something stupid like jumping into an abyss ever, ever again I'll come after you and kick you until your behind falls off!" Between words, she was sobbing; between words, she kissed his cheeks and once, his lips.

If Rage had had the time to think about this beforehand, he might have expected a pang of jealousy at the sight of the two. Keiran was hugging the girl just as tightly as she was hugging him, stroking her hair, comforting her, smiling at her with his special smile just to make her feel better. It made her laugh in a kind of disbelieving way, and she smacked his shoulder whilst simultaneously wiping the tears off her cheeks. They looked very fine together. Close in age. Both beautiful, both—despite the past events—innocent and young and free of scars, regrets, and lost chances.

Rage knew the girl was in love with Keiran. Right now, he could see that Keiran also loved Luca, in his way.

And it didn't bother him. There was no jealousy, just relief that the girl was safe, at least for now. They would have to find a way to sort out their personal mess—there was a baby in the picture now, and the question of who had fathered it—but this could wait.

After all, the empress or the princess or Wulfric might order their deaths at any moment.

Wulfric, who'd looked at Keiran and Luca for a moment like everyone else, shook his head in mild amusement and dragged a chair into the middle of the room. "Please, Your Highness, take a seat," he said. "Finally, we are all together. Finally, we can solve a problem or three."

Keiran looked up, still holding Luca in his arms.

The princess. She'll attack you!

Keiran's warning came just in time. Still holding the toy horse, the princess had taken a large jug from the table and would have smashed it onto Rage's head if Keiran hadn't seen her move. She missed him by an inch, the jug only brushing his arm before hitting the wall and breaking into four large, deathly sharp pieces. The water seeped into a thick, woolen carpet. Left in the princess's hand was the handle.

Swinging it, she sliced Rage's chest. Then she dropped it and went for his throat, dropping her son's toy along the way.

"Kayla!"

The empress's voice wasn't loud. It was an old woman's voice, strained with age and sorrow, but it made her daughter turn nevertheless.

Hands raised and tears streaming down her face, Kayla looked at her mother. "You ordered this. You hired the assassin," she whispered, a terrible smile spreading over her bloodless lips. "My Leon died because of you. I will kill him. And I will kill you."

Heavily, the empress fell onto the chair Wulfric had offered. The little monk stood next to her, hands folded. Waiting; watching.

Rage was next to Luca and Keiran with a few strides. Standing before both of them, protecting them. In his hand was his knife, and Jack had raised his walking stick, which could, if necessary, become a deadly weapon.

"Rage," Wulfric said. "Dear boy. Listen, if you please. And forgive a grieving mother. An accusation has been made. Won't you tell us what happened last night?"

The princess, moving slowly now, dropped the handle and picked up the toy horse. She stepped up to Rage. The madness lingering behind her eyes was bright and brilliant, and he recognized it instantly. It was the same madness he'd harbored for the better part of the winter, and it was born out of the same reason. Losing a loved one was heartbreaking. It ate up your strength, your hopes. Your life. It broke you.

When Keiran had died, he'd beaten his killer to death. Rage couldn't blame Kayla for wanting to do the same.

"You killed my son," she croaked.

"I did."

Behind him, he heard Luca gasp.

"My Leon. My sunshine. I loved him so deeply. I miss him so much, and I will kill you first, and then I will kill my mother because she has ordered his death. Has she not?"

Looking at the old woman's sad face, Rage said, "She did."

Kayla swayed. She would have fallen if Rage hadn't taken her by the shoulders and pushed her onto the sofa he'd placed her onto once before, when she'd been felled by Wulfric's potion.

He knelt before her. It was important that she understand what happened, or the madness would eat her up. It had happened to him. He'd like to spare her the experience.

Only, as usual, he didn't find the right words. And when his silence lasted a fraction too long, she snapped, would have slammed her fist into his face if he hadn't caught her wrist. "You are a cruel, coldhearted killer. I do not want to hear what you have to say. I want you dead!"

It was Keiran who intervened. Silently, he stepped next to Rage and lowered himself to his knees so he could look into the princess's face. Swiftly, he put his hand over Rage's, who still held Kayla's wrist.

Let him tell you.

Shocked, the princess wanted to free her hand, but Keiran didn't let go of her.

You can hear me. Let me help you understand.

"Oh my, how utterly fascinating," Wulfric murmured, but no one paid him any attention.

The princess stared at Keiran, her gaze flickering to their entwined hands. "Understand what?" she whispered.

Keiran looked at Rage.

Think of the prince. Picture as many details as you can. Begin at the tavern. Ending up here, in this room. Don't skip memories. I don't know why I know this will work or how I am doing it, but I know I can't do it without your help.

"Whatever you ask." Slipping his free hand around Keiran's waist and pulling him closer, Rage closed his eyes, blanking out everyone else in the room. Everyone apart from Keiran, whose heart he could feel beating against his ribcage, and Princess Kayla, her bony wrists in his fingers.

The night before last seemed a lifetime away. Back then, there had been only one concern: how to save Luca. An easy enough task given that both he and Jack knew the city well, and even easier given Jack's many connections.

The tavern—which one had it been? It had been crowded, and he'd told Keiran about his time in the city and why he'd turned his back on it. They'd drunk a beer each. Being so close to his lover and still unable to touch him had been much harder than Rage had expected.

And then Wulfric had found him and offered him a deal. He'd followed him into the night, hoping beyond reason the little monk would find a way to solve his problem.

Remembering was easy so far. Rage could taste the beer on his tongue, hear the noise, he even remembered the stains on the table, the sticky floor, the landlord's trembling hands when Wulfric had entered.

Somewhere, there was Keiran. Close; skin to skin. He was Rage's anchor—without him, he might have very well stayed lost in thought, unable to find his way back into the here and now. The intensified memories were Keiran's doing, and now he asked Rage to move on, to follow Wulfric into the palace, and so Rage did.

Somewhere, there was the princess, holding her breath, waiting, anxious. Close; heart to heart. She was the one who pulled him forward—without her, he might have decided to skip the next memories, the ones where he killed the child. But this was for her and her alone. She needed to know. She needed to see and to feel so she could believe—and understand.

The boy in his big bed looked at him. Once more, Rage smelled the sickness in the room, the looming death. Once more, he talked to the child, soothed him, and promised sleep.

Once more, he killed the boy, softly, painlessly, and with a heavy heart.

Sobbing. A sound of deepest agony, heartbreaking and forlorn.

A voice, distant and faint. Meaningless words though spoken in earnest.

A hand on his face. Real, warm, and caring.

Rage.

A voice in his head. Keiran's voice, just as it was Keiran's hand touching him.

Confused, Rage shook his head. It seemed full of cobwebs, with no room for thoughts or emotions or memories.

Rage. Look at me.

Light pierced his eyes. Rage blinked, then became aware of the floor underneath his knees, Keiran's hand on his face, and their hands, still entwined with the princess's.

He couldn't have said how much time had passed.

Kayla wasn't crying anymore. Where there had been nothing but pain and madness, there was now a solemn grief. She was still. Slowly, she set the toy horse aside. "How did you do this? I was *there* when Leon died. I saw what you did. I felt it." She frowned. "I did not know Leon was in such pain. I did not know he wished to die so badly. Why did I not see it?" She looked at the empress. "Why didn't you tell me?"

"What mother could see a thing like that?" Wiping her eyes, the empress looked at her daughter. "Which mother would be strong enough to do what I have done—ask an assassin to kill one of her children?"

"*You* saw it," Kayla said. She got up, her hand slipping out of Rage's clutch. She stepped to her mother's side. "You visited Leon, didn't you? Although I had forbidden it?"

"I had nothing to do with his injury, Kayla. I was not responsible for his fall. I did not poison him. I never wished him harm. I loved him, my daughter." She sighed. "I did order his death, though."

One by one, Kayla looked at everyone in the room. "Then his injury was truly nothing but an accident?"

Rage guessed that this would be the hardest part—accepting that no one had planned this, no one was responsible.

No one to blame. No one she could make pay.

"Ahm, lady, I might be of a different opinion here." Wulfric shed smiles and mannerisms like an old, smelly coat. "Prince Leon's 'accident' was certainly no accident. It took me a long time to find out what happened the day he went into the stables."

"He fell off his pony." Kayla's voice was hard.

"Oh yes, he did. Buttercup. A fine animal, friendly and careful. Fairly small—ideal for an eight-year-old child. He loved it. He sneaked into the stables after dinner to groom it. Once or twice, he fell asleep in the straw. Always, a guard found him and carried him back into his rooms."

Kayla's eyes brightened at the memory. "How often have I told him that sleeping in the stables is not for a little boy? He never listened. So I had Gabriel watch over him. He always knew where Leon was even if I didn't."

"The day Prince Leon fell off his horse, Gabriel was sick," Wulfric said thoughtfully. "I didn't know until recently. Gabriel was reported as missing from duty that morning. Apparently, he'd been drinking too much the previous night. When I asked him about it a week ago, he began to stammer. It took some persuasion before he admitted he could remember having gone into a tavern—but not how he'd gotten home or with whom."

The little monk folded his hands over his nonexistent belly.

"There were no reports of anything out of the ordinary." The empress looked at her daughter. "I made inquiries. So did you, Kayla. This is the first time I've heard about Gabriel not being on duty that day.

Wulfric shrugged. "As I said, I found out myself only recently. I was in the stables, wishing to know what happened to Prince Leon's pony. Call it a gut feeling, Your Highnesses. I was certain something had been at odds that day. I asked everyone. I even had a little chat with Buttercup." He smiled, looking ruefully at Rage. "If necessary, I can pry an animal's brain just as well as a human's. Though they like it even less."

"Understandable," Rage replied flatly. "It hurts."

Wulfric looked stunned. "It does? Really? Oh my, if only I had known." He winked at Rage, then turned back to the empress and her daughter. "Anyway, reading a horse's mind is usually wasted time as they simply don't think like we do. So I went in there with a clear picture in my mind: Leon, lying on the floor screaming. I hoped I would get something I could use in response, and I did.

Buttercup tried to flee. The horse connected pain and panic with the day Prince Leon fell off its back, and that made me wonder. So I asked some more questions until one of the stable boys showed me the pony's saddle."

Rage didn't need to read minds to know what would come next. "It had been tampered with?"

Beaming at him, Wulfric nodded. "Underneath the saddle I found several of those spiky little seeds. I can't remember the name of the plant. Round, green, they look fluffy until you touch them."

Fiddleneck?

"That's the one. Thank you, young man. However, they could never have got underneath the saddle by themselves. Gabriel wasn't there to check the gear. It all feels like very foul play to me. The pony shied the moment Leon was lifted into the saddle. He fell and broke his leg. The rest we know."

"Why keep the saddle?" Rage asked. "Any killer with a brain would destroy the evidence immediately."

"I assume whoever tampered with the saddle thought a missing saddle would cause more ruckus than leaving it where it is. When digging around a bit I found a stable boy with a sick mother and a very bad conscience. With a bit of help from my trusted guards, he admitted that he'd been paid to put the seed under the saddle and that afterwards, he'd been too scared to go anywhere near it. He cried throughout the whole interrogation, begged me to believe he didn't have a chance of saying no, or his mother would have died an untimely death, and that he was sorry."

The empress and her daughter had joined hands. Both women's faces were hard. "Who paid him?" Kayla asked. "Get me their names, Wulfric."

Wulfric shook his head. "He did not know any names, Princess. The situation was dire. The two of you had stopped speaking to each other, the barons and lords plot behind your backs, no one trusts anyone else—an impossible way to rule a kingdom. So eventually, I saw no other solution but to scheme this little plot to bring all of you together into one room. So that maybe I might find some answers I have not been able to find before." He smiled a shy little smile. If Rage hadn't known him better, he would have believed him to be nothing but a concerned, helpful, anxious monk eager to serve his empress.

It was not easy, though, to fool the old woman. "Why have you not told me this before?" Rage noticed that suspicion against the little monk laced her voice. "What else do you know and hide?"

More than just suspicion. Anger, disappointment, and the will to unravel this riddle at all cost.

The monk saw it too. Soothingly, he raised his hands, a look of concern on his face. "Your Highness, please do not draw wrong conclusions. I had nothing to do with Prince Leon's accident."

He thinks one of them is involved, Keiran's voice sounded alarmingly loud in his mind. Rage turned to him, frowning.

Tell them, before they call the guards, and we all end up in prison once again!

For a moment, Rage hesitated. In his opinion, clearly supported by every one of his aching bones, Wulfric would be a much better man dead than alive. The monk was like a spider, sitting in the web's middle and waiting until the prey had managed to get itself completely wrapped up in its sticky threads. Wulfric lied, manipulated, controlled every step and every word inside the palace as well as outside, and Rage would have loved to keep his mouth shut and await either the empress or her daughter calling in the guards. Wulfric would end up in the same dungeon cell Rage had escaped from, and it would serve him right.

Sadly enough, it was very likely that not only Wulfric would be escorted away.

Putting his hand to his still aching shoulder once more, Rage was tempted to let it happen, but only for a mere second. Luca was quiet enough to make it abundantly clear how scared she was. Jack would fight any guard no matter the cost. This was a lose-lose situation, and when Princess Kayla opened her mouth to call the guards, Rage interrupted her. "The monk thought either you or your mother were pulling the strings. That's why he kept what he knew to himself, hoping that if he got the both of you into one room and told the truth about the pony, one of you would drop her mask. Am I not right, Wulfric?"

The monk just smiled.

"You brought me into town. You lured me into the palace. It was your idea to hire an assassin to end the prince's pain. I bet you could have done it yourself, but this way, you had a chance to confront mother and daughter with your suspicions face-to-face and stay out of it at the same time, innocent as always."

Wulfric wriggled his eyebrows and shook his head. "Had I given the prince anything, even a sip of water, the princess would have had me beheaded. And I knew you would be gentle."

Keiran put his hand on Rage's leg. *I saw him in the marketplace this morning. He told everyone the prince had been killed. He described you. It was because of him I found you.*

"Quite right, young man," Wulfric said. "And by the way, you absolutely desperately need to learn how to properly focus your words. Yes, I spread the rumors, knowing you would hear them and free Rage. I also got the young lady out of Well Prison—just in time, by the way—before your friend Jack would have vanished with her. I needed her in this room because I knew my dear boy Rage would come and get her. And bring his extraordinary young friend, who has such extraordinary magical abilities despite the fact he's mute. Easy, actually. A bit complicated on the planning side, with lots of maybes and perhapses, but easy nevertheless. Besides, I am truly glad neither of you planned this. I couldn't be sure. I apologize for any inconveniences, of course."

Princess Kayla stood. "Inconveniences?" Her calm voice was worse than any scream. "My son's injury, his pain, his suffering—inconveniences? His death—inconveniences? So many sleepless nights, so many tears—inconveniences? You even thought I had this planned? Had ordered my own son's accident? How dare you, worm!"

Her mother held her back, lest Kayla smash the monk's head with that vase from the table.

For once, Wulfric didn't come up with a witty remark. He stood pressed to the wall, wide-eyed and clearly completely dumbstruck by the princess's reaction to his words. "I did not mean to insult you, Princess," he finally managed. "I apologize."

Kayla wasn't in the mood for forgiveness. "I want to know why this happened. All of it. Why poison Gabriel so he couldn't watch over Leon? Why hurt the pony? Why make him fall? Tell me why—Mother, Wulfric, anyone!"

Luca, who'd been quiet so far, snorted from behind Rage's back. "You don't have much contact with the common folk, do you? Or worry about money? Because if you did, you'd know." Pushing away Jack's hand, she faced the princess. "This is about war, lady. And about lords who think war would earn them more money than they could spend in a lifetime. It is about greed and cruelty. And your son was just a pawn."

"Brighter than I thought, that girl," Wulfric murmured, though not loud enough for the princess to hear.

Kayla focused on Luca. "War. There will be no war."

Luca raised her chin. "War is practically around the corner. You and your mother hate each other. The throne is all but empty because the lords made you suspicious of each other, because you fight all the time, and with the little prince's illness, it got worse. When have you last conferred with your ministers, Empress Deoris?"

"I—"

"Months," Luca continued. "You are not present anymore, Empress. And the people notice. They are worried, and the lords are eager to talk about nothing else but war. I've been in the town for only a few days, and still I know all about it. From the guards, from gossip, from the old man who cleaned the floor outside my cell. A good war puts money into the pockets of the ones who run it. Like— your Lord Chancellor. Or Lady Evangeline. Counselor Howlett—now he will sell his horses in no time once war is declared, never mind that they're crap and scared of noise. It was not just one person planning this. It was a whole group of people. The names I just mentioned are in the mouths of most people in town, so you should start looking into their business. Your own lords and ladies are responsible for Prince Leon's accident. I could swear an oath on it. And it is your fault they made it this far because you two can't talk to each other."

Jack took her arm and pulled her back. "You better shut up now, Missy, or you won't see another sunrise," he whispered into her ear.

Princess Kayla just shared a look with her mother. Something like a secret conversation took place, possible only between people who knew each other very, very well. Finally, the empress nodded.

"We have to talk," she said quietly. "The four of you will stay in the palace until morning. As our guests," she clarified. "You are free to leave, but we would prefer another word with you. Wulfric, see they get chambers. Then come to the throne room."

CHAPTER
Nineteen

JUDGE FEDERICO sat at the breakfast table when the knock sounded at his door.

Unusual, a visitor this time of day. Everyone knew he liked to sleep in, and everyone knew he hated to be disturbed at breakfast. Or any other mealtime, come to think of it.

Methodically chewing the bite he'd just taken, Federico decided to ignore the knock. Whoever it was would either give up entirely or come back later, and by then, he wouldn't be home anymore.

A sip of wine helped the bite get down. It was his first glass and the first bottle—he was shockingly sober, and Federico didn't hold with sobriety anymore. Not since his house rang with silence.

Another knock, more insistent this time and accompanied by a voice.

Sounded like a guard.

Hmmm.

Federico put the chicken leg down and licked the juice off his fingers. Never had a guard knocked on his door for so long. There was no reason—he did his duty, he never missed a court appointment, he did as he was told. And there was no trial today.

He might as well have a look. Life was boring nowadays. Maybe the knocker was someone interesting for a change, and not just another client with a bribe.

Federico pulled a face when he heaved himself out of the chair. His muscles protested, so did his joints, and his stomach demanded the chicken leg. But his brain, which stayed in working order no matter how much he tried to drown it in alcohol, demanded to know who was at the door.

By the time he'd made it downstairs, the knocking had turned into a pounding. They'd break the door down if he didn't hurry.

"What?" the judge snapped, ripping the door open. The door handle nearly slipped out of his greasy fingers.

Outside was only one guard. He knew her—she served in Well Prison, and she'd been looking after the pregnant girl who hadn't killed her father and who he'd sentenced to death nevertheless. Well, by now, Jack would have freed her, so no harm done.

Anika handed him a roll of parchment. "Urgent message, Judge Federico," she said, standing straight. "I am to escort you to the palace for a trial. Sir."

Federico snorted. "Sure. The palace. And pigs can fly, eh?" No one would ever order him to judge there. Only members of the royal family were judged in the palace. And in such an unlikely case, it wouldn't be him to speak the verdict.

"Don't know about any pigs, sir, but if you open the parchment, sir, you'll probably get an explanation. Princess Kayla gave it to me less than twenty minutes ago, and she said if I didn't bring you, we'd both be in real deep shit."

Federico looked at the sigil. It belonged to the royal family. "She said that, yes?"

Anika grinned. "Not with such nasty words, sir, but the meaning was clear."

Federico broke the sigil and unrolled the parchment. Not that he expected anything to be written on it—this surely was a joke— but he was curious nevertheless.

When he read the first words, he belched. The chicken, eggs, ham, and the pancakes wanted to get out of his stomach again, quite desperately to boot.

"It is signed by the empress," he said weakly. "I am to go to the palace."

"Just what I told you." Anika took the judge's arm to steady his step and led him to the waiting carriage.

LORD BARNARD had been up since dawn, pacing his room and cursing the judge who'd stopped him from taking over Babylon Manor. Instead of ordering the death sentence to be carried out immediately, that bastard had postponed it for three days, claiming the hangman's workload.

Three days!

Back in the courtroom, he'd managed to calm down enough to smile and nod, accepting the verdict no matter how hot the hate had burned inside him. Federico, fat and useless as he was, still had the power to put him into prison, and prison was a place Barnard would like to avoid at all cost.

But—three days!

Had the damn judge done his job properly, the bitch would be dead by now. She'd have been taken to the stake immediately, and that strange little monk would have been too late to take her away. But no, Federico had to talk to her! Had needed to hear her opinion, and instead of two minutes, the whole farce had taken closer to an hour.

Cursing under his breath, Barnard opened and closed his fists constantly, wishing it was the bitch's throat he was squeezing, not just air. So close, he'd been so close to getting her land and Babylon Manor! If only the judge had done what he'd been paid for.

"I should teach him a lesson," Barnard murmured. "Pete is watching his sister, and I never ordered him to get back. So I could let him know I want an accident to happen. A small one. Nothing too drastic."

He grinned. For Pete, "nothing too drastic" didn't mean the same thing it did for other people. By nightfall, Judge Federico would have one sister less.

Barnard heard the knock on the door but didn't think about it. If it was important, one of his servants would get him.

Irritated at the silence outside, Barnard opened the door to his private rooms to take a look himself—usually, there was some shouting and a lot of laughter when someone who should not call on his mercy was taught a lesson.

The city guards seized him the moment he stepped outside. One twisted his arms behind his back, and the other one took his sword belt as well as his boot knife. His servants stood pressed to the wall, wide-eyed and frightened, kept in check by a fierce-looking woman.

"You're making a mistake!" Barnard croaked. "I'm—"

"Lord Barnard of Compton Manor. Direct neighbor to Babylon Manor, owned by Lucinda of Babylon. That correct?" The guard had a parchment in his hand, checking the names written on it.

Barnard gulped. His heart gave an extra beat, and he began to sweat—he had to be careful with his heart; it tended to race on occasions, leaving him weak and out of breath for hours. "That's me," he said, trying to free his hands. "If you know who I am you also know there is no reason for force!"

"Got orders to take you to the palace. I'm Gabriel, Princess Kayla's personal guard. She sent me. Made it urgent. Boys, take him away. The princess hates to wait."

"You're making a huge mistake!" Barnard screamed, kicking and fighting and not giving a shit about his heart. "I'm Lord Barnard, close personal friend to the lord chancellor, and if you don't release me immediately, I'll make sure you get hanged!"

The guard cast him a smile. "Want to ride in a carriage, or shall we throw you over the back of a horse, my lord? Makes no difference for us."

They were dragging him outside his house, and they didn't care a damn about his status or his money or anything else. They wouldn't... they couldn't....

Horses and a carriage were waiting before his door. When the guards dragged him to a sorry-looking mare, Barnard finally realized this morning wouldn't go as planned "Not the horse!" he bit out. The guards threw him into the carriage instead.

Barnard's heartbeat sped up, making his lungs go all wheezy, and his hands began to shake. Someone would pay for this. As soon as these idiots got it into their thick heads that they'd taken the wrong man, he'd have a nice, long chat with his friends.

Pressing a hand to his chest, Barnard fought hard to get his breathing under control. It was about time the war began. It was about time the lord chancellor took over the kingdom's affairs and got rid of the old woman pretending to be an empress.

Judge Federico, descendant of a long line of judges but about as far away from ever becoming a lord as he was from becoming thin, had never had the honor to set foot in the palace. When he had been younger—and slightly healthier—he occasionally had walked along its huge gates and wondered how it might look inside, but he had never suffered from the delusional wish to ever get an invitation to the royal court. Therefore, he was very nervous when the carriage stopped and Anika helped him out. He was nervous when he was led upstairs and through corridors, and he was out of breath when they finally reached the courtroom.

Only the most valuable members of society were judged here. Only a lord was allowed to sit in the judge's chair, and really, he shouldn't be here. This was a mistake, and a big one on top of it.

A guard saluted him when he entered the courtroom. Federico nearly jumped.

Slowly, he climbed up the steps to the judge's chair, awaiting shouts and hands pulling him away and angry faces at his insolence.

There were none.

The chair didn't feel much different from the one in Well Prison. It was a bit larger and maybe a bit softer.

He relaxed ever so slightly. This here was common ground no matter the circumstances. This here was a courtroom, he was a judge, there were files, and well, until someone explained to him what was going on, he might as well have a look at them.

He was stunned to see the files were his own. His handwriting; his comments.

His signature under the verdict.

Federico frowned. Why drag him here when the verdict was already spoken?

The courtroom became unimportant, so did the people who streamed in and took their places. He glanced—there weren't many. Hmmm. Some of them were quite important members of the city's aristocracy. Well. Probably, they didn't have anything else to do today, and anyway, they could wait until he got a clearer picture of the situation he'd somehow ended up in. Luckily, Anika stood next to him. Leaning over, he asked her to organize him something to eat so he could calm his nerves a bit.

Flipping through the pages, Federico quickly understood it was the case of the girl he'd sentenced to death not too long ago. Brother Wulfric had snatched her away moments after he'd signed the verdict—the very one he now held in hands again.

What the hell? he thought, and then Anika returned with a pile of sandwiches. Federico groaned at the sight of them. He hated sandwiches. Squishy and a mess to eat. But well, better than nothing.

Taking the first bite, he suddenly realized no one had told him how to judge.

He dropped the sandwich, the taste of ham and egg on his tongue turning to ash.

No one had bribed him. No one had threatened to kill his family. No one apart from Lord Barnard, who sat in first row, two guards to the left and right of him. He looked miserable and even more nervous than Federico felt, so probably he couldn't count on judging according to the lord's wishes. The man wanted the girl dead, and Federico had sentenced her to death. This should be over.

Instead he was here and didn't know what was expected of him.

His hunger vanished. Given the dread filling his stomach, he guessed he wouldn't eat anything anytime soon.

"Rise!"

A guard had called out, and everyone in court stood up. Only Federico remained seated—he was too heavy, and anyway, a judge didn't stand for anyone.

The girl was led in and took her place in the suspect's stand. She wore a richly embroidered dress, her hair was done properly, and surely they didn't expect him to honor her by getting to his feet?

Most people in the courtroom looked as bewildered as him.

"Princess Kayla," the guard called out, and heads turned, and a murmur arose. It was unheard of for the princess to attend court sessions. But there she was, dressed in deep blue and not wearing either jewelry or weapons.

Federico remembered the rumor of her son's death, wondered if it was true, looked at her face, and knew the answer was yes.

He knew how she felt right now. Which didn't change the fact that he had no idea what was going on here.

Federico wished his legs would obey orders, but they didn't, and so he remained seated.

"Her Highness, Empress Deoris," the guard called out, and this time, there were shocked outcries and people stood on their tiptoes so they wouldn't miss the empress taking her seat.

Somewhat amused, Federico noticed the lord chancellor swaying as if he'd taken a blow to his head. Several lords and ladies were whispering frantically, and a few were about to leave the courtroom when the guards secured the doors. No one was about to come in again, but much more importantly, no one was to get out either.

His nervousness vanished, and the sweat on his hands and face dried. He was the judge, and no one had bribed him. The empress was here, her daughter, many of rank including the lord chancellor—this should become interesting. Finally.

They were all here for an unimportant, rude young girl he'd taken a liking to and who, somehow, had managed to befriend Jack, a former assassin.

Who was, not surprisingly at all, here as well.

"Take your seats," Federico said, relived his voice sounded steady and powerful. "Your Highness, my princess—I am most honored to be blessed with your presence in this case. May the verdict be just."

There. He'd said it. The old formula to be spoken by every judge before he signed the verdict and which he'd refused to say ever since his wife and daughter had died.

No one had bribed him. The girl's case was of interest to the empress and her daughter, no one had bribed him, and he would speak just.

Federico cleared his throat and hid his hands underneath the table so no one would see them shake. "I have sentenced Lucinda of Babylon to death already," he said, looking at the empress. "The verdict was signed. It is here on my table. As this is a unique case, I would like to know if it is legal to dismiss it and take a fresh look at the case."

The empress nodded.

A fair trial. Federico couldn't believe it.

Then his eyes fell on Lord Barnard's smiling face, and he knew his short dream of justice was over already. The man had bribed him. He had someone at his sister's house; he'd told him when he'd handed over the money. Federico was certain Barnard was threatening his family even now while they were both in the palace, and there was no way he could do anything but sentence the girl to death again.

He could feel himself going pale, the blood rushing from his face as if it were a leaking bottle. His hands underneath the table shook so badly he couldn't have picked up a sandwich even if he had wanted to.

The empress expected a fair trial, and Federico was sure she knew everything he had written into his file including his doubts about the girl's guilt. She wouldn't accept a death sentence, but if he spoke a different—and honest—verdict, his family would suffer for it.

For the first time this day, Judge Federico longed for a huge jug of very strong beer.

"Is there a problem?"

The empress's voice cut down every whisper. All eyes were on her.

Federico didn't know what to answer. The truth was not an option, so he stayed quiet.

The empress leaned over to her daughter, said something, and everyone in court saw the princess nod in agreement.

Nearly the complete audience paled at the sight.

"We understand there have been issues concerning the safety of your family," the empress said. "To guarantee a fair trial, we hereby elevate Judge Federico to the status of a lord. Any harm coming upon him or his family will be considered as the worst crime imaginable. Anyone committing such a crime will be mercilessly hunted down. Anyone so much as trying to order such a crime will be taken into the Main Dungeons immediately." She gave a small sign to one of the guards, who left instantly. "And just in case, we have sent guards, making sure Judge Federico's family is well and safe."

Maybe Federico imagined it, but he thought her eyes were right on Barnard. And given the terrified look on Barnard's face, he understood the implications of her decision just as well as Federico.

Lord Federico.

He gulped, wondering whether he would wake up soon or if this nightmare would continue much longer.

Lord. Him. And his sister, her husband, his nephews, and his father would be safe forever no matter how he judged. Bribery wouldn't be an issue ever again. Fear wouldn't be an issue again.

Federico, too sober for his own liking and more scared than he had been in a very long time, put his suddenly steady hands flat onto the file in front of him. "In this case, I judge the young lady, Lucinda of Babylon, charged with the murder of her father, Lucius of Babylon, as not guilty."

Maybe he should ask for a short break so he could go and find a nice, quiet corner so he could throw up.

On the other hand, watching Barnard desperately try to keep control over his emotions and failing more and more with every breath he forced into his lungs was worth a bit of an upset stomach.

"You judged quite quickly," the empress said. "Are you certain?"

"Absolutely. There is no evidence whatsoever she killed her father or ever visited the inn where the deceased's head was found. On the day of his death, she was not at Babylon Manor. Not guilty, Your Highness."

"She hated him! She wanted him dead, she always interfered with his decisions, and whenever he tried to bring her to heel, she called him a useless coward." Lord Barnard had jumped up, his face bright red with anger and frantically fighting against the guards who tried to pull him back onto his seat.

Before Federico could say anything, Luca leaned forward, spitting at Barnard. She missed him, but only barely. "And you know that because you regularly had a drink with Lucius. I heard you laugh. I saw the two of you getting drunk, and twice, you killed one of my dogs. Yes, I hated him. But I didn't kill him."

Wulfric—*when did he come in?* Federico wondered—raised a hand. "If I may? She doesn't lie. Truth magic, Your Highness. Unusual and awfully complicated to weave, I know, but I thought it would be of help here."

Federico signed the verdict. It felt good. Maybe he shouldn't be surprised—it had been ages since he'd judged fairly.

"In this case, I demand to become her legal guardian." Barnard looked decidedly ill. Underneath the red color on his face he was pale, his skin waxen. He was sweating, and his breath came in short gasps. Still, he stood tall and proud, facing the judge and playing out his last card. "She's not yet of age. She's too young to run a manor. Since Lucius is dead, she needs a legal guardian. As her next door neighbor and because Lucius has promised me her hand once she's of age, I am the logical choice for the part."

"In your dreams you are," Luca said acidly. It earned her some laughs, mainly from the guards. "And anyway, you're too late. I'm already married. With a husband at my side, I am to be considered legally of age, and you can shut up now, Barnard."

As the empress didn't intervene, Federico decided to sort out this problem as well. "Can you present your marriage certificate?"

Luca held up her hand. "I married the old way. We shared a bed and a meal. I willingly gave him my virginity, and willingly, he took me into his bed. I wear his ring I wove from both of our hair and if you ask him, he will tell you this is the truth."

"All true," Wulfric cast in. "Just in case anyone is interested."

Barnard waved his hand dismissively as if swatting away an annoying fly. "A wedding ring can be forged. Where's your husband, Lucinda? Anywhere near?" The smirk on Barnard's face showed how certain he was that he would win this game.

From the shadows, a man in black stepped into the light. He was tall and pale, and right behind him was a younger man. Federico hadn't seen either of them ever before, which didn't matter since he knew an assassin when he saw one. "I'm Rage," the man said, and Federico thought he could hear a faint rasp in his voice as if he'd overdone it recently. Probably too much shouting in a tavern.

"Judge, my wife has been cleared of all charges. I want her out of the offender's stand."

The girl, not awaiting Federico's nod, pushed past the guards and slipped her hand in his.

Federico just had to grin at that, especially as he saw Barnard blinking in confusion and staring at Rage disbelievingly. Full of hate, he shouted, "She's been promised to me! By Lucius of Babylon. Her father. We shook hands over it. She's been *promised* to me! She cannot go and marry someone else just as she pleases without facing the consequences!"

"Oh, oh," Wulfric murmured, nodding sadly. "Another truth, I fear."

"Lucius, he promised me her hand. He"—Barnard pointed a finger at Rage—"he stole her from me. I want, I want, I want compensation is what I want. For, for a lost future with a loving wife. Yes. That's what I want."

Rage raised an eyebrow. "A loving wife? Luca? Are you kidding me?"

Laughter rippled from the audience when Luca kicked Rage's shin, but was quickly stilled by the empress's hand. "What is it you want, Lord Barnard? What kind of compensation do you have in mind?"

Barnard grinned a cruel smile. His eyes fixed on Rage as if trying to figure out who he was, he said, "One night. I want a night with his beloved. It's only fair, isn't it? He's had all the pleasure. He'll get the land and the title. All I want is one night. I promise I will be… gentle."

"You worthless, lousy, creepy little bastard!" Luca shouted, to the delight of several women in the audience.

Rage put his arm around her waist. He seemed to seriously consider the offer. "Fine," he finally said. He looked at Luca. "One night with my beloved."

"Rage!" Luca screamed, balling her fists but unable to step far enough away from him since he didn't let go of her. "I'm not—"

Rage flashed her one of his rare smiles, and she stopped midsentence.

"Agreed, Barnard?"

"Agreed!" Barnard could barely sputter out the word in his haste to close the deal.

Rage's smile vanished. He put his free hand onto the young man's shoulder. "Keiran. You don't mind, beloved? I've got the strong feeling Barnard hasn't had much experience in getting fucked by a guy. Just"—and here he grinned—"be gentle."

"What?" Confused, Barnard looked at Luca, then turned to the empress for help. "The boy? No, I meant her, Lucinda. I didn't agree on the boy. She's—"

Federico, following with all his senses the drama unraveling in his courtroom, leaned forward to get a better look. He knew better than to interfere. This here would sort out itself, if he wasn't totally mistaken.

Rage walked straight up to Barnard. Behind him, the girl and the young man joined hands.

Good.

Rage reached out and grabbed Barnard's collar, pulling him up from his seat where he was trying to hide. "I don't give a damn what you *meant*. I asked what you want, and your answer was clear. One night with my beloved. You did not mention a name. The one I love is Keiran. Have a night with him. Don't come running if he does things with you that you might consider unpleasant." Letting go of Barnard, he stepped back.

Barnard struggled for breath upon falling back to the bench. He was pale and sweaty. Wiping his hands on his trousers, Rage went back to Luca and Keiran.

Wulfric clapped. "Well, Barnard, Rage spoke the truth," he said mildly. "The boy is his beloved. I—and everyone else, I believe—knows you're fond of young girls, but not of young boys. Pity, really. If I were a bit younger, I'd court the young man myself."

Barnard swallowed dryly. "You know that's not what I meant. He tricked me. It's not fair!"

Judge Federico belched. "Enough of this. Lord Barnard, we all heard what you said. Are you taking the offer? If not, this case is closed."

After a long moment between harsh intakes of breath, Barnard shook his head in disgust.

He wasn't willing to give up, though. Still staring at Rage, his hands gripping the bench he was sitting on, his eyes suddenly widened.

He turned around, scanning the audience.

Whatever he saw there, it made him raise his chin. He stood up, swaying. "This man," he said, and behind him, the audience became restless all of a sudden. "When Wulfric came to get the girl, he said her husband had murdered Prince Leon."

People shuffled in their seats. Feet tapped nervously on the floor, and hands wiped sweaty brows. Barnard, though, did not stop talking.

"He's a killer," Barnard shrieked. "I mean, you can even see it. He's an assassin! We never wanted the prince to die. We just wanted the princess distracted and the empress too busy for reigning. A war would solve so many problems!" He turned, looking at the audience. What he saw made him frown, and he faced the empress. "Can't you see it? We need a war! We need some money coming in. We need to discourage the southern territories eyeing our borders, we need—but you don't want this to happen, so we acted!"

Slamming his fists to the barrier in front of him, Barnard didn't even notice the guards appearing to the left and right of him until they put their hands on his shoulders.

"Thank you, Lord Barnard." Wulfric rubbed his hands. "I see you have a deep understanding of current politics. Would you mind terribly telling us who else is involved?"

Several people from the audience were on their feet, trying to hide behind others. There were muffled cries of shock, there were only very few genuinely confused looks, and there was, in general, every effort made to look innocent.

Wulfric smiled. "Actually, I would like to ask all of you a few questions. Your Highness, with your permission?"

The empress, looking grim, nodded. The guards who had been securing the doors stepped forward and arrested protesting lords and counts, men and women alike.

"What?" Barnard looked confused amidst the chaos. "What's happening?"

Wulfric patted his cheek in a nearly friendly manner. "I finally found someone who I can talk to." He was hopping, cheerful like a child. "Why, oh why did I know you would turn out to be the weakest link in the chain? Only the Lady knows. However, in the Main Dungeons we will have all the time of the world for a nice little chat. Which, in a way, I am terribly sorry for, but well, this is how it is going to be. It means I will not get to bed early again tonight. Truly, is no one thinking of my health but me? Anyway. Some call me careless, and some think I am, in fact, completely out of my mind, but I do not want a war, I do serve my empress, and I deeply dislike little boys dying. Get him out of here."

"No, but—" Barnard began, but Wulfric obviously didn't listen anymore. He made sure the room was cleared, and together with Federico, he watched the empress and Princess Kayla leave.

Anika stepped up to Federico. "May I help you?" she asked and offered him her arm.

He allowed her to help him up, but instead of leaving, he quietly told her to walk with him into a dark corner ideal for overhearing ongoing conversations.

"I am getting too old for this," Wulfric sighed. "Two nights in a row without sleep—do you have any idea what that means for a man as ancient as me?"

He looked at Rage and smiled. The silence in the courtroom was disturbing. Dust stirred by restless feet was settling quietly on the benches. It would be not very long before other verdicts would be spoken here.

"I think it is time you are going home," Wulfric said. "All of you."

"You suspected Barnard. Why?" Jack asked.

"Because of his greed. At first, he was just a welcome tool to lure you to town, dear boy. But then I began to think, which, for me, is always a pleasure. I thought, 'Why is he so eager to get his hands on Babylon Manor? Is it just because he wants to add to his already considerable wealth? Is it, maybe, because he actually has a weak spot for young Lucinda here? Or is it because in case of a war he could do with the large meadows perfect for raising battle horses?' Apparently, it was the latter. And obviously him losing everything made his tongue a bit careless." Pressing his hands to the small of his back, he sighed again, deeper this time, and longer. "However, the young lady is with child, and it is not good to give birth here in the city if one is accustomed to the countryside. Do get home, if you please."

"You'll let us go just like that?" Luca sounded as if she didn't believe a single word the monk had said, and Federico, silently watching, could only agree.

Wulfric shook his head. "Sad, really, the distrust young people show towards a man of the Lady nowadays. Yes, I will let you go. I have more pressing matters to attend, and for some reason I believe that you would cause more problems staying here than you ever could on your nice manor. Give birth to your daughter, Lucinda of Babylon. When she is old enough, I will come by and pay you a visit. I have the distinct feeling this child will be special." He took a step, raising his hand in an attempt to put it on Luca's belly.

With one step, Keiran was in front of her. And although Federico didn't hear a thing, he had the strange feeling that the boy was shouting at the top of his lungs.

And Wulfric winced, staggering backward. "Ouch," he groaned. "That hurt! By the Lady, young man, you need tutoring. I want you back in the city sooner rather than later. Rage, make sure he actually finds his way here, or I will find methods to make your life miserable. If he does not learn to control his new skill, he will go mad anyway." He smiled his disturbing little smile. "Somehow, it is a riddle to me why you didn't go mad, dear boy. But then, it is none of my business. You did your job. You were paid accordingly. Now get out of my sight."

Federico saw the man in black reaching out, ready to strangle Wulfric, and he saw Jack putting a soothing hand on his arm. This was a strange quartet; that much was for sure. The girl slipped her hand into the assassin's, and Rage took a step back.

"I should kill you, monk," he said, and there it was again, the hint of hoarseness, the hint of past pain. Federico decided to do a bit of research, just to quench his curiosity.

"And will you?" Wulfric tilted his head.

"Not now. Now, it is time to go home."

With that, the man in black turned, leaving Wulfric behind, who stared after him with a calculating look on his friendly face.

CHAPTER
Twenty

THE JOURNEY out of the city was much harder than anticipated. Spring couldn't decide whether to stay or play hide-and-seek with winter for another little while. The nights were cold, the ground hard, and Luca way too unwell to perform magic that would have warmed anyone but herself.

"We all need a break, but you especially," Rage finally said, ending the debate over whether they should head for Dragon Spring Farm or Babylon Manor. "We'll stay at Jack's house until the baby is born. The man who runs Babylon Manor, can you trust him?"

"Eli is a crook, a liar, and a thief," Luca replied. "I do trust him, but I want to go home, anyway."

"The babe will be stillborn if you don't agree to rest," Rage snapped. "Jack's place is days closer than yours. Shut up and do what you are told at least once in your life."

Luca stared at him and began to cry. She fled into Keiran's arms, who held her close, soothed her, and even shared a blanket with her during the night, when Luca tended to have nightmares. Without him, the journey would have been even harder; without him, she truly might have lost the baby.

Rage, keeping watch during the night and dozing in the saddle during the day, began to feel every bone in his body, and not in a good way. He ached, and with the pain slowly but inevitably increasing, he stopped talking, stopped eating, stopped sleeping.

"Not much longer, cub," Jack told him each morning. "Wish we could go faster, but with you falling apart and the girl throwing up every other minute, it's just a little bit longer."

Rage didn't even grunt. He just rode on.

When they finally reached the farm, it was as if they'd just escaped hell.

Marit came out to meet them. "All of them staying here? How long for?" she demanded to know, clearly disapproving of anyone staying apart from Jack and—maybe—Rage. "The girl will clean out the pantry in no time, old man. And the boy, will he sleep with master Rage or with the girl or with both of them or what? I'm not holding up for this lewd behavior and such, I'm telling you. Find yourself another housekeeper—"

Jack clenched his fists. "Marit. One more word, and I'll personally gag you and throw you into the henhouse. Draw a bath for Rage. Food for all of us in an hour. Cub, after the bath and after you've eaten you'll sleep unless you want me to club you. Keiran, take Luca to the spare room and make sure she lies down. Stay with her, and get her whatever she wants. Other than that, I don't want to hear or see anything until tomorrow morning. Now do what you are told. All of you."

And they did.

From then on, things finally began to improve.

MONTHS LATER, Jack had picked up his habit of spending his nights with one of his various mistresses. Luca, raiding the pantry far less than Marit had feared, was due to deliver the baby any moment now. Rage had left pain and nightmares behind, with the help of regular sleep, Marit's food, lots of hot baths, and lots of sex. True, there had been visitors and letters from the empress. True also that Keiran had been in the city twice so far, for five days each time, alone. He'd gone unwillingly, but he'd gone nevertheless, and when back home, his grip on his impossible magic had strengthened.

Other than that, it had been a peaceful few months at Dragon Spring Farm.

It was a truly warm day. Keiran, bathing in the sun near the well, stretched and let his hand dangle in the water. Lazily, he discarded the thought of getting up for something to eat. Instead, he rolled around and sprayed the wet, cold drops onto Rage's sun-heated skin.

Rage didn't even open his eyes. He was lying on his back, mostly asleep after a long, languid morning of lovemaking. "Don't tell me you are still not satisfied." His left hand found Keiran's ankle. Circling the joint, he brushed his thumb over the sole.

Keiran grinned. *Maybe I'm in the mood to play.*

"I'm too lazy to play." Rage yawned. "Tonight, maybe."

Scooping up some water, Keiran let it rain onto Rage's groin.

A smile spread on the assassin's face. "I thought we played enough. Seems I was wrong."

His cock stirred. When Keiran sucked it into his mouth and Keiran's cool fingers rolled his balls, Rage moaned softly and spread his legs a bit wider. *Thought you were too lazy to play?* Keiran mocked. With a last, hard suck he brought his lover to the brink, but let his cock slip out of his mouth before he could come.

He didn't need to touch himself to get hard. The thought of what lay ahead was more than enough to make his whole body tense with excitement.

He traced his fingertips down to Rage's ankles, leaving a wet trail in their wake. Twice Keiran dug his hand into the water until his lover's skin was decorated with dozens of tiny pearls. Some ran down his sides; Keiran could see from Rage's twitching lip that it tickled and that it was most arousing. He would come long before Keiran could fuck him if he wasn't careful.

Swiftly, Keiran sat up and shifted between his lover's legs. Rage's eyes fluttered open. Lifting his head, he watched Keiran, waiting.

He trusts me, Keiran thought, still considering it a miracle and, as it happened sometimes, disbelieving what he had gotten himself into. A long time ago, all he had wanted to do was find his friend Luca. What he'd found was not only Luca but the assassin, and the same night they'd met, he had seduced him.

He trusted me even back then.

Circling Rage's entrance, Keiran watched as his lover's cock twitched. Rage had remarkable self-control, and he wouldn't want to spill his seed too soon. Keiran could play this game as slowly as he liked. Usually, it was Rage who was top, and it was Rage who determined the speed.

Today, it would be the other way around if this was to work.

Keiran would have to control Rage's magic.

He slipped a finger into Rage's entrance, feathering over Rage's sweet spot until his lover bucked against his hand, one foot pressed to the soft ground, the other still outstretched.

A bead of sweat showed on Rage's face, but maybe that was from the sun's heat. But his breathing was ragged now, his eyes glued to Keiran's face, and there was that hunger again, the need, and the love that had replaced the hole in his heart.

Keiran smiled when he felt his lover shudder under his touch. He leaned down and kissed one of Rage's nipples, rolling it between his teeth, sucking it until it was hard. He'd nearly stopped fingerfucking his lover; by now, it was more like a soft caress.

Keiran moved down and kissed the velvety head of Rage's cock. Simultaneously, he removed his fingers, dipped them into the water once more, and drew small, cold circles on Rage's balls.

Rage moaned in a soft, helpless way, something he never did when on top.

And the magic inside him uncoiled. It did so always, at some point during their lovemaking. In the past few days, it had been later rather than sooner, but always, Rage needed to tighten the net, to reign in the wildness inside him. It distracted him, in a way, and it stopped him from losing himself to their lovemaking.

It also bothered him, although he'd never said a word about it and probably never would. Rage's magic was, in his eyes, his problem.

Keiran, though, was nevertheless able to tell the exact moment Rage shifted his focus from simply having pleasure to that place inside him where his magic tried to break free.

Today, he didn't want that to happen. Today, he wanted Rage to enjoy this without having to worry about anything, and least of all his magic.

Gently, Keiran sucked Rage's cock, tasting the salty drops whilst stroking his lover's balls. He was hard himself, had been for ages, it seemed. He wouldn't be able to wait much longer.

Please.

He'd waited for this, the silent plea, the wordless begging to get fucked. But it wasn't enough.

Please what?

It was how it had to be if Rage was to lose control completely. When he was drunk or high, he gave up easily. When sober, it took more to unravel him, and it was Keiran's task to get him there.

He let Rage's cock slip out of his mouth and moved upward until he was face-to-face with his lover. *Please what, Rage? Please kiss me? Please stop? You need to tell me what you want, or I won't do it.*

A hint of uncertainty, barely visible, maybe barely there. Wild magic roared, eager to escape, to hurt, and to kill.

Rage's focus shifted away from him.

Keiran felt it too and quickly placed his hand on Rage's chest, pressed his whole body to his lover's. *Don't. I know what I'm doing.*

Rage hesitated. His concentration was sharply centered at the net he had to weave, but in the past months, Keiran had learned a few things under Wulfric's tutoring. He knew how to weave the net.

Let me do this.

Rage relaxed. His eyes fluttered closed, and his breath became a bit more regular. The iron-like grip of his mind around his magic softened.

Keiran leaned in and kissed him.

Rage's arm locked behind Keiran's neck. *Please, beloved! Fuck me.*

Keiran's cock tightened along with his. Greedy with lust, he spread Rage's legs; quickly, he slipped on top. His hand guiding his cock, he found Rage's entrance slack with need, and he didn't take much time to ease his way in—there had been enough preparation, he was way too hard to wait, and anyway, if he thought about this any longer, he might get too scared to actually do it.

Take control.

One hard push. A strangled cry from Rage's lips, raw and low.

Keiran reached inside, found the net, and tightened it.

Control. For now.

Not enough, not by far.

A push; a hold.

Again.

Keiran fucked Rage slowly, always holding back himself because this was not for him but for Rage and because he needed to keep control over his lover's magic. Reaching inside someone's head and heart wasn't easy, never had been even after Wulfric had showed him how it was done. When all he wanted was to find his release, it was a task that needed a lot of concentration.

But Rage trusted him.

Keiran could feel Rage's mind slip away to the dark spot deep inside him, where his magic rattled at the bars of its cage.

It was now or never.

Wait, Keiran said into the silence behind Rage's closed lids. He reached out, touched the cage's bars, and gently pushed Rage back to the light, where there was nothing but pleasure and the promise of a fabulous orgasm.

A second; a blink, even—Rage hesitated.

And then he gave up control.

Slowly, steadily, Keiran moved body and mind. The wild magic was roaring. He strained to keep it under control and not lose his rhythm at the same time. He barely managed it.

Rage was now groaning regularly, his pelvis grinding against Keiran's cock. Both his legs were wrapped around Keiran's hips, and each time Keiran drove into him, it felt deeper than before.

Keiran caught one of his lover's arms and held it down, restricting his movement, holding him, keeping him under control. It was easier for him that way because it helped him focus his mind.

And the magic stayed caged, even though Rage didn't hold the net. Keiran did.

The groans became small yelps, then short, breathless screams. Rage lost himself in pleasure, careless of consequences, and certainly not in any state to control anything anymore.

Keiran, watching him, kept control.

Holding Rage down with his left hand, he placed his right on Rage's hip, to keep his weight off his lover and to drive into him with full force now. Slow was over. Fast and hard replaced the gentle rhythm.

One last hard thrust, and Rage came, crying out Keiran's name with his voice as well as his mind.

Sweat pouring down his face, Keiran clenched his jaws, keeping a hold on Rage's magic, and came himself.

He collapsed on top of Rage, then slipped off him. Keiran flopped into the grass beside Rage, and because this part was always bittersweet for him, it was easy to part with Rage's soul as well, releasing his grip on the magical net and retreating silently, unnoticed, whilst the magic went to sleep just like that.

For a heartbeat, he felt lonelier than ever before, the close physical and mental contact undone, though he'd believed but a moment ago it would last forever.

A low, contented sigh caught his attention. Rage pulled him close until his head rested on his shoulder. Only now, Keiran realized how badly he trembled; only now he realized how much energy this had cost him. The sun was low over the horizon. Luca would be waiting for them to come home.

Not yet, though.

Rage didn't talk, his heartbeat slowing gradually. When Keiran, out of a sudden need for closeness, hugged him, he just tightened his grip.

The evening wind blew across the short grass and dried their sweating bodies. A lone bird began to sing now that the day's heat broke.

Rage turned his head, brushing a kiss against Keiran's temple.

Not knowing how to phrase his worries, Keiran just asked, *You all right?* hoping what he'd done hadn't been too much.

Rage pushed himself up, resting on his elbow and looking down at Keiran. *Yes. I need a word with Wulfric, though. The things he teaches you are troublesome.*

Wulfric said it would be madness, trying it. Still—

Taking Keiran's face between his hands, Rage kissed him.

They took a bath afterward, playing like little boys, laughing and chasing each other as if there had never been dark and painful times. Right now, neither thought of what lay ahead of them.

Luca would be going back to Babylon Manor after the baby was born.

Keiran needed to go back to the city for further lessons with Wulfric.

Rage had been summoned before the empress.

Right now, all that counted was that they were together, that the water was cold and refreshing, that dinner waited for them, and that tonight they would sleep in one bed with no chance for nightmares.

They got dressed and were about to leave when they heard footsteps and a constant, annoyed mutter.

"Why do you always have to hide here?" Marit growled, standing in front of them, a leaf or two showing in her hair. "It's a long way, and I am old. Not that anyone would care."

Rage put his shirt on. "Then why bother?"

"Better hurry up, Master Rage," Marit said, her arms crossed over her breasts. "It is time."

Rage raised an eyebrow. "Dinner can surely wait a little while longer?"

Marit spat on the ground, turning back to the house already. "As if I had time to prepare dinner. It's time for you to get home to your wife, assassin. Stop fooling around with the boy. Hurry, for I need to get old Jack, too, who's somewhere in the village."

Rage and Keiran shared a look. "Something wrong with Luca?"

"Men. Such stupid creatures." Marit smirked. "The missy is in labor. You might be already too late and the little thing has dropped to the floor instead of your waiting hands. Because that's what a father is supposed to do, isn't it? Be with the wife, help her through the hard time, catch the babe when it's born?"

Both Rage and Keiran broke into a run, leaving Marit behind.

"If only I knew which of those two shared the girl's bed," the old woman mumbled. And then she grinned. If she hadn't watched from behind the trees, she could have told them sooner.

EPILOGUE

MOMMY?

"Use your mouth when speaking to me, love."

"Mommy?"

"Yes, love?"

"Papa is coming home today." The little girl, sitting on the kitchen chair and watching her mom prepare lunch, dangled her legs and tried to nick some carrots, only to earn herself a stern look.

"Is he? About time. He's been gone for weeks. Truly, I don't understand why he insists on doing… whatever he does when he's gone."

Sasha hid her smile behind her hand. It was so funny when Mommy tried not to talk about Papa's job. She remembered only at the last moment, and there was always a bit of stuttering around the subject.

"Mommy?"

"Yes, love."

"Do you miss Papa?"

Mommy put down the knife she used to chop carrots. She cleaned her hands on a cloth, picked up the bowl of carrots, and placed it on the table. Then she sat down, surely for the first time this morning. Sasha knew her mom got up at dawn, often forgot to have breakfast, and rarely had a break before way past lunchtime. That she took the time to sit with her now was an unexpected treat.

Mommy took a carrot; it crunched when she bit it in half. "Yes, I miss him," she said, her mouth full. Sasha thought she looked suddenly very young, not at all like a mommy anymore but a teenage girl, especially because her hair wasn't braided properly today.

Actually, mommy's hair was rarely braided properly, a fact that led to constant chatter between the maids. In Sasha's opinion, it looked beautiful. Her whole mommy looked beautiful, even when her arms were dirty up to her elbows after she'd helped a foal getting born, or when her hair was covered in straw at harvest time, or when she was tired and grumpy in the evening.

Mommy seemed to think nibbling the carrots was an all right thing to do although lunch was only an hour away. So Sasha nicked one too. They were always best when stolen.

"But Papa will sleep in Keiran's bed tonight," Sasha said and wished she'd bitten her tongue instead because where Papa slept was something else she wasn't supposed to know. After all, she was only five. Vaguely, she suspected the sleeping habits of parents weren't among the things little girls should care about.

But Mommy was in a cheeky mood today. She smiled and tucked a strand of ink black hair behind her daughter's ear. "You see too much, mouse. What else do you know?"

Sasha blushed. Having her mommy's full attention was as welcome and wonderful as it was scary. Usually, that only happened when she'd done something bad, like spied on Jean, her maid, or listened in on private conversations. In such a case, Keiran always knew, and if Keiran knew, her mommy knew as well.

She hadn't spied in a long time, and she hadn't done anything bad either. Nothing she knew of, anyway.

"I know Papa is tired," she tried, carefully watching her mom's face in case she said something wrong. But Papa was a safe subject. Mommy knew how much she loved Papa and that sometimes she knew things about him she wasn't supposed to know.

"I can imagine that. Once he makes up his mind and comes home, he doesn't take many breaks."

"And he's been helping Uncle Jack," Sasha said. "There was the smell of hay, and he was very hot, and I think Papa brought in the harvest."

Luca laughed. "In this case, he won't be happy finding the pitchfork waiting for him." After opening the string of leather she used to bind back her hair, she refastened it, catching all the escaped strands whilst doing so. "Does it bother you that Papa sleeps in Keiran's bed?"

Again, Sasha had to smile, only this time, she didn't hide it. She'd known about Papa and Keiran ever since… probably since she'd been born. Or at least since she'd learned to walk. It was so obvious that Sasha wondered not many other people knew about them.

"Papa loves Keiran," she told Mommy in case Mommy didn't know either.

But Mommy smiled. "Yes, mouse, he loves him. That doesn't answer my question, though."

The carrots were sweet. Sasha was already taking a third, not only because they were really nice but mainly because she needed time to think about this problem.

Did it bother her that Papa didn't sleep in Mommy's bed? Or, to be honest, that he didn't sleep in Mommy's bed often?

Paula from down the village, who was seven and hence much wiser than Sasha, would giggle and call her stupid had she asked her, although Sasha was her best friend. She'd tell her that mommies and daddies had to sleep in one bed. That it was kind of the law and that everyone knew this, and that she was a baby thinking it could be any other way.

But Papa and Keiran, they slept in one bed too, and they kissed and did other things Sasha shouldn't know about. Only that once this spring, she had seen them kiss, and when they'd closed the door behind them, she'd peeked through the window.

And sometimes, Mommy sneaked into Papa's and Kei's room, and all three of them slept in one bed. And sometimes, when Sasha sneaked into Mommy's bed because her own bed was too large and too dark at night, Mommy wasn't alone, with either Kei or Papa being with her.

To Sasha, this was how it should be. Mommy was working hard, but she was happy. Keiran and Papa, though apart due to Papa's job and Keiran's going to the city every now and then, were happy too. They slept in each other's beds, sometimes in Mommy's, sometimes in Keiran's, sometimes just two of them and sometimes all of them.

"That's fine for me," she finally said, realizing her mother was still waiting for an answer. "Only when Papa's home, there is sometimes not enough space for me in his bed. You know, during a thunderstorm or when a spider crawls over my ceiling. Last time he said I'd stolen the bedcover!"

Luca's lips twitched when she saw her daughter's pout. "Go and tell Keiran about Papa. And then I want you to gather the eggs. Can you do that for me?"

Sasha was already out of the kitchen, storming across the yard. Keiran would be in the stables, and if she was really lucky, he'd allow her to ride Flash.

Keiran?

Hmmm?

It was a relief he didn't ask her to speak aloud. With him, she could be more herself than with Mommy because only Keiran fully accepted she not only could, but preferred to, talk mind to mind.

And Papa knew it too, and if Mommy wasn't around, he loved taking her for a ride, not opening his mouth once but listening to her endless, silent chatter.

Kei, Papa is coming home today.

I know, mouse. With steady, long strokes, he wiped down the horse he'd taken to the village this morning. He'd brought a bag of potatoes and a bag of flour to his parents' house; Sasha could feel his tension ease with every stroke and finally vanish. He didn't like going home much, his stepmother always bitching at him for not taking care of them, for insisting on staying at the manor, and what was he doing there anyway, there was so much work at home, and those rumors about him and the lord....

Sometimes it wasn't easy being able to hear things she wasn't supposed to hear.

Offering the last carrot to the horse, Sasha watched a dark shadow creep across the stable walls. It was lean, and it had white paws—Sammy, as none of his various children had quite inherited his looks. He meowed once, and she believed he cast her a cat smile but only, she knew, because he hoped she'd allow him to sleep on her bed tonight again.

Do you miss him? she asked. Apparently, today was a day for questions.

Oh, hell yes. The answer came fast; Keiran hadn't phrased it with his mind but his heart, and his longing, his love, and his joy at Papa's return hit Sasha hard.

Keiran didn't notice, luckily, or he'd have been worried. Ever since she had spoken her first silent word, he was worried about her and her ability, but only recently there had been talks about a teacher.

Tentatively, Sasha tickled the huge horse's flank. It wasn't Flash—Keiran would never take Flash to his parents' house—and it was softhearted and glad to be in the stables, but it didn't like getting tickled. Its tail swished over her face, and she giggled.

Not that she was done asking questions yet.

If you miss him so much, why do you allow him to leave?

Like Mommy before him, Keiran halted in his task, turning his attention to her. Sitting in the straw, he pulled her next to him. *You don't seem to know your father very well if you believe anyone can stop him from doing what he wants.*

It was a test. He knew this wasn't the question she really wanted to ask, so he made her think and come up with a proper answer herself.

But—he's away for weeks. And Papa misses you too and Mommy and Sammy…. Her silent voice trailed off, and she looked at Keiran for help.

He pulled her close, hugging her in the crook of his arm. *He misses you most. And he leaves because he has to. The empress counts on him, mouse. If there is a task she wants him to do and if this task accords with his code, then he has no choice but to obey her.*

Because of the little prince, and because the empress protects Laure's nunnery, and because of Debbie and her mom and the goats he gave them?

Right, Keiran answered. *I didn't know Luca told you that much.*

Sasha blushed, like she had with Mommy. Only now she realized she'd been caught. No one had told her. She'd just found out.

Sighing, Keiran handed her another carrot, this one from the horse's trough. *You need a teacher, mouse. Wulfric warned us this could happen. I just didn't expect it so soon.*

He hadn't meant her to hear this, but she caught the thought nevertheless.

Which was, of course, precisely why Papa and Mommy and Keiran talked about her needing lessons all the time.

Resting her chin in her hands, Sasha looked at Keiran and wondered, not for the first time, how it could be she had two fathers. She had inherited her father's black hair and his tall, lean stature, she had her mother's face and sharp tongue, but she had Keiran's eyes and his ability to talk without words. Papa had learned this from Keiran, but she hadn't needed to learn it at all as her first word had been a silent one.

Strange.

Kei, how come you and Papa are both my fathers? she asked, merely to keep the conversation going rather than expecting an answer. After all, Jean always told her that asking too many questions only led to confusion and chaos on both sides. And considering the look on Keiran's face, Sasha knew that chaos wasn't far away.

Oops. I shouldn't have asked that. Sorry, Kei! If she needed to, she was quick to apologize. In this case, just for safety, she also added a cute smile.

But Keiran just placed a kiss on the top of her head. *I can't answer that.* His silent voice was careful, the emotions she sensed through the link showed his hesitation as well as his deep love for her. *Not because I don't want to, but because I really don't know. From long before you were born, we wondered who fathered you. Then you arrived, and we thought time would show. It didn't. You look like Rage as much as you look like me. It is as it is, mouse. You are his girl, and you are my girl.*

Another kiss, this time to the back of her hand. Sasha giggled—she always felt like a princess when Keiran did that.

Couldn't you find out with a bit of magic?

We could, probably. Brother Wulfric offered already. But we don't want to know. Is that all right for you?

Sasha beamed. She'd feared that one day, the strange little monk would grab her and look at her and then announce neither Papa nor Keiran were her real father, but someone else and that only he knew, and that she'd have to come to the city with him if she ever wanted to find out.

Keiran felt her sudden fear and the reason for it, and hugged her a bit tighter. *Wulfric won't take you away, mouse. If he wants to teach you, he will have to come here, to Babylon Manor.*

He didn't lie to comfort her; he was telling the truth, Sasha knew it. Relief washed through her, strong enough to nearly make her cry.

Maybe a tiny tear ran down her cheek, but if so, she wiped it off instantly. Crying was for babies, and she wasn't one. *I don't like him,* she confessed. *He smells strange, and he always looks at me as if he wanted to put a needle through me and study me just like Ken does with his beetles.*

A flash of amusement washed through her, originating in Keiran—for some reason, he thought what she'd said was funny. *Your papa would agree with that. He doesn't like Wulfric either, mouse.*

Can't we find another teacher?

But Keiran shook his head. *He's the best, and he's the only one who can control magic as strong as yours. You have a lot to learn, Sasha: how to block your thoughts from others, how to stay out of other people's heads, and how to make sure your magic doesn't lash out when you are tired, hungry, or annoyed.*

That last part especially made Sasha feel ashamed and scared. Papa already told her what had happened to his dog. He had explained to her in clear words that the dog hurt itself and that he'd killed it trying to heal the wound. The story had made her cry. Still, it was only a story, and she hadn't thought about it very much until the incident with one of Sammy's kittens.

Sasha nibbled her lip, and she felt tears well up in her eyes, as always when she thought about it.

She'd been so angry that day. Mommy had told her to do her homework first, and when she'd refused—or rather, when she'd found other more important things to do—had forbidden her to go outside and play. And when Sasha shouted at her and called her unfair, Mommy sent her into her room without lunch.

She hadn't even known her magic, which had been feeble and unimportant until then, could lash out at all. She definitely hadn't known it could hurt others, and when the kitten, just old enough to sneak away from its mom, suddenly squeaked with pain, Sasha hadn't believed she was the reason for it.

Luckily, Papa had been home that day. When the kitten wouldn't stop squealing and when she saw its twisted, tiny paw, she began to scream, and he was there, taking care of her while Keiran took care of the kitten. A broken paw, and he fixed it while Papa talked to her and calmed her and explained how dangerous it was to let her magic get out of control.

Papa's magic is strong, isn't it? she now asked, secretly wiping her sleeve across her eyes. *Nearly as strong as mine?*

Keiran smiled at the hint of pride in her voice. *Yes, mouse. Nearly as strong as yours. And learning how to control it cost him a lot. Wulfric taught him. It wasn't a nice lesson because your papa was much older than you are. It's the reason he never uses his magic. And we think you should learn now so your lessons can be nice and easy. Besides, we will all make sure Wulfric won't put a needle through you.* Placing one last kiss to her brow, Keiran let his fingers creep to her waist where they began tickling her. It ended up in a tickle fight. This time, the tears running down Sasha's cheek were born out of laughter.

Suddenly, they both stopped playing; suddenly, they both looked up, listening.

Papa!

A dark figure stood in the doorway, a larger horse-shaped shadow looming behind it. "I see I wasn't missed," the shadow said. In his voice there was a hint of fatigue, a ghost of a long, hot day on the road. But mostly, there was a smile.

Sasha flung herself into Papa's arms, knowing he would catch her and lift her up and swing her around like always when he came home.

Then she hugged him, her arms tightly slung around his neck. She inhaled his scent, his cheek scratched her face, and she knew he was happy to be home again. This feeling of contentment, of joy burned like a flame inside him, and it embraced her as well as Keiran, who now kissed Papa no matter that she was still in his arms.

Somewhere in the distance, Mommy called for lunch. She must have seen Papa riding into the yard, and probably she was already on the way to the stables so she could hug Papa herself.

Her family. Two daddies and one mommy, and honestly, how could anyone be so stupid and call this anything but perfect?

I love you, Papa, her mind whispered, and he laughed, a deep rumble that always made her laugh with him.

Love you too, mouse. Now let's go and say hello to Mommy.

She loved it when he talked to her in the silent way. She loved it when he was home. Nothing could go wrong when he was home.

RAGE COULD have told her that practically everything could go wrong at any given time, no matter how much one tried to prevent catastrophes. But he didn't. After all, she was only five, too young to know about life's cruel turns.

She'd learn soon enough.

SAM C. LEONHARD lives in southern Germany and is a journalist by profession. Writing has been part of her life since age twenty, but somehow it was never enough to report the latest news about small-town politics. She wrote short stories for friends and family until a few years back she discovered the world of fandom. The Petulant Poetess is where she feels at home; slash became an addiction as soon as she stumbled over the first story.

If not writing—which isn't half as often as she'd like—Sam takes care of her son, her dog, a few cats, the madness at work, and life in general. She likes to believe she's got some humor left after years of dealing with people who usually don't understand what she's talking about when she says she's writing fantasy with gay porn on top of it.

E-mail: sc.leonhard@googlemail.com
Facebook: https://www.facebook.com/sam.leonhard.7

http://www.dsppublications.com

http://www.dsppublications.com

http://www.dsppublications.com

http://www.dsppublications.com

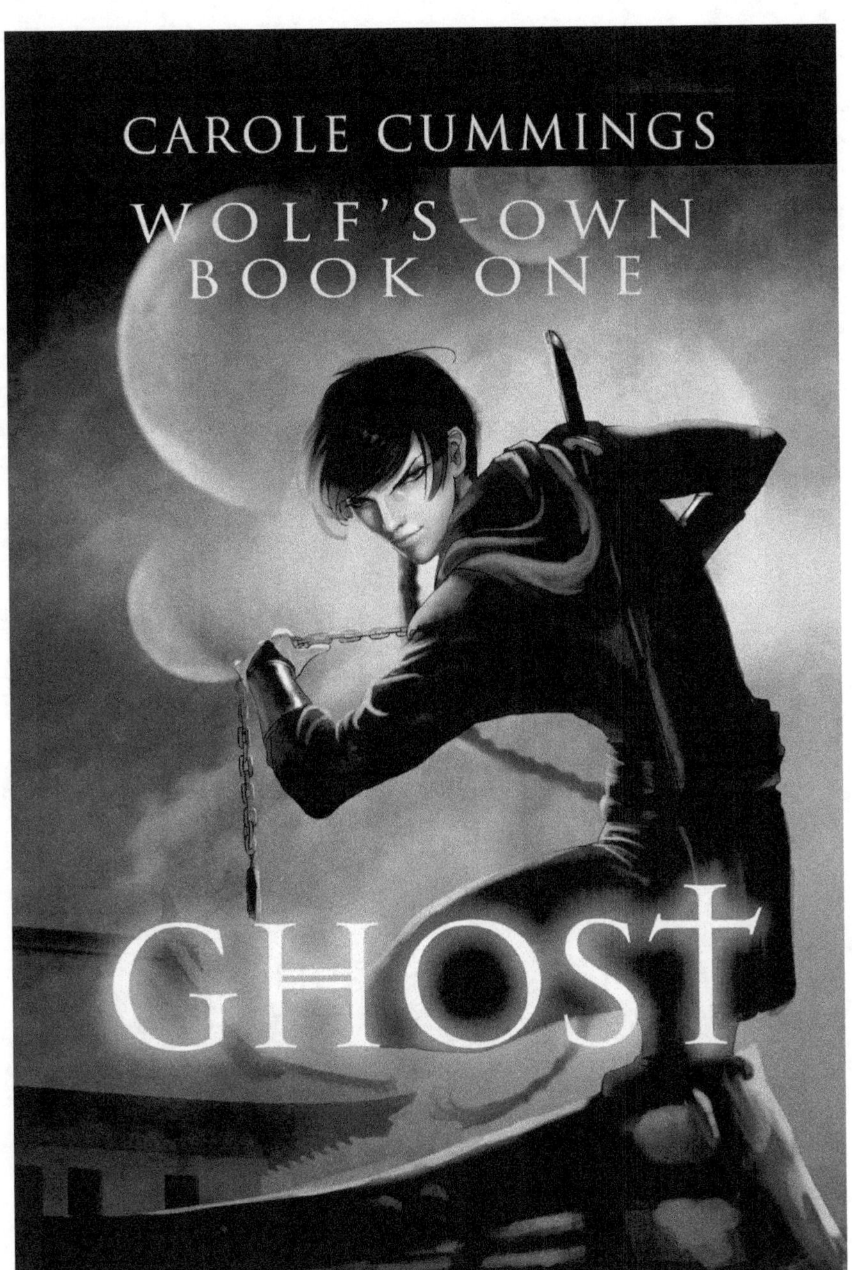
CAROLE CUMMINGS
WOLF'S-OWN
BOOK ONE
GHOST

DSP PUBLICATIONS

visit us online.
WWW.DSPPUBLICATIONS.COM